COLD STEAL

A successful housebreaker who leaves no traces and no clues as he strips Reykjavík homes of their valuables has been a thorn in the police's side for months. But when one night the thief breaks into the wrong house, he finds himself caught in a trap, and the stakes are raised far beyond anything he could have imagined. Gunnhildur Gísladóttir of the Reykjavík police finds herself frustrated at every turn as she searches for a victim who has vanished from the scene of the crime, and wonders if it could be linked to the murders of two businessmen with dubious reputations that her bosses are warning her to keep clear of.

COLD STEAL

QUENTIN BATES

LARGE
PRINT

First published in Great Britain 2014
by
C&R Crime
an imprint of Constable & Robinson Ltd.

First Isis Edition
published 2018
by arrangement with
Constable & Robinson Ltd.

The moral right of the author has been asserted

A catalogue record for this book is available
from the British Library.

ISBN 978–1–78541–475–6 (hb)
ISBN 978–1–78541–481–7 (pb)

Published by
F. A. Thorpe (Publishing)
Anstey, Leicestershire

Set by Words & Graphics Ltd.
Anstey, Leicestershire
Printed and bound in Great Britain by
T. J. International Ltd., Padstow, Cornwall

This book is printed on acid-free paper

For Sacha and Cathy
with grateful thanks for the essential maintenance

Acknowledgements

Many thanks to those good people who cheerfully answer awkward and obscure questions. You all know who you are.

CHAPTER
ONE

Soft feet made no sound on the track leading through the trees. The two men said nothing to each other, communicating instead with pointing fingers, lifted eyebrows and nods. The taller one of the two went ahead, spying out the route and watching their objective while the stockier man came behind and watched the other's back, looking into the distance to see if they had been observed and occasionally looking behind to check for anyone following.

Summer was still a few months away and most of the chalets were empty, boarded up and mothballed for winter. Beneath the bare branches of the trees that surrounded it a warm light illuminated the windows of one chalet and tendrils of woodsmoke drifted upwards, twisting and disappearing in the evening breeze while their smell carried downwind to where two figures in dark clothing left their car tucked away out of sight of the road.

They stopped in front of the chalet as darkness fell, and listened before moving closer and crouching on the veranda each side of the door. The stocky man looked questioningly at the other, who nodded back. Gradually, the tall man lifted his head to peer through

1

the glass of the door, quickly dropping back down and grinning. He pulled at his woollen hat, rolling it down over his face to leave only eyes and mouth visible in the firelight flickering inside, and pointed at the window with a wink.

The stocky man covered his face with a scarf and stood up next to the window. He leaned cautiously to bring one eye in line with the glass and looked inside. He stepped back out of sight and the tall man could see the laughter in his eyes. He pointed to the door questioningly and the shorter man nodded.

He took a hammer from the pack on his back, a sledgehammer with the handle cut off short to make it easily portable. He lifted it, feeling its weight. The tall man took a pistol from the pocket of his camouflage jacket, and although he had checked it only a few minutes earlier, he checked it again.

They took up stations each side of the door, the gunman on the handle side, his broad-shouldered companion opposite him with the hammer ready for a two-handed grip to smash the door inwards in case it should turn out to be locked. The tall man held up four fingers and they counted silently together.

Four, three, two, one, and the gunman pushed the door handle down and stepped into the doorway with the pistol raised, knees bent and feet spread in a fighting stance. His colleague dropped the hammer there had been no need for and stepped inside the room behind him, a pistol now in his hand as the two of them took in the scene in front of them.

2

The brightness of the girl's white socks, the only thing she was wearing other than a gold chain, stood out against her tanned skin. She stared at them first in confusion, then anger and finally in terror as she screeched at the sight of the weapons trained on them. She scrambled to her feet, trying to cover herself with her hands while the man she had until a moment before been enthusiastically straddling looked dazed, his hands straying instinctively to his wilting erection.

"Who . . .? Who the hell are you?"

The stocky man took two rapid steps and grabbed a handful of the girl's abundant black hair close to her scalp, pulling her head to one side and forcing her down.

"Quiet," he ordered, and she whimpered as he pushed her to her knees, holding her head still where she could not avoid watching.

The man on the floor did his best to scuttle backwards across the thick rug. "What do you want?" His voice quavered thin and high. "Look, I have money. How much do you want?"

The taller of the pair took two rapid steps forward, aimed and fired a single shot that caught his target squarely in the throat. A second shot punched a neat hole in the man's forehead and he dropped back to the floor, his head against the base of the iron stove, and the smell of singed hair immediately began to fill the room. It had all taken no more than a few seconds.

The tall man stepped forward and kicked his victim's head clear of the stove, noticing that the sparse hair had already been burned off where it had landed against the metal. He looked at his colleague, who nodded in approval, still holding the girl who was staring at the corpse in shock, hands limp by her sides as she no longer tried to cover herself. He let go of her hair and she dropped to the floor. The stocky man jerked his head towards her questioningly and the tall man shook his head, eyes narrowed in disapproval.

"No," he said. "Leave no traces. Just a witness."

He leaned down and grabbed the girl's wrist, pulling her back to her feet while his colleague whistled his admiration at the slim hips, long legs and supermodel breasts.

"Please don't hurt me. I've seen nothing," she said, her voice choking.

"Little girl, you've seen everything," the stocky man said.

"I won't say anything. Believe me, I won't say a word."

"Don't you get it?" Lines formed around the tall man's eyes as his face crinkled into a grin behind the scarf. "You don't understand, darling. You can tell them whatever you like."

Gunna stretched her hands high above her head, arching her back as the yawn threatened to lock her jaw in position and Steini took the opportunity to shoot an arm under her back and squeeze as she relaxed into the sofa.

"Have I missed anything?"

"An American comedy with canned laughter and no jokes, and a British cookery programme in which the

4

chef didn't even manage to fillet a haddock properly, so the answer to your question is no."

The credits on the TV rolled and this time Steini yawned.

"It must be catching. Where are the kids?"

"Laufey went to see Drífa and promised to be back before ten, and as the news is just about to start, I'd say that's a promise about to be broken."

The titles of the late evening news began as the outside door banged.

Gunna lifted her feet onto the sofa and leaned against Steini's shoulder. "I'd say that promise may well have been kept, this time, and only just," she said as the grey-haired newsreader appeared on screen looking more serious than usual as the opening sequence showed a view through trees swaying in the wind.

"Suspicious death in Borgarfjördur, police are at the scene," the newsreader intoned as the picture flashed to a light aircraft soaring into the sky. "Reykjavík city council faces uproar over airport plans. Questions continue to be raised regarding IceLine's bankruptcy as eighty jobs are lost in Iceland, London and Singapore," the newsreader said in a flat voice as a street scene from somewhere in Asia appeared.

The door burst open and Laufey appeared, puffing with exertion. "I'm not late, am I? I said I'd be back by ten."

"Shhh," Gunna said, sitting up and with her attention on the screen as it returned to the story with footage of a secluded summer house clearly taken from some distance away and with blue flashing lights casting shadows between the trees.

"A forty-year-old man was found dead at a summer chalet earlier today," the newsreader said in a suitably sombre tone. "Police have not identified the deceased and have issued no details beyond stating that they are seeking the driver and passenger of a grey Audi A5."

The camera cut away to a bearded police officer under an umbrella that raindrops dripped from as he spoke. Gunna could see a familiar barrel-chested figure in the background, a phone at his ear.

"Know anything about this, Mum?" Laufey asked.

"Nope. I've been on leave for a week, and I haven't heard anything. If it was anything to do with me, I guess Ívar Laxdal would have called by now," she said and looked at Steini with pursed lips as her phone began to buzz. "Speak of the devil," she added.

CHAPTER
TWO

With her fingers encased in mittens encrusted with clinging snow, making them more clumsy than usual, Gunna fumbled with the rifle in her hands. It was an old-fashioned bolt-action weapon and although she had never fired one before, she instinctively knew what to do. There were only three cartridges. One was in the rifle's breech and the safety catch was off. Another was in her hand, safely inside the mitten to be sure of not losing it, the last one tucked away inside layers of clothing. They were precious and she knew that every one would be needed.

The house was an old one. It looked forlorn and abandoned from her position on the bank above it. The door hung half open and broken, the interior of the old place in deep darkness. Sharp grains of snow carried by the wind stung Gunna's face as she watched intently, her attention fixed on the door. The snow around it had been churned up, streaked with black and red, raked with prints.

Gradually her attention on the door relaxed as she felt she herself was being watched. There was no sound other than the whisper of wind that tugged at the ripped curtain hanging on the smashed door. She looked around and then quickly back at the door, waiting for movement, not knowing if it would come from inside or out.

When it came, it took her by surprise, and from behind. A rushing sound and a sharp animal smell made her look over her shoulder in alarm and she rolled over to aim the rifle, hoping to be fast enough. The animal seemed on top of her, a vast dirty-white presence that appeared in front of her face, and she knew already that she was too late to bring the rifle to bear. She could see the calmness in its eyes as it grunted and felt the animal's raw power as a paw as big as her head and set with claws swung towards her.

Gunna sat bolt upright, her eyes wide open with the vision of the bear in front of her until it faded. The room was dark, with only a narrow strip of weak light coming under the door. She breathed deeply, the dream still vivid, and pushed hair damp with sweat from her face.

"What's the matter?" Steini mumbled, stretching out a hand from under the duvet to rest it on her thigh. "You all right?"

"Yeah. Bad dream, that's all."

"Reckon you can get back to sleep?"

"Hope so," Gunna said, lying back on the pillow as she tried to convince herself that the dream, in utterly convincing technicolour, even down to the animal's piercing reek, had been nothing but her imagination playing tricks. She knew it would be hopeless trying to get back to sleep and she could feel her heart still racing while Steini's steady breathing told her that he was having no such problems.

Gunna swung her legs out of bed, eased open the door and slipped into the kitchen.

Orri had left Lísa in bed. Their relationship was an odd one, dominated by them both working shifts, Lísa managing a canteen at a factory where production was only ever halted for a day at Christmas, and him at a freight company's depot on an industrial estate on the city outskirts. His other activities also ate into his time and he had never got round to telling Lísa that he had volunteered to work reduced hours when the company had been forced to make cuts. In fact, all but a few of the mostly middle-aged staff had taken a cut in hours, and it didn't seem to have mattered. The old boys just worked harder to make up for it, which was something Orri failed to understand.

He yawned as he clocked in, already wearing his overalls and steel toecap boots, his helmet under his arm. He looked into the coffee room where two of the old boys were leafing through newspapers a week old and grumbling about the state of the country.

"Good morning."

"Good morning, Orri," the one facing him replied while the other one, a corpulent man with a roll of fat at the back of his neck, the sight of which made Orri feel queasy, continued to look through last week's small ads. "And how might you be this fine day?"

"Not so bad."

"You're early today. Your Lísa must have been at work last night?"

"Nope. She's still asleep."

"The lazy bitch. I'd have kicked her out of bed, demanded eggs, bacon and coffee be brought to me, and an early morning roll in the hay to kick off with."

Orri snorted with laughter. "Yeah, right," he retorted. "I've seen your old woman and it'd be a brave man who told her to do anything."

At the next table, Dóri the foreman closed his newspaper and stood up with a slow smile. "That's what you youngsters can't get into your heads. Gentle touches. That's all it needs. That's what has them eating out of your hand and running to get your breakfast when you whistle for it."

"If you say so," Orri said, already bored with the non-stop talk of women and their bizarre habits that seemed to obsess his older colleagues. "What are we starting with today?"

"Six pallets to go to Akureyri. Two for Raufarhöfn on the same truck, so those need to go to Reykjavík today. There's a couple of crates to go to Djúpivogur and another shipment for the Westmann Islands, but that's not on pallets yet. Eight collections to make in Reykjavík, two in Keflavík and there's a delivery from Akranes due at eleven that's being forwarded to somewhere or other. It has to go to the airport, anyway," Dóri reeled off in a flat monotone as he read the list from a clipboard.

Orri yawned. "What am I doing then, boss?"

"I'm not the boss, young man, but I'd suggest Alex does the Keflavík run from Hafnarfisk in the fridge truck as usual and you do the Reykjavík collections in the Trafic. Does that meet with your agreement?"

"Alex is in today?"

"He'd better be if he wants to keep his job, that's all I can say," Dóri said, taking off his glasses and folding them away in the breast pocket of his overall. "Late yesterday. Late today and late twice last week. Not good enough and I wouldn't put up with it, but I'm not the boss, as you know."

"I'll have a word."

Dóri looked at him with his face screwed into a frown. "Up to you. But the old man doesn't need to put up with Alex being a dick. There are a dozen immigrants a week knocking on the door asking for work."

As the old man left him to it, Orri tapped at his phone, put it to his ear and listened to Alex's voicemail kick in with a few sentences of rapid Latvian that he ignored.

"Hi. It's Orri. Where are you, man? You're going to get sacked if you keep coming in late," he said in bland English as he walked through the door and saw Alex swagger towards him with a smile. He paused and dug in his pocket, raising a finger at Orri as he did so.

"Don't bother. It's a message from me," Orri called out. "Telling you not to turn up late again if you want to keep your job."

"Hey, don't worry. He can't fire me," Alex said with a grin. "I didn't mean to be late." He whistled. "That

11

girl. Man. She just wouldn't let me go. Know what I mean?"

"Yeah, yeah. I know. But she won't like you so much if you're under her feet at home all day, will she?" Orri said.

"You have some stuff for me? I have space next week if you have some goods to deliver."

She was early for her midday shift, arriving at the Hverfisgata station with an hour to spare, certain that Ívar Laxdal would be looking for her. In two years with what had been formed as the Serious Crime Unit, she had found that serious crime seemed to occur in fits and starts, and Gunna and her colleagues had found themselves investigating anything from car theft to a cartel of youthful but computer-savvy mobile phone thieves, as well as the occasional crime so brutal that she asked herself repeatedly if this was something new. She wondered if people were reporting things that had previously been sorted out behind closed doors, often with more discreet violence.

Ívar Laxdal found her in the detectives' office as her computer was powering up.

"Gunnhildur," she heard behind her as she typed in her password. "I hope you feel better for the break?"

She swung her chair around and saw the granite face of the National Commissioner's deputy, his blue eyes sparkling with an intelligence and humour his deadpan expression rarely betrayed.

"Not bad, I suppose. Another week would have been good, but you can't have everything."

12

"Indeed, and someone has to right wrongs and lock up bad guys." He looked around the deserted office. "Where's Helgi?"

"On leave, as of yesterday. Gone up north for a week."

"And Eiríkur?"

"He should be here at twelve — first day after a month's paternity leave."

"Paternity leave," Ívar Laxdal said as if the words hurt him. "In my day there was no such thing. I was at sea when my eldest was born and didn't even see him until he was almost a month old."

"Thanks for the call yesterday. I was just watching the news when you rang up. Anything new?"

Ívar Laxdal rubbed his chin, his thumbnail rasping against the bristles.

"Yes. The victim is Vilhelm Thorleifsson, forty-one years old, resident in Copenhagen since 2009. His name hasn't been released yet."

"He was shot? Any more details yet?"

"Strangely, it was two rounds from a .22 weapon. I'd have gone for something heavier if I wanted to finish someone off, but if you're accurate and it's at close range, it'll do the job well enough. There's a witness as well, not that it seems she can tell us much."

"Serious stuff."

"As you say, serious stuff," Ívar Laxdal said. "The witness is nineteen years old, saw the whole thing at close quarters and is now traumatized and sedated. So we'll see what comes out of it all."

Gunna saw with dismay that the screen of her computer was filled with emails demanding immediate attention.

"What do you want me to do? Is Sævaldur looking after this one?"

Ívar Laxdal let fall a rare smile. He was aware of the friction between Gunna and her chief inspector colleague and she knew that he preferred them not to clash.

"Of course Sævaldur is involved. He was at the scene half the night with the forensic team and they're still up there knocking on doors, if they can find anyone at this time of year. But this one is mine, I'm afraid, instructions from . . ." He lifted his eyes to the ceiling. "You know what I mean. To start with I want Sævaldur and his team investigating the scene. I want you and Eiríkur working on the victim's background."

"You said he lived in Copenhagen?"

"That's right. His wife and daughter will be here this evening. I'm sure she'll be delighted when she finds out what he was up to."

"All right. You want me to meet her at the airport, or is that being done by family?"

"Leave her until tomorrow. Start on his business background today."

"Another shady businessman?"

Another rare smile. "I know how much you enjoy the company of men in smart suits, even if they're dead," he said, silently leaving the room and contriving not to bang the door.

14

"Yeah, right. Especially when they're dead," Gunna muttered to herself.

Natalia dragged hard on the last millimetres of her cigarette and threw the butt out of the window, where it joined the ones from the week before and the week before that on the roof of the garage.

"Someone has been here," Emilija said, as if that were an offence of some kind. "The toilet has been used. I'm sure of it."

Natalia shrugged. "So? Somebody must live here, surely?"

Emilija let herself sink deep into the leather sofa that filled one end of the apartment's living room, directly opposite a vast TV screen that filled almost the whole of the opposite wall.

"If whoever lives here had left the remote on the table, then we could have TV on while we work," she said wistfully.

"Nobody lives here," Natalia said.

All winter the three Reindeer Cleaners had arrived to clean houses in this smart, half-built suburb. Today's job was to scrub the kitchen and the luxurious bathrooms, vacuum the living room and dust the bedrooms that rarely appeared to be slept in. The job had become easier and easier as there was so little to be done. The apartment was always as spotlessly clean as it had been when they left it the previous week. Nothing was ever out of place. The kitchen was never used and the bathroom remained pristine.

"Who lives in this place?" Emilija asked. "I want to know who can afford to leave a place like this empty. If I knew who it was, hell, I'd screw the life out of him and live here myself."

A wicked smile flashed across Natalia's sharp face. "A rich man, yeah. If I knew, I'd have him first."

"As long as he's old and won't last too long," Emilija mused.

"Men again?" Valmira asked, appearing in the doorway with the vacuum cleaner tucked under one arm. "Are we finished?" She put the vacuum cleaner down by the door and ticked the boxes on her list. Everything had been done, even though nothing had needed to be done, but she still walked around the place to check.

"Why do we clean this place, do you think?" Emilija asked, letting herself fall backwards onto the deep sofa next to Natalia and lifting her feet onto the long coffee table, a deep grey slab of stone on four steel legs. There were bags under her eyes and she wanted to close them and spend the rest of the afternoon on that welcoming sofa.

"A friend of the boss owns it," Natalia said. "I heard him talk about it once on the phone. He said he'd have the place cleaned every week. He thinks I don't understand what he says," she added, grinning wickedly.

"I'm not so sure. I reckon he wants you to think that," Emilija said.

"Why?"

"I don't know."

"No, Viggó's a pretty stupid guy."

"It belongs to a friend of Viggó's father," Valmira said thoughtfully, appearing in the doorway from the echoing hall and walking to the window. "Natalia, you'd better stop throwing those cigarette ends out of the window. Someone's going to notice them. Anyhow, we're back here tomorrow."

"Tomorrow? Not possible," Natalia said with a flash of anger in her voice as she sat up straight.

"Down the street. Booked for tomorrow afternoon."

"Shit, why not now?" Emilija asked, getting to her feet. "That means we have to come all the way out here tomorrow and we're not paid for travel, are we?"

Valmira walked stiffly away from the window and the others recognized the look on her face, knowing there was a depth of trauma in her that they could not understand properly and had never felt comfortable asking about.

"Ready, are we?" She asked, trying to sound bright.

Middle-aged people were the best. Orri preferred not to steal from the elderly, not because his conscience might trouble him, but because there was something about the old that disturbed him. People who had retired had a strange smell about them, they lived among clutter and rubbish, and their valuables were scattered in the unlikeliest places.

Middle-aged people had more of the easily disposable toys that were worth money, computers and gadgets that fetched good money and which the Baltic boys could sell easily enough. While the younger generation had its own expensive toys as well, those houses were more likely to have an alarm that worked or, worse, small children in the house.

No, people in comfortable middle age with cash to spare and their offspring long gone were the best option. They were the people with everything in order: cash in a sensible place, a wad of dollars or euros left over from that last holiday, a smart laptop that had hardly been used, antiques on display in glass cabinets rather than at the backs of drawers full of ancient oddments. These were the people who had sat on their cash, not the mortgaged-to-the-hilt people in their thirties who had come out of the crash so badly.

Orri wondered why he was in the old couple's house, considering his aversion to the young and the elderly. But the answer was simple enough. The back door had been left unlocked. Hidden by a hedge on one side and in the shadow of the garage, it was just too easy to walk in and help himself. With a slim torch held between his teeth to cast a pool of light in front of him, Orri went through the bedroom drawers systematically. Some housebreakers would gleefully scatter everything in their wake, breaking anything that might be in the way and leaving trails of muddy footprints and worse. That wasn't Orri's style. He felt that making a mess was unprofessional. Ideally, he wouldn't leave a trace, and sometimes days or weeks would pass before people realized there had been a visitor, by which time any trail had long gone cold and the goods had been safely disposed of.

This time he was lucky. There was gold and silver to be had, a dozen krugerrands, a heavy necklace and a couple of bracelets and chunky pendants that he quickly stowed in his bag without looking too carefully. Metal was good and the Baltic boys would give him a price for it. Melted down, it became untraceable, and there was always a market for it.

A leather wallet made of some soft skin yielded a handful of cash in a variety of currencies, which he stuffed into a trouser pocket before he decided that enough was enough for a few quick minutes of easy work. It might take weeks for the couple whose bedroom he had invaded to notice that the cash and jewellery had vanished, and he made a swift exit. He clicked the back door locked. He dropped the torch into his jacket pocket and froze, standing with his back to the wall between the house and the garage.

He heard car doors slam twice in quick succession and a bang as the house's front door shut, and he hurried on silent feet to the corner and saw a BMW parked squarely in the drive. Lights were being switched on inside as he looked around and made a dash for the street. It took a matter of only a few seconds before he was off the drive and walking along the road towards where he had parked the van around the corner, still loaded with boxes to be delivered.

His heart still in his mouth, he got in the van and was gone in a few seconds, still waiting to hear cries of anger and the slap of flat feet on the wet pavement. At the traffic lights at the end of the road he watched the mirrors carefully, but there was nothing to be seen, no cars behind him, nobody on foot. He peeled off his latex gloves and dropped them into the passenger side footwell as he congratulated himself on a job well done, laughing out loud as he left the quiet street behind him.

It was Eiríkur's first day back and he looked tired, with bags under his eyes and a hangdog look about him.

"Welcome back," Gunna greeted him. "And congratulations. How's the little one doing?"

Eiríkur's smile lit up his wan face. "He's the most beautiful baby in the world, of course. But he's been keeping us up, and so has his sister."

"Jealous, is she?"

"A little. But we've been trying to give her as much attention as we can, but it's not easy."

"Tell me about it," Gunna said. "I'm afraid you have to be firm as well as loving, unfortunately, and it can't always be painless."

"I know. I'm not really sorry to be back at work, to be honest," he said, dropping his voice as if he were confessing a sin.

"Don't worry about it. I could never have stopped working. I'd have happily sold both mine if I'd had to spend all day every day with them."

"Where's Helgi?" Eiríkur asked, looking at Helgi's unusually tidy and clearly empty desk.

"On holiday. He's driving to Blönduós today and he'll spend the next two weeks in some remote valley helping sweet baby lambs into the world, and I imagine in the autumn he'll want another week's holiday to go

20

and help his brother round up those same lambs and send them off to be slaughtered."

"Oh," Eiríkur said, and sat down at his own desk and watched his computer start up. "I didn't realize he was on holiday. Are we busy? You want me to take over any of Helgi's caseload?"

"There's an assault case that Helgi's working on which I need you to do some work on. It's a hit-and-run thing, but it seems that it might have been deliberate. You'll find the notes on the system, so you'd best have a read through it and I'll fill you in on the details afterwards. Then there's a couple of muggings that seem to have got out of hand, with a little more violence than usual. That's a lowlife by the name of Thór Hersteinnsson. We know it's him, but there's precious little hard evidence and nobody he knows wants to give a statement."

Eiríkur's face fell. "I've encountered this Thór before. Not the pleasantest of people, I have to say."

"He has an alibi for both muggings, provided by various of his friends and therefore dubious, so if you could crack one or both of those, we'll be doing nicely."

"That's it?"

"Oh, no. We have a dead businessman to deal with. Don't you watch the news?"

"I thought Sævaldur would have been looking after that as we were both off?"

"He is, but so are we. All of us under the Laxdal's eagle eye. Briefing at two, so I'd better find something out about this man. You'll be on this as well."

Eiríkur sat back in his chair and gazed at the computer screen in front of him and the piles of paper between it and him, all of which demanded attention. Gunna could see his eyes starting to glaze over at the prospect.

"Small, Medium and Large," Viggó announced from behind the desk in the corner of the garage. "Bang on time, my darlings."

"You go fuck yourself, fat boy," Natalia grunted with Viggó out of earshot, but only just; he cupped an ear.

"Hey, what d'you say?"

"I say, nice to see you, boss," she replied with a broad smile and exaggerating her accent almost to a parody of herself.

Viggó's eyes narrowed as she bustled past with her box of cloths, brushes and sprays, and Valmira handed mops, buckets and the two heavy-duty vacuum cleaners out of the van to Emilija.

"Hey, Small, Medium and Large!"

This time Natalia's eyes narrowed while Emilija and Valmira pointedly ignored the names he had given them.

"What is it?" Valmira finally asked.

"Which of you three has the first aid certificate?"

"We all have first aid training. It's in the contract, and you made us pay for it as well. Remember?"

Viggó spread his hands wide in innocence. "I don't make the rules, girls. It's not up to me."

"You not the boss then?" Emilija asked, stacking the equipment on racks against the wall.

22

"Yeah, I'm the boss."

Emilija shrugged. "You don't make rules. You not boss. Simple," she said, without stopping what she was doing. Both she and Natalia kept their conversations to the simplest Icelandic they could while Viggó was anywhere near, leaving Valmira to speak for them. None of them found it odd that they all used Icelandic every day between themselves as the only language they all had in common, but were careful not to let Viggó find out they could understand everything he said.

Valmira was different, they felt. She had come to Iceland with what remained of her family as a hollow-eyed child refugee from a war-torn part of the Balkans that she never spoke about. Only the limp that stiffened in cold weather and the occasional suppressed hiss of pain as she bent to pick something up gave away the old injuries they had never dared ask about. Valmira, or Large, as Viggó preferred to call her, had been in a proper office job before the financial crash had bankrupted the import company she had worked for practically overnight, and she spoke a dozen languages, including Icelandic as well as any local, apart from an accent that only tiredness brought out.

"I'm the man in charge here and don't you forget it," Viggó warned, his face reddening.

"You daddy. He boss. Not you," Natalia said with venom behind her sweet smile.

"You be careful, Small. Mind your manners or you'll be sacked."

23

Natalia smiled again, just as sweetly, her tiny teeth bared. "You daddy, he love me. He don't sack people who work hard."

"Viggó, we're doing another house on Kópavogsbakki tomorrow," Valmira asked, anxious to interrupt the banter between Viggó and the girls before it became a squabble. "Is there a reason why we couldn't do it at the same time as the one we did today? I mean, it would save us a drive, and you know we lose out by having to drive all the way there twice."

Viggó sat down again and propped his feet in their smart trainers on the desk. "We'll do it tomorrow because that's what's on the rota," he said in a sour tone.

"I know. I'm just asking. If we do the downstairs flat again next week, can we arrange to do them together? It saves time."

"We'll see," Viggó decided. "It depends how I feel. But it has to be tomorrow, because that's what the client asked for. Simple," he said, mimicking Emilija's accent and eliciting an angry sideways look from her as she stalked to the canteen, leaving him to giggle to himself at his own cleverness.

"You all know each other so no introductions needed," Ívar Laxdal announced to the room. A dozen people sat haphazardly in hard chairs. "Sævaldur, begin, if you please."

The force's red-faced and newest chief inspector stood up with his beefy arms folded.

24

The victim is Vilhelm Thorleifsson, forty-one years old, resident in Copenhagen. Married with one child," he began.

Ívar Laxdal made an impatient circular motion with one hand, a silent encouragement to get to the point, but Sævaldur either failed to notice or else would not be moved, as he went through the victim's school and university qualifications before getting to the point.

"The killing took place in a summer house in Borgarfjördur, owned by one of the victim's companies. He was shot twice with a .22 calibre weapon, once in the throat, once in the head. We are looking for two people and we have practically nothing to work with. There are no prints at all that can't be accounted for. There are a couple of footprints outside, but they could have been made by any of a dozen people. We do have a witness, Yulia Bushuyeva, says she's nineteen, but she's twenty-three according to her passport. Russian national, speaks reasonable English and doesn't know more than a few words of Icelandic. According to her, the two men spoke English, but she's not able to say whether they had accents or not."

"How long after the killing was the alarm raised?" Ívar Laxdal asked as Sævaldur paused.

"The girl isn't certain. She raised the alarm by dialling 112 but she wasn't able to describe where she was, so it took a while for the local force to get there, and by that time she had gone running to a neighbour, who took her in after he had seen what had happened. So, plenty of confusion."

"Any other witnesses?"

"A man walking a dog claims to have seen a grey Audi A5 along the road that evening, but he didn't pay much attention. It turned out he had spent the afternoon in front of the football on TV and was so drunk he could hardly walk. We've been knocking on doors all day and that's all we've come up with."

"Can we be sure it's an A5?" Eiríkur asked.

"He may have been drunk, but he's a car dealer, so yes. We can be pretty sure of that."

"It doesn't look promising, does it?" Ívar Laxdal said.

"It looks professional," Sævaldur agreed. "Not least because according to . . ." he consulted his notes. "According to Yulia Bushuyeva, one of the two men made sure she saw Vilhelm being shot and told her to 'tell them what you saw'. Or so she says. And the only piece of evidence we have is a hammer."

"What sort of hammer?"

"A sledgehammer with the handle cut off about halfway, to make it easier to hide, I guess. I'd imagine they planned to break the door down, but according to the girl, it wasn't locked and they walked right in on them. Screwing by firelight," he added with a leer.

"So we comb every hardware shop in the country until we find someone who sold a sledgehammer recently?" Gunna suggested. "I take it this was a new hammer rather than an old one?"

"It looks brand new. It's at the forensic lab now being checked for prints and anything else it might tell us."

"Gunnhildur?" Ívar Laxdal said in a bleak voice. "Background?"

"Businessman. University drop-out. Married, one child. Supposedly lives in Copenhagen, but seems to have been on the move a lot in the last few years. He had business interests all over, but it seems he saw which way the wind was blowing a few years ago and disposed of most of what he had in Iceland before the financial crash, which was when he decamped to Copenhagen."

"So no fool, then?"

"Not stupid, at any rate. Vilhelm Thorleifsson had interests in Lithuania, Latvia, Denmark, here and also at one time in West Africa."

"Africa?" Sævaldur asked. "How did that happen?"

"Shipping," Gunna said. "He's from a fishing village in the Westfjords."

Sævaldur smirked. "A relative, maybe?"

"Not as far as I know," Gunna shot back. "My relatives tend to be of the poor but honest variety. His father owned a boat and he sold it for him, after which he worked for a shipbroker and did very well selling tonnage and quotas on his own account. The Africa connection is something I haven't got to the bottom of in the couple of hours since I came back from leave. I gather he was contracted to sell a ship, sold it to himself at a knock-down price, and ran it himself, so there's one of probably many unhappy clients there."

"Do you think it's relevant? Unhappy clients with grudges to settle?"

Gunna spread her hands in question. "Who knows? If there's some serious money involved, then it certainly could be."

"Next move?" Ívar Laxdal asked.

"I'll be speaking to his wife in the morning. Eiríkur will be digging into our victim's business affairs and has already contacted police in Denmark and various Baltic States to find out if they have anything on him. We also need to consult financial crime. It seems Vilhelm Thorleifsson was investigated for insider trading in the aftermath of the crash, but there was nothing that could be nailed down, even though he came up smelling of shit."

Ívar Laxdal clapped his hands once.

"Go. All of you. Get on with it. Gunnhildur, a word, if you please. Sævaldur, come and find me before five. That's it," he ordered and the room cleared in seconds. "You and Sævaldur can thank your lucky stars that upstairs wants me to head this. None of us is going to come out of this well," he warned her in a low voice once the room had emptied.

"You think so?"

"What do you think, Gunnhildur? A contract killing carried out by two professionals, probably foreign, who have undoubtedly left the country by now and the weapon is at the bottom of Borgarfjördur. We don't have a hope in hell of cracking this without a very lucky break somewhere along the line."

"I hope you're wrong about that."

"I'm always right," he said. "You know that. But," he added and paused.

"But what?"

"Sævaldur will get nowhere. With luck he'll get a sighting of one of these people and possibly a description. If we get anywhere, the answers are going to come from his business background. So dig as deep as you like."

He sorted the haul in the basement, leaving Lísa upstairs, rolling pastry with a look of concentration on her face and a smudge of flour on the end of her nose. The silver went into one pile, the gold into another, and then into bags. One thing he had put into his bag without looking at it closely was a heavy bag of stiff, old paper that crackled between his fingers as he spilled its contents onto the bench. He fingered the eight heavy gold clasps and let the long chain coil itself into a pile. He scooped it into his palm and weighed the chain in his hand, hundreds of finely wrought links that flowed like water through his fingers with a single gold cylinder at one end, and a single decorated gold tube as big as his thumb and which clunked as it landed heavily on the bench.

Orri knew what it was and for the first time ever he wondered if he should not have taken something. His grandmother had owned a similar collection, the clasps and chain from the ornate bodice of a set of national dress of the kind worn by a well-to-do lady of maybe a century ago, while the heavy gold tube would have formed part of the long tassel of the black cap that would have topped the ensemble. The clasps were a little worn and the rich gold gleamed dully under the single harsh overhead light in his storeroom. Someone had treasured this and kept it carefully, just as his grandmother had done, keeping hers for her own daughter in the vain hope that the girl's inheritance would not be sold at the first opportunity and converted into a weekend's solid partying or the down payment on a car.

Running the gold chain through his fingers and arranging the clasps in their two rows on the rough timber bench, he wondered who had owned the set. It was something he had never done before. Gold was money, and money in the bank was, supposedly, security. He cursed briefly. Laptops, fancy mobile phones and iPods had none of the patina of age and affection that the old woman's gold had, and he decided involuntarily that this was not something for the Baltic boys to melt down.

He sighed, disturbed at his own thoughts. Orri put the clasps and chain back in the paper bag and placed it at the back of the drawer under the bench. It was certainly not something to hold on to, so he would have to find a buyer for it somewhere; someone local. Conscious that a risk accompanied this, he knew that at least this way it would probably find its way onto a set of national dress. Plus it would fetch more than it would for scrap. He had no use for the thing himself, although Lísa would admire it if she ever got to see it, knowing that she had a set of national dress that she occasionally brought out for weddings and suchlike events that he preferred to steer clear of. But then, Lísa had a proper family made up of ordinary people she got on well with, not like the untrustworthy crowd of drunks and shysters that made up his motley group of relatives.

As always, Valmira drove. Natalia sat by the window and smoked in direct contravention of company rules, her head half out of the window. Emilija sat in the middle seat of the van and wrinkled her nose as each blast of smoke-laden air wafted into the cab.

"Do you have to?" she demanded. "Can't you wait ten minutes until you get home?"

"Hey, don't be like that. Just because you gave up's no reason to stop me having one."

"She's right," Valmira said from behind the wheel. "You always smoke in the van and I wish you wouldn't. It stinks."

Natalia threw her half-smoked cigarette away and wound the window closed, trapping the poisoned air inside while Valmira drove in silence and Natalia stared sulkily at the pavements and shop windows. She got out by the shop near her flat in Breidholt without a word and stalked away, lighting another cigarette as she walked, as if to prove a point.

"We've upset her now," Emilija said with a sly smile.

"Yeah. And it wouldn't be the first time. I hope she turns up in the morning. I don't want to see her lose her job."

"That's not going to happen, is it? She just turns on the charm when she needs to and Viggó melts when she gives him a smile."

"It's not something you can miss, is it? She does the same with his old man as well. Have you noticed? Still, hopefully she won't be sulking tomorrow."

"You know what these hot-blooded South Americans are like. She'll have forgotten it by the morning."

"I know," Valmira said with a sigh. "And it's not going to stop her smoking in the van, is it? You OK for tomorrow?"

"I am," Emilija said, yawning and stretching her hands behind her head. "The boys are going to their father tonight, so I have an evening to myself for once."

"It's a shame you'll be on your own," Valmira said, shifting down a gear and listening to the van's gearbox complain.

"Says who?" Emilija asked with an arch smile.

"What? A new guy? Tell me!"

"Early days. But who knows?"

"Local boy?"

"No." Emilija laughed. "Not again. He's a sweet guy and he's from Latvia."

Valmira looked dubious. "He's OK, this guy, is he? Not like . . .?"

"No, nothing like him, I'm pleased to say," Emilija said with a shiver.

CHAPTER
THREE

"Oh, did I wake you?" Drífa asked as Gunna blearily appeared in the kitchen. "I'm sorry. I was trying to be as quiet as I could."

"It's all right. You didn't wake me up and I have to be in early anyway."

"I thought you weren't at work until the afternoon?"

"Something's come up. Can't you sleep?"

"I was hungry and Kjartan needed a feed."

There was a newspaper on the table that Drífa had been reading, scattered with the crumbs of a sandwich. Gunna poured herself orange juice, squinting at the clock and dismayed to see it was a few minutes past five and there was light outside beyond the kitchen curtains. "That's both of us then. Too early to be up and too late to be going back to sleep," she decided. "I'd best make some coffee."

Drífa watched as Gunna set the percolator to run and disappeared back to the bedroom, emerging in uniform trousers and shirt.

"Have you heard from Gísli?" Gunna asked

"Yesterday. He should be back tomorrow."

"Already? That was a short trip, only two weeks. What did he say?"

"He said he's staying ashore for a few weeks now."

Gunna nodded and listened to the percolator hiss and mutter. She was dreading her son's return from sea, hoping that she would be able to contain the bitter recriminations she wanted to let fly at him over his having given her two grandsons in the space of a few weeks. At the same time she longed to have their old close relationship back, while admitting to herself that it could take years and effort on both sides for them to regain that old intimacy.

She knew that Laufey missed her big brother and that the two of them were in touch, something that was a comfort while she and Gísli had become estranged for the first time in their lives. There was a bond between the half-siblings that she appreciated and which was something she had missed in her own upbringing with two considerably older brothers who she felt still treated her like an irritating youngster.

"They're docking in Hafnarfjördur," Drífa said, startling Gunna from her thoughts. "Steini said he'd go and pick Gísli up from the ship."

"Oh, that's good of him."

"I don't think Steini minds. He and Gísli really get on, don't they? Is it because Gísli . . . ?"

"Because Gísli what?" Gunna asked.

"Because Gísli's father was never about?"

She could see Drífa biting her lip, as if the question might be a step too far.

"Could be," Gunna admitted. "Or it might be because Steini doesn't have sons of his own."

34

"Oh, I see," Drífa said, relieved that the question hadn't elicited a sharp reply.

"Thanks for letting us stay the night," she added after a pause.

"Don't be silly. You're always welcome."

A little over a year ago a heavily pregnant Drífa had appeared on Gunna's doorstep, deep black hair in disarray, mascara in streaks down her face and looking for a sympathetic shoulder to cry on. Since then the mascara made only rare appearances and the black hair dye had grown out as Drífa's priorities had been forced to change dramatically.

"Just as well," Gunna muttered to herself.

"Sorry?"

"What?"

"You said something?"

"It's all right. Just thinking to myself."

Drífa lapsed back into silence as the percolator hissed to a standstill. Gunna poured her first mug of coffee of the day and pulled back the curtains to let in the first thin hint of pre-sunrise daylight.

He had finished his collections and was unloading when Alex returned from his pick-ups. Orri drove carefully, cautious not to let the forklift slide on the rain-wet concrete as he lifted the pallet that had weighed down his van on the way back. The forklift whined and complained but did as it was asked, under protest, unwillingly depositing its load on the warehouse floor. Orri hoped that it would lift it onto the truck later when it came to be collected.

Alex stood in the doorway and lit a cigarette, watching as Orri moved the forklift across the floor to the charging bay on the far side and plugged it in.

"You have anything for me?" he asked with a dramatic look around him as Orri stood outside and took a breath of cold air.

"A few bits. Not a lot."

"What sort of gear?"

"A couple of electric drills, good brands, no rubbish. An iPad. A couple of phones. A couple of good watches. A bit of metal."

Alex wrinkled his nose. "Not much," he said dismissively. "You not working too hard, are you?"

"Just being careful. That's all."

"Bruno won't be happy."

"Bruno can kiss my arse," Orri replied. "If I get caught, you guys aren't the ones who'll be doing time for it."

Alex looked shocked for a moment, and then smiled. "Maybe Bruno don't buy from you if you don't have the goods."

Orri shrugged elaborately to demonstrate his lack of interest. "Plenty of people willing to buy good stuff," he said with a wink just as theatrical as the shrug. "There are other buyers than just Bruno out there. You know, sometimes I wonder if this Bruno guy really exists."

Alex's eyes widened in unconcealed curiosity and he ground out his cigarette beneath the toe of his boot. "You believe so? Not so many now, I think." He made a play of elaborately extracting another cigarette from its packet and looked into the grey distance as he lit it. "I have a few contacts as well," he said quietly. "Just so you know."

"You're telling me that you're in competition with Bruno? That might be a dangerous game."

This time Alex shrugged and Orri sensed the bravado. "Bruno is not so much here now. He's busy back home. Some of his friends there come to me and ask if I can send to them. Tools, electronics," he said. "Metal."

Orri could see the gleam in his eye and understood that Alex desperately wanted to be a kingpin himself, not just the messenger boy who ran the risks.

"Yeah, right," Orri said. "What happened to Juris? I think it's a risky game you're getting into, Alex."

Alex snapped his fingers and winked again. "Juris was careless. I have friends. Juris didn't have friends like mine."

Vilhelm Thorleifsson's wife was remarkably composed for a brand-new widow, Gunna thought, and her mind was inexorably dragged back to Raggi's sudden loss. It was a long time ago, she told herself ruthlessly, but someone else's loss always reminded her of that devastating shock and the terrible aimless year of depression that followed it. The fact that it was a long time ago made no difference on the occasions when the thought caught her unawares and the misery came flooding back.

"Gunnhildur Gísladóttir, I'm with the CID team investigating your husband's death. My condolences," she offered, knowing in advance that they would not be wanted.

Vilhelm Thorleifsson's wife sat stiff on the edge of a leather sofa at her parents' vast house where nothing was out of place and Gunna wondered if dust would ever dare to get past the front door, let alone settle in the corners.

"What happened?" She asked in a blank voice.

"Your husband was murdered by two attackers," she said baldly, deciding that Saga probably had no desire to be shielded from any gory details. "He was shot, twice, at close range."

"Was it quick?"

"Probably."

"That's a shame. Was his extremely personal assistant with him?"

"Personal assistant?"

"Yulia. The Russian girl."

"Yes, so it seems."

"And was she hurt?"

"Physically, no."

"That's a shame as well."

"I take it you didn't get on?"

"Me and Villi or me and the Russian girl?"

"I meant you and your husband."

"We had our moments. But not for a few years. He led his life and I lead mine."

She sat almost immobile, her face a mask that Gunna guessed had to be artificial to achieve quite such an unnatural lack of mobility. Saga's knees were pressed together as she sat on the edge of the sofa, her back straight. Her skirt and jacket looked to Gunna's eyes as if they had been tailored from the same supple leather as the sofa's covering. A starched blouse was buttoned to the throat and ink black hair shrouded a narrow face that might have been attractive if it were to see a little animation.

"How long had you been living separately?"

"We live together, just in separate rooms. Villi chased his businesses from country to country and I'd given up asking him when we were likely to see him next."

"How about his business affairs? Did you have any involvement in his work?"

"No. Nothing. Occasionally he'd give me something to sign as I was a name on some of his companies, but I just signed without looking too closely."

"Isn't that rash? Signing something without reading the small print?"

"Villi was a shit husband, but he knew how to make money. Cashwise, I could trust him. But not dickwise."

"We'll need to take a look at his business affairs."

"Good luck. Most of Villi's business was in his head, and what wasn't there is in his laptop, if you can get into it."

"Property?"

"The house in Copenhagen is mine. I made sure of that when the first personal assistant showed up five or six years ago."

"There's more than one?"

"Three to my knowledge. Maybe more. They're always bright and beautiful. Gold diggers. That's why the houses are in my name only. I hold the real estate;

Villi got to play. It was — what do you call it? — a mutual understanding."

"Holiday? What's that?"

Emilija looked up, the toilet brush held in front of her like a sword.

"I just asked," Natalia said, propping herself against the basin and feeling in her pockets for a cigarette before reminding herself that smoking on the job was a sackable offence. "When did you last have a trip home? When did you last see your parents?"

"I'm not sure. Three, four years ago," Emilija said, applying herself to the toilet, even though it was virtually in its original pristine state. "It was before Anton was born, and before the divorce. So four years, I think. And you?"

Natalia scowled. "Ten years."

"What? As long as that?"

"At least," Natalia growled, spraying and polishing the mirror over the basin. She stopped, tensed, placed her hands on the edge of the granite slab the two basins were set in and jumped. She stood on the slab to polish the top half of the mirror. "Hjörtur will never agree to let Nonni out of the country. He thinks I wouldn't bring him back."

"And he'd be right, wouldn't he?"

Natalia looked at herself in the mirror and pulled a face. "Yeah. Probably. But it's a long time to not see your home, parents, friends, all that stuff."

"Finished, ladies?" Valmira asked, appearing in the doorway.

"Almost," Natalia replied. "I'm just finishing polishing the mirror and Emilija's busy with some old bastard's shit-stained toilet. Apart from that, we're almost done."

Emilija used her shoulder to push from her eyes a strand of hair that had come adrift.

"Hey, Vala. When did you last get to go home?"

Valmira looked at her sideways with disquiet.

"What do you mean? Home?"

"You know," Natalia said, jumping neatly down from the granite slab and wiping off the marks her trainers had left. "Home. Yugoslavia. The place you lived in before."

"This is home," Valmira said shortly. "I've never been back and I don't intend to," she added sharply before leaving the room.

"Not a good question," Emilija said quietly.

Natalia scowled. "What did I say?"

"It's sensitive. Valmira had a bad time, what with the war there and everything. She was in hospital a long time when she was a kid. Didn't you know?"

Natalia flushed the toilet and gave it a final squirt of bleach. "Hell, no. I didn't know that. I don't know her as well as you do."

"I don't know much either. I don't ask and I don't think she wants to tell. But she lost some of her family in the war; I don't know what happened to Valmira, but she was hurt, anyway. So now you know."

"She won't be upset, will she?"

Emilija shrugged. "A few minutes, then she'll be OK again. Don't worry."

41

"Is that why she's alone? No boyfriend, no husband?"

"Nothing," Emilija said with a shake of her head. "There's an uncle and some cousins. That's it. I'm not even sure she's ever . . . You know."

"Played hide the sausage?"

"Yeah. That's it. Not that she wouldn't want to, I reckon. But Valmira has a few big problems in that department. Best not to ask too many questions. Come on. Let's get this finished and we can pack it in for the day."

"Would anyone have wanted to do Vilhelm harm? Anyone you can think of?"

"I don't know." Saga had hardly moved and her voice was toneless. "There must be plenty of people who would have happily broken his nose, but I don't imagine they would have gone as far as killing him. But someone did, I suppose, and I don't really know what sort of thing he was getting up to in Russia and Lithuania."

"Any business partners?"

"Not really. Not any more. Villi was solo more or less, as far as I know. Not that he told me too much."

"All right, is there anyone in his business circles who might know more?"

"Try the assistant. She might know who he was in bed with." Saga leaned forward and extracted a cigarette case and a lighter from a handbag at her side, camouflaged in the same leather as everything else around her. "Apart from her, that is. Although maybe

42

not. The assistants tend to be decorative rather than useful." A lighter clicked like a pistol and she sent a plume of smoke up into the sterile air. "But if anyone knows, it'll be his friends. The few he had left, that is."

"Names?"

"Elvar Pálsson, Sunna María Voss. Those are the ones he seemed to take care not to piss off too much. I suppose a man needs to hold on to a few friends."

A pale face appeared in the doorway and a girl in her early teens appeared. Gunna saw the same sharp cheekbones and thin lips as Saga's, but framed in a younger face.

"Mum?"

"Not now, darling. I have to talk to this lady."

"About Dad?"

"Yes, dear. About your father." The last word dropped from Saga's lips like a curse.

"Are you going to find the person?" The girl asked, looking at Gunna.

"I hope so. We're doing our best."

The girl nodded and withdrew, apparently satisfied with Gunna's answer.

Gunna wrote down the two names. "Elvar Pálsson?"

Saga nodded slowly.

"And Sunna María Voss?"

"That's her. They were at university together, all three of them. Elvar has been Villi's partner in a lot of shady ventures. Sunna María married a dentist. We went to their wedding in Antigua. It was lovely," she reminisced and her face softened for the first time.

"They are both here in Iceland?"

"Sunna María and her dentist live here. Kópavogur somewhere. Elvar? Yeah. He's around somewhere. He seems to pop up. Villi always knew where he was."

Winter was best, dark all the time and no problem getting about without being noticed. When it was cold and dark, people also hurried more and didn't hang around watching to see who that was across the street bundled up in a padded coat and hat. Summer could be good as well, but different. That was when people were away and left their stuff there for the taking, Orri thought, wishing it could be summer again and knowing that it wasn't far away.

The street he was interested in was a new one, a row of low-slung houses with flat roofs, the street deserted and silent as only a cold morning could make it. He could see that each one had its lower storey dug deep into the ground as a basement while the long tinted windows above showed that these were houses for people with money, or access to it. The concrete of the walls was still a shiny grey, with a sheen that a year or two of weathering would dull if it were not painted, and the gardens were wide open. The straggling twigs at the edges would one day be hedges and trees, but for the moment they were little more than sticks scratching for a foothold and waiting for winter to end.

Deliveries in this exclusive half-built suburb had sparked his interest in the area. This part of Kópavogur on the older western side of the main road was fertile hunting ground for a man of his talents, he felt. As the area was hardly a fashionable one, it was populated by

44

mostly prosperous middle-aged people, his preferred type of homeowner.

The waterside houses of this new street had all been finished, but on the landward side was a row of plots in various states of completion; one that was clearly weathertight and ready for work inside, while another was still a concrete foundation and another was not even that far advanced, still a series of trenches with the steel mesh in place, ready for the foundations to be poured.

He rubbed warmth into his hands, the rubber of the thin latex inside sticking to the wool of the gloves he wore over them. He had been discreetly walking around this quiet end of Kópavogur for a few days, paying particular attention to the street of new houses and making a habit of going purposefully the same way, so the neighbours would assume he lived there, or at least somewhere close by. Orri reckoned that being part of the scenery helped as he checked out the houses on the city side of the street. These were the smartest houses, the ones with nothing but rocks and water behind them.

Less chance of being noticed, he mused. Once behind one of the houses, there would be nobody to see him taking his time finding a way in around the back. The downside was that a rapid retreat by taking a short-cut over someone's garden was out of the question. The slope down to the sea, not a problem in summer, was slick with melting ice and would take him only to the sea-smoothed rocks of the shoreline.

On a day like today, with a hint of spring in the air and the days finally getting longer he reflected that it was between two seasons. Maybe it would be better to cash in a few of his investments or raid his own bank account and spend a week or two in the sun, even though he had been determined not to take a holiday quite yet, telling himself that a few more jobs were needed to lift his finances first. He worried about the amount of gear he had managed to collect recently, all of which needed to be turned into cash. That was where he felt his business plan had failed him.

Looking quickly along the street behind him, and with nothing to be seen either way, Orri ducked along a footpath at the side of a square house and kept close to the wall as he went rapidly around the back. Like the rest of this brand-new street, it was a big house, built with its big corner window overlooking the sound separating the old end of Kópavogur from the newer suburb in Gardabær, where smart blocks of flats had replaced the shipyard and slipway where he remembered his father working a long time ago, coming home with his face blackened from welding and the persistent cough that had finally finished him. He peered in through the basement windows and wondered whether or not he should call the house's landline number. He had found out who roughly half the inhabitants of the street were and had their phone numbers stored away. He knew where some of them worked, what cars they drove and in some cases how many children they had. This house he knew belonged to a couple with a dental practice in the Kringlan shopping centre. There were no children as far as he had been able to work out, and although he knew the couple's names, he wasn't sure of their age group. There could be children who had left home, or there could be house guests, or even elderly parents visiting from some godforsaken dump in the country. That was information that couldn't be gleaned from phone books and the internet.

As he scanned the doors and windows, his mind drifted back to business and the gap in his way of working. Finding cash in any serious amount was almost unheard of these days now that everyone used plastic, and credit cards were of limited value, even though they could be picked up anywhere. A good, modern phone, a camera or an iPad would be worth grabbing. Sometimes there were old books or ornaments in glass cases that a dealer might take. While jewellery was always worth having, it was getting harder to fence and Orri didn't like dealing too often with the Polish and Lithuanian boys who melted down gold. It was only a matter of time before one of them was collared and spilled his guts to the police, and Orri regretted there was no honour among honest thieves. The hard boys from the Baltic had their ways of spiriting merchandise away to Europe, but if it came to the crunch, any one of them would drop him in the shit before one of their own. Not that he blamed them, he thought, hand on the handle of the back door as he eased it open. If one of the Baltic boys were to be shipped home after squealing to the law, his kneecaps wouldn't last more than a week at the outside.

Orri stiffened as he listened at the door. The sound of a radio could be heard faintly and the house had a warm feeling to it, telling him there was someone inside. He made his way through the dim basement and up a spiral staircase, taking care to place his feet gently on the metal steps. At the top he listened at the door but could hear no sound of movement. Orri eased open the door and cursed as it squeaked, hearing at the same moment the rush of water from a running shower and seeing steam billowing from the open door of the bathroom opposite him.

"Hi, sweetheart, you're early," a woman's voice sang out playfully. "Shut the door, will you? There's a draught. Come and join me, if you want."

Orri stood transfixed. Through the open bathroom door he could see that the entire wall opposite him was a mirror. It was half misted over, but at the centre of it he could see the reflection of a tall woman with a wet helmet of hair swept back over her head, eyes closed and energetically soaping breasts and a taut belly beneath pounding jets of hot water. He wondered for a second what to do, unable to tear his eyes from the steam-shrouded vision in the mirror.

"Hello?" The woman called out. "Is that you?"

There was a note of uncertainty in her voice that decided him. Dealing with people was not his style. He gently shut the door and made his way back the way he had come, taking advantage of the house's windowless end wall to hop unnoticed over the low fence into the unkempt garden next door.

He pulled some sheets of glossy paper from his pocket and held them ready in one hand. It wasn't a great cover, but delivering flyers for a pizza delivery place was at least a reason to be standing next to someone's front door if he were challenged.

Orri walked round to the front of the house, stuffed a flyer through the door, listened to the clack of the letterbox echo in the hallway behind it and scratched his head as he tried to remember who lived in this house. He went with confidence down the path and back to the dentist's house, taking his time stuffing a flyer through the letterbox as he listened for signs of life inside.

It wasn't fair, he decided on the way back to the street. People used to leave their cars outside as a decent indication of whether or not they were home. Putting the car in a garage that any normal person would use to store junk was downright unnatural and could confuse an honest housebreaker.

He continued along the street, posted a few flyers into more letterboxes and made his way back to where he had left his car, disturbed by the sight of the blonde woman in the shower and his mind unable to settle on anything else. He made himself walk at an unhurried pace. He had left the house fifty metres behind him, walking stiffly with his hands deep in his pockets, when a slate grey car swished through the puddles past him, drew up and parked opposite the house. A tall man with a look of furtive excitement jumped out, hurried across the road and looked both ways along the street before disappearing behind the building, along the same path Orri had taken.

Gunna never felt entirely comfortable during her infrequent visits to the financial crimes division. Her own confusion when faced with figures longer than a telephone number and a vague guilt at never having mastered long division left her in awe of people who could look at a company's annual report and pick holes in it.

Björgvin looked older than when she had spoken to him last, which was more than year ago. There were hints of grey at his temples and a now permanent furrow in his high forehead, but he still had the same engaging smile.

"*Hæ* Gunna. Good to see you," he greeted her, mug in hand as he made for his desk. "You want one?"

Gunna shook her head. "No, thanks, First smoking, then caffeine. I tell you, it's no fun being middle aged."

"Get away with you. Middle aged? I can look up your date of birth easily enough."

"I'll save you the trouble. Forty-one and a grandmother. Twice."

"In that case, congratulations. So what can we do for you? Or is there anything you can do for us, maybe?"

Gunna sat down, pulled a single sheet of paper from her pocket and unfolded it on Björgvin's desk.

"I'm hoping we might be able to help each other out here," she said, running a finger down the names. "Vilhelm Thorleifsson, dead. His business partner is a character called Elvar Pálsson, who's sometimes in Iceland and sometimes not."

One of Björgvin's eyebrows lifted and he cradled his chin in one hand as she spoke.

"Then we have the dentist and his wife, Jóhann Hjálmarsson and Sunna María Voss."

"The names ring a bell," Björgvin said thoughtfully. "A company called Sólfell Investment, which went bankrupt a while ago for quite a few million and with no assets. I've encountered Vilhelm Thorleifsson and Elvar Pálsson before. Not recently, but their names have cropped up. This is the character who was murdered in Borgarfjördur, right?"

"That was Vilhelm."

"He had been involved in some investments, but I gather his business isn't in Iceland these days. You know the kind of thing with companies owning shares of other companies and the trail going dead in Cyprus or Tortola? He had been a shipbroker a few years ago and did some deals in West Africa, something to do with landing illegal fish outside the EU and getting it repacked with all the right certificates. There was an EU investigator enquiring about him not long ago, but I don't think it came to anything."

"But are he and Elvar Pálsson working together?"

"Probably." He smiled wryly. "It's not a big country, you know. Iceland's business community isn't that large, so you can keep tabs on who's doing what even when it's nothing we need to take a direct interest in. The hard part is when we do have to take an interest because it gets so complex."

"Why does all this stuff have to be so complicated?" Gunna asked, knowing that the question was a stupid one but still determined to ask.

Björgvin shrugged and smiled weakly. "It's hard to tell," he said finally. "I suppose it's fashionable to tie things up in knots, and it keeps the accountants and lawyers in business. Let's say that if there are many entities involved, then ownership can get very complex, with percentages of this owned by one company and a share of something else held by another, and so on. That's one reason," he said and paused.

"And the other?"

"It's the obvious one. It's to discourage people like you and me from figuring out what's really going on. The more complex the ownership, especially when foreign subsidiaries are involved, then generally the more reason there is to dig into what somebody wants to keep quiet." He sighed and leaned back. "And it's worth keeping in mind that much of this is aimed solely at avoiding paying tax. It's when it becomes evasion rather than avoidance that it gets sticky."

"Rather you than me, Björgvin. But could you have a look at these people, or have a trawl through the archives?"

He rocked gently back and forth in his chair, chin in hand. "I've heard these names before, Jóhann Hjálmarsson and Sunna María Voss. Any relation to Jón Vilberg Voss, by any chance?"

"I'm not sure yet, but it sounds likely."

"Ah." Björgvin's face lit up. "I know him, slightly. He's practically a relative, actually. His ex-wife is my cousin."

"Small world."

"In the rest of the world there are supposed to be six degrees of separation between any two individuals. That's the theory. In Iceland, it's something like two degrees at most. Like I said." He grinned. "It's a small country. What's your theory on all this?"

Gunna splayed her palms wide. "The murder says payback to me. Very professional and no traces, no leads. I'm wondering if he did a deal that went sour and someone is settling a score, maybe to maintain face. If it's anything to do with the companies that these four people owned, or still own jointly, then I really don't want the others to be blasted on my patch."

Orri found he was sweating by the time he reached the van. His breath gradually slowed and his heart stopped racing as he wondered if almost being seen had given him the shock, or if it had been the unexpected sight of the dentist's statuesque wife in the mirror that had given him a turn.

He switched on the engine and listened to it hum as he conjured up the sight again in his mind; he shivered as he realized what could have been if he had been a few minutes earlier or later. He could have walked straight into the woman, or else her boyfriend could have found him on those metal stairs with nowhere to go. Orri felt slightly sick at the thought. He had been inside countless people's houses and never took chances. His visits were careful and he made sure people were at work or on holiday when he arrived to relieve them discreetly of their valuables.

Orri felt he had let himself down and couldn't understand why he had gone against his instincts by breaking his own rules twice in quick succession. He slipped the van into gear and headed back to town. Shaken, he drove more slowly than usual. By the time he pulled up outside his flat at the less fashionable far end of Kópavogur his growling stomach insisted it was lunchtime.

His heart sank as he noticed Lísa's tired Ford parked in his space. He tried to remember if she had mentioned she was coming over today, and he was tempted to drive away and have an hour or two to himself, but the thought of another spell in heavy traffic without anywhere particular to go wasn't appealing and he got out of the car. He liked the girl, and she clearly liked him a lot. How they had become a couple was something he didn't quite understand. It had been a rare one-night stand for each of them, as they both felt they had long grown out of spontaneous Friday night couplings with virtual strangers. But Lísa hadn't gone home the next morning, and within a week it was as if they had been married longer than Orri's grandparents.

He took the flights of steps at a run, wondering if Lísa had come to cook, if a takeaway was more likely, or if she expected him to take her out. Orri had no desire to go out and a takeaway would be his preferred option, he decided. A meal, an afternoon in front of the TV and an uncomplicated screw, either in bed or on the carpet if Lísa were feeling adventurous. But the smell of spices hit him before he had even reached his front door and he knew that he would have to be complimentary about something experimental.

Lísa was hunched over a pan on the stove, her glasses teetering on the end of her nose as she pushed onions and peppers around in the sizzling oil.

"*Hæ*, sweetheart." She smiled. "All right, are you?"

"Not so bad," he allowed, dropping his jacket onto the back of a chair and disappearing into the spare room that he had used to accumulate junk of various kinds, although it was all ordered and he could put his hand on anything he wanted. He put the torch, his phone-jamming device and the lightweight backpack that folded down into a package the size of a wallet into a drawer and went back to the kitchen. Normally he would have stashed his burglary gear in the storeroom in the basement, but by now there was meat sizzling in the pan and the smell was making him hungry.

He wondered if Lísa suspected what he did on odd afternoons and weekends, and why when he wasn't at work he was so often out of touch. He poured a glass of the red wine that Lísa had brought with her.

"*Skál.*"

"*Skál*, honey," she replied, pouring the onions back into the pan with the chopped meat and adding a little water and a big squeeze of tomato paste. "Hot, or very hot?"

"What?"

"One chilli or two?"

"Two," he decided. "Good day?"

"Breakfast shift, so I've been up since five."

"Early night, then?"

She pushed her glasses up and smiled invitingly. "If you say so. How was your day?"

"Y'know," he said, sipping wine and thinking of the dentist's wife and her voluptuous figure, which contrasted with Lisa's spare frame. Still thinking of the figure in the shower, he gave Lisa a hug from behind, easily cupping her breasts in his hands.

"You smell of swimming pool," he said, his nose in her still damp hair.

"Forty lengths," Lisa said, wriggling free in his embrace as she stirred the pan. "Get me the big pot for the pasta, will you?"

CHAPTER
FOUR

Gunna already felt frustrated at the lack of progress. Sævaldur and his team were busy with the murder scene in Borgarfjördur and she had to keep telling herself that she and Eiríkur had not been sidelined. She reminded herself several times that Ívar Laxdal had told her clearly to leave Sævaldur to his part of the investigation and that she should concentrate on the victim's background. One aspect that she had to admit to herself made it less easy to get to grips with the case was that Vilhelm Thorleifsson had been a deeply unsympathetic character. Every morsel of information she uncovered about the man convinced her that it would only have been a matter of time before he was murdered, as his companies went bankrupt leaving fuming creditors in their wakes, while he continued to live a charmed life.

One contact whispered bitterly that it wasn't just the impending financial crash that had sent him to do business overseas, but the fact that so few people in Iceland were prepared to trust him any more.

A few hours on the phone, including a short conversation with the man's estranged wife, had told her that the victim's business partner Elvar Pálsson was living in London, as far as anyone knew, but had business interests in Britain and the Baltic States. Gunna reflected that half a dozen foreign police forces were now probably getting sick of repeated requests for information on this pair of Icelandic financial cowboys.

Although what appeared to be the pair's main business vehicle in Iceland, Sólfell Investment, had ceased trading more than a year earlier, she found the names of Vilhelm Thorleifsson and Elvar Pálsson listed among the directors of a dozen companies. One had its address registered at the chalet where Vilhelm Thorleifsson had been murdered. Two were registered at an address in Kópavogur and the rest at the Reykjavík address where the defunct Sólfell Investment had been based. The national register showed her that Elvar Pálsson had his legal address registered overseas and the phone book listed a couple of the companies at the same Reykjavík address.

After half an hour of producing a chart of ownership and cross-ownership on a whiteboard, Gunna stood back and admired her handiwork, shaking her head at the criss-crossed red, green and blue lines. With Vilhelm Thorleifsson's name in the centre of the board, it was clear that there was a network of people with reasons to wish him harm as well as those he had collaborated with. But as well as Elvar Pálsson's name, the multi-coloured strands pointed repeatedly at two more names and Gunna went back to the national register and the phone book to track down Sunna María Voss and Jóhann Hjálmarsson.

Orri had done his homework. The house he had visited belonged to Sólfell Property ehf, a limited company owned by Sunna María Voss and her dentist husband, which was no surprise. There was nothing unusual in rich people putting their property into the names of relatives or companies. What was a surprise was that several more of the bunker-like houses in the street were owned by the same company, along with two more at different stages of construction, one of them weathertight and the other still a set of half-dug foundations. He found that Sólfell Property even had a website of its own that listed several exclusive properties available for short- or long-term lease via a letting agency.

A few canny investments there, Orri decided as he spent an afternoon researching the street's residents still further. He reckoned that around half of the twenty houses in the street were owned by their occupants, the rest could be owned or rented and therefore less easy to find out much about the occupants.

"The dentist is dabbling in property." Orri laughed to himself as his fingers skimmed the trackpad of the laptop he had bought legally. He knew better than to have stolen goods lying around the flat. Merchandise was best disposed of quickly, he felt. Comparing the photos on Sólfell Property's website with satellite images, he was able to work out which houses were theirs and wondered if these would be worthwhile targets. It would be worth scouting around, at least. Anyone in the market to rent a house like that would be no pauper, although the research might be a little more involved than with someone who had lived in the same house for years.

Orri snapped shut the laptop and stood up, tossing his keys from hand to hand. A little drive out to the wealthier end of Kópavogur would not be a bad idea. Lísa wouldn't be back for a few hours yet and maybe he'd be nice to her for once and take her out for a meal. Nothing too fancy, mind, no waiters with waistcoats or any of that stuff. A pizza, or a fish meal at one of the trendy places near the harbour that were half-empty outside the tourist season.

Heading for the door with his fleece over his arm, he thought again about the dentist's wife and the vision of her, eyes closed with water coursing over her face and jutting breasts, past the taut belly to the dark triangle below. The thought added a spring to his step as he promised himself he was only going to observe.

The elderly lady was agitated and her husband fumed, standing up to take a few angry paces before sitting down again.

"You've no idea when this happened?" Eiríkur repeated wearily.

"Of course not," Matthildur Sveinsdóttir squawked, fingers busy with the frayed tassels of a shawl draped over her shoulders. "It wasn't until I saw my clasp in Aunt Bertha's window that I realized."

"Aunt Bertha?" Eiríkur asked.

"It's a shop."

"It's in Reykjavík," her husband explained, filling in the gaps. "They sell all kinds of old junk there."

"Antiques, he means," Matthildur corrected. "Ævar, why don't you go and look in the garage and see if anything's missing there?"

"Don't be stupid, woman. I always lock the garage. Unlike you, who's always leaving the back door unlocked."

"I do not!"

"Excuse me, can we get back to the matter in hand?" Eiríkur demanded, trying to sound as stern as he could. The old man stamped from the room, banging the door behind him. "Could we start again?"

Matthildur Sveinsdóttir took a deep breath. "Yes. Well, Ævar and I went downtown to do some shopping, like we usually do once a week or so because we like to have a walk around the centre and have a coffee in Hotel Borg or somewhere. Ævar misses town so much since he retired, you know," she prattled and Eiríkur groaned inwardly.

"I appreciate that, but what did you see in this shop?"

"That? I told you, didn't I? I saw a gold clasp just like mine, the one that came off my mother's best dress that she had from her mother. I'd been meaning to sew a new bodice for it for years and never got round to it, and now that the arthritis is playing merry hell with my fingers I probably never will, but I was going to pass it on to my daughter one day, you see, that's why I kept it in the drawer upstairs."

"So you are sure it's the same one as yours? How do you know?"

"Well, I said to Ævar straight away that it looked just like mine, and so we came straight home and I looked in the drawer upstairs and it was gone," Matthildur said with aggrieved triumph.

"You didn't go into the shop and look at the . . . what was it? A clasp? What is it exactly?"

The old lady pursed her lips in impatience. "A clasp. A set of gold decorations for national dress. Surely you know what I mean?"

"Gold? Was it worth much?"

"I don't know, young man, but Aunt Bertha had a damned respectable price tag on it. Surely you'll go and look? It was in the window an hour ago."

Eiríkur nodded, pretending to understand. "Is anything else missing from the house?"

"Ævar's watch, the smart one that he hardly ever wears, and I think Ævar said there was some money in the drawer as well."

"And you have no idea when these items disappeared?"

"They didn't disappear. They were stolen," Ævar's voice boomed furiously from the door. "There's nothing missing from the garage."

"You checked all the cupboards, did you?" Matthildur asked.

"Of course I did. You don't think I went out there and didn't have a proper look, do you?"

"Do you have a list of what's missing?" Eiríkur asked quickly, hoping to nip another squabble in the bud.

"Well, not really," Matthildur said after a moment's thought.

Eiríkur closed his notebook. "In that case, I'm going to go down to this Auntie Bertha place now. I need you two to go through the house, put together a list of what you think is missing — as detailed as you can make it — and to think hard about when you last saw these items so we can have an idea of how long they have been missing."

"Why do you need to know that?"

"Because that will give us an idea of when the break-in might have taken place," Eiríkur said, calling on reserves of patience. "And that means I can try and tie it in with other similar incidents, and hopefully get an idea of who might have been responsible."

"All right," Ævar growled. "You do that, young man, and when you find out who it is, I want to break his fingers one by one."

He drove past a couple of times and was pleased there wasn't a soul to be seen; not that the streets being deserted said all that much. In this kind of neighbourhood people walked from the door to the car and no further. The exclusive cul-de-sac where he could see the dentist's house at the end was quiet. There was no car to be seen and no lights on inside. It was the same further along the street at most of the houses on the seaward side, the ones he was most interested in, and at this time of the afternoon, experience told him that people could be unpredictable in their movements, though middle-aged people generally kept office hours.

He pulled on his gloves before leaving the car. Normally he preferred to simply walk in while the owners were at work or preferably on holiday somewhere far away, giving him time to concentrate without interruption. This time of day was dangerous and Orri knew he was taking a risk, reproaching himself again for breaking his own rules. People could appear unexpectedly, but he admitted to himself that it gave him a buzz of excitement.

He patted his pockets, made sure his torch was in his pocket and switched on the phone jammer, a little device that would interrupt any mobile phone traffic within 15 metres once it was switched on, not that he had needed it so far.

Orri padded silently though the still house, the back door lock opened easily with a strip of plastic, the torch between his teeth and a pool of light sweeping the floor ahead of him. The living room was a vast open space of hardwood floor with a nest of deep sofas in the centre, and just a few ornaments scattered here and there, mostly modernist artworks that his professional eye dismissed as being too heavy to carry as well as too easy to identify and trace.

A narrow room parallel to the living room was a more fruitful hunting ground. He wondered about the slim laptop on the desk, along with the battery charger the owner had thoughtfully left with it, but decided against it, reasoning that first he would look for the smaller, more easily portable stuff. A drawer yielded an iPhone, not the latest, but presumably the one the owner had upgraded from and still worth having. A digital camera from another drawer found its way into his backpack, along with the handful of foreign currency that every house seemed to have somewhere. This time it was a bundle of dollars and an envelope stuffed with assorted euros and some Swedish and Norwegian notes.

The bedroom was where he caught his breath and Orri could not stop his rising excitement. He started with the old-fashioned dresser. Sunna María Voss clearly had expensive taste in jewellery, and the necklaces, pendants and a couple of heavy silver bangles were an interesting haul, but he felt there had to be more if he searched for it.

The top drawers in a chest glided open and he slid a practised hand under and behind the contents of each one in turn, feeling for packets of boxes without disturbing anything. The dentist had nothing hidden among his socks and underwear, but he felt his heart beat faster as he went to Sunna María Voss's side of the wide bed and opened the first drawer. He leaned forward and bent his head close to inhale the lavender scent before he felt under and behind the frills inside to pull out a jewel case. He snapped open and was disappointed to find a necklace of pearls that gleamed palely in the light of the torch. Clearly old, and strung on a thread with a heavy silver clasp, he regretfully closed the case and replaced it. Pearls were old-fashioned and difficult to sell, not something that could be melted down into an anonymous lump.

He reflected that in the old days people kept their bank books in their bedrooms, but these days everything was online and traceable. Large amounts of cash had become an increasingly rare find, even in these difficult times when nobody trusted the banks as they had done only a few years ago.

Sunna María Voss's bedside table in the pool of pale light thrown by the torch revealed nothing but a few paperbacks, a jar of lube and a pack of condoms that gave Orri a sudden rush of excitement, a few half-consumed packets of painkillers and fluff in the corners.

Deciding that he had seen enough, Orri went slowly through the living room and along the hall, where he inspected the pictures on the wall. Paintings could be worth money, although not worth stealing other than to order. There were only large black-and-white portraits of the dentist and his wife, singly and together, the dentist clearly older than his wife by at least a decade, Orri guessed.

A sound startled him and he recognized the rumble of a garage door, followed by the double thunk of car doors closing somewhere below him and the clang of a footstep on the metal staircase from the basement. He guessed that the house's occupants were returning, cursing himself for having taken so much longer than he had needed to.

He cast about quickly, trying to decide where to go, and with the newcomers coming up from the garage in the basement, he made for the lobby and shut the door behind him. He had a moment of panic as he realized that the heavy front door was deadlocked. Although this would not normally be a problem to pick, there was no time to concentrate. He stood instead among coats and scarves hung behind the internal door, breathing long, deep breaths as he stayed calm, his hand on the handle.

A throaty laugh came from the stairs as the door leading up from the basement burst open and swung back to bang against the wall.

"Be a little bit patient, lover," the husky voice said teasingly as heels clattered on the tiles of the hall and he could hear a man's growl.

"I've been patient all day," the second voice said and Orri could feel the urgency in the man's tone. He risked putting his eye to one of the frosted glass panels on either side of the lobby door and could make out an indistinct image of a couple in a writhing embrace, mouths locked together.

He listened with mounting excitement as there was a rustle of clothing in the hall. There was a slow rip of velcro being pulled apart and he could hear the fumbling and giggling from both of them as they pulled at each others' clothes.

"You said Jóhann's away, didn't you?" The man's voice gasped.

"Sweetheart, he's enjoying himself in Frankfurt with his little Fraülein right now; you don't need to worry about him," the woman's voice assured her friend. "We have all the time in the world." She laughed. "Well, until tomorrow night, anyway."

"Come on, I want to see you without that dress hiding everything," the man almost panted.

"Then you'd better help a lady with it, hadn't you," she replied in a coquettish voice. "If you're in that much of a hurry."

Orri stood guiltily spellbound. He saw through the patterned glass as Sunna María Voss wrapped her arms around her lover's shoulders and he lifted her off the floor as she twisted her legs around his waist. Orri prayed that the door would withstand the punishment it was getting as the man's desperate thrusts impaled her against it, transmitting shock after shock to the door that rattled in its frame until he groaned and her moans subsided, then the two of them sank to the floor.

"Well done, big boy. Well done," he heard Sunna María Voss say to her hoarsely panting lover. Orri looked around and saw with relief that there was a key hung on a hook inside the coat rack. "Now it's my turn, maybe?" she suggested in a sardonic voice as Orri clicked the lock, swung open the door, closed it quietly and fled into the twilight.

Aunt Bertha was in one of the old houses at the older end of the city centre, surrounded by shops selling overpriced sweaters and mass-produced plastic elves and vikings. Eiríkur looked in the window first, and in spite of his height, he had to stretch to see the knick-knacks displayed in the narrow window of the old house that had been built on a concrete basement in the old-fashioned way.

He wondered how Matthildur Sveinsdóttir had been able to see anything in these same windows as he went up the steps and pushed open a door that chimed a tune as he entered the stuffy, scented room. He peered around him at the racks of second-hand clothing, the shelves of fashionably antique porcelain and the old posters and photographs of forgotten movie actors on the walls.

"Can I help?" A voice asked. Eiríkur had to look around to see and found that it came from a woman in a black-and-white dress and a hairdo held in place as if by magic. A closer look as he approached the counter told him she was probably closer to his own age than the look she had adopted would have indicated.

Eiríkur opened his wallet and the woman looked at it with surprise.

"Eiríkur Thór Jónsson. I'm a detective with the city force. There's a clasp in your display case, a gold clasp and set from a set of national dress. Could I have a look at it?"

"I . . . er. I suppose so," the woman said, clearly in doubt, pausing for a moment for a second look at Eiríkur's wallet before she took a key from the till and opened a glass-fronted display case. She placed a tray in front of him. The clasp and chain gleamed in the afternoon sunshine streaming through the windows.

"There's a problem?"

"It seems that this may be stolen goods," Eiríkur said, letting the heavy chain run through his fingers. "So, unfortunately, I'm going to have to take this away with me."

"What? But . . ."

"I'm sorry. But until this is sorted out, I have to confiscate it," he said, taking a form from his folder and starting to fill it in. "Your name?"

"Svandís Búadóttir."

"And you're the manager?"

"I'm the proprietor," she said, pushing out her chin and stretching herself to a height that almost reached Eiríkur's shoulder.

Eiríkur completed the form and turned it round on the counter. "Sign here, please."

"You really are a policeman, aren't you?"

"The genuine article. Now, I'd like you to tell me how this came to be here."

"What business is that of yours? I mean, this is intrusion, surely? It's intolerable."

"I'm sure the old lady whose bedroom drawer this was taken from thought the same."

Her hands went to her mouth. "You mean it really is stolen?"

"Very much so. Where did you get it from?"

"Such a pleasant young man," she mumbled absently. "And such a beautiful set. He said it had been his mother's."

"Did this pleasant young man leave his name?"

Svandís took a receipt book from under the counter, looked over Eiríkur's shoulder as a couple entered the shop and smiled at them before her sour expression returned. She flipped through the carbon copies of receipts until she found the page.

"There."

He read, "Jewellery received from Halldór Birgisson," followed by an identity number and a price that prompted Eiríkur to do a double-take.

"Is that how much this stuff costs?" He asked, picking the price tag off the tray the jewellery had been placed in and calculating that Svandís expected to charge roughly double what she had paid for it.

"It's old. Nineteenth century. This stuff doesn't grow on trees."

"I need to take this as well," Eiríkur said and watched Svandís open her mouth to protest as he pocketed the receipt book. "Don't worry. You'll get it back. I don't suppose that's his real name, so what did this guy look like?"

Svandís immediately looked blank. "Just average, I suppose."

"You don't have CCTV in here, do you?"

"No."

"Then when was he here?"

"Look at the receipt. The date's on it."

"Saturday? Two days ago? What time of day was it?"

"I'm not sure."

"Right. So what did he look like? Tall? Short? Hair colour? Facial hair?"

"Oh, I don't know. Taller than me but shorter than you."

"That applies to probably just about everyone in Iceland," Eiríkur said, putting a finger to his shoulder. "This tall?" He asked, moving it up. "Or up here?"

"That's closer."

"Just under two metres, then? Hair?"

"Ordinary. Brownish. Quite short."

"Beard? Moustache?"

"Stubble."

"Anything special you noticed about him? Any distinguishing marks?"

"Like what?"

"Scars, tattoos. That sort of thing."

"No. Nothing. Just a nice, ordinary young man. He said it was his mother's and that she'd died a few years ago and now he needed to stop his house being repossessed, so he had to sell it."

Eiríkur sniffed. "I'm sure. What was he wearing?"

"I'm not sure. I always look at the eyes, you know."

"Well, was he wearing a suit?"

"No. A coat of some kind. I think it was green."

"Now we're getting somewhere. Dark green? Light green? A long coat or a short one?"

"Short. It was one of those ones all the young people wear these days. Like the one you're wearing, only dark green."

"A fleece?"

"If that's what they're called. And it had some yellow letters on it."

"I don't suppose you remember what?"

Svandís put a hand to her forehead. "No. It's gone," she said, as if remembering was something painful.

"So we have a brown-haired man with stubble, roughly one metre eighty tall, wearing a dark green fleece with yellow lettering on it. Age?"

"I don't know. Under forty?"

"All right. How much under forty?"

"Thirty, maybe," she decided with an effort.

"Thank you. That all helps," Eiríkur said, zipping up his own fleece.

"When will I get that back?"

Gunna rang the bell, then hammered on the door that swung open in front of her to reveal a dark lobby.

"Who are you?"

She was confronted by a startled woman in a dressing gown that had clearly been hastily pulled on.

"Gunnhildur Gísladóttir, city CID. I'm looking for Sunna María Voss or Jóhann Hjálmarsson, or preferably both of them," she said, flicking open her wallet.

"CID? What's it about?"

"Are you Sunna María?"

"I am." She crossed her arms and cocked her head on one side. "Look, this really isn't convenient."

"Maybe not, but it is urgent."

"So urgent it can't wait until the morning? It's half-past seven and I'm about to go out."

"If it wasn't urgent, I'd be at home myself by now. Can I come in? This really is important."

"Tomorrow, please."

"You know Vilhelm Thorleifsson?" Gunna asked.

"Villi? Of course. Why?"

"He's been murdered."

"Murdered?" Sunna María asked. "You're sure?"

"I'm absolutely sure, which is why I'm here on your doorstep at seven thirty in the evening and not at home with my feet up. So are you going to let me in?"

"Æi, it's not exactly convenient . . ." She looked quickly over one shoulder and then back at Gunna.

"And it's not exactly convenient to be stood here in the dark," Gunna said with determination and took a step inside as Sunna María backed away.

"Wait here."

Sunna María disappeared into the darkened house, leaving the door open while Gunna pulled the outside door shut behind her. She could hear whispers and a chuckle from inside the house.

"This way, please. We'll go into the kitchen."

Gunna saw as she followed her along the corridor that Sunna María had brushed her hair and the dressing gown had been swapped for a silk kimono. Every door along the corridor had been shut and a slash of light from the kitchen at the end cut through the darkness.

"I don't even have coffee in the house," Sunna María apologized. "Jóhann drinks coffee in the mornings but I don't."

"That's all right," Gunna said, placing her folder on the table and opening it. "You knew Vilhelm Thorleifsson?"

"Of course. We've known him for years."

"We?"

"My husband and I."

"I take it that's not him in the other room? So can I ask where your husband is?"

"Germany, as far as I know. But he might have gone somewhere sunnier for a while. We lead pretty independent lives these days."

74

"It hasn't been released to the press yet. Vilhelm Thorleifsson was murdered three nights ago."

"That was Villi they were talking about on the news? Shit. I had no idea he was even in Iceland."

Gunna studied Sunna María's face as she chewed her lip and fidgeted with her hands. She stood up and walked around the room nervously and sat down again. "What happened? Can you tell me?"

"All I can say right now it that there was nothing accidental about it. You knew him well? I'm looking for anyone who might have held a grudge against him, anyone he may have pissed off enough to want to kill him."

Sunna María cupped her chin in her hand. "There's no shortage of people he owes money to. I mean," she said in a sudden show of confusion. "How? Who did this?"

"We don't know. It's under investigation and we don't have many details yet. You knew him socially or through work?" Gunna asked, although she already knew the answer.

"I was at college with him. Villi, me and my husband, we used to own a company together. Several companies, in fact."

Sunna María's lips puckered in a worried line.

"Including Sólfell Investment?" Gunna asked.

"That's one of them. It was wound up a few years ago."

"I understand it was bankrupt, wasn't it?"

"Well, yes." Sunna María shrugged and her mouth curled downwards as she shook her head dismissively.

"It's beside the point, anyway. We are looking at the very real possibility that there's a connection with you and your husband, and you might be in danger."

"You think so?" She said with a theatrical gasp. "Here in Iceland? Come on."

"I'm completely serious. It's not something we can rule out. I'd advise you not to stay here alone, and I'd go so far as to advise you not to stay here at all."

"Can't I get police protection if you think I'm in danger?"

Gunna wanted to smile at the suggestion. "Right now, no. We simply don't have the manpower available. It's something we'll be discussing tomorrow when we have more details."

"Was Villi murdered at that chalet he keeps in the country?"

"So I understand. You don't seem surprised?"

"The dirty devil. He used it as a hideaway so he could entertain his girlfriends. His wife was furious when she found out about it."

"I'm not exactly surprised. Had he owned the place for long?"

"Five or six years. Something like that. He had a share in a web design company. The company bought the chalet for team-building weekends, things like that. When it went out of business, I suppose he must have been able to hang on to it."

Gunna nodded and shuffled the papers in her folder. "Where can I find your husband?"

"Like I said, Germany. He was at a conference and then he was going somewhere else after that. I'm not sure where. I don't try and keep track of his travels these days."

"You have a phone number?"

Sunna María stood up and opened a drawer. "Plenty of them," she said, handing Gunna a card and pulling an iPhone from the pocket of her kimono.

Gunna looked at the card and saw Icelandic, Danish and German contact numbers. "Can I have that?"

Sunna María took the card and wrote a number she found on her phone on the back.

"That's the secret number he thinks I don't have," she said. "Call that one if you want to surprise him."

CHAPTER
FIVE

It was a bright evening and the sun bathed the mountains that Vestureyri sprawled under with a warm glow. There was hardly a breath of wind and the town could be seen reflected in the glassy water of the harbour. Gunna sat on the step at home with the schoolbooks she knew she ought to be reading, but English grammar had always been a trial. Stuffy stories of perfect families shopping and going to restaurants of the kind the little town certainly didn't boast had little meaning or interest, while the American films that the local cinema showed were another matter entirely. Somehow the English the heroes and shifty-eyed villains on the big screen spoke was a different world to pointless schoolbook English, and the strange and more exotic patter of the travelling Australian boys working in the fish factory was even more beguiling, scattered with abbreviations and crude slang that they would wryly explain if asked. Everyone knew that one of the girls at the factory had become very friendly with one of the travellers and a baby in the spring was being gossiped about already. Gunna wondered if Ríkey would be leaving with her Gary, or if they would stay in Vestureyri, or, more likely, the boy would simply move on and forget about the roots he had put down in this distant fishing village in the far north.

Danish with its back-of-the-throat vowels was even more of a battle and she put down the story of the little black Volkswagen in disgust as an engine roared through a cracked exhaust in the next street and she could hear the squeal of a fan belt that needed tightening. The tyres squealed and she stood up to look over the bushes by the gate to see if she could make out which of the local boys was pushing an old banger beyond its limits when she heard a sickening crash followed by silence. A few moments later there was a babble of angry calls and Gunna ran down the slope and around the corner of Old Togga's house to see a sleek grey car with steam coming out from under a crumpled bonnet. It had ploughed hard into the driver's side of a dark green car that she recognized with horrified despair as the one her father had spent long weekends and evenings restoring.

Gunna couldn't sleep. Yet another dream had woken her long before dawn and she leafed listlessly through yesterday's newspapers while the shards of the nightmare scene that had left her father crippled played out repeatedly in her mind.

The percolator bubbled and she padded to the bedroom door to close it, knowing that the aroma of coffee would bring Steini out, bleary-eyed and concerned that she had not been able to sleep. Gunna poured herself a cup of coffee and a bowl of cereal, and set them both on the Sunday paper with its alarming headlines. As she munched, she flipped uninterestedly through the pages, more than half of them to do with the upcoming council elections. Years before when she had taken an interest in local politics, she would have read every word. But now the overblown assertions and what looked suspiciously like downright lies failed to be convincing.

She finished the cereal and drank the remaining milk from the bowl as her phone quietly buzzed a text message.

Hi Mum. Are you around? Today? XXXg

Gunna nodded to herself, frowned her eyebrows into a single dark bar across her forehead and wondered what her errant son might want.

Sunna María was well into a late breakfast at Harbourside Hotel when Gunna walked in and watched her for a moment, delicately spooning up a bowl of chopped fruit. There was no sign of the invisible amorous companion whose presence had been unmistakeable at the house on Kópavogsbakki the night before.

"Good morning," Gunna said, sitting down without being asked and reaching for a cup as a waiter appeared.

"Are you a guest?" he asked. "Breakfast is for guests only."

"No, I'm not, but I could do with a cup of coffee all the same," Gunna said, unzipping her coat and hanging it on the back of her chair.

At the sight of her uniform, the waiter decided not to push the matter, disappeared on silent feet and returned with a flask.

80

"I spoke to your husband," Gunna said. "He's in Munich and flying home today, so I'll be back to speak to him this evening."

Sunna María slit open a roll as if she were cutting its throat. "I'm sure his Fraülein will be disappointed that her sugar daddy is leaving her," she said with satisfaction.

"That's something I didn't ask about," Gunna said in a sharper tone than she had intended. "He wasn't aware of what had happened to your former business associate."

This time there was a note of chagrin in Sunna María's voice. "He has other things to think about, I should think."

"What I'm looking for is a link to the killer, or killers, and I have to assess whether or not you are in danger yourself," Gunna said, looking at her over the rim of her coffee cup. "Do you feel you need protection? Have you upset people who might want to go to these extremes, or is there someone out there looking to settle a score? I gather there's another partner in some of these businesses, Elvar Pálsson?"

"Elvar ran Sólfell Investment. The rest of us were really just sleeping partners. But between them they must have upset lots of people, so I guess there are plenty to choose from." She smiled. "Jóhann and I came in as partners later, so maybe we haven't pissed off quite so many people."

"Where is Elvar now?"

"I don't know," Sunna María almost snarled. "We're old friends, but I don't keep tabs on him."

"Who would bear a grudge against Vilhelm Thorleifsson?"

This time she rolled her eyes. "Look, Villi was a businessman. There must be hundreds of people who have been sticking pins in wax effigies of him over the years. Then there's his wife, of course."

"Saga? Why do you say that?"

"You've met her. Surely you can figure it out."

"I can. But I want to hear your take on it."

Sunna María sighed. "Villi didn't have a faithful bone in his body. He physically wasn't capable of keeping his dick in his trousers, and a man with money to throw around doesn't need to. He had a constant stream of mistresses and girlfriends."

"Does that include you?"

"Please . . ."

"I can't not ask. You must realize that."

"All right. Yes. But it was a very long time ago. When we were at university. Long before he met Saga and way before I met Jóhann. Does that answer your question?"

"How come you and Jóhann came in as business partners?"

Sunna María sat back and dropped the roll she had buttered back on the plate. "I knew the boys because we were at college together. Jóhann had some money to invest back in 2003 or 2004 and we wanted to do more than just fix people's teeth."

"Your husband's a dentist?" Gunna asked, although she had already found this out and had called the smart practice in the Kringlan shopping centre the day before to see if he might be there.

"And a very good one. He bought a practice not long after he qualified, years ago — bought out an old boy who was ready to pack it in and retire to the golf course. Well, after a couple of years it turned out the building off Lindargata was worth a fortune, so he sold it to a developer who built a petrol station and a 10–11 store on the site. Jóhann banked the cash, got himself a smart financial adviser and rented a new place instead. That's when he started investing here and there."

"And that's where Vilhelm and Elvar came in?"

"Something like that. By 2006 they had figured out which way things were going to go here, so they started moving their business out of the country. Nothing flashy, just buying up smallish companies that weren't doing so well, putting in a project manager to split them up or turn them around, and once the books looked more positive, selling them on. It was good business. It still is. Elvar is still busy, but Villi had taken something of a back seat."

"And Jóhann and you?"

"We still have a couple of companies that are active with Elvar and Villi."

"So what about Sólfell Investment? That didn't do so well?"

Sunna María looked uncomfortable for the first time. "That didn't go as successfully as it should have done. It was an investment vehicle with a few other partners to develop some real estate here in the city."

"What went wrong?"

"I knew it was a mistake from the start and Elvar didn't like it, said it was too risky. In 2007 we bought some land. That's our other company, Sólfell Property, which has been doing rather well ..." She looked up and smiled, waving across the room.

A slim young man in a silver jacket appeared by the table.

"Why are you here, darling?" he asked, almost pleading and staring at Gunna's uniform in surprise. "This place is just so plastic."

"I know, Siddi. I'm so sorry, but I had some problems at home and had to move out for a few days while they're sorted out."

"Plumbing again? I remember telling you there was something wrong with the water."

"Yes, Siddi, and you were quite right." She picked up her room key from the table and handed it to the young man. "I'm in three oh five. You just go up and wait for me, I won't be long."

"Pedicure," Sunna María explained when Siddi had departed towards the lobby and the lifts. "Siddi works wonders."

"I'm going to need a list of companies, and a list of people."

"Suspects, you mean?"

"People who could conceivably be suspects, and I'll need it today."

Sunna María looked horrified. "Today? My diary's already full."

"In that case you'd best cancel a few things, because this isn't going to wait," Gunna said. "You've time to get your feet scraped, but after that we need to go through the details and get all the names together.

Unless you're not concerned about us being able to figure out who murdered your friend, of course? You were talking about police protection just now."

"Well, yeah. Of course I'm worried," Sunna María said, a sulky look on her face. "And of course I want protection if I'm in danger."

Orri had been bad-tempered all day and snapped at Lísa that morning, leaving the flat without a word. He came back from work to find that she had left him an unwelcome sinkful of washing up. He scowled, ignored the plates and cups, and made himself a couple of generous sandwiches.

Leaving the block of flats and still hungry, he was grateful for the darkness that matched his mood. Although it was cold and the days still felt short, there was an undeniable smell of spring on the chill air. A few more weeks and there would be real daylight well into the evenings, which would push his darkness break-ins into night-time proper and the occasional thrill of exploring houses while the owners slept, although that meant that the easy springtime crop of power tools from sheds and garages would become a larger part of his activity.

He drove past Sunna María Voss's house. There were lights on in almost every room and a car in the drive, a black four-by-four Mercedes that gleamed in the light of the street lamps. He shook his head, trying to push her from his mind and telling himself to concentrate. The two houses he had in mind for that night both

85

looked to be quiet as he drove past, turning at the next junction and parking the car in the street above.

Orri walked back, patting his pockets as a final check that he had everything before slipping quickly behind the large detached house further along, which he'd already identified as being rented. Situated where the street curved gently, the back of the building could not be seen from the neighbouring houses. Creeping silently and with all his senses alert, he was sure there was nobody inside as there was no sound to tell him of any occupants. Normally a burbling TV somewhere was enough to tell him someone was home, although it wasn't an infallible rule. People made noise, or generally surrounded themselves with sound, and the deep silence around this house told him there was nobody home.

This time it was the garage door that let him in. Like every house in the street, there was an integral garage built into the basement, and this one had both an overhead door and an ordinary door next to it. He tried to slide his strip of plastic past the door jamb, but the fitting was too snug and he fell back on the set of tools from his wallet, starting with a lever in the keyhole to provide tension, then quickly raking the lock in the forlorn hope that it was cheap enough to give easily. When that didn't work, Orri looked over his shoulder, the sweat starting to appear down his back in spite of it being a cool night. He selected a hook pick and inserted it, feeling the pins click one by one until the torsion lever turned the lock and the door swung open.

Orri grinned to himself in triumph. Picking locks was a skill he had painstakingly taught himself.

The garage was practically empty. The steel rack of shelves was clear of the usual paraphernalia that families collected and stored out of the way. He peered into the basement and saw it was empty, too, and with disgust, Orri realized that he might have spent time and effort breaking into an unoccupied house. There were the usual white goods in a row, but there were no power tools of the kind that he guessed Alex had a ready export market for.

He ascended the stairs and eased open the door at the top into the house itself. His soles whispered on the pale wood floor as his torch threw a narrow beam of light ahead of him. Like the basement, the kitchen was vacant apart from a few empty pizza boxes and cartons that had once contained noodles, stacked neatly on the worktop.

So there had to be someone here, he decided, wondering if they were preparing to move. There were cases in the living room, all locked, and he did not feel inclined to try picking the locks, at least not until he had checked the rest of the house. A tablet or even a decent smart phone would do the trick, he thought, that would be enough to have made the trip pay for itself.

In the bedroom there was a vast double bed, bigger even than the one he had seen at Sunna María Voss's house the night before. This one was bare of any bedclothes but had a couple of cases stacked on it. It was one of the smaller bedrooms that was in use, with the bed meticulously made and only a very few personal items to be seen.

Back in the main bedroom, Orri clicked open the first case and immediately shut it again. A ThinkPad laptop, more than few years old and therefore worth next to nothing. Another case revealed another laptop, sleeker and newer, but still not modern enough to be worth taking, although it might do as a last resort, Orri decided.

The contents of a heavier case were what made him catch his breath as he snapped the clasps and lifted the lid. The metal parts of the pistol were nestled snugly in foam cutouts, waiting to be plucked and assembled. The case had a faint, sharp smell of oil and he wondered if the weapon had been used. Orri felt a sudden fear as he knew this was far beyond anything he could have expected. Even with his limited knowledge of firearms he could tell it was a specialist tool that gleamed malevolently in its padded case in front of him, a murder weapon designed for one purpose only.

He closed the lid and fastened the clasps again. The sweat broke out along his back as he felt an anxious hot flush of fear. In a rush of realization, he knew that the people who owned a weapon like that were not ones he would want to meet, and he wouldn't even want them to know they'd been visited. He backed away, nervously keeping his movements as deft as they had been on the way in, terrified that he would knock over some pretentious ornament and set alarms ringing along the street. His feet made no more sound than they had when he'd entered the house. The torch was switched off and he made his way along the hall and back to the door leading to the basement and way out, reasoning that the clear route through the front door was too obvious.

At the top of the steps, Orri felt his breath coming in gasps and consciously made himself breathe more slowly, at a measured rate that also settled his mind and helped him think logically. There was no hurry. If there were anyone here, they would have raised the alarm. The place was silent. There was nobody here. Although there was no reason to hang about, he told himself there was no need to move as silently as a cautious mouse.

He crossed the basement in almost complete darkness and gulped in relief at the sight of the door, but relief morphed slowly into panic as the door refused to open. In desperation he rattled the immobile handle and turned to go back into the house and seek out another door, upstairs and out through the front door. He'd be in full view of the street, but what the hell?

At the bottom of the steps he paused at a sound a few inches behind his head. It was a full-bodied click, the snick of engineered metal that he'd heard often enough in movies but never expected to hear in real life.

"Stand still," a voice behind him instructed. "Lift your hands up."

Just like he had seen in the movies, Orri lifted his hands above his head and panted with fear. "I don't mean any trouble. I'm leaving. I haven't taken anything and I haven't seen anything," Orri forced himself to say as clearly as he could.

"Name?" the voice continued in its accented English.

"Orri Björnsson."

"And what are you doing in here, Orri Björnsson?"

"I'm a burglar," he admitted; it was the first time he had said the word out loud, and it felt distinctly odd to be saying it in English.

"You steal from people's houses?"

"Well . . ." Orri began, twitching as swift hands began to delve in his pockets. A light flickered into life behind him.

"A professional, I see," the voice said as the phone jammer was lifted from Orri's pocket. "Not a particularly good model, but it'll do the job well enough at short range."

"Look, I . . ." Orri said, turning his head to look behind him.

"Don't turn round," the voice said softly, administering a sharp kick to Orri's calf muscle that made him gasp in pain and force himself not to cry out. "So who are you working for?" The voice immediately demanded.

Orri sniffed and blinked back tears that appeared unbidden. "I work for myself," he said finally.

"You work alone?"

"Look, who are you?" Orri said, trying to think fast. "You're not a cop, are you?"

"Who do you work with?"

"A friend."

"And your friend, he knows where you are and he'll come and look for you if you're not back at the right time?"

"Or he'll go to the police."

This time there was a snort of laughter behind him. "That does not sound likely, Orri Björnsson. A thief going to the police because another thief is late getting home. I don't think so."

"Who are you?" Orri asked again. "Listen, I can help you. I can hear you're not from here and I could . . ." he said, but his voice faded away lamely.

"I think we need to go for a walk, Orri," the voice said softly and his hands were swiftly hauled downwards and taped together behind his back. A second later a bag descended over his head and the faint light of the torch behind him was blotted out. Then he was spun round in a circle several times in each direction and roughly dragged, before his knees were kicked from under him and he collapsed in a heap. He could hear the voice making a joke in a language he didn't understand and the sound of something scraping on the concrete floor before everything went quiet, even though he hadn't heard anyone leave.

Gunna could see that Jóhann was tired. He looked younger than his fifty years, she thought, although he had clearly put effort into keeping himself trim. He was a slim, spare man with a mop of curly hair that had turned an incongruous pale silver grey. It made him look oddly youthful, Gunna thought, deciding that he must have been a striking man in his younger days. He fiddled with his glasses, turning them over in his fingers and putting them on to check the laptop in front of him that chimed at intervals.

"Vilhelm Thorleifsson," Gunna said. "You knew him well?"

She saw the corners of his mouth droop in disapproval and he glanced at Sunna María, who sat impassively. They made an odd couple, Gunna decided, the prosperous dentist older than his wife by ten or fifteen years, she guessed, wondering what had brought them together.

"I didn't know Vilhelm well, I have to admit," he said in a dry voice. "I wouldn't call him a friend as such."

"But I gather you were more involved in your business dealings with him?"

A second rapid glance that passed between the two of them did not go unnoticed by Gunna as Sunna María left the room.

"I have been maybe more involved in the day-to-day business activities. But my wife is aware of the overall picture," he said, his voice dry.

"I don't intend to delve unnecessarily into your business affairs, other than what could concern Vilhelm Thorleifsson. Is there anyone who would bear him a grudge, enough to have him murdered?"

Jóhann smiled briefly, displaying teeth that looked less than perfect. "Not that I can imagine," he said. "Vilhelm's business affairs were complex and extensive. Our involvement has been modest."

92

"Sólfell Investment and his shipping ventures, you mean?"

"Precisely."

"That's all?"

"There have been a few other ventures. We have a property concern that Vilhelm put some finance into, and we were fortunate to have concluded our business. We handed over our stakes in his and Elvar Pálsson's business in exchange for Sólfell Property being put solely into our hands."

"Any other business partners, other than Elvar Pálsson?"

She watched the blood leave Jóhann's lips as they pressed tightly together for a moment in disapproval.

"No. I'm in the final stages of winding up any business relationships with Vilhelm and Elvar, other than companies that we both hold a share in. But we have an overseas investor in Sólfell Property and a company called Vison that is at start-up stage at the moment."

"You didn't get on with Vilhelm and Elvar?"

"No."

"Any special reason?"

Jóhann hid a yawn behind his hand. "Call it a gut feeling," he said and Gunna sensed immediately that there was more than just dislike behind his comment.

"You didn't trust them?"

"No. Not at all," he said sharply, as if the question had touched a nerve. "Elvar's a relative of my wife's, but not a close relative. My personal feeling is that he's this far from being a criminal." He glanced at the closed door and held up a hand with a narrow gap between his thumb and the tip of the forefinger. "So, no. I have never been able to trust him and have done my best not to entangle our affairs with his. It's a delicate matter, as my wife is fond of him."

Gunna nodded. "I see. When you say he's this far from being a criminal, in what way?"

Jóhann grimaced. "It's not easy to say. You understand that I have nothing concrete to base this on. But his opinions, the way he does business, everything. Elvar Pálsson would sell his first-born child if he thought there was a profit in it. Everything has a price, and Vilhelm was much the same. You can call it a generation gap if you like. But you understand?"

"Gut feeling again?"

"More than gut feeling, I think."

He looked up as the door creaked open.

"Finished?" Sunna María asked, standing behind her husband with her hands on his shoulders. "Jóhann's tired. It's been a long day. Hasn't it, darling?"

"I think we've discussed everything for the moment. Of course, if either of you hear of or from Elvar Pálsson, then I'd appreciate it if you let me know."

"He's in danger, do you think?" Sunna María asked, eyes wide.

"I've no idea, but until we can find out what happened to Vilhelm Thorleifsson, then I can't rule anything out."

"Do you have any leads?" Jóhann asked, biting his lip.

"I can't say. My colleagues are handling the investigation in Borgarfjördur, and I won't know until tomorrow what progress has been made today."

"Are we in any danger, do you think?"

"I can't say, but I'd recommend that you take care. Don't answer the door to anyone you don't know. Don't go out alone."

"How about protection?" Sunna María asked. "Shouldn't we have protection? I mean, if you think Elvar's in danger, so could we be, surely?"

"To be honest, we don't have the manpower, unless there's a very pressing reason."

"You mean, if someone killed one of us, the other one would be entitled to protection?" Jóhann asked, and his face cracked into a wintry smile.

"Something like that," Gunna said, and tore a sheet of paper from her notebook. She quickly wrote a number on it.

"It's not cheap, but try this person if you want some protection right away. I would have to convince my superiors that you need protection, so going private's your only option. At least until someone starts breaking your windows."

"I need to piss," Orri said, trying to sound angry, but his tone came out as plaintive.

"Piss, then," the voice said. "I'm not stopping you."

"Let me up, then."

"I didn't say anything about getting up. If you need to piss, then you'll have to do it where you are."

Orri wondered how long he had been sitting in the chair. It felt an age and his bladder was bursting. He wondered if it was still night, or if it was daytime by now.

"What time is it?" he asked suddenly.

"Why do you want to know?"

"I want to know how long I've been kept here against my will."

"A little while, Orri Björnsson. Not as long as you might think, believe me."

He could hear the swish of soft footsteps on the concrete floor.

"Who are you?" he demanded, his voice cracking as he began to panic and he fought against the bands of thick tape that fastened his hands together, struggling to stand up, but stopping as he found that more bands tied his feet to the legs of the chair.

"Be careful, Orri Björnsson," the voice said softly. "If you tip the chair over nobody is going to help you up."

He heard the legs of another chair scrape across the floor towards him.

"Stay still, you fool," the voice snapped and Orri obeyed. "Full name?"

"Orri Sigurgeir Björnsson."

"Date of birth?"

"Eighteenth of March 1978. Why do you need to know that?"

"Address?"

"I'm not telling you until you tell me why."

Orri gasped as he was immediately doused in freezing water, and he guessed as he struggled to get his breath back that the voice must have had a bucketful ready.

"Address?"

"Ferjubakki twenty."

"Which floor?"

"Third," Orri answered in confusion, wheels turning in his mind at the curt questions.

"Your mother's name?"

"Why do you want to know?" Orri demanded, expecting another dousing, or worse. "It's none of your fucking business."

Instead there was silence for a moment before the voice spoke again, with a soft menace this time. "Your mother's name?"

"Her name was Ingibjörg Theódórsdóttir. She's dead," he added without knowing why.

"And you have a sister, Margrét Hildur Björnsdóttir, right? Does the name Elísabet Sólborg Höskuldsdóttir mean anything to you?" the voice asked softly as Orri felt his mouth go dry and both the need to pee and the chill of the water soaking into his clothes were forgotten.

"Yes," he croaked.

"Good," the voice said with evident satisfaction. "As you can guess, Orri, while you have been sitting here in the dark, I've done a little research and know quite a bit about you, and by the time you get out of this place I'll know a lot more. It never ceases to surprise me how much you can learn from a person's phone. You're a rather foolish young man, but it seems there are a few skills there that we might be able to use."

"We?" Orri asked. "Who's 'we'?"

"That's something you don't need to know, Orri. Just be happy that we haven't decided to deal with you in a way that we normally would with someone who interferes. You understand? Normally you would have disappeared," the voice said smoothly. There was silence while the disembodied voice allowed its words to sink in. Orri gasped for breath inside the bag. "Tell me, Orri. Do you know who this house belongs to?"

"Yes," he gulped. "Do you?"

"I want to know how good your information is."

"It's owned by Sólfell Property."

He wondered if the voice was even listening.

"Normally someone like you would have vanished. Maybe lost in the hills somewhere, but it would be many years before you might be found. Understand?"

"I understand," Orri replied, his mouth dry, but his heart hammering with relief at the thought that whoever had put a bag over his head and tied him to a chair was going to let him live after all.

The voice spoke softly and Orri strained to listen through the bag that was gradually suffocating him.

"In a few minutes I will be gone. This place will be empty, so there's no need for you to search around for anything worth stealing because there's nothing here. In a few days you might receive some instructions. You would be well advised to do what you are told."

"And if I don't?" Orri asked. The words were out of his mouth without thinking. There was silence for what felt a long time.

"I thought I had made it plain that I know where you live. I know who your girlfriend is, where she works and where she lives. I know where your sister and her children live. Do I make myself clear?"

"Yes," Orri whispered.

"I don't care about your other business, but it would be as well for you to not get caught," the voice said in a silky tone.

"But . . . that was nothing to do with me," Orri said desperately and heard the voice's chair pushed back as its legs rattled on the concrete.

"Goodbye, Orri Björnsson. Watch out for instructions."

"Hey, how do I get out of here?"

"You'll find a way, if you're smart enough."

"But . . . what if I can't get out?"

"If you're not that smart, then you're no loss. Consider it a test, Orri Björnsson."

"Take the bag off, at least, will you?" Orri pleaded as he heard the soft footfalls recede and the door at the top of the stairs shut.

"Go home, Gunnhildur."

She looked up from the papers she had been engrossed in to see Ívar Laxdal at the end of her desk.

"I can't make head nor tail of this stuff," she said. "I just see company names and who owns which percentage of some company that also owns bits and pieces of something else. It's an absolute minefield."

"Go home, like I told you."

Gunna squared the sheets of paper she had been poring over and tucked them into her folder.

Ívar Laxdal's eyes narrowed. "You're not taking that lot home with you, are you?"

"I am. I'll have another read through it all tonight and see if I can make sense of it."

"No." Ívar Laxdal shook his head. "Don't waste your time. If nothing jumped out at you right away, then it's probably not going to. Take the whole lot to a specialist over at financial and ask them to guide you through it. But you have some names, at least?"

"There's no shortage of people who would like to do this group of people a bad turn," Gunna said. "But murder? I don't know. I have a list of the companies that Sólfell Investment and all the other companies that this bunch bought and sold over the last few years, although I doubt it's a complete list. A lot of them are in Denmark and Sweden, one or two in Germany and there's one in Britain as well. My guess is that we're spoilt for choice for people who would happily knock these shysters off."

"So where do we start?"

"That's the problem. I'm also concerned about Elvar Pálsson, the missing link. Is he going to turn up as a corpse? Or is he sunning himself somewhere a long way south of here? My feeling is that this character is either keeping out of harm's way or else he's already been dealt with."

"Or he's involved?"

Gunna shivered. "Sending a message or taking care of unfinished business?"

"Could be either. This woman's husband is back tomorrow, right?"

"No, he's already back. I've just come from meeting the two of them. He's not saying more than he has to, and he looks frightened."

"He's a dentist?"

100

"He is. A wealthy dentist."

"Is there any other kind?"

"Wealthier than most, I understand."

Ívar Laxdal's thumb scratched the stubble on his chin. "Gunnhildur, go home. You have five minutes to be out of the building."

"Make it ten."

"Not a moment longer."

"Who are you?" Jóhann asked, clearly intrigued by the slight young woman sitting in front of him while Sunna María hovered behind him.

"My name's Bára. I do the kind of work I think you're looking for."

"How do you know what we're looking for?"

"Because you called me."

She studied Jóhann and could learn little from the man's tired face, while Sunna María's nervous fingers told her more. Jóhann's face was impassive, with lines that radiated from behind his eyes and she could sense that on a good day there could be a quick humour there, but he had come straight from the airport after a day's travelling and it was clear that his patience was thin.

"What do you offer?"

"Personal protection. I stay with you, watch your back, keep bystanders away, that kind of thing. A lot of it's gauging the temperature, understanding what's going on around us, avoiding dangerous situations before they occur rather than having to deal with them when they happen," Bára said. "Although that's naturally part of the brief as well. But it depends, and I'd have to have an idea of what to expect."

"What are your credentials? Experience?"

"Five years as a police officer, and I was at the embassy in Brussels for a year. Is it the press you're having problems with?"

Sunna María looked at Jóhann and shook her head rapidly. "You tell her."

Jóhann cleared his throat. "A friend of ours has been murdered," he said. Bára took care not to show any surprise.

"Here in Iceland? You mean the man who was murdered in Borgarfjördur a few days ago?"

"Yes," Jóhann said in a dry voice. "Sunna, would you?" He asked, nodding at the minibar in the corner of the room. "Ach, I seem to spend half my life in hotel rooms, and now I come home and have to spend the night in yet another one."

He sipped the whisky Sunna María handed him. "Drink?"

Bára shook her head. "I'm at work."

"Not just Villi," Sunna María broke in. Nobody knows where Elvar is."

"There could have been two murders?"

"We don't know that," Jóhann said. "Elvar appears to have dropped off the face of the earth, but it's not as if that hasn't happened before. Both of these men are . . . were business acquaintances of ours."

"So you feel you could be subject to some kind of similar attack?"

"Exactly. I'm not too worried, but my wife is concerned, as you can imagine."

"I see."

"What can you do?"

"What do you want? I can provide advice on where to go and not go, what to do or not do, places to avoid, things to look out for. Or I can accompany you if that's what you feel you need."

Sunna María looked anxiously at Jóhann and nodded while he rested his chin in one hand.

"Round-the-clock or daylight hours?" he asked.

"It's up to you. I can sleep in the same room as you if that's what you feel is needed."

"I'm sure that won't be necessary," Jóhann said with a tired smile.

"Can you tell me anything about the circumstances of these murders, so I have an idea of what we are talking about here?"

"Villi was shot," Sunna María said, her voice welling up with pent-up anxiety.

"I thought that was a drug-related killing?"

"I don't think so." Sunna María said.

"So what can you do?" Jóhann asked. "Anything?"

"No guarantees. I can't stop a bullet but I would expect to be able to keep you out of a dangerous situation."

"Good," Jóhann said with the air of a man who has made a decision. That's what we'll do. Can you be here from nine to nine?"

"Of course."

"Fine. We'll see you here tomorrow morning."

"You don't want to know how much I charge?

"No." Jóhann covered a yawn. "If I get murdered then I'm not going to be here to write any cheques, am I?"

Orri shouted out but heard only his own voice coming back at him. He strained at the tape holding his hands together, and in a fit of panic he pulled frantically, the broad tape cutting into his wrists as he did so.

Panting with anger and fear, he stopped and sat motionless, the unbearable pressure in his bladder forgotten as he felt blood trickling over his hands. He made himself think, banishing his loathing of the voice from his mind as he concentrated on how to free himself. Hands, feet, eyes, he thought. Any one of those would make it easier to deal with the other two problems, and after that he could think about escaping from this terrible house that he fervently wished he'd never set foot in.

He forced himself to relax, and as he did so he felt the chair shift under him. He wriggled in his seat and wondered what kind of chair he had been bound to, hearing it groan. He guessed wood from the sound it made. He tried to stand up, straining to straighten his body, and was rewarded with feeling the chair start to loosen its grip. He kicked frantically, both feet at a time, feeling the tape cut this time into the skin above his ankles as the chair complained and finally collapsed under him. It left him winded on the floor in its wooden wreckage, but he was able to slide his bound ankles over the ends of the chair legs, and the back of the chair had broken, leaving his hands taped loosely together.

Cautiously he sat up and shook away the remnants of the chair back that his arms had been tied across, finding that he could at least move them. He struggled to his feet awkwardly and took a few slow steps forward, blundering into a wall hard enough to make him see stars. With the wall against one shoulder, he stumbled cautiously around the room, trying desperately to remember what he had seen in it before he had been ambushed.

Just as he recalled having seen a set of shelves with a steel frame, he found himself walking into it, giving himself a knock on the side of the head that almost sent him reeling back in pain as he fought back his rising panic. Turning his back, Orri felt clumsily along the bottom shelf at waist height, his fingers becoming increasingly numb, and groaning with relief as he found the end, and with it the sharp edge of the steel angle bar that supported the shelf.

He sawed frantically, stabbing blindly to pierce the tape with the shelf's sharp end and feeling it weaken further with each lunge, providing his wrists with further grazes and scratches, which he ignored in the frenzy to free his hands. When the tape finally tore under the strain he rubbed his wrists furiously to restore circulation. Before attacking the bag still over his head, Orri tore at his trousers with nerveless fingers, finally freeing his flies and groaning with relief yet again, this time as a stream of hot piss steamed in the cold air.

Finally he leaned uncertainly against the shelf and clawed at the bag over his head, dragging down deep breaths as he emerged into the semi-darkness. Orri looked around in suspicion, certain that he was being watched. He crouched down as he recovered his breath and the panic began to fade, leaving him drained after the effort of escaping from his bonds. As his heart stopped hammering, he took deep breaths and stood up, feeling faint, and made for the stairs. Listening to the muted rattle of the steel steps, he stopped and paused before carrying on and eased the door at the top open.

The apartment was empty. There was nothing to indicate that the voice or the voice's companion had been there. The cases had disappeared. The beds had been stripped. Even the kitchen looked spotless in the glimmer of moonlight through the window. Outside the street looked cold and peaceful in the dull orange glow of the street lights.

He tiptoed back downstairs, feeling his pockets, and was worried to find they had been emptied. In the basement he took the chance of switching on the lights, and as they flickered into life, he was sickened to see the wrecked remains of a wooden kitchen chair in a pool of cooling urine laced with streaks of his own blood. Casting about quickly, Orri's heart leaped to see his belongings neatly arrayed on the floor next to the back door. He quickly pulled on his shoes and stowed his keys, torch, lock picks, phone jammer and wallet in his pockets, and peered at his phone to check the time, seeing with a shock that he had been in the house for almost five hours; more than four hours longer than he had intended to be there. He also saw missed calls from Lísa and a couple of text messages, including one that read simply, If you're reading this, then well done. I'll be in touch soon.

That set his heart beating with anger as he kicked the door. To his surprise it swung open gently. A flood of cold air stole into the basement and he escaped into the night, certain that hidden eyes were watching him.

"*Hæ*, Mum."

Laufey lay on the sofa, legs crossed at the ankles, absorbed in the iPhone she had recently become the proud owner of.

"*Hæ*, sweetheart," Gunna said, lifting Laufey's legs, sitting down and laying the legs across her lap as she did so. "How's things?"

"We were wondering where you were."

"Where's Steini?"

"Gone out. Some friend of his has a car that won't start, so he went to give him a hand."

"So there's nothing to eat?"

Laufey's phone whistled and she put it down. "There's what's left of a casserole in the slow cooker. It's a bit heavy on the garlic, though. Drífa couldn't eat it. If you ask me really nicely, I'll do you some pasta while I warm it up."

"That would be very welcome, darling daughter."

"All part of the service to the republic's guardians of law and order, dear mother," Laufey said, swinging her legs from Gunna's lap. "You've been busy? That guy who was shot the other day?"

"You know better than to ask. But, yes. That's about the shape of it."

"Are you going to catch whoever did it?"

"I hope so," Gunna said grimly. "Is Drífa here?" She asked, her question answered immediately by a wail from the next room.

"Yep. You weren't here, so we invited her to come and eat with us. Steini played with Kjartan until his friend called and asked him to help him get his truck going."

"Fair enough. Do I have time to run for the shower before they appear from the bedroom?"

"If you're quick," Laufey said.

Under the hot water, Gunna reflected that Drífa had become part of their household over the last year, until she had been allocated a small social housing flat in the village. Since then, Drífa and baby Kjartan Gíslason had become a frequent presence, particularly with Laufey spending much of her time with the pair.

Gunna had found herself getting closer to the girl, who had clearly come to rely on her as a replacement for her own mother, who hadn't spoken to her since the baby had come into the world the previous summer. Now Drífa and Kjartan staying the night in Gísli's long-abandoned bedroom was an occasional occurrence when she could see the girl was feeling particularly lonely.

Almost to her own surprise, Gunna found herself warming to the girl and sympathizing with her, but the question of which of the two Gísli might settle down with still nagged at her. Sensible, sharp-tongued Soffía would have been her preferred choice of daughter-in-law, and she still felt that Drífa was too young for parenthood, although Kjartan's arrival had forced her to grow up rapidly.

She could sense that Drífa had made an effort to be independent and not to impose more than she had to on Gunna, who admitted to herself that she would not complain if the girl were to impose more, and she realized with discomfort that Steini saw more of her grandchild than she did herself.

Laufey was as good as her word. A plate of chicken casserole and pasta waited on the table as she emerged from the shower, scrubbed and fragrant, while Drífa sat on the sofa and Laufey held Kjartan. The little boy looked at his grandmother with wide eyes and held on tight to Laufey.

"That's granny," Laufey whispered to the little boy. "She locks up bad people, and if you're naughty she'll lock you up as well . . ."

"Hæ, Drífa," Gunna said, blowing on a forkful of hot food. "How's things with you? The little man's getting bigger, isn't he?"

"He looks like his father," Drífa said. "And he has the same temperament."

"Awkward, you mean?" Laufey asked. "We get that from Mum."

"Yeah, and I get it from a long line of Westfjords wizards and bandits, so beware. Speaking of which, Gísli's ashore now?"

"Yep, yesterday."

"Hell," Gunna swore, fumbling for her phone. "He texted me this morning and I clean forgot to get back to him."

"He probably thinks you're a bad mother now," Laufey chided, holding Kjartan's hands as he stood in front of her on unsteady feet. "Your granny's a bad example to us all," she told the little boy as he laughed and gurgled back at her.

CHAPTER
SIX

Two of the men had moustaches, bristling moustaches that slashed their lined faces in half. Kalashnikovs slung over their shoulders, they brought with them the smell of smoke and anger, but the menace came from the slighter, younger man with the clean-shaven face and beady eyes at the back of the group.

Valmira watched with a feeling of disbelief as the young man inspected the kitchen and stepped forward to point at her father and brother, jerking his head towards the door. The other two nodded, as if carrying out an everyday job of work. Valmira's father got to his feet and looked one of the two men in the eye, grunting a greeting that was returned in kind. Her brother scowled as he stood up from the table, quickly squeezing her hand as he did so, and she could see the fear he was bottling up inside.

Her mother was silent, arms tightly folded. Her father smiled at his daughters and muttered a blessing as he left. The clean-shaven man was the last to leave, turning to look at the woman and the two girls, giving them a thin smile that made Valmira shiver.

Outside they watched the truck make its way slowly down the potholed road, loaded with a dozen men and boys who did not look to see where they were going, while by the tailgate two men sat with Kalashnikovs cradled carelessly in their hands.

That night there was a crackle of gunfire in the valley below and Valmira's mother began packing what belongings could fit into one suitcase and an old army backpack. They left on foot soon after dawn, letting the goats and the chickens out to fend for themselves, and Valmira looked back at her home for the last time as the three of them walked down the road, following the path the truck had already taken.

She woke with a start, the image of the white-painted house with its sagging tiled roof as fresh in her mind as the confused clucking of the chickens they left behind them. She shook off the dream, one that returned several times a year and which she knew from bitter experience would mean no more sleep that night. She slipped out of bed and went to make coffee in the kitchen, where she could sit and watch the day break over the sea in the country she now called home.

Valmira stopped the van outside Natalia's house, gave a short blast on the horn and was relieved to see her come running across the grass, her trademark puckish smile in place.

"Hey, Emilija, how'd it go with lover boy?" She asked, taking the seat at the end as Valmira pulled away, the van bumping through puddles and splashing gritty grey water in all directions.

"Ach. You know. Men," Emilija said.

"Younger? Older?"

"Younger, a bit."

"Young guys are useless," Natalia declared. "Find yourself an old boy. They're so much better, and they're grateful as well."

"I know." Emilija sighed. "You keep telling me."

"So how was he?" Natalia asked slyly. "Did you . . .?"

Emilija sighed again. "No. He ate everything I'd cooked and then Anton woke up, and after an hour trying to get him back to sleep, lover boy decided to go and meet his friends in some bar."

Valmira shook her head and tutted while Natalia tittered, her brilliant toothy smile running around her dark face.

"What's this one called?"

"Alex. He's a sweet enough lad, but he's . . . you know. Childish."

"Get an old guy. Fifteen years difference is about right. He'll be pushing sixty and thinking about nothing but golf while you're still young enough to have some fun."

"Yeah, just like your older men," Emilija said sharply. "We see how long your old guys hang around."

"It's the kids. Guys don't like teenagers," Natalia said defensively. "It's all right for you, yours are still young."

"Which is why I pay a fortune for childcare, so I can work all day and earn peanuts," Emilija said. "I'd be better off on benefits, I'm sure of it."

"So why don't you stop working?" Natalia asked, stung by Emilija's tone.

"You know. Because if I'm on benefits Ingi's family will do everything they can to have the children off me, and then where would I be?"

"Try old Jakob. He probably hasn't had it since the last century."

Emilija opened her mouth to deliver a sharp retort, thought better of it and instead turned to Valmira. "Is it that house in Kópavogsbakki again?"

"It's the one we were at yesterday plus another one further up the street. Two for the price of one," she said with a wintry smile. "It's just the annexe flat at the first one, then the whole place at the next one."

"Is that all for today?"

Valmira braked gently to allow a car waiting at a roundabout time to get onto the road ahead of them.

"That's what I was going to ask you about. There's an office in Gardabær that Viggó has signed up for a month's contract."

"So why ask us?"

"Because it's overtime. Cleaning has to be done between six in the evening and six in the morning. Four hours each evening, but it has to be evening because the place is in use during the day."

Emilija looked dubious. "I could do with the hours, but it depends on the children. I'll do it if I can get a babysitter," she said.

"Get your young guy in," Natalia said with a snigger. "Feed him, screw him, and when he's asleep you can run out and do two hours cleaning. If the kids wake up, he can read them a story."

"Listen . . ." Emilija said, her irritation starting to boil over into anger.

"Now, then," Valmira said loudly. "That'll do, ladies. Let me know, will you? But I need to know tomorrow, so I can tell Viggó if we need to find someone else to do evenings. Maybe you could rotate it somehow, do a couple of evenings each?"

"If I can find a sitter," Emilija said.

"OK for me," Natalia decided. "I leave Nonni with food and TV, no problem."

"Otherwise I'll do it myself until you can sort yourselves out. All right?" She said, turning the van off the main road and through Kópavogur towards the street of quiet mansions overlooking the Sound.

Lísa watched him suspiciously as he dropped his work boots, sat back and sighed. She had seen the cuts on his wrists and rather than ask, had merely given him a stern look that invited answers, but he brushed it off. Lísa slept with her back to him that night, arms folded over her chest in a way that told him an explanation would be required before any fun could be had.

Orri was less worried about that than about the voice he constantly expected to hear whisper in his ear in that peculiarly accented but clear English he had heard in the basement of the house. He carefully checked the apartment for anything that might indicate that someone had been in there. He put a new lock on the front door, fitting below the worn Yale a mortice lock with a key that felt heavy in his hand.

Lísa glared at him as he handed her the new key.

"Orri, what the fuck is going on?"

"Just . . ." he floundered. "I just want us to be safe," he finished lamely as she rolled the key between her fingers and pursed her lips in irritation.

"Is there something you should be telling me? Like how come you didn't come home until the middle of the night?"

"I have to go. I'll be back at six," Orri said quickly as he scuttled for the door. "You'll lock up when you go to work, won't you?"

She heard his boots clatter on the concrete stairs as he hurried down them and she looked at the new brass key. It was as long as her little finger and dwarfed the rest of the keys on her key ring. She shook her head and wondered what Orri had got up to. Lísa knew well enough that he had some kind of dubious racket going on and that he stored boxes and bags in the basement storeroom that would disappear and be replaced at intervals. He rarely mentioned where he might be going when he left the flat, and while she was fairly sure that whatever he was doing didn't involve drugs, she was less and less happy about the fact that this man she was increasingly involved with was up to something dubious.

Lísa looked out of the kitchen window and surveyed the car park. Orri's car had gone, and as he had taken his working boots, that meant he had a shift that would keep him out of the flat for at least six hours. In the bedroom she shuffled through his bedside table, turning up old electricity bills, decade-old birthday cards, obsolete mobile phones, a few ancient Christmas cards, coins and broken ballpoints, but nothing useful.

She stood in the middle of the room at the foot of the sagging bed and thought before turning on her heel and leaving the flat to clatter down the stairs to the basement.

There had once been a laundry down there, lined with washing machines. But now that people preferred to have a washer and a dryer in their own apartments, the washroom had been stacked with bicycles that had seen better days.

Next to the washroom was a long storeroom of steel cages, one for each of the eight apartments. Orri's store was the tidiest. There was a bench against the wall lined with boxes and an old chest of drawers next to it, all out of reach behind the padlocked door. Lísa tried every key from the handful she had brought downstairs with her until she had no choice but to give up, glaring at the chest of drawers as if it had personally offended her.

Natalia and Emilija shivered as the wind blew along Kópavogsbakki. Sprawling modern houses squatted heavily on their half-submerged basements and huge blank windows stared blindly at the houses opposite. Valmira fumbled with the bunch of keys for the day and finally found one that opened the door, which swung open into a dark hallway.

Once gratefully inside out of the wind, she dropped the heavy vacuum cleaner and shivered.

"Empty house this time. The people have just moved out, so it only needs to be made presentable for the next tenants."

"Top to bottom, is it?"

"Every corner," Valmira confirmed. "And we have all morning to do it. So who feels like doing what?"

"Same as usual," Natalia said. "I take kitchen, Emilija does bedrooms, you living room, and we do bathroom last?"

"Bathrooms," Valmira corrected, looking at the list in her hand. "There are three."

"Three?" Emilija echoed. "Are there ten people living here, or what?"

Valmira shrugged. "People with money." She shouldered the vacuum cleaner with a wince and set off along the hall, flicking light switches as she went. "If you make a start, I'll check out the rest of the place. All right?"

Natalia made a start on the kitchen, a long room tiled in dark slate that she decided with a frown was perfect for highlighting every spillage and speck of dust, and fitted with discreetly opulent appliances with matching dull steel fronts. She began at the top, walking on the worktops to wipe down the walls from the ceiling down, and as everything was already clean, a rapid wipe-over was all that was needed. She hummed as she worked, occasionally breaking into a few words of a half-remembered song in Spanish, satisfied with the steel extractor hood over the stove when she could see her face in it.

"Hey, Emilija!"

There was a muffled answer over the whine of the vacuum cleaner in the distance.

118

"Hey!" Natalia called again, wiping the doors of the cupboards after she had checked they were both empty and spotlessly clean.

"What is it?" Emilija asked, her face in the kitchen doorway.

Natalia sat down on the worktop, her legs dangling into space, and wiped a bead of sweat from her forehead.

"I don't think anyone's been here. The place is perfectly clean. Weird, isn't it?"

"The beds have been slept in, so someone's been here."

"How's Valmira getting on? It must be time for a smoke break for some of us by now."

Emilija looked along the hall. "I heard her a while ago but I'm not sure where she is now. I'll go and have a look when I've finished in there," she said and left, pushing her thick brown plait over her shoulder.

Natalia jumped down lightly. With her soft shoes and slight frame, she landed soundlessly. She decided that a break was needed and stepped outside the front door into the icy wind, lighting up under the shelter of her jacket and sending a plume of smoke to be whipped away by the wind.

"Talia!"

"What?" She called back, holding the cigarette outside while leaning into the hall.

"Come here, will you?" Quick."

Natalia regretfully took a long drag and flicked the rest of the cigarette into a puddle next to the set of steps leading to the house's front door and stalked along the hall to see Emilija with panic on her face at the door to the basement.

"Down here, quick. It's Vala."

"She's hurt?" Natalia asked, imagining her falling down the stairs.

"Hell, I don't know. Come with me, will you?"

Their feet clattered on the steel steps into the wide basement.

"She's here . . ."

Emilija crouched down and put an arm around Valmira's shoulders, where she sat immobile with her back to the wall.

"Vala, it's all right. We're your friends," she crooned while Valmira stared into space, her eyes blank and focused on thin air.

"What's all that stuff there?" Natalia asked, bewildered.

"I don't know. But don't touch it. Something's happened here."

"What do we do? Call Viggó?"

"Call the police. Then you can call Viggó."

Natalia's mouth set in a thin, hard line. "The police . . .? You're sure we need them?

"Jesus, Talia. Look at all that blood, will you?"

"But the police. Police is bad news. We take Vala home, tell Viggó she's sick. Clean it all up. Nobody needs to know."

"You're joking, aren't you? Look at all that stuff. Someone's been hurt here, or killed. We don't tell the police and they find out afterwards, we'll be in prison ourselves."

Natalia pouted. "In Chile . . ."

"We're not in Chile, Talia. This is Iceland. The police aren't going to throw you in jail for reporting something. Jesus, call an ambulance, will you? Vala's in a bad way."

Emilija brushed a lock of Valmira's dark hair away from her eyes and saw a tear on her cheek.

"It's all right, Vala. Natalia's getting help. You're going to be just fine. You hear me?"

Gunna saw that the ambulance and a squad car were there before her as she strode up the path to the gaping door where a small figure with a look of outright distrust on her pinched face glared at her.

"Good morning," Gunna offered, stepping past her and looking about.

"You police?" asked the small woman in the jacket wrapped tightly about, her fists thrust deep in her pockets.

"That's right. I'm a detective. And you are?"

"Natalia."

"You called us, did you?"

"Yeah. Emilija, she said call you," Natalia said and Gunna could hardly make out her words through the thick accent.

"All right, where's this Emilija, and the officers who are already here?"

Natalia jerked her head towards the recesses of the house, every sound inside echoing of the bare walls and uncarpeted floors. "In there. Downstairs. I stay here."

Gunna's footsteps sounded loud on the smooth wood floor and she heard voices as a figure in paramedic's overalls appeared from a doorway, a thickset woman on his arm and leaning heavily on him as another paramedic followed them.

"*Hæ*, I'm Gunnhildur from CID, what's the situation?"

The woman with the dark fringe over her blank eyes and clutching the paramedic's arm did not appear to be injured and Gunna wondered what the problem was.

"Your guys are downstairs and I guess they'll tell you the story," the paramedic said in a patient bedside-manner voice. "This lady's had a shock and we won't be leaving quite yet. We'll be in the ambulance if you want to catch up with us in a little while."

"Thanks, will do," Gunna said, and made her way down the stairs.

At the bottom two officers in uniform surveyed a broken chair in the middle of the floor.

"Ah, the cavalry's here."

"*Hæ*, Geiri. What's the story, then? Who did what and who got hurt?"

The heavily built officer stepped back while his colleague, a young woman with a sharp face, frowned at the debris on the floor.

"Three cleaners arrived to give this place a scrub. They're all foreigners; they work for some outfit called Reindeer Cleaners. The house is rented and the tenants left a couple of days ago, so it's being cleaned for the next tenants. Anyhow, it looks like one of the cleaners came down here, and I can't really make out what happened. Whatever, one of the others came down here and found her sitting on the floor as if she'd been knocked on the head."

"Had she?"

"Apparently not."

"Fallen over, maybe?"

"No injuries as far as the paramedics can tell."

"There's blood here," the male officer said, leaning forward and picking up a leg of the smashed chair.

"Hold on," Gunna ordered, hurriedly snapping on a pair of surgical gloves to take it. "Best if you get back and don't touch anything," she added, holding the chair leg under the light to inspect it. Ragged lengths of ripped duct tape stuck to the wood and the dark stains looked suspiciously like dried blood. She stepped back, surveying the floor where the remnants of the wooden chair were scattered, and quickly made out the other leg, also bound with ripped tape, and patches of blood that had stuck to the polished cement floor.

"Right, back upstairs, both of you," Gunna said decisively. "Geiri, will you seal this off and I'll have forensics look the place over before this goes any further. No point muddying the waters before they get here. Tinna?"

"Yes?"

"I'll talk to forensics to start with. While Geiri gets his rolls of smart blue tape from the car, will you have a word with the two cleaners upstairs? Leave the casualty with the medics, but get names, addresses, phone numbers, who they work for, and get all the keys to this place that you can lay your hands on. All right?"

"Yep."

"Good. Go on then," Gunna said, pulling her phone from her pocket and selecting a number.

Outside Gunna found the ambulance's back door open. The dark-haired woman with the broad shoulders sat hunched inside with a blanket over her shoulders, shaken by sobs as she stuttered words in short bursts between bouts of hyperventilation, one of the two medics holding her hands as she reassured her.

"What's the score?" Gunna asked the second paramedic, a young man with cheeks reddened by the cold wind.

"Hysterical. Something's given her a colossal shock, and my colleague's in there trying to calm her down a little before we take her to hospital."

"Any idea what?"

"Nope," the man shook his head. "Couldn't say. But she shied away as soon as she saw me in that house. She only wanted to see my colleague."

"You have a name?"

"Valmira. That's all I have so far. We'll get her name and identity number when she gets to the hospital. I reckon she'll need to be sedated, but we'd need a doctor here for that."

"So she's not a local?"

The man shook his head. "Not sure. Her Icelandic is very good, but she was babbling in some other language to start with. She switched to Icelandic once she calmed down," he said, and looked past Gunna to the ambulance's open door.

"Ready?"

The female paramedic looked down and nodded. "She's not good. I can't remember seeing anyone with no physical injuries quite so distressed. I'll stay in the back with her, but we had better be quick." She raised an eyebrow at Gunna. "Police?"

"Yep. You're going to the National Hospital?"

She looked dubious. "You want to interview her?"

"Oh, yes."

"You'll have to check with the doctor. I'm not sure she'll be in any fit state for a while."

The forensics team did its work behind closed doors while Gunna sat in the scrubbed kitchen and made notes. Emilija and Natalia sat opposite her like naughty schoolgirls, one wide-eyed and fearful, the other wearing a truculent scowl.

"How long have you worked with Valmira?" Gunna asked,

"Four–five year," Natalia said.

"A couple of years."

"So you both know her quite well? You socialize outside work, or are you strictly colleagues?"

"I see her sometimes," Emilija said. "We started this job around the same time because we both lost our jobs in the crash."

"What were you doing?"

"I was a chef at Bryggjubar. Then it closed down when the banks . . ."

"I get the picture. And Valmira?"

"She worked for an export company, worked there a long time. It went bankrupt a few months after the crash. But there's always shit work to be had and we've both been here since," Emilija said without any bitterness.

"How about you, Natalia? You know Valmira well?"

Natalia put out a hand, palm down and shook it from side to side. "A little."

"You understand what I'm saying, don't you? Where are you from?"

"From Chile," Natalia said with a thick accent as Emilija shook her head and looked away.

Gunna looked into Natalia's defiant black eyes and put her pen down on the notebook in front of her, waiting for Natalia to look away. Eventually her stare dropped guiltily to the table.

"Listen," Gunna said softly. "I can see you understand every word I've said to you and I'd appreciate it if you didn't play the stupid foreigner with me. Understood?"

Natalia's jaw squared in defiant dislike, but she nodded.

"Fine," Gunna said. "Just so you know, this isn't a formal interview. I'm only making a few notes for background, nobody's been arrested and I'm not even sure if a crime has taken place, although I will probably have to take formal statements from you at some point. All right? So, Natalia, how long have you lived in Iceland?"

"Eleven years."

Gunna was gratified that even in those two words the fake accent had disappeared immediately.

"And you, Emilija?"

"About eight years."

"Tell me about Valmira. Where is she from? Married? Children? Does she has any family here?"

Emilija shook her head. "There are some cousins who live somewhere outside Reykjavík, Ólafsvík somewhere, I think. Her name's Valmira Vukoja, and she's from Bosnia originally, although I know she has lived in Iceland for a long time, much longer than Talia or me."

"She's not married, no boyfriend or next of kin?"

"No. As long as I've known Vala she has kept to herself. Not many friends, definitely no guys. She has relatives here but she doesn't talk about them much."

"And you all work for what? Reindeer Cleaners? I'd best have a word with them as well. Where's the office?"

Emilija and Natalia exchanged a thin smile as Gunna wrote down the address.

"What's the manager's name?"

"Viggó. Viggó Jakobsson. He runs it, sort of. But his father owns the company, I think."

Picking on the smile that flashed between them, Gunna's antenna twitched. "This Viggó. How do he and Valmira get on?"

"Why do you want to know?" Natalia asked, breaking into the conversation for the first time.

"I don't need to know, but it could be useful. I'd like to find out what's happened to your friend, and anything you can tell me helps build up a picture. You all spend a good few hours every week at work, so someone's working environment is an important part of it. So do Valmira and Viggó get on well or badly?"

"Well . . ." Natalia said, and paused.

"She gets on well with old Jakob," Emilija said. "He employed her to start with after the company she worked for collapsed."

"But now his son runs it?"

"Yeah. And he's stupid," Natalia said with emphasis.

"She's right. Viggó knows that Valmira could run everything better than he does," Emilija added. "But he's the boss's son, so . . ."

Gunna made quick notes. "Understood. There's some friction there?"

Emilija nodded. "But only on Viggó's side. Valmira doesn't want his job, but Viggó thinks she does."

"You work as a team all the time?"

"Yes. There are three teams," Emilija said.

"All foreigners," Natalia added.

"All? Nine people?"

"That's right. All foreign women, plus Viggó."

"I'll go and have a chat with him," Gunna promised. "When you got here this morning, was there anything unusual?"

"Well," Natalia began, and looked doubtful. "Not really. It's just that . . ."

"Just what?"

"It looked like the place had already been cleaned. It was too clean. There was hardly anything for us to do."

"The whole house?"

"I did the bedrooms and they were spotless," Emilija said. "Talia did the kitchen; was it the same?"

"Yes. All I needed to do was polish the surfaces. It was like the place had already been cleaned before we got here."

"Is there anywhere you didn't clean?"

"The bathroom was all that was left. Otherwise we were almost finished. I heard Valmira vacuuming the front room and then she went down to the basement. I'm not sure if we were supposed to clean down there or not and I haven't seen the list."

"What list?"

"We get a log sheet from Viggó for each day with the jobs on it and instructions, quick clean, deep clean, which rooms, that sort of thing. Valmira ticks everything off as we go. I don't know what was on the log sheet for today, but there's another job this afternoon, somewhere in this street."

"Any idea where the log sheet is?"

Natalia shrugged and Emilija looked blank. "Probably in the basement," she decided. "Valmira must have had it with her."

"Anything interesting?"

"Well . . ." Gunna paused, wondering whether or not to involve Eiríkur, knowing that he had enough work to do already. Although they worked well together, she hadn't built up the same close relationship with him as she had with Helgi. Eiríkur was a city boy and of a different generation; it was less easy to bond with him than with someone who shared a similar background. Gunna had come to Reykjavík from a small town in the far west of Iceland and Helgi from a farming district in the north, and while Eiríkur's parents had come from the countryside, he had grown up in the city and had little feeling for what went on outside its limits. She couldn't help wishing that it was Eiríkur who was still on leave and not the solidly dependable Helgi, who had chosen precisely this week to be away.

"It's something odd," she said finally. "Some contract cleaners turned up at a house in Kópavogur to spring clean a house that had been rented, so it would be all fresh and clean for the next tenants. But in the basement they found a smashed-up chair, bits of duct tape and a lot of bloodstains on the floor."

"That sounds unpleasant. Torture of some kind, do you think?"

"I don't know what to think. Forensics have been over it and taken every sample they can think of. It screams dubious to me, but unless there's a DNA match or something else, I doubt we'll ever get to the bottom of it."

"So you have no victim, no idea what happened or when, and you don't know where to look? Sounds good to me," Eiríkur said brightly. "How about . . .?" he pointed a finger towards the ceiling. "What does the Laxdal say about it?"

"I'm going to ask a few more questions before I mention it to him. The really odd thing about it is that one of the cleaners, the one who found the stuff in the basement, seems to have had a fit and was taken away in an ambulance. I'm getting the feeling there's more to this than meets the eye, and that these Reindeer Cleaners aren't telling me everything."

"Reindeer Cleaners? Is that what they're called?"

"Yup. Tasteful, isn't it? It goes without saying that they're all immigrants."

130

Gunna stood up and pulled on her jacket. "I'll leave you to continue with Vilhelm Thorleifsson's background. Can you see what else you can find out about Elvar Pálsson as well? I'm going to ask the manager at Reindeer Cleaners a few pointed questions."

"Another immigrant?"

"Not this guy. I gather he's the only one working there who isn't foreign."

"All these foreigners, nothing but trouble," Eiríkur sniffed.

"What do you expect when Icelanders don't want to do shit work and import people who are prepared to do it?"

"People would do these jobs if they were paid properly, surely?"

Gunna looked out of the window to check the weather before leaving the building. "And there you have the other half of the problem. If you pay shit wages, then you'll find yourself employing the people who, for whatever reason, can't find anything better."

"A bit like working for the government, you mean?" Eiríkur asked with a faint smile and Gunna was taken aback for a moment by the first hint of a rebellious comment from him.

"Getting that way, Eiríkur, I guess," she said, hiding her surprise.

The young man with the big ears was far from pleased to get an unannounced visit from the police.

"Viggó Jakobsson?" Gunna asked, knowing already that she had the right person. "Gunnhildur Gísladóttir.

I'm with CID and we're investigating Kópavogsbakki fifty, where a squad of your cleaners found something unpleasant in the basement."

"I don't see what this has to do with me," Viggó said, not bothering to conceal his impatience as he spun a set of car keys on his finger. "And I do have an important meeting in a few minutes."

With almost twenty years as a police officer behind her, Gunna had almost managed to suppress the instinct for making instant decisions about people, but it was difficult not to take an on-the-spot dislike to Viggó Jakobsson as he stood up behind his desk.

"I understand that the company belongs to your father, so I guess if he's the one who runs things, he's the one I ought to be talking to," she suggested.

Viggó sat down quickly and dropped his keys into his jacket pocket. "No, you don't want to be doing that," he said hurriedly. "I can tell you anything you need to know."

"Can you now? Who owns Kópavogsbakki fifty? You do contract work, don't you? So you're working for the owner, I take it?"

"I . . . er. I'm not sure I can tell you that," Viggó stammered and Gunna raised a questioning eyebrow. "We have a contract with an estate agent. Actually, we look after about fifty houses and apartments on behalf of that agency, and four of then are on Kópavogsbakki. I'm not sure, but I think fifty belongs to someone who has been out of the country for a few years. Who owns these agency places isn't our affair."

"So how frequently do these houses get cleaned?"

"Normally at the end of the lease, and again before they're let if there's a gap of more than a week or so between people moving out and others moving in. Some tenants also take up the option of having the place cleaned for them once or twice a week, but not this one."

"And Kópavogsbakki fifty? Had people moved out or were they about to move in?"

Viggó looked blank. "You'll have to ask the agent. We just get a call asking for a cleaning squad."

"I thought you said you could tell me anything I need to know?" Gunna said and watched Viggó's face turn pink. She opened her folder. "All right, let's try another tack, shall we? The three cleaners who were there, Valmira Vukoja, Natalia Rodriguez and Emilija Plaudis. All reliable staff, are they? They've all been with you for some years?"

"Small, Medium and Large, I call them." Viggó laughed, but the laughter died on his lips as Gunna looked at him impassively. He coughed. "Small — Natalia — she's been here the longest, seven or eight years. She started here when my old man was still running the company."

"Small?" Gunna asked and Viggó quailed at the sight of her frown.

"Yeah," he explained with a careless, forced laugh. "Those three always work together. Natalia's the little one with the temper, Emilija's a sort of normal shape and size, and Vala's the big fat one." He laughed again while Gunna looked at him stone-faced.

"I see," she said eventually as the grin faded from Viggó's face. "Very flattering, I'm sure. I take it all their work permits and papers are in order?"

Viggó opened his mouth and closed it again. "I think so," he said. "They all have identity numbers and they pay tax, so they have to be legal," he added triumphantly.

"How long have Emilija and Valmira worked for you?" Gunna asked. She knew the answer but wanted to see if Viggó knew as well.

"Since around 2009, I think. After the crash."

"You must have records of their employment history."

"You want me to look it up?"

"That's what I'm here for."

Viggó opened a laptop in front of him and waited for it to whirr into life, leaning over it with his chin in one hand and an elbow on the desk. He tapped and prodded at the keyboard with his free hand.

"Small started here in March 2006," he said.

"Natalia, you mean?"

"Yeah, Natalia. Large —"

"Valmira?"

Viggó coughed. "Yeah. She started here in February 2009 and Medium. Sorry, Emilija, started in April."

"Any problems with any of them?"

Viggó's eyes stayed on the screen in front of him. "No, not really. Small —"

"Natalia."

"Yeah, Natalia," he corrected himself. "She's late now and again, but that's all. She can be a bit of a

134

handful, and she has a temper. You know what these fiery Latin types are like." He laughed.

"Not really, but I'll take your word for it," Gunna said, taking notes. "And the other two?"

"They're no problem at all, work hard and no complaints."

"You mean from them or the customers?"

"Of course I get complaints from them. I mean, they're women, aren't they?" Viggó said and a second hollow laugh died in the face of Gunna's stare. "No complaints from the clients, no. Never, in fact."

"Perfect staff, you might say?"

"I suppose so."

"I'm sure they appreciate being referred to as Small, Medium and Large. Now, which agent lets the house on Kópavogsbakki fifty?"

"Listen, I have a little job for you."

Gunna heard Eiríkur sigh into the phone and carefully suppressed the urge to tell him to get a grip. Privately she decided to give him the benefit of the doubt. He was tired after a month of paternity leave, the new baby's arrival had been stressful — premature by several weeks — and Eiríkur's wife had not had an easy time of it.

"Go on."

"I need you to get on to the Directorate of Immigration and ask for details of some people. Nothing fancy, just how long they've lived here and if they're fully legal. The names are Valmira Vukoja,

Natalia Rodriguez and Emilija Plaudis," she said, and reeled off the three ten-digit national identity numbers.

"All right. Want me to call you back with on that?"

"Only if there's anything that looks urgent. Otherwise it can wait until I'm back. You might want to run those names through our system as well, just to be sure."

"OK, will do," he said with a little more enthusiasm, indicating that the old Eiríkur might be back, and Gunna felt some relief as she looked at the floor-to-ceiling windows in smoked plate glass behind which she expected to find LuxRental.

The place didn't look as busy as it might once have been, but she made allowances for it also being early in the day. The open-plan office stretched back into the distance, and as she walked through the nests of cubicles, it seemed that fewer than half of them were in use as pairs of curious eyes followed her.

"Can I help you?"

The reception desk was situated in an odd position in the middle of the long room, an island in the midst of a sea of squares made up of four cubicles each. A young man with round glasses and hair that stuck up at an alarming angle looked expectant.

"I'm interested in Kópavogsbakki fifty," Gunna said, giving him a smile. "I understand it's empty."

"Er . . . Yes. I think so. If you wait a moment I'll see if I can find someone to help you. Take a seat," he invited. "There's fresh coffee in the flask," he added, indicating a small table next to a deep sofa against the wall.

Gunna sat back and waited, a cup of fragrant black coffee in her hand, as she flipped through her notes from the meeting with Viggó Jakobsson and looked up to see an older version of the young man in front of her, beaming a chiselled smile at her from beneath coiffured grey hair instead of a gelled-up quiff.

"Good morning, I'm Óttar Sveinsson. I gather you're interested in one of the houses on Kópavogsbakki? We deal with several of those properties, but they are rather exclusive and the costs match that exclusivity, you see," he said and Gunna felt immediately that she was being put in her place as someone who didn't look wealthy enough to afford a house with quite such an exclusive sea view.

Gunna returned Óttar Sveinsson's fixed smile. "It's actually Kópavogsbakki fifty in particular that I'm interested in, as I gather it's recently become vacant. That's right, isn't it?"

He sat down next to her on the sofa, perched on the edge and holding a sheaf of papers in his lap. "Actually there are a few technical issues with Kópavogsbakki fifty that we expect to be resolved in a few days. Essential maintenance. But that means that the property is temporarily off-limits for viewing. Maybe we could interest you in other properties in the same area?"

Gunna hauled herself unwillingly from the sofa's clinging embrace to perch on its edge next to him. She dug in her pocket for her wallet and flipped open her identification. Óttar Sveinsson blanched.

"I'm only interested in Kópavogsbakki fifty, and as I already have a house of my own, I'm not looking for somewhere to live, thanks."

He gulped. "I'm not sure we can supply that kind of confidential information. Client confidentiality and all that," he said with a weak, apologetic smile.

"You can, I assure you." Gunna could see his resolve weakening. "In fact, I'm sure Viggó Jakobsson has already given you an idea of what's going on. As something that doesn't look good has happened in a property that you're responsible for and have access to, it might be in your interest to be co-operative."

Óttar wasn't sweating, but the moment for the first drops to appear on his forehead could hardly be far away. Gunna gave him a look intended to be reassuring, and he responded with a glassy smile of his own that looked to have been painted on.

"This is a respectable agency," he struggled to say and looked up at the young man from the reception desk. "Svenni, would you leave us, please? Ask Hildur if there's anything you can help her with, would you?"

Eiríkur looked stressed. Gunna wondered how many times his wife had called that morning before dismissing the thought as uncharitable.

"How did it go?" He asked, pushing a lock of fair hair back from his eyes and looking up from the screen.

"Kópavogsbakki fifty is owned by Sólfell Property ehf, ostensibly," she told him.

"So we need to look up who owns that."

"You can look it up if you like," Gunna said, dropping into Helgi's vacant chair next to him. "But according to Óttar Sveinsson the smooth-talking silver fox of an estate agent, it's a company owned by a group of people including the couple along the street at Kópavogsbakki forty-two, and I can tell you right away that Sólfell Property is owned by friends of Vilhelm Thorleifsson and Elvar Pálsson."

"Big shots?" Eiríkur asked with a downward curl of one corner of his mouth. "More twats in suits?"

"Eiríkur! What's got into you?" Gunna said in feigned shock. "You're not turning into one of these dangerous radical types, are you?"

"Ach. Five years of watching the news, prices going up and all the rest of it. Either that or I've been working with you and Helgi for too long."

"That might be it," Gunna admitted. "But this is very interesting as the directors of Sólfell Property are Jón Vilberg Voss, Sunna María Voss and Jóhann Hjálmarsson."

"Curiouser and curiouser," Eiríkur said, with lines that Gunna had never seen before appearing on his forehead as he frowned. "That's too much of a coincidence, isn't it?"

Gunna cracked her knuckles. "Let's say that once I'd overcome his reservations about telling the police things his clients might not want us to know, Óttar Sveinsson became very talkative."

"He's an estate agent, what do you expect?" Eiríkur snorted. "They're just snake oil salesmen under the skin."

"You really have developed a cynical streak while you've been off, haven't you?"

Eiríkur sighed and looked around. "You know," he started and Gunna sat back and looked at him expectantly, "I'm wondering if I'm cut out for this, to be quite honest with you."

"You mean police work in general, or CID?"

"Both, I suppose," he said and screwed up his face in a frown that Gunna felt didn't suit his normally fresh, open features. "These last few weeks haven't been easy, what with the baby and the missus both being sick. It's been hard on her and it hasn't been easy on any of us. There have been a good few sleepless nights and a lot of time to think things through." His voice faltered and he looked past her at the window and the shreds of ragged white cloud scudding across a blue sky behind them. "I mean," he faltered. "You had a hard time of your own, what with your husband and all that. How did you manage? Did you think about packing it all in?"

"What? And go to live with my mother? Not at all. If anything it was the thought of going back to work that was one of the fixed points when everything else was going haywire," Gunna said, suddenly serious, and she felt a wave of recollection that brought an unbidden lump to her throat. "It was very difficult after Raggi was lost," she admitted. "We'd only been married a year or so and Laufey was two, something like that. I didn't know what the hell was going on and it was a truly dreadful time, but we all have our ways of coping, I

140

guess. So what's really bugging you, Eiríkur? Is it the job or is it you?"

"Me, I suppose. I just don't feel like I'm doing the right thing."

"And what should you be doing?"

Eiríkur hesitated. "I, well. You know I did the first two years at university before I joined the force?"

"Of course. You think I haven't seen your CV?"

"That's what I'm thinking. Going back to finish university."

"Theology?" Gunna stared. "Tell me you're joking."

Eiríkur shook his head. "I'm deadly serious."

"You want to be a priest? Why?" Gunna asked. "I mean, it can't be for the humungous salary or because the Church needs you more than the police force does?"

"I believe the Church does need people like me," Eiríkur said in a low voice. "You see the priests the Church has these days? All those earnest young things with years of university behind them and precious little else. It needs people with some idea of real life. There are too many people there in jobs for life, taking part in committees and meetings."

"Like the public sector as a whole, you mean?"

"I've given it a lot of thought these last few weeks; months, even."

"And your mind's made up?"

"No. But it's getting closer."

Gunna stood up and wondered what to say. Eiríkur's confession had taken her completely by surprise. While she knew that he was the youngest child of fairly elderly parents, and that he'd been brought up in the shadow of the church in a Reykjavík suburb where the old man had been the parish priest, she hadn't realized that he was actively religious or that his thoughts had been moving in that direction.

"What does your wife think of all this?" Gunna asked.

Eiríkur was about to speak when the door opened and Sævaldur Bogason, one of the senior detectives and someone neither Gunna nor Eiríkur got on well with, nodded to them as he stalked to a desk in the corner, whistling tunelessly as he logged on to a computer.

"I'll talk to you about it later," she muttered, and Eiríkur nodded in agreement. "Right now I need a word with the Laxdal."

"Something juicy, is it?"

Gunna looked sideways at Sævaldur Bogason as he put down his tray and sat down opposite her in the canteen. He was the force's newest chief inspector while she was still a sergeant, even though they had graduated in the same year. The difference, she told herself, was that Sævaldur had spent all his career in Reykjavík, while ten of her years as a police officer had been spent on a rural beat with few prospects of promotion in the provincial backwater where she still lived, preferring to commute an hour each way every day than move to the city.

"To be quite honest, Sæsi, I'm not sure. It looks unpleasant, but who knows? It may have been some kind of role-play, or something completely innocuous."

142

He smiled glassily in a way that projected neither humour nor amiability. He and Gunna had crossed swords more than once in the past and had disagreed on practically everything on the occasions they had worked together. But their relationship had improved as they got used to each other in the detectives' office at the Hverfisgata station, while each took care to leave the other space to manoeuvre.

"There's blood on the floor? Doesn't sound playful to me."

"It doesn't sound that way to me either. But with no body, no victim in casualty and nobody knocking down the door here to protest at ill-treatment, it doesn't look like it's going to go anywhere. How are you getting on up there in Borgarfjördur?" Gunna asked, to steer the conversation away from her case and towards Sævaldur's.

"A nightmare. No dabs, no sightings, nothing at all. One drunk witness who might have seen a car that could have been relevant. That's all."

"And the hammer?"

"Nothing. We've been around every hardware shop in the country and haven't found anyone we couldn't account for who bought a sledgehammer in the last month. Have you any idea how many sledgehammers are sold in Iceland every year? Dozens of the damned things. The slugs are being analysed, but I don't believe for a second they'll tell us much."

"A dead-end case, for the first time in how many years?"

Sævaldur forked pasta quickly. "Who knows? There have been unsolved disappearances, like the woman a few years ago who took her dog for a walk and was never seen again. But you're right, an unsolved murder hasn't happened since . . ." He tore at a roll and messily mopped up some sauce. "Not since long before our time."

"How about your housebreaker?" she asked to change the subject, although she knew it was a sore point and that he was concerned it could become something of a joke.

"He's a sly bastard," Sævaldur growled, tapping too much pepper onto the remains of his lunch. "Not a damned clue, no fingerprints, no CCTV, no sightings."

"Sure it's just one person?"

Sævaldur took a mouthful and swallowed it down without chewing, while the pepper made him cough and his already red face went a shade darker.

"That's what the Laxdal said. I reckon it's just one housebreaker. Ívar thinks it's a gang, or else more than one burglar operating separately, stealing stuff to order."

"So why do you reckon it's just one man?" Gunna asked, gradually losing her appetite as Sævaldur forked down a few more rapid mouthfuls before replying.

"Law of averages. One, we know most of the villains in the city. If it was a group of some kind, we'd get a whisper of it from someone sooner or later, because these people can't help falling out or getting drunk and spilling the beans somewhere," he said, putting his fork down. He bent one finger back with the forefinger of

144

the other hand. "Two," he said with emphasis, now with two fingers bent back, "the chances of a small place like Reykjavík producing two skilled housebreakers operating at the same time is just too slim. Three, there are too many similarities."

He released his fingers and returned to wielding his fork like a man who'd been starved of a square meal.

"Unless it's a gang from somewhere or other?"

"Lithuania or Poland or somewhere? Yeah, could be," Sævaldur conceded.

"Different times of day or night, all kinds of properties. You sure it's just one person?"

Sævaldur narrowed his eyes but didn't stop eating. "He's versatile, that's all."

"But that also indicates more than one pattern, don't you think?"

"No, there are still too many similarities," he said, pushing his plate away and opening a tub of yoghurt. "No entry damage, which is unusual in itself. He never forces anything. Locks are picked or he uses doors that are left unlocked. There's no mess. He doesn't empty drawers and cupboards all over the place. He's so discreet that some of his victims don't know they've been robbed until they go to look for something and it's not there. Consequently we have no idea when many of these break-ins took place, and I'd guess there must be a bunch of them out there that haven't even been noticed yet. On top of that, the stuff never shows up, ever."

"Zero recovery?"

"Absolutely nothing. This guy is taking cash, mostly foreign currency, or so it seems. He's taking jewellery, electronics, that sort of stuff."

"So it's going abroad?"

"That or it's being stashed away somewhere for a rainy day, which is unlikely, I reckon," Sævaldur said, staring moodily out of the window.

"None of this stuff ever appears?"

"Nothing. Not one single piece. We have serial numbers, photographs of valuables, all sorts. We've been watching the small ads on the internet, the flea market at Kolaport, even eBay. Nothing so far."

"It's going abroad, no question."

"Just what I thought," Sævaldur said, as if reluctantly agreeing with her. "I'm going to be leaning hard on all the fences we know, and I'd better make some progress before a journalist notices and Reykjavík's silent housebreaker hits the newspapers. So if you know anyone worth leaning on that we don't have on our list, let me know and I'll go and give them a kicking."

"No one that I can think of," Gunna said, pushing her plate aside. "But you might want to have a word with Eiríkur. An old lady called the other day about some jewellery she'd seen in a shop window that looked like hers, and when she got home, she found that she'd been burgled and hadn't noticed."

Sævaldur's eyes shone. "Really? None of our guy's stuff ever shows up, so I don't expect it'll be the same one. but I'll ask Eiríkur what he's found. A damn shame I'm having to look after this and the Borgarfjördur case on my own with half of my crowd of layabouts on courses or sick leave. These next few days I'm leaving my boys to continue knocking on doors up there and I'll manage things from here, which means I can get back to looking for our sneak thief," he said, letting his fork clatter onto his plate. "Eiríkur's doing all right is he?"

Gunna opened her mouth and was on the point of telling Sævaldur of her concerns about Eiríkur, but then she remembered how often she and Sævaldur had clashed in the past and thought better of it.

"Ach, I don't know. He's had a rough time, what with the baby being premature. He'll be all right when he's back into the routine."

"Pussy-whipped, I reckon," Sævaldur said in a loud voice, and a girl from the social insurance office across the road that shared the police canteen gave him a dirty look that Sævaldur completely failed to notice as he inspected the point of a toothpick he'd used to excavate behind a molar. "In my day . . ."

"In your day women were pregnant every year, didn't drive cars and did as they were told," Gunna said in a louder voice than was strictly necessary. "They had a hot meal ready at seven on the dot every night, did it twice a week in the missionary position and were damned grateful for it, right? But since then we have found our way into the twenty-first century and one or two things have changed."

"More's the pity," he said wistfully. "All right, it was just an opinion. No need to come over all feminist on me, Gunna."

147

* ★ *

"Now, did you check those three out for me?"

"Yeah, I did." Eiríkur shuffled through the papers that were already accumulating on his desk and came up with a sheet of notes. "Right. Natalia Rodriguez, Chilean citizen. She's lived in Iceland since 2003. She has a child with a local guy called Hjörtur Helgi Grétarsson. She's here legally, work permit and residence permit in order. Emilija Plaudis, Latvian citizen, and as an EU citizen she's here legally. Divorced, her former husband's Icelandic, name of Ingi Antonsson. Two children. Been here since 2006," Eiríkur read out.

"And the casualty? Valmira?"

"Valmira Vukoja. She's a naturalized Icelandic citizen, originally from Krajina. Came to Iceland in 1996 as one of half a dozen families of refugees with her mother, sister and an uncle. The mother died a few years ago. The younger sister went back to Krajina about five years back and the uncle still lives here, married to a local woman in Hellissandur and isn't going anywhere."

"All that's in the Immigration Directorate's files?" Gunna asked. "They don't normally come up with answers that fast."

"Well, not quite. But I know someone who works there and she gave me a little background detail. There's more, actually," Eiríkur said, and Gunna was aware that Sævaldur on the far side of the room was listening carefully, in spite of his show of being engrossed in his computer. "Valmira Vukoja was quite badly injured at some point, and patched up as well as could be expected in the circumstances, considering where she came from was a war zone at the time. So she spent quite a lot of her first year or two here in and out of hospital. But she did extremely well at school, learned the language quickly and well enough to get through university with a degree in business and modern languages."

"A model citizen. So what's she doing working as a cleaner?"

"The crash happened," Eiríkur said with a shrug. "According to what I've been told on the quiet, Valmira was the office manager at a company that was importing clothes and shoes, and was branching out into importing furniture from somewhere in the Far East. That company went out of business very quickly once the banks stopped lending."

"So the former office manager with the degree and six languages is now cleaning rich people's houses instead? That's a comedown, isn't it?"

"There but for the grace of God go we . . ." Eiríkur said and Gunna gave him a sharp look, unsure if he was serious or not.

"Anything on our system?"

This time Eiríkur smiled. "Oh, yes. Natalia Rodriguez has a record. Two counts of assault, four of public drunkenness and one for shoplifting."

"And the back story, if there is one?"

"There's an extremely volatile relationship with the father of her son, this Hjörtur character, and also with Hjörtur's wife."

"The guy has a wife *and* girlfriend? That's always going to be a recipe for a quiet life, isn't it?"

Valmira's eyes were unfocused, set on a point somewhere beyond the wall of the room at the national hospital as Gunna glanced through the window.

"Injuries?" Gunna asked the doctor who repeatedly pushed his glasses up his nose and let them slip down to look over them.

"No, nothing physical."

"Up here?" She pointed to her own temple.

"Ah. Who knows?" The doctor asked with a wry look. "That's hardly my department, I'm afraid. But probably, I'd say."

"I'm all right to speak to her, though?"

"Go ahead. But I'd appreciate it if you let me know whether or not she tells you anything that might be useful. Come and find me afterwards? I'll be in my office."

He left her to look through the window in Valmira's door, the soles of his rubber clogs squeaking against the scrubbed floor.

"Good morning. Valmira?" Gunna offered, closing the heavy door behind her and causing Valmira's eyes to snap back to reality.

"Hello," she said uncertainly.

"My name's Gunnhildur Gísladóttir and I'm a police officer. I'm investigating what happened at the house you were working at yesterday and what you found there," Gunna explained, watching Valmira for a

150

reaction. "I understand you were brought in here yesterday. Are you feeling better? Well enough to talk?"

She sat on the chair next to the bed while Valmira smiled and fluttered. "I'm really sorry for all the fuss. I'm fine." She sighed. "It was just that . . ." she said and lapsed into silence.

"Just what?"

Valmira shook her head. "Memories. Bad memories."

"Yesterday you turned up at this house at eight, and it was schedule to be a four-hour job, right?" Gunna asked and got a nod in response. "There was another house to be cleaned in the same street in the afternoon?"

"That's right. First number fifty, and then forty-two in the afternoon."

"Had you cleaned this house before?"

"Fifty? Yes, I think so," Valmira said and Gunna listened carefully for the traces of an accent in her voice but was hard-pushed to hear any, although occasional lapses in grammar gave away the fact that she was not a native speaker. Not that that's any indicator, she thought to herself, reflecting that the younger generation's grasp of its own language had weakened alarmingly in the face of the influx of English to practically every facet of life in Iceland.

"And forty-two? I understand they're owned by the same people."

"I don't know anything about who owns what. As I remember, we did fifty quite a long time ago, maybe a year, but we look after number forty-two regularly. There's a dentist and his wife who live at forty-two. Maybe they're both dentists, I don't know. Anyway, we

151

normally clean that place once a week, always an afternoon job."

"Can you tell me what happened yesterday? You went down to the basement of number fifty and what? Were you supposed to clean the basement as well?"

Valmira sighed a deeper sigh than before. "No, I wasn't supposed to go down there. But we have to sign off the worksheet at the end of the job saying that we have left the house secure. So I always check garage doors, back doors, that kind of thing, to make sure it really is all locked up."

"And what happened? Was there someone there?"

"No. There was nobody," Valmira said in a blank voice, her eyes again focused on something in the far distance. She sat for a moment and hugged her arms around herself, her thick dark hair shrouding her face. "I switched on the lights as I went down the stairs and saw what was there, the broken chair and the blood on the floor, and so much came flooding back. I don't know if I fainted, but it was as if I had been taken back to . . ." she paused.

"Back to Yugoslavia?"

"Yugoslavia?" Valmira said bitterly. "That's what it was called when I was a child. Everyone hated that old bastard Tito, but at least he kept people from murdering their neighbours."

"I see. I'm sorry to hear it. So this took you back to . . ." Gunna paused, not sure what to say. "Back to something you'd rather forget?"

"No. I don't want to forget that my father and brothers disappeared and were probably shot in a forest

152

somewhere because their names were a little unusual. But I can do without the sudden reminders of what happened."

"You were lucky to escape, surely?"

Valmira nodded vigorously. "Don't imagine that I'm not aware of that and that I don't remember every day that this place is safe and here nobody is going to knock on the door in the night and take away people whose faces aren't quite right, or who some official has a grudge against."

"So it was a shock?"

"It was a shock to see the same way of doing things. I had never expected to see this in Iceland. I know what went on there."

"What, then?"

Valmira shrugged. "I guess someone was tied to a chair and questioned, in a very painful way."

"Torture, you mean?"

"Exactly. I try not to think about it. But I think you can be sure that he told them everything they wanted to know."

Soffía looked radiant, her red curls tied back as Ari Gíslason suckled contentedly. "You were just passing, were you?"

"Well, let's say I was visiting someone nearby. How is he?" Gunna asked, peering at the tiny head, its eyes closed.

"He's fine. But he seems to be hungry all the time."

"The same as Gísli was. He was on a bottle when he was four days old. I couldn't keep up. Mind you, things were different then." Gunna sat down and gazed at the baby. "He has your hair."

"Red?" Soffia laughed. "That means a temper, doesn't it? I'm already looking forward to him being a teenager."

"He'll be fine."

"Yeah, but you're his grandmother. Kids can do no wrong as far as grandparents are concerned."

The word hit her with a force she could not have imagined.

"Grandmother. It still hasn't sunk in," she said. "But don't you believe it. We're not all a soft touch."

"How's Drífa?" Soffia asked, her face turning serious, clearly with an effort.

Gunna winced. "I don't know. She's all right one minute and in tears the next."

"I think he's asleep," Soffia decided, looking down at the baby and gently detaching him to lift him over her shoulder. "I hope she's all right. It's not her fault that . . . Well, of course it is. These things don't happen out of thin air. But you know what I mean."

"I know. She's not having a wonderful time of it right now. Her parents desperately want her to go home, and she's equally determined not to, so there's a battle of wills going on there."

"And you're caught in the middle?"

"You could say that. Drífa's mother is in the middle of the world's longest-lasting sulk and has hardly spoken to her since Kjartan was born. My brother Svanur calls once or twice a week, not that it's me he

154

wants to speak to. He's just checking on Drífa. He's been to see her, but his wife hasn't."

The baby burped and gurgled.

"You want to hold him?"

"Go on then."

"And is she all right?"

"I think so." Gunna held the little boy tenderly, looking intently at the placid, sleepy face. "I hope so, at any rate. It's not easy to tell. Drífa is a very bright girl, but she's a dark horse and doesn't give too many secrets away. As far as I can see she's coping, but it's not easy for her and she's always broke."

Soffía smoothed her shirt, not knowing what to do with her hands now that Gunna was holding the baby. "I ought to see her."

"Drífa? You think so? You're probably right."

"It's not her fault that . . ."

"Come on, Soffía. It takes two."

"I know, but I'm not going to harbour a grudge. Life's too short. Ari and Kjartan are half-brothers, so we owe it to them to bury any differences and let them grow up with as much of a relationship as we can."

Ari Gíslason yawned in her arms and opened one eye a crack to look up at his grandmother.

"You're quite right," she said and crooned to the baby in a way that would have Eiríkur, Helgi and Ívar Laxdal wondering if this was the same person. "Would you like me to speak to Drífa? I see her most days."

The scabs on his wrists and ankles were hardening, while Lísa's attitude was starting to soften. Orri told

155

himself that he should have made up a story of some kind to explain why he had been out so late, but there was no way he could explain all those cuts, so he simply didn't try; he just kept his mouth shut and waited for it all to blow over.

It had been a frosty day. Lísa had hardly spoken to him after he came in from work, but in some ways that was just fine, as good as a holiday, with no discussions about curtains, vacations or any of those increasingly clunky dropped hints about acquiring a permanent home together, or pets, or children or weddings. Orri liked his independence. Living alone and having Lísa stay with him a few nights a week was about right, he felt, although he could see that what had been a night or two had become practically the full week and his flat was overflowing with Lísa's stuff.

Lísa appeared from the shower, one huge towel wrapped around her and another around her head, bare feet slapping the kitchen's plastic floor tiles as she passed him and trailed a hand over his shoulder. She rooted through the bottom drawer as Orri admired the curves under the towel stretched tight as she bent over.

"Wasn't there an extension lead in here?" She asked, turning her head to look at him accusingly.

"In the cupboard, I think," he answered, his mouth full of toast. "What do you need it for?"

Lísa stood up and pulled the towel tighter. "Hairdryer. The cable doesn't reach far enough."

"There's one behind the TV," Orri said, reaching for his phone as it buzzed with an incoming message.

"I'll use this one," Lisa decided, the towel slipping slightly as she passed him.

"Coming?" she asked, her voice dropping to an inviting tone.

Orri grinned. The offer of a quick one was an olive branch. Things were getting back to normal.

"That's an offer a man shouldn't turn down," he said, reaching out to pinch an end of the towel between thumb and fingers as Lisa swept past, leaving him with a fluffy white heap on the floor as she giggled her way to the bedroom. He heard the whine of the hairdryer as he thumbed the button on his phone to display the text message, and as he read it his world went silent.

Hi Orri Björnsson, he read in English. Pleased to make your acquaintance the other night and sorry I haven't been in touch before. I have a little job for you, nothing too difficult. Check your mailbox on the way to work. You'll find written instructions there and the equipment you'll need is on the back seat of your car.

He sat and stared at the screen, his head buzzing in shock. He had pushed what had happened to the back of his mind, convincing himself that the man who had tied him up would not really call on him, telling himself that he had just wanted to give him a fright.

"Orri."

He scrolled down to see if there was anything more, but there was only a blank screen and no caller's number to reply to.

"Orri," Lisa called from the other room.

Orri stared, his mind in a whirl as the memories of that night resurfaced.

"If you're not coming, then I'm getting dressed," Lisa called from the bedroom.

He shook his head hard, as if to scatter the bad memories and collect his thoughts. He got up abruptly, pushing the chair back as he did so. Lisa sat cross-legged on the bed as she brushed her hair.

Orri forced a lecherous smile that didn't suit his mood in the least.

"I thought you weren't coming," she said, tossing the hair brush onto the dressing table and lying back as Orri pulled at his jeans, his mind elsewhere.

CHAPTER
SEVEN

Eiríkur scratched his head. "Gunna?"

"What?"

"Something interesting here."

She looked up, catching the tone in Eiríkur's voice that indicated as much excitement as he was ever likely to display.

"Let's hear it, then."

"The woman in that Aunt Bertha shop described a man with stubble, medium height, brownish hair, quite short."

"You're still working on that?"

"Well, no. I was going to come back to it when I have time. But when we were knocking on doors along Kópavogsbakki yesterday, one of the people in the street reported seeing a man who answered to the same description. It seems this guy has been observed more than once."

"That's all well and good, but that description could apply to around a third of the male population."

"Yeah. But both Aunt Bertha and this old boy at Kópavogsbakki specifically mention a green fleece with some kind of yellow logo."

"How come you've only just noticed this?"

"I'm going through the notes the uniformed officers collected from the neighbours. Tinna and Geiri knocked on a lot of the doors and this is one of Tinna's. She spoke to a retired gentleman who appears to have too much time on his hands, according to her notes."

"Then you'd best get out there and start asking questions, hadn't you? Did you pass this on to Sævaldur?"

Eiríkur shook his head. "No. He's busy enough as it is for the moment."

"Good. Go on, then. Get yourself out to Kópavogsbakki and chase it up, will you? That way if the Laxdal asks if we're getting anywhere I can tell him truthfully that you're following a lead."

Orri trudged along the narrow street in the western end of Reykjavík. He had the location memorized and the black Chevrolet was not quite where he had been told to look for it, though close, a few hundred metres further along and parked badly by the side of the road, with one wheel on the pavement.

He looked around quickly to see if anyone were about and felt nervous. He would have preferred darkness and walked further along the street. He felt ravenously hungry, and at the bottom of the street where it widened to join another road he found a snack bar and bought himself a hot dog and a drink.

Orri's hands trembled as he ate the sausage in its bath of ketchup and remoulade in a just few gulps, washing it down with a can of fizzy drink and asking himself why a man who revelled in the thrill of not being seen as he explored people's houses was so nervous. He knew the answer as he downed the last sugary drops from the can and tossed it into an overflowing bin. Working for himself, he was in charge and in control. This time, he was someone else's puppet, doing their dirty work for a wage instead of a bounty.

He stared moodily through the scratched clear plastic of the snack bar's windows, leaning on the chest-level bar that ran around the unheated inside of it and watching a few people walk past, heads bowed into the fresh wind. Lamp posts along the street shivered in the uneven gusts.

The door banged behind him and he thrust his hands into his pockets, one fist clasped around the little back box as he walked back towards the hulking black car.

This time he approached it from the rear, the end he was supposed to get to. Orri looked around smartly, made sure there was nobody about and dropped to one knee. He reached up high under the wheel arch and put the box in place, feeling the magnets snap it firmly to the American steel of the bodywork. In only a few seconds, he was back on his feet and walking fast.

He took a side street, then another to zig-zag back to the harbour where the work van was parked in a corner of a public lot. He hardly dared breathe until he was hunched in the stream of traffic heading back to the depot, his hands gripping the wheel tight to stop them trembling.

Gunna spied the blonde mop by the check-in desk first, before Bára turned round and saw her.

"Thanks for the gig." She grinned. "I might even get a couple of weeks on a beach somewhere hot out of this."

"You're welcome. Charging a decent rate, are you?"

"Fairly respectable," Bára said. "A hundred thousand a day."

"Cash, or are you going to be honest?"

"Probably a combination of the two." Bára winked. "A week for me and a week for the government."

"Very wise. But I guess you're working for it?"

"Twelve hours a day, seven days a week until further notice. Which would be fine if they weren't such a pain in the neck."

"How so?"

"Sooner or later I'm going to have to have a little discussion with Sunna María about just what I'm supposed to be doing, as she seems to think that a security consultant is some kind of gopher. It makes a change from collaring shoplifters by the clothes racks, though."

"And Jóhann?"

Bára thought. "I'm not sure. Haven't seen a lot of him so far as he's mostly stuck behind his laptop, but he seems to be humouring her."

Gunna cracked her knuckles. "Well, I suppose I'd better go and make their acquaintance. You won't forget to drop me a line if anything suspicious crops up?"

"Me?" Bára said in mock shock. "Haven't you heard of client confidentiality?"

"I have indeed. But I've also heard of doing discreet favours for pals who recommend your services."

"Touché. There'll be a text if anything turns up that doesn't smell right. But can you tell me what happened to shake them up so much?"

Gunna looked around before replying. "A man was shot in his summer house with a .22 handgun, very professional, according to what we're being told. So far there are no leads, and it's as if the killers have just vanished. The man was in business with your clients, so watch your back."

A serious look stole over Bára's face. "You're sure you think you're doing me a favour with this?"

"Ach. You'll be fine. It's them these villains want to knock off, not you."

"Somehow I don't think a hundred thousand a day is enough to take a bullet for."

"Far from it. And before I forget, both of them are screwing other people on some kind of semi-regular basis, just to make the security issue even more complex."

"Oh, that's just wonderful."

"But Jóhann's likely to be less of a headache on that score as it seems he keeps his in Germany, according to his wife."

"Is it a serious case?" Geir Einarsson asked eagerly. The overheated front room was stuffed with books from floor to ceiling. Eiríkur looked at them as the old man shuffled towards a chair by the window, and saw that they were predominantly crime novels, mostly in English and a few translated into Icelandic with lurid covers.

He fussed with a pipe and moved a book that had been placed open, face down on a footstool.

"What happened over there? This is such a quiet neighbourhood normally."

"I'm sure you understand that we can't say too much, other than that it appears a crime has taken place."

"Say no more." He tapped the side of his nose. "Of course. Walls have ears."

"My colleague tells me you've observed some suspicious activity around here?"

"I wouldn't say that, young man. But I sit here by the window most of the day and see everyone who goes by."

"You're retired, I take it?" Eiríkur said.

"Long ago, my boy. I'm past eighty. You think that people of my age can walk into a job just like that? Not that I would, even if there were jobs to be had."

"So you sit and read all day long? That sounds like the kind of thing I dream of."

"It was wonderful for the first few months, but these days I'd rather be outside, and I hope I will be when the weather's warmer. For now, though, I'll stick to indoors."

"Right, can you tell me what you've seen?"

"Better than that. I can show you my log." There was pride in the old man's voice as he strained to lean down for a folder that had fallen to the floor. "I've been reading crime stories for years, so I know how important it is to be precise. Look."

He pointed to a list, made out day-by-day, of people passing by the house. It wasn't a long list, as Eiríkur guessed that relatively few people other than residents walked along the exclusive cul-de-sac, but Geir Einarsson had carefully listed them.

"I'm particularly interested in a man wearing a green fleece with yellow lettering on it."

"Ah. Stripes."

"Stripes?"

"That's what I call him. I've noticed him passing now and again. I don't think he lives around here, but I could be wrong."

"What makes you think that?"

Geir Einarsson tapped the side of his nose a second time. "Ah, intuition." He smiled gleefully. "Is that what you sleuths depend on most of the time? Flashes of inspiration and intuition?"

Eiríkur wanted to retort that results were normally obtained by endless mundane questions and cross-checking, but decided not to shatter any illusions.

"What's your villain done, I'd like to know? No, I know you can't possibly tell me, so I'll not ask. Merely a rhetorical question."

"He could have been a witness to an incident and we'd like to be able to rule him out, that's all," Eiríkur assured him. "Nothing sinister."

"What a shame." The old man chuckled. "I was hoping for a criminal mastermind being brought to book, but we can't have everything, I suppose. What do you want to know about Stripes?"

"When have you seen him? What time of day? And how many times?"

"I keep a close eye on the neighbourhood, and not just because I don't have anything else to do. I was brought up in this street, and until a few years ago this house was all on its own. The rest of these homes are all new. I thought at first that Stripes was a workman on one of those new houses they're building at the end of the street, but there hasn't been any work going on there for weeks. Too cold for concreting, I suppose. But even with no work in progress, Stripes still takes a walk around the district."

"When did you last see him?" Eiríkur asked, hoping that sooner or later a question would hit its target. "And I'm interested to know why you think he might not be local."

"Because people round here don't walk; they drive. Even to the shop on the corner. They might go for a run, swaddled in latex . . ."

"Latex?"

"You know, those stretchy clothes that young people wear."

"You mean Lycra."

"Latex, Lycra. Whatever. That's what I mean. They'll run around dressed in clothes that leave nothing whatsoever to the imagination, but they don't walk anywhere. Stripes walks. People who live in this district wouldn't dream of doing anything as ordinary as just walking."

166

There was clear disdain his voice, and Eiríkur could only agree, trying guiltily to remember when he had last walked any further than to the car.

"It's like America, where nobody walks. I went there once and didn't like it much," Geir said.

"'Stripes'," Eiríkur reminded him. "Why 'Stripes'?"

"Why Stripes? Because of the two yellow stripes," Geir answered, as if speaking to a child, putting a finger to the opposite wrist and running it up to his shoulder. "I just told you, he has two yellow stripes up one arm of a green jacket. You can't miss it."

"And lettering as well?"

"Ah. I could see there's a badge of some kind on his sweater, but I'm afraid he was always too far away for me to make it out."

"But you can describe him?"

"I can," Geir said with relish. "Not only can I provide a description, I write it all down, so I can give you the times and dates that he walked down the street."

Jóhann's half-moon glasses slid almost to the end of his nose and he smiled warmly at Gunna.

"Good afternoon, officer. Unfortunately you find me in slightly uncomfortable circumstances."

"Pleased to see you're following advice."

"Obviously I would prefer to be at home, but . . ." He shrugged and closed the laptop on the desk in front of him. "What can we do for you? Coffee?"

"Why not?" Gunna said, wanting to see if he would ask Bára to fetch coffee, but instead he called the front

167

desk and ordered it through room service. "I wanted to ask you about Kópavogsbakki fifty, which I believe you own?"

This time Jóhann's stare became harder and lasted a moment longer than was comfortable as Gunna met his gaze head-on, refusing to be overawed.

He took a deep breath through his nose and let it out slowly as he tapped the table.

"I, that is to say we, own a share in a company that owns Kópavogsbakki fifty."

"And three other properties, including the house that you live in at Kópavogsbakki forty-two?"

"That is correct. I'm sure you know all this already, officer."

He looked up as there was a knock on the door and Bára stood up, stepping into the lobby and closing the door of the suite behind her.

"I like her. Quiet and confident," he said as soon as Bára had shut the door behind her. "A friend of yours?"

"A former colleague," Gunna said. "Sólfell Property ehf. That's you and who else?"

"It's me, Sunna María and Jón Vilberg Voss."

"This isn't something that Elvar Pálsson and Vilhelm Thorleifsson have been involved with?"

He looked up as Bára escorted a young man in an ill-fitting waistcoat into the room, pushing a small trolley in front of him. He waited for the waiter to leave before answering.

"They were initially, but then we went our separate ways. The land was an investment some years ago and we have been building ever since. Vilhelm and Elvar

168

never saw their futures in Iceland and they aren't involved in our property venture. They started out in the shipping business and became typical export raiders, if you want to use that hackneyed phrase, except that they were good at it, weren't over-greedy and kept themselves out of the limelight. Sunna María and I both live in Iceland and as far as I know we expect to stay here, so investing in property here was logical. So we bought four houses and live in one of them ourselves. One is rented and two are plots that are under construction."

"And Jón Vilberg Voss? Your brother-in-law?"

"Exactly. He's in the diplomatic service and has been based in Paris for some years. But like us, he'll want to retire to Iceland one day, not to some semi-tropical shambles." Jóhann sat back, his glasses in his hands as he fiddled with them, bending the frames in his fingers. "Why the interest in the houses? I assure you everything is above board and legal with the tax authorities."

"I don't work for the taxman," Gunna assured him. "Is there any connection between Jón Vilberg and Vilhelm Thorleifsson?"

Jóhann shook his head. "Hardly. They move in very different circles."

"An incident took place a few nights ago at Kópavogsbakki fifty. That's why I'm interested to find out if there might be a connection."

Jóhann's expression hardened and a new glint appeared in his eyes. "Incident? What kind of incident?"

"An assault. It's still under investigation. Have you been aware of any unusual traffic in the street? Anyone calling? Any signs of attempted entry at your home?"

The set of his jaw softened, although the intense gleam stayed in his eyes. "I haven't been at home very much recently. Conferences in Germany and Hungary, and a trade fair in Munich have kept me away for a while. You had better ask my wife."

"She's here?"

"In the other room."

"You spend much time abroad?"

"More than I'm comfortable with at my age. Coffee?"

He poured a cup for Gunna from the pot on the trolley while Bára looked on impassively. He poured one for himself and sat back, brooding; Gunna looked closely at him as he stared into space. The lines of tiredness around his eyes were deeply etched.

"Officer, I have to admit I'm more puzzled than worried. Can you tell me what the hell is going on? An acquaintance is gunned down. You have been hinting that I need to be careful, so we move to this fiendishly expensive hotel for a few days. Am I to understand that I'm also on some kind of maniac's hit list?"

"If I knew, I'd tell you, and I'd be a lot happier if I knew where Elvar Pálsson is. But I have to be cautious. Is there anyone else who might be at risk? Any other business activities or partners?"

Jóhann drained his cup and placed it carefully on the saucer, rotating it so that the handle lay parallel to the table's sides. "No. Sólfell Investment and the associated

170

companies have all been, or are being, wound up. Sólfell Property will soon be the only one left apart from my dental practice, and Vison, which isn't much more than a registration number."

"Were you and Sunna María aware that Vilhelm was in Iceland?"

"No. It was a surprise that he was murdered here," Jóhann said with a wintry smile.

"Not a surprise that he was murdered, just that it happened in Iceland?"

"Let's just say that these boys haven't made too many friends over the years. We knew that Villi was due to come to Iceland sometime soon as part of the winding-up process of various companies that he and Elvar own here, but it was a surprise that he had arrived without letting us know first. Not that he was ever too free with information."

"You have any children?"

"Sunna María and I are childless. I have two boys from a previous marriage who are now grown up and have families of their own."

"You had better give me names and addresses, just in case."

"Hjálmar lives in Akureyri. Smári lives at Furuás eighty-five. He works with me, so he's at the practice most days."

"You don't have much to do with letting your houses?"

"Nothing at all. We leave all that to Óttar Sveinsson. He gets a respectable percentage, but we make him work for it. The construction work on the other two houses is looked after by Sunna María after we decided that she could do a better job than the project manager we used before."

"So you have no idea who might be there at any particular time?"

"None at all. At one time I used to watch to have an idea of what the people who had rented the houses looked like, but now I never bother. As long as the rent comes through, I don't pay any attention. I normally know if one of them is empty as there's always some minor maintenance or decoration to be done, and Óttar checks before he spends my money," Jóhann said slowly. "Although it's normally Sunna María he speaks to. I guess she's less tight-fisted than I am."

"So you weren't aware of who was at number fifty?"

"Officer, I've been out of the country for the last two weeks. Sunna María said something about the place needing to be cleaned and that's all I can tell you."

Óttar Sveinsson didn't look pleased to see her and jumped up from behind his desk to head her off into a quiet corner. By the time his hurried steps coincided with Gunna's he had managed to summon a smile.

"What can I do for you this time, officer? Looking for a house, maybe?"

"The same one, actually," Gunna said and watched the smile fade. "I'm here to take all the paperwork related to Kópavogsbakki fifty for the last twelve months."

"All of it?"

"Every tiny snippet of information down to the last detail. I'm assuming you keep records going back a few years?"

"We keep everything. But we don't keep it all here."

"Where's the rest of it?"

"At our storage facility."

"You don't mean your garage, do you?"

Óttar Sveinsson looked hurt. "Of course not. If it's not here it'll be stored at our other office in Kópavogur. Excuse me," he said, and went over to whisper in the ear of a young man sitting behind a desk.

"No, right now," Gunna heard him say in an urgent tone. "It's important."

"One moment, please," he said, returning to the corner where Gunna had decided against sinking into the all-enveloping sofa. "My colleague is fetching everything."

"Who makes the decisions on repairs to the houses you rent out?"

"One of us will do that, normally. We inspect properties that we manage regularly, as long as the rental period is longer than six months, otherwise we only inspect at the end when the tenants leave."

"So is that your job?"

"Most of the time."

"And if it's something major that needs doing?"

"Then we consult the owners. We don't have the authority to embark on significant costs without their consent. Minor expenses aren't a problem and that comes out of the payment to the owner."

"Let's just say," Gunna said. "Let's imagine a tenant carries out some work. Is that acceptable?"

"If it's authorized, yes. Otherwise tenants aren't allowed to carry out modifications."

"So when the basement of Kópavogsbakki fifty was painted throughout, was that your doing?"

Óttar Sveinsson stopped short. "I really don't know," he said after a moment's thought and looked across to where the office boy was not exactly hurrying to bring them a bulky file. "Thank you," he said tartly as it was handed over.

He opened the folder and started to flip through it, going through checklists and receipts.

"No," he decided. "If the basement was painted, then it wasn't done by us or on our instructions."

"Thanks." Gunna took the folder and opened it.

"We will get that back, won't we?"

"Eventually. Are the details of the tenants here as well?"

"At the back," he said, extracting a plastic sleeve and from that a sheaf of papers.

"I suppose you photocopy identification?"

"Naturally," Óttar Sveinsson said, taking the sheaf of paper and flicking through it with practised fingers before taking a slower second look. "I, er . . . I'm sorry, but it seems those papers are missing. This is the previous tenant, not the one who has just moved out."

"That's convenient."

Óttar Sveinsson shuffled his feet and mumbled in embarrassment. "I can't understand it. We're so careful. It must have been misplaced in the wrong folder."

174

"So who were the tenants?"

"They were two gentlemen, here on business, I understand, for a few months."

"Names?"

"I really don't recall."

"Local?"

"No, they were Danish, I think. Or German."

"Surely they had references?"

"Normally, yes, we would expect references. But Sunna María told me that she knew them and she was happy to skip the formalities."

"Anything?" Gunna asked. "Anything at all?"

Ívar Laxdal's face was set in its usual impassive mask. "Nothing at all. Sævaldur has nothing, literally nothing. The slugs are nothing that can be identified and match no firearm on any records. The witness saw nothing that was of any use, and as the girl is from Russia, she doesn't speak English well enough to be able to tell if the killers spoke with an accent or not. There's no description beyond two men, one about one metre seventy-five and one about one-eighty-five tall, both heavily built, with dark hair judging by their eyebrows. That's all."

"No vehicle in the area or anything like that? If it wasn't a hired car, then where did it come from?"

"Gunnhildur, you think Sævaldur's incident room hasn't been through all that?"

"Sorry. It's frustrating, though." She sensed that he was impatient, unusually for someone who exuded calmness and control while others around him struggled to keep abreast of their workloads. "You're getting shit from above about this?" she ventured to ask, and saw with a flush of satisfaction that the question had taken him by surprise.

"No. Not yet," he said with a faint smile. "But rest assured that I will."

"There is something else. The cleaner who found that pool of blood in a cellar yesterday and freaked out?"

"What about it? No victim, so no case, I'd imagine."

"That would be my feeling as well, except that the house is owned by Sunna María Voss and Jóhann Hjálmarsson."

"The dentist and his wife? Who have been in business with the victim?"

"That's them," she said. "It seems the wife is the one who has been in business with Vilhelm Thorleifsson. The husband's lukewarm about him, and also about the missing partner, Elvar Pálsson."

Ívar Laxdal sat silent for a moment and placed the palms of his hands together in front of him, his fingertips beating a tattoo against each other as he thought.

"It's a mess, isn't it? Have you located this other character?"

"No. He's abroad as far as I can make out, but nobody knows where."

"Keep an eye on things, would you, Gunnhildur?" He said slowly. "If this man . . ."

"Elvar."

176

"If he doesn't show his face soon, then are we looking at a missing person enquiry? Could he have gone the same way?"

"Who knows? He travels to the Baltic States, and it seems he has business in London as well. So it's anyone's guess."

"Not in Iceland. Someone will know where he is. Family?"

"He has an ex-wife who has been an ex-wife for a very long time, no contact there. He's dissolved most of his business activities here, and the little he does have left in Iceland includes the bankrupt firm that the dentist and his wife were involved with."

"And how are they coping with all this?"

"Living in the lap of luxury in the Harbourside Hotel. But they can afford it."

"They're still asking for protection?"

"Not at the moment. They have a security consultant looking after them."

Ívar Laxdal's eyes rolled and he groaned. "Not some hoodlum, I hope?"

"No, Bára Kristinns who used to be at the Keflavík station."

"Ah, then that's all right," he said, brightening. "A very sharp young woman. A real shame we couldn't keep her on the force."

"Yeah, and for a hundred thousand a day I'm tempted to go into that line of business myself."

Gunna scrolled through the report with mounting frustration. The basement of Kópavogsbakki 50 had been examined by the forensic team, who had come up with nothing conclusive. There were no recent fingerprints anywhere in the basement other than those of Valmira and the other cleaners. The dried blood on the floor was real enough and was identifiable as the overwhelmingly common type O, but it was doubtful that a DNA profile could be obtained.

She chewed her lip, knowing that even an urgent DNA analysis request could take weeks and cost money that would come from the department's already thin budget. Costs had been cut and cut again, to the point that she had started bringing in a few lightbulbs and toilet rolls that filled a drawer of her desk in case the day came when there was an empty store cupboard.

The door had not been forced, although scratches indicated that the lock had been picked, and it was clear enough from the bloodstains on the tape and the splintered remnants of the wooden chair that matched three remaining chairs in the kitchen upstairs that someone had been tied to it.

"So who the hell are you and why were you there?" Gunna muttered to herself, rattling her fingernails on the table.

The smashed chair indicated that the victim had broken it to escape, in which case, whoever it was had been left alone long enough to break the chair, bite through the tape and escape. Examination of the grey duct tape used to bind the victim to the chair had yielded some threads of a dark green material, and this had also been found on a corner of the shelves, as if the victim had snagged some clothing on it.

"Interesting," Gunna decided. "But when? "When did this happen? How long ago?" She picked up the phone and started dialling when the door swung open and a paper cup of coffee appeared, followed by Eiríkur, a folder of notes under one arm.

"Hæ," Eiríkur said, dropping into his chair. "I had no idea that we lead such exciting lives."

"Oh, yes," Gunna agreed, her eyes skimming the rest of the report. "Non-stop thrills and spills at CID. That's why you wanted to be a policeman, isn't it?"

Eiríkur stretched and yawned. "Well, I certainly didn't join up to be lectured on police procedure by an old boy who seems to have spent his retirement reading thrillers and knows more about police work than I do."

"No joy here, I'm afraid. Whoever was tied up in that basement appears to have been born without fingers as there isn't a print to be found anywhere. No luck with your elderly crime fan, then?"

"Maybe." Eiríkur grinned. "You know the Aunt Bertha guy, described as medium height and otherwise completely unremarkable, but wearing a green fleece with a yellow logo on it?"

"Go on."

"Old Geir Einarsson has logged the appearance of a man in his late twenties or early thirties on ten occasions walking along Kópavogsbakki wearing a green fleece with a yellow logo on the front and two yellow stripes down one arm."

"That means there's a possibility our mysterious victim could be whoever robbed the old lady's house. Sævaldur's phantom housebreaker, maybe?"

"How do you figure that out?"

Gunna tapped the side of her nose and scrolled back through the report. "Traces of Polyethylene tera . . ." She stumbled. "Polyethylene teraphthalate found on the gaffer tape in the basement of Kópavogsbakki fifty, and also on a sharp edge of the shelves. That's the stuff that fleece jackets and whatnot are made from. Colour: dark green."

"Wonderful. Will you tell Sævaldur or shall I?"

"You know he'll be furious if he doesn't figure this one out for himself."

"I know. I can't wait."

"I don't suppose your elderly armchair sleuth saw what the logo was?"

"Nope, sadly not. Too far away," Eiríkur said. "But he seems to have walked the same route, mostly in the afternoons, and he was seen at various times from soon after midday to just before dark."

"There you go, then. You'd better get back to Aunt Bertha and see if you can jog that woman's memory, or find out what CCTV there is around there that he might have walked past. If you can figure out the logo, you might have him."

"She did give me the time, so I'll see what I can find."

"Good man. Now get on with it before Sævaldur comes back and you have to tell him what you've found out," she said, reaching for her desk phone as it rang.

Orri saw Lísa's car parked outside and muttered a curse that she had managed to park it across two spaces. He switched off the engine and sat in silence for a while, listening to the car ticking as he gathered his thoughts. He had been surprised at how nervous he had been sticking whatever it was to that car downtown that morning, scared of being noticed and questioned. Orri felt that under normal circumstances his nerves were strong, but being unable to choose the time and place was uncomfortable, and not being able do his usual research troubled him, removing the illusion of control.

Eventually he sighed, pulled the keys from the ignition with a click and made his way inside, his heavy work boots in one hand and his high-viz vest over his arm.

In the lobby he rattled his postbox and was surprised to see there was a bulky padded envelope there with no stamp, just his name on it in typed capitals. Puzzled, he ripped it open and found inside a folded wad of notes circled with a rubber band. Looking around quickly to see if he was being watched, Orri counted the notes and decided as he did so that the hour's detour that morning had maybe been worthwhile after all. The wad of 5,000 krónur notes was equivalent to a good week's wages.

He was on his way up the stairs with a spring in his step that had been lacking all day when his phone buzzed and he read the message as he pushed open the door of his flat and walked into the smell of something heavy on the spices.

Orri stopped dead, leaving the door half open.

Good evening, Orri Björnsson. You did well today. We have another task for you. Instructions for the job and on where to collect the equipment will be in your mailbox before morning. Reply with a blank message to acknowledge.

In a daze, and with the feeling deep inside that he was doing the wrong thing, Orri thumbed the reply button and sent a blank message back with the door of his apartment still open.

"*Hæ.* Who was that?" Lísa asked. "Anything important?"

Orri dropped his boots and his fluorescent jacket by the door, and shook his fleece from his shoulders.

"Nah. Work stuff. What's cooking?"

CHAPTER
EIGHT

Bára sat in a café a few minutes' walk from the Harbourside Hotel and waited for Gunna.

"Working you hard are they?"

Bára's smile was thin. "I'll have them house-trained in a few days, I hope."

"So what are you doing here?"

"Checking security. Back entrances and fire doors, that sort of thing," she said. "And getting a break from madam upstairs."

"How are they getting on?"

"He's all right. He's in bed by eleven and working at his laptop by seven in the morning. She sleeps to midday and is up until three. He's worried, Gunna," Bára said, looking around her. "It's easy enough to tell. There are phone calls that are clearly not friendly ones and I'd love to have a really good look inside his laptop, but there's no chance of that happening. He never leaves it open and I suspect there are a dozen passwords to go through to get to anything."

Gunna looked over Bára's shoulder at the morning activity unfolding. A ship was manoeuvring slowly in the still water of the harbour, assisted by a tug snapping at its heels to shove it into a berth. She shook her head irritably.

"All right, are you?" Bára asked with concern.

"Yeah. I'm OK. Haven't been sleeping well recently. Things have been awkward at home for a while."

"Are you and Steini not getting on?"

"Steini's lovely, as always," Gunna sighed. "He's patient, always in a good mood and he cooks. So there's nothing whatever to complain about. It's my boy that's causing me grief. You're out of the loop if you haven't heard."

Bára looked blank. "In that case I'm out of the loop."

Gunna took a deep breath. "Last year Gísli and his girlfriend —"

"Soffía?"

"That's her. A sweet girl. Soffía got pregnant and the little boy, Ari, was born in April."

"Congratulations!" Bára beamed. "Wow, Gunna a grandmother! That's wonderful, surely?"

"That's the good part. Not long after Soffía got pregnant, Gísli, Laufey and I all went up to Vestureyri for my grandmother's funeral. I stayed there with Laufey for a few days, but Gísli drove south the day after the funeral as he was going back to sea that night. He took a passenger south with him and the passenger got pregnant on the way."

Bára sat in silence. "Shit," she said finally. "That's terrible. When . . .?"

"Did baby number two appear? Kjartan made his appearance about two months after Ari."

"Shit," Bára repeated. "So who's the girl?"

184

"That's what makes it all even better. She's my brother Svanur's stepdaughter, and at the beginning of last year Drífa showed up on my doorstep in floods of tears, and she's still there."

"She's living with you?"

"She was until last summer when we managed to get her a social housing flat in the village, so she and the baby are living around the corner and my Laufey seems to spend as much time there as she does at home."

"Life's never quiet or easy around you, is it?" Bára said with a wan smile. "And there's me moaning about having to shepherd these two snobs all day. Speaking of which," she said, looking at her watch. "I need to be there in a few minutes."

Outside the café Bára turned up the collar of her coat against the sharp wind.

"You want a lift?"

"No, it's all right. The Harbourside is right there and I need to have a walk around the back as well anyway."

"Fair enough. I'll need to come and grill them again later today."

"Gunna," Bára said and hesitated. "Client confidentiality aside — you know how old habits die hard — and between ourselves."

"Yes?"

"Jóhann's as worried as hell, like I said. He tries to hide it, but it shows. She's up to something as well, with all the calls and texts she leaves the room to take, but I haven't figured out what it is yet."

* ★ *

Orri's back ached as he got slowly out of the truck, his high-viz jacket draped over one arm. In the canteen he listlessly changed out of his boots while his cup of coffee cooled on the table next to him.

"All right, are you?" Dóri asked, pushing his glasses up onto his bald head and putting down the crossword. "You look like shit, Orri."

"Slept badly."

"Never mind. Can you do a couple of hours tomorrow? Overtime?"

"Yeah. Should be OK. Eight?"

"Eight would be fine. Go on, go home and get your head down."

Orri nodded. His head was heavy and the few hours of sleep had been no rest at all. On top of that, he found himself concerned at Lísa being so suspicious of him, not that he could blame her, he told himself ruefully. He extracted his phone from his jacket pocket and keyed in a text message to her, ending it with a smiley face that he would never normally have used, hoping it would get him out of cooking that night.

Alex stood in the corridor and smiled as Orri made to go back outside.

"*Hæ*," Orri said.

"Hey. Bruno ask about you," he said quietly.

"Why? Is Bruno worried about my health?"

"No. But maybe you should be, if you don't get Bruno some goods."

"You tell Bruno he can go screw himself," Orri snarled in an angry retort. "I'm not at his beck and call,

186

and you can tell him so. If there's some gear, then I might let him have it, if he's lucky. Or I might not."

He stalked out without waiting for a response from Alex, who was startled by Orri's unexpectedly angry outburst. In the year they had worked together, Alex hadn't even heard Orri raise his voice, let alone snap back in fury, and he wondered what was wrong. Girlfriend trouble probably, he decided as he walked after him.

"Orri, man. What's the problem?" He asked, hoping to sound friendly. "I said, Bruno asks about you, nothing else."

"You know, Alex," Orri said. "Sometimes I wonder if this mysterious Bruno really exists or not."

Eiríkur felt his eyelids droop. He had watched half a day's footage spanning the downtown streets of central Reykjavík from four of the series of cameras with not a sign of anyone in a green fleece dark enough and with distinctive stripes to match the fibres found in the basement of Kópavogsbakki fifty.

The cameras closest to Aunt Bertha were the ones he began with, and while the shop's owner was far from sure what time of day it had been when the man came in, he started each recording a few minutes before Aunt Bertha opened its doors at ten. Two hours later he had fast-forwarded through two hours of footage from the four closest cameras and was starting to wonder if the woman had the right date.

He took a break for half an hour, chatted with the communications centre's staff and went outside for a few minutes' fresh air to clear his head before starting again. He decided to stick with the same four cameras as before and told himself to keep to the area around the shop before going to the cameras further away.

By now the streets were busier, with a thicker mass of pedestrians. Eiríkur paid attention to those walking with purpose rather than the ones who ambled the streets looking in windows here and there. After midday the streets began to fill with people in hiking boots and padded anoraks and he cursed the fact that a cruise ship must have been at the quay and disgorged a few hundred tourists to spend a couple of hours looking at the sights.

The ticker in the corner of the screen said 15.32 when a nondescript figure in a yellow waistcoat walked past, and Eiríkur hardly noticed the dark green fleece with two narrow yellow stripes down the sleeve until the man had passed the camera and was out of sight. Suddenly he was wide awake and rewound the figure's progress, this time with his eyes intently on the screen. He replayed the sequence as the man walked under the camera and away from it, slipping off the waistcoat as he walked and stuffing it into a pocket.

He stopped the replay and called out to one of the others. "Hey, how do I follow this guy?"

"Found a villain, have you?"

One of the communications staff, a headset on one ear with its lead trailing at his side, leaned over the monitors.

"This guy," Eiríkur said, pointing at the round-shouldered figure stopped in mid-stride.

"All right. That's Austurstræti. You know where this guy is going?"

"A shop called Aunt Bertha."

"The shop full of old crap on Ingólfsstræti?"

"I think they like to think of it as an antiques shop, rather than a place full of old junk. But yeah, that's the one."

"In that case, we should be able to follow him over the street into Bankastræti."

His fingers flickered over the keyboard and a click of the mouse later they saw the dark green fleece appear, walking towards them, and this time Eiríkur could see the man's face.

"Stop it there for a second, can you?"

The communications officer clicked. The picture froze and he zoomed in. Eiríkur found himself looking at eyes that glanced sideways out of the picture, shoulders hunched and a deeply ordinary face. Short brown hair and a few days' worth of stubble surrounded a squat nose. There was a determined look on the face, its lips pressed together as if the man was concentrating and defensive, keeping the rest of the world at bay.

"Can I save that as a still image?" Eiríkur asked.

The mouse clicked a couple of times. "Done. You want to see where he's going?"

As the image unfroze, the man continued, looking to left and right, until he disappeared around a corner. The communications officer looked expectantly at Eiríkur. "That's Ingólfsstræti, and the shop he's going to is a hundred metres away."

"Hell, I had hoped for a better view of him."

"Let's wait, shall we?" He said, fast-forwarding through the recording. "He'll be coming back the same way, I expect."

The ticker had clicked to 15.56 when Eiríkur saw his target approaching, walking jauntily this time, stepping past the camera without noticing it. The communications officer switched the camera viewpoint to Lækjargata and then Austurstræti as they watched him retrace his steps, walking with quick steps that marked him out among the throngs of slow-moving tourists.

"Didn't take long, did he?"

"He must have a car parked somewhere," Eiríkur said.

"Or else he lives in the west end of town. I'll bet he's parked next to Bæjarins Bezta."

"Then he'd have cut through to Hafnarstræti. Unless he was going somewhere else first? Let's look at Hafnarstræti and Tryggvagata, shall we?"

The camera switched and they scrolled through enough footage without any sign of him.

"We lost him," Eiríkur said despondently. "Shit."

"But you got a picture of him."

"I know. I was hoping for a car. A number would have taken me straight to him."

The communications officer yawned and stood up to go back to his desk. "What's this character done, anyway?"

"I'm not sure. He's been the victim of a violent assault and for some reason hasn't reported it," Eiríkur

190

said. "And I have a feeling that he might well be the phantom housebreaker Sævaldur's been looking for."

The communications officer hid a smirk. "See if you can catch the bastard before Sævaldur does. He'll sulk until Christmas if you do."

"You called, young man?" Gunna greeted Björgvin as he took off his glasses to rub his eyes.

"Yes. Thanks for dropping by."

"No problem, I was about to disappear off home, so you just caught me."

"And you just caught me as well," Björgvin said with a bleak smile. "I'm finished in half an hour and won't be back until Thursday."

"Excellent, a long weekend."

"We're moving house starting tomorrow, so I expect we'll need every minute of it. But that's nothing to do with why I asked you to come over."

"You weren't going to ask me to help you shift furniture?"

"Not unless you're offering? But we have plenty of spare hands," he said, lifting a folder from the top of a filing cabinet behind him. "This is what I wanted you to have a look at."

Gunna pulled up a chair, sat down and watched the rows of figures on the document Björgvin ran his finger over blur into one.

"I'm not great with numbers, you know."

"That's all right. You don't need to see the amounts." He reached for a notebook and started drawing circles. "I just wanted to give you an outline of it all."

"Elvar Pálsson and Vilhelm Thorleifsson had both been in the shipbroking business at one point, and as far as I can make out, they both still have interests in shipping. In 2007 they were able to get a loan of around ten million dollars from a pension fund."

"Ten million? Good grief."

"It gets better. With a partner, they were able to buy a factory ship that operated in the Pacific, and it made a profit. Not a huge profit, but it did well enough. In 2010 it shifted to West Africa and worked there, where it did very well in 2010 and 2011. We estimate it earned between twenty and twenty-five million dollars in those two years."

Björgvin's grey eyes lifted and looked into Gunna's.

"A profitable venture, surely?" she asked. "Now you're going to tell me the pension fund never saw a penny of its investment back?"

"You're way ahead of me, but this is where it gets interesting and also difficult, as none of this happens in Iceland. The ship, *Bright Spring II*, was registered in Belize, owned by a company in Cyprus and managed by a company in the Isle of Man, and both of those companies were subsidiaries of a company in Luxembourg."

"Were?"

"That's the operative word. The whole operation went bust early last year. It seems the ship's main engine failed and it was sold off to a Norwegian company based in Morocco to be either scrapped or repaired, but that's neither here nor there. All of that complex ownership and management structure is purely there to avoid paying tax anywhere, and what is interesting is that all of those companies are brass plates, with no staff or offices, and it's not easy to track down who the directors are, or were. But what is quite clear is that *Bright Spring II* was in fact managed by Elvar Pálsson from his office in Reykjavík."

"Before he moved abroad."

"Exactly. He moved to London not long after the ship was sold and the companies were wound up."

"And the pension funds?"

"Out in the cold," Björgvin said, his bleak smile returning. "There's no sign of the original ten million dollars, or the proceeds of the ship, or the approximately twenty-five-million dollars it earned in the roughly two years it operated off West Africa."

"It may be a stupid question, but where did all that money go?" Gunna asked, her mind reeling.

Björgvin shrugged. "Your guess is as good as mine. We have no power to investigate these foreign companies unless their authorities are prepared to co-operate."

"And they're not, I take it?"

"Not a hope. The whole point of using companies in these jurisdictions is to keep out inquisitive types like me," he said and reached for another folder. "But this one is closer to home."

Björgvin smoothed out a sheet of notes and again reached for his pad.

"More circles?"

"I'm afraid so. But not so many this time. Sólfell Investment was set up in 2005 and didn't do anything at all for two years. The directors were Sunna María Voss, Jóhann Hjálmarsson, Vilhelm Thorleifsson, our other errant shipowner, Elvar Pálsson, and a gentleman called Boris Vadluga."

"That's a new name. Who's he?"

"A Latvian businessman who likes to invest his money in profitable schemes."

"Legally profitable, or otherwise?"

Björgvin smiled briefly. "I don't think he's worried either way, so long as there's a profit involved in such a way that he's not going to find himself in court, and guess who the partner in *Bright Spring II* was? Anyway, in 2007 Sólfell Property invests a very substantial chunk of cash in land in Kópavogur, right by the water."

"That's the dentist and his wife and her brother. So three of them."

"They pour cash into the construction of ten of these very smart houses. No expense spared. Remember this was post-crash and construction contractors were scratching for any work that would keep them ticking over. So, all but four were sold, and those are still owned by Sólfell Property."

"So where's the scam? There has to be one, surely?"

"The original vehicle, Sólfell Investment, went bankrupt, leaving zero assets. Sólfell Property spends a stack of cash on land and development. So where did all that money come from? Sólfell Property didn't have that kind of finance at its disposal, so my guess is that this is cash from overseas." Björgvin sat back and put his hands in his pockets. "The question is, where did all

194

that money come from to start with? It's still very unclear, except that it appears to have originated from an account in Luxembourg. My guess is that this is at least partly the *Bright Spring II* profits."

"Laundering?"

"We didn't start looking at these people until you mentioned them the other day." Björgvin stretched and crossed his ankles under the table. His lanky frame seemed to go on endlessly and Gunna wondered if his feet stuck out past the desk. "But that's my best guess. Someone wanted to clean some dirty money through a profitable little property business in Iceland. Buy some land, build some expensive properties, sell them. That way the money is the result of property speculation, and not wherever it came from to start with."

"Drugs?"

"No doubt," he said with a lopsided smile. "It could be all kinds of stuff. Drugs, vice, protection rackets, gambling, loan-sharking. These guys are spoilt for choice and all they need is a way to wash the smell of shit off their money."

"No? Definitely not? All right, thanks," Eiríkur said, putting the phone down and pushing it away.

"No luck?" Gunna asked, looking long and hard at the prints of the man in the green fleece that Eiríkur had produced, including close-ups of his face and of the logo on his jacket.

"I've searched for the face and the logo and I can't find either anywhere. You'd have thought that logo and the stripes would be something special, but I can't find anything. If there were some letters that would be a help. I've called every shop in Reykjavík that sells this kind of thing and all the manufacturers I can get hold of, and nobody's familiar with it."

"It may have come from abroad?"

"Then we're no nearer than we were."

"You have a face."

"Put out a media appeal?" Eiríkur suggested.

Gunna dropped the prints back on the desk. "The trouble is, your suspect will then see it as well and he'll lose that fleece like a shot."

"Ach, somebody will know him. Even if it's just his mother."

"Yeah, and his mother's going to shop him to the police."

"She might if she's a particularly law-abiding mother."

Gunna sat with her chin in her hands, looking at the face of the man in the green fleece. Under the crop of brown hair, he looked ordinary, the sort of face nobody would notice. Taken when he had been walking towards Aunt Bertha, the face had a strained look about. The split-second of footage chosen had caught him chewing his lip, as if he'd been stressed or hadn't slept properly. He looked tired, Gunna thought, and wondered what kind of guilty conscience he might have.

"No," she decided. "I don't want it released, not yet. Circulate his picture internally first. It might take a day or two but we'll see if anyone comes up with anything. If nobody knows anything we'll think again, but on

Monday you'd best tell Sævaldur that you have a lead on his phantom housebreaker."

Eiríkur retreated behind his computer and Gunna could hear him tapping at the keyboard. He hit send with a flourish and sat back.

"Done," he said. "Time for a coffee, I think. Want one?"

"Not for me, thanks. I have to go up and see if I can find the Laxdal before he disappears home."

She heard Eiríkur pottering in the coffee room, the clink of mugs being washed and Gunna reflected that Eiríkur's wife must have done a good job of training him. She stood up and pulled on her jacket as Eiríkur's phone rang.

"Eiríkur!" She called and cursed when there was no reply. "Eiríkur Thór Jónsson's phone," she said as she lifted the handset.

"Is Eiríkur there?"

"He's about somewhere. Who's this?"

"Lárus Erlendsson from station at Selfoss. It's about the pictures Eiríkur emailed to everyone."

"Ah, in that case, you can tell me. Eiríkur's one of my team."

"Oh, right? And who are you, my love?"

"I'm Gunnhildur Gísladóttir, and I'm not your love," Gunna glowered. "You recognize the man in the picture?"

Lárus Erlendsson laughed. "No, not a clue who he is."

"In that case, what can I do for you? I don't suppose you wanted to chat about the weather?"

"No, don't be stupid. It's that logo he sent as well. The one on the guy's fleece."

"You recognize it?"

"Of course I do. I'm a member myself; I'm on the committee. It's the Kjölur Equestrian Club."

"That's a great help, thanks. I'll pass on the message," Gunna said, put the phone down and yelled, "Eiríkur! A trip to the country?"

Gunna met Bára outside the hotel, where she parked the unmarked Golf in the manager's parking space.

"What's happened? All right?"

"No. Jóhann's disappeared."

"Shit."

"And I'm supposed to be looking after them."

Gunna thought quickly. "Disappeared as in wandered off or disappeared as in snatched?"

"No idea. He said he was going down to the lobby for a newspaper and hasn't come back."

"How long ago?"

"An hour," Bára said.

"And her ladyship?"

"Sitting upstairs calling all his mobile numbers one after the other. It's taken the best part of half an hour to get her to agree to call you."

Gunna thought quickly and looked around the hotel's lobby. "OK, get me Jóhann's phone numbers, would you? I'll see if we can put a trace on them. Where's the duty manager in this place?"

A minute later Gunna was in a room behind the reception desk watching jerky black-and-white footage of guests coming and going, amazed at the sheer number of people passing through the doors. Finally Jóhann appeared. He emerged from the lift with a group of people, walked across the lobby, spoke briefly to someone standing by the restaurant door and picked up a newspaper from a pile. Gunna watched him leaf through *Morgunbladid* for a few moments before looking around him and walking quickly out of the main doors.

Gunna switched to the camera outside and saw him open the door of a taxi and get in, taking a seat in the back and shutting the door with the car already moving. Gunna wrote down the number, thanked the mystified girl at reception and headed for the lift.

Sunna María sat in her suite, her face thunderous.

"Well? Do you know where he went?"

"It looks like he just went out," Gunna said. "Had he had any calls or messages before he went downstairs?"

"Probably. His computer and his phone ping out messages all day long." She glared at Bára. "You're supposed to be looking after security, aren't you?"

"That's right. But I'm not here to stop either of you going somewhere of your own free will."

Gunna shook her head. "There's nothing for me to do here. If Jóhann wasn't abducted, then there's nothing for me to investigate," she said, her hand on the door handle. Sunna María stood with her back to them, staring out over the slipways below them.

"He could be in danger, couldn't he?" she asked, turning to face them.

"Could be," Gunna admitted. "There's nothing suspicious on the CCTV and it looks like he just got in a taxi and drove away. If Jóhann went somewhere, he clearly went of his own free will. Has he done this before?"

"Disappeared without a word? No. But he hasn't been well recently," Sunna María said, turning round with a look of concern etched onto her face. "He forgets things and he's been depressed. I can't help being worried about him."

Alex felt good about himself and the world around him. It was dark and cold and he'd been working all day, but a hot shower had eased the aches and pains. He poured a slug of vodka into a glass and looked forward to the evening, especially the night, which promised to be a busy one.

Maris was sitting with his feet on the table and the television in front of him rattled as the crowd at Old Trafford roared their appreciation. His feet were surrounded by cans and Maris leaned forward, lifting and shaking them one by one to find a full can. Both Maris and the can sighed as he popped its ring pull and took a long swallow.

The apartment was nothing special. The bedroom belonged to Alex as he had been there longer and Maris, as the newcomer, slept on the lumpy couch. While the place wasn't exactly dirty, it was far from clean, with bags of cans and garbage by the door, which nobody bothered to take out until they started to smell. When he'd moved in all those months ago, Alex had found bags of garbage stacked on the balcony and the living-room windows tightly closed to keep out the smell.

"Score?" Alex asked, drying his hair vigorously with a towel and leaving it standing up in all directions.

"Two–one to our boys," Maris said, excitement in his voice, one foot pumping up and down in agitation as an evening of the score was narrowly avoided.

"And only five minutes to full time?"

"Where are you off to?" Maris asked. "Emilija again?"

"Yep," Alex said, spraying his armpits, wrinkling his nose and waving a hand to disperse the astringent cloud.

"Again? You'll be married before you know it." Maris laughed.

"Not me," Alex said, slapping his bare chest with one hand and lifting his glass. "You don't marry women like Emilija. Chicks with kids are all right for keeping you warm, but when it comes to the long-term stuff, a man wants a model with not so many miles on the clock."

"Solid bodywork? Better upholstery?"

"Precisely. No dents. Maybe one careful owner." Alex grinned and looked up with his glass in front of his face as there was a sharp rap on the door. "You expecting someone?"

Maris shrugged. "Don't know. It might be the boys. They were talking about going into town," he said, his attention on the screen as the crowd roared again.

Alex opened the door and immediately tried to push it shut. "Maris!" he yelled, as the door ground gradually open in spite of his best efforts to stop it, until it swung back and he was sent flying back into the room with it. He jumped right over the couch and Maris, who looked up bemused as a big man loped into the room and a smaller man with a narrow, lumpy face sauntered after him.

Alex found himself on the balcony, shoeless, shirtless and cold, looking at a long drop into the darkness below as a patter of chilled rain whispered on the concrete.

"Evening, boys," the narrow-faced man said as his burly companion turned the key, locking Alex out on the balcony to shiver and look in through the window, wondering what they were saying. "Your pal's not very friendly tonight, is he?"

Maris looked up in confusion. "What's up? Who are you guys?"

The big man picked Maris up by the front of his shirt, which ripped as he was hauled forward and deposited face down over the table that his feet had been resting on a moment earlier.

"You've not been doing as you've been told, have you, Alex?" the little man asked as the big man planted a foot on his shoulder with all his weight behind it and Maris thrashed in panic. "Hush, Alex," he said softly. "Don't make a noise. We don't want to disturb your neighbours, do we?"

"I'm not Alex," Maris pleaded. "That's Alex out there on the balcony. I'm Maris. Maris Leinesars. Alex is out there," he gabbled, trying to point towards the balcony. "I haven't done anything, honest."

The big man grunted and spat on the carpet. "Does it matter?"

"Not really," the little man sniffed, taking a hammer from his pocket.

With his face pressed hard to the top of the table, Maris could see nothing of what was going on behind him, while Alex watched in growing horror as everything was played out in eerie silence. It wasn't a big hammer, a delicate tool of the kind used for fine joinery work and tiny nails, and Alex wanted to be sick as he saw the big man lean down and spread Maris's hand out over the table top

Maris squirmed and jerked his hand away. The hammer hit the table, leaving a half moon of a dent in the surface.

"Keep him still, will you?"

This time the hand was splayed on the table, with the big man's fist planted over the wrist to keep it firmly placed.

In spite of the double glazing, Alex could hear the first half of the screech of pain before the big man grabbed Maris's face and stopped any more noise. He could see him struggle frantically in the big man's grip. The little man broke all four fingers of his left hand with the delicate hammer, using deft, sharp taps that shattered bones and joints. Then he looked up and stared into Alex's eyes for a long moment, winked and nodded to the big man, who slowly released Maris from his grip.

The big man lifted Maris up again and deposited him on the couch, where he sobbed in shock, cradling one ruined hand in the other as his team scored again moments before the whistle and the crowd howled its joy. The two men slipped away into the night and Alex frantically rattled the handle of the balcony door.

Orri had already decided he didn't like it, but his instructions were clear. He had dressed himself in black, as usual, his balaclava rolled into a hat that nestled just above his eyebrows and his hands thrust deep into the pockets of his black jacket. It was a cold night and even with two extra layers he found himself shivering as he walked in a wide circle.

He didn't like industrial estates. Far too many businesses were taking security seriously these days, and while alarms were more or less an occupational hazard, it was the unobtrusive cameras that worried him; just like the box of tricks in his backpack.

The building was dark, and the faint glow of street lamps across the road did little to illuminate the dark front. As he had already been past a few times during the day, Orri knew that the building's sheet steel cladding was painted matt black from ground to eaves. A few years ago it had been the offices and workshops of a company manufacturing machinery for bakeries and pizza shops. The building had then been sold to a charitable body that everyone knew was actually a motorcycle club whose members referred to themselves as the Undertakers, living in uncomfortable rivalry with at least two other similar charitable organizations in the city.

Orri knew it wasn't a sensible place to be breaking into. If he were to be found, the Undertakers were more likely to live up to their name than call the police, and he reasoned that a job like this should mean danger money.

The back door leading to the old workshop, now converted lovingly into a spick-and-span engineering space, complete with a lathe against one wall, had been left conveniently unlocked. There were no blinking lights anywhere to indicate an intruder alarm and Orri assumed that the Undertakers were simply confident that nobody would dare break into their clubhouse.

He found the office at the top of the creaking stairs. His torch picked out details as its narrow beam swept around the room. A painted emblem filled one wall with the Undertakers' black and silver crest, and a large black desk with a computer on it sat in the middle of the room surrounded by chairs. The ashtrays, mugs and glasses showed the place was used. A red light on the far side of the room gave him a moment's disquiet, until the torch's beam picked out a coffee maker that had been left switched on. He was on the point of switching it off, but thought better of it.

Orri was relieved to see that plastic trunking studded with power, phone and ethernet sockets ran around the wall at waist height, a relic of the room's former role as the sales manager's office. Kneeling, he prised open the cover and set to work. He had to admit to himself that it was a clever piece of equipment. The new double power socket looked the same as the old one once he'd installed it, but behind the white plastic of the trunking there lurked a listening device which he guessed was voice activated, along with a slot for an SD card and a small black box clipped to the back of the socket. Orri hoped this was a device that would allow the sound files to be wirelessly transferred, as he had no desire to come back and retrieve the SD card.

He stood back, put the socket he had replaced into his bag and admired his handiwork. There was no outward sign that the socket had been tampered with and there were no marks on the floor. The plastic bags he had pulled on over his shoes had left no prints. Unfortunately the Undertakers weren't big on housekeeping up here, unlike in the spotless workshop downstairs, and he could see that the dust had been disturbed but hoped that nobody would notice.

As a parting gift, he went to the computer on the desk and took out a flash stick that was in the slot, replacing it with one from his pocket. As instructed, another anonymous flash stick was dropped into a jar of oddments on the desk.

Orri checked his tools. Nothing had been left behind. He was at the bottom of the stairs when the deep-throated rumble of motorcycles outside made him freeze. The sound dropped to an idle and he could hear that they were parked on the forecourt at the front of the building as he wondered how many there were. Two? More? At least two, he decided, and stole across the workshop, slipping out of the back door and shutting it behind him just as the big double doors at the front swung open and lights flickered on.

He broke out into a cold sweat as he jogged through the deserted industrial estate, stopping only to take the bags from his feet and roll off the surgical gloves, dropping them into a waste container outside another dark building. Forced by the arrival of at least a few of the Undertakers to take a roundabout route, it was a long walk back to the car, during which he reflected that he'd had a very lucky escape. Gradually his nerves turned to euphoria as the familiar buzz stole through him. He walked faster, rolling his balaclava back and fighting back an urge to laugh out loud and punch the air.

CHAPTER
NINE

The hammering on the door gradually worked its way into her consciousness and Emilija fumbled for the clock. The sight of a luminous 0420 was not a welcome one and she moved carefully to avoid waking the toddler asleep next to her. She padded to the door, a dressing gown thrown on hurriedly and tied around her as she pushed strands of hair away from her face.

He clicked on the outside light and could see a shadow on the other side of the door.

"Who is it?"

"It's me, Alex. Let me in, will you, Emilija?"

"What do you want? It's four in the morning. I have to go to work in a few hours."

"I just wanted to see you."

There was a plaintive quality to his voice that she hadn't heard before as she debated with herself whether or not to let him in.

"What's the matter, Alex? Are you drunk, or something?"

"I'm not drunk, I swear."

"That's what you said last time."

"Please, Emilija. I swear, I just wanted to see you."

With a sinking feeling that she was doing the wrong thing, Emilija clicked the lock and Alex practically fell through the door, shutting it quickly behind him with a sigh of relief that he could not hide.

"Thank God," he breathed, and threw his arms around her.

"Alex, what do you want?" Emilija demanded. "It's the middle of the night."

"I know. I missed you, darling," he wheedled, lifting a hand to her cheek to stroke it.

"Get off," she said, slapping his hand away. "What's happened? Have you been thrown out of your place?"

"No, of course not."

Emilija turned and made for the little flat's living room with its bed against one wall. She perched on the edge of the bed, and when Alex made to sit next to her, she pushed him away.

"No, sit there," she ordered, pointing to the only armchair. "And don't make a noise. Anton's asleep."

"Ah, he's such a sweet child."

"Yeah. That's not what you said when he cried in the night."

"I'm sorry. I was drunk that time and it won't happen again."

Alex's eyes flickered around the room, stopping repeatedly on the window, as if he were expecting to be followed.

"What the hell have you done this time?"

"Nothing." Alex protested. "Nothing at all. I couldn't sleep and I was thinking of you all the time."

"So you got up at four in the morning to make sure I wasn't asleep as well? Or to make sure I didn't have anyone else here? Is that it?"

"Don't be silly, Emilija. I trust you."

"Alex, we're not a couple. I slept with you a few times and you walked off as if it meant nothing to you."

"But it did," Alex said, standing up and coming across to her. "Of course it did. I'm sorry, I've been so busy."

"And you think I haven't?"

He shifted to sit next to her and clasped her hands in his. "Emilija, I'm so sorry. I shouldn't have been so thoughtless."

"You're a heartless bastard, Alex."

"Emilija," he breathed, stroking a wisp of loose hair away from her face and moving closer for a kiss as he wrapped his arms around her. Emilija felt herself sink into his muscular arms and returned his kiss, surprising herself at her own eagerness. Alex's hand plucked at the dressing gown and pulled it from one shoulder while the other slipped inside. She felt herself being gently pushed back onto the bed as Alex ran one hand through the thick hair at the back of her head.

"I've missed you so much," he crooned as he pulled the dressing gown wide open and a hand was suddenly under her T-shirt and cupping a breast.

"No, Alex. Not now, not again," Emilija whispered unconvincingly as she made to sit up and shake him off.

"Come on, sweetheart. You don't know how much I want you."

210

"No, stop. Alex. Stop," Emilija said firmly, and pulled herself upright as a moan from the other side of the bed called her to where Anton was sitting up and rubbing his eyes.

"Mummy. Who's the man?"

He crawled across the bed and into her arms as Alex retreated. Emilija pulled the dressing gown closed around herself and Anton.

"It's all right, my darling. It's only Alex. You remember Uncle Alex, don't you?"

Anton nodded sleepily and huddled closer. As Emilija rocked back and forth, his eyelids drooped and he gradually fell asleep in her arms, but not before Alex was also stretched out and snoring.

Eiríkur's quick response took Lárus Erlendsson by surprise, arriving at the Selfoss police station with his sheaf of screengrabs from the city surveillance cameras before he had even had his first mug of coffee.

"They're good pictures, aren't they?" He observed as he leafed through them at Eiríkur's side in the tired Polo from the police car pool.

"You could make out someone's Visa card number if you wanted to," Eiríkur said. "Where is this place?"

"Straight on past the farm at Mýri and it's the next left after that."

Eiríkur understood that he was expected to know the farm at Mýri, but said nothing and waited for a sign. When it finally appeared from the flat landscape, he dutifully signalled and turned, bumping the car down a dirt road.

"This is it?"

"Over there."

Lárus Erlendsson pointed to a row of low buildings that looked dilapidated from a distance, but as they approached turned out to be immaculate stables painted the same shade as the dun-coloured hills that rose gently behind. Eiríkur stopped the car and the silence after the rumble of the gravel road from Selfoss flooded in as he opened the door. The quiet and the view took him by surprise, even after the drive over the Hellisheidi heath that morning. The only sounds to be heard once the car's engine had been shut down were muffled laughter and conversation from the stables and birdsong all around, while a mountain of towering white cloud formed a backdrop to the distant mountains where sunlight made the white tips glitter.

Eiríkur followed Lárus into the stable and wrinkled his nose at the overwhelming smell of horses and hay that met him and made Lárus breathe deep.

"Ah, that's better," he said.

"You keep horses as well?"

"We have six horses here, me and my wife between us."

"Are there many members?" Eiríkur asked, inspecting a noticeboard pinned with announcements and cleaning rotas.

"About sixty, altogether."

"Sixty? I'm amazed."

"Why's that?" Lárus grunted in a tone that indicated offence had been taken.

"I didn't expect this place to be so big. I thought there might be a dozen people."

Lárus looked dismissive as he pushed open a door and grunted a greeting to the group of people gathered around a long table.

"My colleague Eiríkur Thór Jónsson from Reykjavík," he announced, the word "Reykjavík" dropped as if it had a foul smell to it. "He's brought some photos as part of an investigation, so if you'd like to have a look at them . . . Eiríkur?"

"Er . . . hello," he said to the group of middle-aged people staring at him as he placed the pictures in the table, dealing them like cards. The pictures began to circulate and the group whispered and muttered. "This is a person we are looking for. We don't know who he is, but as you can see, he's wearing a fleece that should look familiar to you," he said, looking around the room and noticing several identical fleeces.

"What's this fellow done?" A corpulent man at the end of the table asked.

"I can't tell you at the moment," Eiríkur answered. "It's a sensitive matter."

"Not a banker is he?"

"No, not as far as we know."

"Anything exciting?" A young woman asked, smiling. "I wonder how come he's wearing one of our fleeces?"

"I take it he's not a member, then?"

Heads shook around the table.

"He's not anyone we've seen here," the corpulent man said. "And I should know."

"Gulli's the chairman," Lárus explained. "He knows all the members."

"How many of these fleeces did you buy?"

"A hundred, I think it was. We still have forty or fifty of them left. Every member had one at the time and we give one to every new member."

"In that case, I'd like to borrow one."

"What for?"

"I'd like to get some tests carried out to check against a crime scene."

"Ólöf, would you?" Gulli said without looking up, his eyes still on the picture in his hands. "This person's definitely not a member, so I'd certainly have a few questions to ask him about why he's wearing one of our fleeces. Our logo is on it," he pointed out needlessly as the young woman opened a cupboard and handed Eiríkur a new fleece, folded into its bag with the logo showing through the transparent wrapper.

"Where did you order these from?"

"A company called PeysuPrent. The guy who ran it used to be a member here so we got them at cost price, but it closed down a while ago."

"He's still a member?"

"No. Sold his horses and packed it in."

"How long ago did you order the fleeces?"

Gulli inserted a little finger into one ear and twisted it around thoughtfully. "Five, six years ago. Something like that," he decided finally.

Eiríkur tucked the fleece in its bag under one arm. "But you're all sure that this man isn't anyone you recognize?" He asked the room at large and heads shook in response. "All right, in that case, thanks for your time. I'll leave some photographs with Lárus, just in case anyone needs to take another look, and I can be reached at the police station on Hverfisgata," he added, handing out cards. "This is turning out to be more serious than a handful of burglaries, so if anything comes to mind, I'd certainly appreciate a call."

"Sorry nobody could help you," Lárus said as they walked back to the Polo. If you don't mind, I'm just going to have a quick look at my mare," he said and walked towards a stable without waiting for a reply.

"Eiríkur?"

He turned to see the young woman who had handed him the fleece walking towards him.

"Yes?"

"Listen. I didn't want to say anything in there in front of the rest of them. But . . ."

"You know who this guy is?"

"Actually, no. I don't know his name. But I think he is, or was, the boyfriend of a girl who used to be a member here. She moved to Reykjavík a couple of years ago. I don't see her very often these days, but we've kept in touch. I met her in town about a month ago and I'm sure this is the guy who was with her. But I could be wrong," she said, looking around guiltily, as if she were betraying a secret.

"And where can I find her?"

"I'm not sure. She works at a factory outside Hafnarfjördur and I'm not sure where she lives now."

"You have a phone number?"

"Not any more," Ólöf said. "She changed her number a while ago and I don't have the new one."

"So how do you keep in touch?"

"Just through Facebook normally. We meet up every few months when I have a reason to go to Reykjavík, which isn't all that often."

"Understood. What's her name?"

"Elísabet Sólborg Höskuldsdóttir. Everyone calls her Lísa."

Gunna peered at the man's smashed hand as the doctor showed her the X-ray.

"Deliberate?"

"No doubt," the doctor said. He had black rings under his eyes and Gunna realized he had to be much younger than he looked.

"That's why you called us?"

He shrugged. "Standard practice. There's no doubt in my mind that this wasn't the result of some accident. You can see how the damage is confined to particular areas. I've been here for a while and never seen anything that looks remotely like that from an industrial injury."

"How's the patient?"

"Shocked and sedated."

"Other injuries?"

He shook his head. "Not that we're aware of. But it's not as if there's a chance of a full examination."

"This couldn't have happened with something falling on his hand?"

216

"I don't know, I'm not an expert. But the breaks aren't in line, so this looks like four separate fractures, not four fingers that have been fractured all at once."

"How did he arrive? Ambulance?"

"No, he turned up in a taxi. He wouldn't be able to drive himself with his hand in that condition."

"I'd best go and have a quiet word. He's still sedated?"

"He's painkillered up to the eyeballs," the doctor said cheerfully. "Good luck."

Maris lay back in bed with his left hand rested on his chest, swathed in a bandage. Gunna sat next to him and saw that behind the drawn face he was relaxed, courtesy of the painkillers. She wondered how soon the pain would set in again and if he would ever recover the full use of his hand.

"Good morning," she said. "My name's Gunnhildur Gísladóttir and I'm a detective with the city police force. You speak Icelandic, or is English easier for you?"

Maris winced. "English is better."

"The medical staff have a duty to report to the police anything that appears not to be an accident, which is why I'm here."

"Accident."

"Go on. Tell me how this accident happened," Gunna said, relieved to hear that her slow English was better than his.

"I was moving . . ." He winced again and pointed with his good hand at the other side of the room. "Like that."

"A cupboard?"

"Yes, cupboard for clothes."

"And what happened that broke all of the fingers in your hand so neatly?"

"I drop it."

"On your hand?" Gunna's tone left Maris in no doubt that she disbelieved him.

"Yes. It fall. From table."

"You put the cupboard on a table, and it fell off, onto your hand?"

"I was not looking. It fell." He put out his good hand again, flat, as if this would demonstrate how the accident had occurred.

"I think you're lying to me, Maris. That is your real name, isn't it?" Gunna said. "In fact, I know you're lying. I've seen the X-rays of your hand and there are separate breaks on each finger that don't line up. So who did this to you?"

"Accident."

"Who attacked you, and why?"

"Accident." His face set firmly. "It was accident."

"Who did this?"

"Accident," Maris repeated doggedly.

Gunna shook her head. "So whoever did this is going to walk around knowing that you're in here and your hand will never be any use again. You realize that?"

"What you say?"

Gunna sighed. She didn't need to ask any more questions to know that this was going to be a struggle.

218

★ ★ ★

He blinked at the square of bright light on the wall and wondered where he was. His head felt heavy. It took a little while for him to work out that the intermittent buzzing he could hear was in his head. Otherwise, there was silence, but not the silence of insulated walls and windows that he was used to. This was an absence of sound, not sound carefully excluded. After a while, he lifted his head from whatever it had been resting on and felt it with one heavy hand, wondering if someone had hit him.

Eventually he forced himself to sit up and found that he ached; not just his head, but every part of him seemed to hurt. Hauling himself to his feet, he supported himself against a windowsill, a graveyard of last summer's flies, and looked out through the cracked panes. The square of light on the opposite wall had been cast through this window, and he was instantly dazzled by the brightness that stabbed into his head. His glasses had gone and only things that were far away were in focus. The rising distant hills were clear, sparkling in the morning sun and white with a delicate scattering of snow, as a cake is dusted with powdered sugar.

He wondered where he might be. He remembered leaving the hotel and getting into a taxi that appeared by magic, as if called, and leaving it to get into the lift at . . . Where was it? Who had called him? It wasn't easy to remember and he found himself trying to claw back memories of what he told himself had happened only a day or so ago, but which felt like ancient history.

Sounds gradually started to impinge on his consciousness. There was an occasional distant drip of water somewhere behind him. A bird sang outside beyond the cracked window. There was the slightest rustle of wind in the dry grass outside and he felt a sudden overwhelming hunger.

He was in a cubicle, a grey box that had once been a room, and the door hung at an awkward angle on one of its hinges. He shuffled to it and looked past into a corridor that he gingerly went along, hands on the walls to support himself.

At the end was another room, the glassless windows open to the elements and their long-broken panes shadows of shards in the deep layer of dust on the floor. What had once been a kitchen was open to the elements and Jóhann shivered. Spring was on the way but summer was still a long way off as he again wondered where he could be, gazing around him as he gathered his wits.

There was a gaping hole in the wall for what had once been the flue for a stove of some kind. Any cupboards or furnishing had long been stripped out, but a rickety table against one wall and a chair next to it looked clean, as if recently wiped down, and to his surprise, he saw his belongings stacked neatly on it. The jacket he had been wearing had been folded. He shook it out and gratefully put it on. In the pockets were his wallet, the cash and cards still there inside, and his phone, its battery dead. He tried to switch it on several times without success before pocketing it and finding his glasses there. The left lens had cracked with a starburst of fine lines at one corner, but he almost wept with relief as the world jumped back into focus and he was able to take in his dismal surroundings.

Work was quiet. The old boys did most of what needed to be done and Orri drank coffee as he read a weekend's worth of newspapers in the canteen, trying not to think about the package under the seat of his car that someone had delivered during the night. The instructions were clear and the task seemed simple enough, and he wondered who the victim might be, but the thoughts were pushed from his mind as Dóri came in, poured himself a mug of coffee and fetched his sandwiches from the canteen fridge.

He sat opposite Orri and started to munch a sandwich heavy with the aroma of home-made meat paste. "Anything interesting?" He asked, gesturing at the open weekend newspaper with the uneaten half.

"Nope. Same old shit. Country going to the dogs because of the government, according to the opposition. Country gone to the dogs because of what the opposition did when they were in power, according to the government."

"You're getting cynical in your old age, Orri." Dóri smiled. "It's nothing to do with the government, as anyone who takes an interest in these things will tell you." His voice was soft and persuasive. People stopped talking and listened when Dóri said anything, and Orri wondered how he did it, reckoning that it was something to do with Dóri having been a teacher for many years. Retirement had not been as comfortable as

221

it should have been and Dóri had watched his savings become virtually worthless in the wake of the financial crash. Orri wondered why Dóri wasn't bitter, or maybe he was, though he hid it well?

"Why d'you say that?"

"It's as clear as day if you look at it from the right perspective. Our elected representatives have next to no real power," he said with a smile that dripped sadness. "Business has this country sewn up tight in every way. People who own fish quotas or have access to power, or companies with monopolies on imports, that's where the real power lies."

"Come on, Dóri. It's not as bad as all that, surely?"

Dóri let his glasses drop from his forehead to the end of his nose and spun around the newspaper Orri had been browsing through. He tapped the cover.

"Look at this. There's been an argument about joining the European Union going on for years. It's not a popular point of view, but it would be overwhelmingly better for you and me if we were part of Europe. Right now wages are two-thirds of what they are in say, Denmark. OK? And food prices here are roughly double. Food and power prices would stabilize, and index-linking would have to go, so the cost of living would fall, not right away maybe, but over a few years ordinary people like you and me would see ourselves better off."

"Yeah, but what about the fishing grounds? They'd be wide open to foreigners, wouldn't they?"

"You might think so, but there would still be quotas and they'd be held by the people who hold them now.

222

So those fishing grounds wouldn't be open to foreigners unless the quota holders were to sell up to someone in Spain or Norway."

Orri looked confused. "You're sure about that?"

"Absolutely. Look, Orri, you're no fool but you walk around with your eyes closed. The government wants to do something that business doesn't like, and what happens? Business whips up a storm of protest."

"You mean in the papers?"

"The newspapers, TV, radio, everywhere. Who do you think owns the newspapers?" He patted the folded newspaper on the table in front of him. "Who publishes this? Do you know?"

Orri looked at the paper with its bright orange logo. "No," he admitted.

Dóri opened it and flipped through the pages. "The gentleman who owns this also owns the supermarket that sells all this stuff," he said, pointing at a double-page spread of meat and vegetables on offer that coming weekend. "And he owns this as well," he added, opening it at a spread of televisions and sound systems. "Now, do you really think this lovely man, undoubtedly a philanthropist who loves his mother dearly, has any interest in welcoming the competition that being part of the EU would bring? Of course not. How come he can have his company's accounts prepared in euros or dollars while plebs like you and I have no choice but to use a currency that's being steered by hand by a government that does what the owner of *Dagurinn* tells it?"

"I don't know," Orri replied, feeling uncomfortable. "Does he?"

"He does, my boy. He does. That's why this delightful country of ours, which we proudly think of, for some bizarre reason, as a bastion of democracy, is run by a small group of men in suits who own banks, ships, land and a few other things."

Dóri sat back with a satisfied look on his face.

"So why doesn't anyone do anything about this?"

"You think people haven't tried? Old Jörundur did his best, and look what happened to him," he said with a smile that ran around his face. "I was a radical for all the years I was a teacher, stood for Parliament and the city council a few times, marched on the Yankee base at Keflavík once or twice as well. Not a hope. The good people of this nation, like people the world over, are sheep who are happy to be led to the slaughter, in that they'll listen to any snake-oil salesman in a cheap suit ready to convince them to vote against their own interests."

Orri looked askance. "People aren't that stupid."

"No?" Dóri asked gently. "Maybe not everyone, but enough to ensure that nothing changes." He sighed. "But now we had better get some work done before the others notice that we're taking it easy. Alex isn't here. He called in this morning and said he'd be late."

"What's wrong with him?" Orri asked with a sideways look.

"Something to do with an abnormal fluid intake, I gather." Dóri grinned. "It's not what I'd call an illness,

224

but just for this once he can have the benefit of the doubt."

"Anyone else would have been given the sack by now if they were as late as Alex is half the time," Orri grumbled.

Dóri leaned forward, elbows on the table, and beckoned theatrically.

"What?"

"Orri, tell me. You know who owns this company?"

"Óli Hansen, isn't it? Not that we see a lot of him."

Dóri shook his head and leaned further forward, his voice was so low as to be inaudible. Orri strained to hear what he said.

"Óli Hansen started the company and he still owns some of it."

"But, what?"

"Óli is just a glorified manager these days. We have owners who have their offices in a city a long way east of here," Dóri said. "Don't even think about why Alex is here, but he's here for a reason and that means he can turn up late five days a week and still not get even a verbal warning."

Orri looked baffled. "So, why?" he asked as Dóri put a finger to his lips.

"Don't ask. Don't look too closely at what comes in and goes out. Don't be too friendly with Alex. That way when someone asks, you can say truthfully that you had no idea."

"No idea of what?"

"Hell, Orri, you're dense today for a smart lad like you," Dóri said with a knowing look that made Orri shiver. "I don't ask and I don't want to know. I have a disabled wife and a bone-headed single-parent daughter to support, and I need this job for as long as it lasts. Now, the reason I asked you to come in is because we have a fish delivery to make today."

"Alex always does those, doesn't he?"

"Normally he does, yes. But Alex hasn't turned up."

"So you want me to do it?"

"Got it in one. It's easy enough. Hafnarfisk have seventy boxes of fresh fish to go to the airport for the London flight this afternoon. You know where the cargo terminal is at Keflavík, don't you? Just follow the signs and someone will show you where to go."

It was one of those impersonal blocks of flats almost as far from the city centre as you can get without being in the countryside. Eiríkur pushed at the outside door and was not surprised that the lock was broken as it swung inwards.

He'd been able to get Elísabet Sólborg Höskuldsdóttir's address from the national registry, an easy enough exercise as there was only one person to be found with that combination of names. But he knew from bitter experience that the listed legal residence was, for many people, where their parents lived, where they had an address for work reasons, or often simply a place they had lived at one time and had long since moved on from without bothering to register the move.

Although the registry specified the address, Eiríkur's suspicions came true when he saw it was a block, with no way of knowing which of the eight apartments

226

would be her one — and there was no name on the list of doorbells that looked likely.

He knocked at the first door he found and got no response. The next door had pounding music coming from inside, which presumably drowned out his puny efforts at knocking, so he went a floor higher and tried again.

The door was ripped open while his hand was still in the air.

"Who the hell are you?"

The face looking out at him from the darkness of the doorway snarled and Eiríkur backed away half a step. "I'm looking for Elísabet. She doesn't live here?"

"There's no Elísabet here," the man said and made to slam the door.

"How about the other flats here? Upstairs, somewhere?"

"Don't ask me," the man snarled and this time the door did close in his face, hard enough for the door frame to shake.

Eiríkur shrugged his shoulders and carried on upstairs, knocking at two more doors before he got a reply. This time a middle-aged woman opened the door and looked at him curiously.

"Good afternoon. I'm looking for someone called Elísabet who lives in this block. I'm sorry but I don't know which flat, so I'm having to knock on doors."

"I don't know any Elísabet, young man."

"Who is it, Margrét?" A quavering voice called from inside.

"It's all right, Dad," she replied and looked back at Eiríkur. "I'm sorry. I don't know any Elísabet."

"I'm a police officer," Eiríkur said, opening his wallet to show his identification card. "I understand there's a woman called Elísabet Höskuldsdóttir who lives in this block, but I don't know which flat," he explained a second time.

"I don't know," the woman said, frowning doubtfully, and looking around to see an old man with white hair slowly approaching along the dim hallway, supporting his gradual progress with a stick in each hand.

"He means the girl upstairs, Margrét. I'm sure of it," the old man said.

"You're sure? The one above, or on the other side?"

The old man pointed one stick at the ceiling, while Eiríkur expected him to fall over, holding his breath until the old man was again supported by two sticks. "Upstairs. Lovely girl," he said as Margrét scowled.

"If you think so, Dad." she sniffed. "How do you know?"

"She talks to me on the stairs sometimes, which is more than any of my other miserable neighbours do, and especially that idiot downstairs who plays deafening music all the time."

"Yeah. I can hear it," Eiríkur said. "It's disturbing you, I take it?"

The music itself was hardly audible, but a persistent bass pulse could be felt rather than heard.

"It is a little irritating," the old man admitted. "But it's not as if I can go down there and punch him like I could have done forty years ago."

"I'll ask a patrol to stop by and have a word with him," Eiríkur promised. "But you're sure it's Elísabet who lives upstairs."

"I'm sure," the old man said. "Margrét here doesn't like her, but she always says hello to me, and she told me her name's Lísa, so I assume that's short for Elísabet."

A few minutes later and after a quick phone call, Eiríkur was knocking on the door upstairs. He could hear his knocks echoing inside and knew that nobody was going to answer. He clattered down the stairs again to find the old man's door still open and both the man and his daughter waiting for him.

"I could have told you she wasn't home," Margrét said.

"I haven't seen her for a while," the old man added.

"She hasn't moved out?"

The old man shook his head. "No. I'd have noticed. There's been no coming and going for a while."

"You don't know where she works, do you?"

"I'm afraid not. All I can tell you is that she works odd hours, coming and going early in the morning or late in the evening. Something to do with food, I imagine, as she often wears those white clothes that chefs wear on the TV."

"And you don't have a phone number for her, or know what car she drives, or anything like that?"

"I'm sorry, young man," the old man wheezed. "I'm not sure I can help you any further."

Eiríkur thanked the old man and made his way down the stairs as two officers in uniform stepped into the building.

"G'day, Eiríkur, you called?"

"Yeah, that was me. Just follow the racket, would you, and maybe have a quiet word with the occupant about anti-social behaviour?"

The taller of the two officers tilted his head to one side and listened for a moment. "*Cradle of Filth*," he decided. "That definitely constitutes anti-social behaviour."

Gunna looked up as Eiríkur arrived, breathless and excited at the hospital.

"Found it," he announced.

"What have you found?"

He grinned in triumph. "Our friend's girlfriend. I know where she lives, and with a bit of luck she should lead us to him. That's her," he said, placing a sheet of paper in front of Gunna.

"Our mystery man's girlfriend?"

"Elísabet Sólborg Höskuldsdóttir. I found the riding club the logo belongs to and someone there confirmed that she had seen the guy in the picture with this Elísabet. So, find her and we find him," he said. "I hope."

"And have you found her?"

"Not so far. I know where she lives and I have her driving licence photo. There's a grey Ford Ka registered to her, so at least I have a little more to go on."

"You've put an alert out for the car?"

"Already done it."

Gunna looked closely at the picture and saw a young woman looking blankly past the camera. Unruly hair had been pushed back behind her ears and she saw

230

thick lips and a stubby nose that gave the strong face a determined look, offset by the steel ring looped through the lower lip.

"Distinctive," Gunna said. "But that photo's almost ten years old, so she might well look very different now."

"Could be," Eiríkur said. "But at least I have some idea what she looks like, and if she can lead me to her boyfriend, so much the better."

"That's brilliant," Gunna said and nodded at the computer monitor showing the shattered hand. "But she'll have to wait. Take a look at that."

"Hell, that must be painful. Deliberate?" Eiríkur asked, staring at the X-ray image of Maris's smashed hand. "That's no accident, surely?"

"That's my feeling," the doctor said, looking up from his desk at the other side of the room. "But you'd better get a specialist opinion on that."

"Listen," Gunna said, flipping through her notes. "Eiríkur, listen. The victim lives at Lyngvangur in Hafnarfjördur. Number 45, top flat on the right. I want you to get over there right away and have a good look at the place before we do much else. Take pictures and dust for prints. But I really want you to see if you can figure out how this happened. According to this gentleman," Gunna said, gesturing to the doctor who was again engrossed in his computer. "The victim had some kind of domestic accident."

"You think he's lying?"

"I don't think he's lying. I know so. So go and check it out while I have another word with him."

Orri would have given almost anything to be somewhere else. Houses were much more familiar and easier to deal with. Offices had never been his style, and daylight even less so, but after the gut-wrenching experience of the motorcycle clubhouse, this had turned out to be easy, far easier that he had expected.

His experience that a man carrying a toolbox and wearing overalls and a yellow waistcoat attracts no attention was again proved right.

Not that this office had been a difficult one to get into, he reflected as he padded between the desks. He might as well have been invisible. The fire escape at the top of the external steel staircase was clearly this office's smoking spot and it had been easy enough to open the door with a screwdriver jammed into the worn mechanism.

He froze as the front door of the office downstairs at street level rattled and he peered cautiously out of the window of what he assumed was the director's office to see a security guard with a dog on a lead walk away, satisfied that the place was locked up, and not expecting anyone to break into an office on a Saturday afternoon.

The dog whined and pulled at its lead, aware of something that the man in the official cap and jacket with a logo on the back was clearly not worried about. The dog came to a stop, looking longingly at the upper floor windows and Orri jerked his head back, certain that it had seen him.

"Pack it in, will you?" He heard the security guard irritably scolding the dog as he made for the comfort of his van and Orri briefly felt sorry for the animal that was being prevented from doing its job, but relieved that the guard was too lazy to do his own job properly.

He quickly did as he had been told. Standing on the desk, he lifted the ceiling panel, put the little control box next to the light fitting and opened the aerial. He clipped the two tiny crocodile clips to the wires leading to the light and saw an indicator on the control box begin to glow. Using a ballpoint pen, he pushed a hole through the ceiling panel, relieved that the old-fashioned fibreboard was soft and there was no need to use the drill he had brought with him, and pushed the barrel of the camera into the gap. With droplets of sweat breaking out on his back in spite of the chill, he replaced the panel and hoped that he had fitted everything correctly. He swept off the desk, even though he had left no footprints, and made for the other office, where he went through the same procedure before heading for the back door.

He was down the fire escape and back in his car within a minute, the high-viz tabard identifying him as a contractor rolled up under the seat, and a few seconds later he was speeding through Kópavogur towards the main road and home. Orri smiled to himself. The sight of the covert camera in its package in his postbox had given him an idea and it had taken only an hour or two to find just what he was looking for.

There had been no call from the Voice and Orri decided to see if he could turn the tables.

An hour's shopping later, he pulled up outside the block of flats. In the lobby he made sure there was nobody about before he used his picks to tease open the lock of the postbox above his own, which he knew belonged to a flat that had been empty for months and was likely to stay that way. Using lumps of modelling clay, he fixed a small camera of his own in the postbox to stare out through the gaps in the grille, shut the box and checked it to be sure it wasn't visible except to someone taking an exceptionally close look. He jogged up the stairs feeling like a man with a good day's work behind him and knowing that he would be able to download the footage from the camera direct to his phone.

A nurse had come to attend to Maris and change the dressing on his hand, giving Gunna the opportunity to make a few phone calls from the corridor.

"*Hæ*, Eiríkur, anything interesting?"

She could hear his phone crackle and his voice echoed in the bare flat.

"Nothing much. I'm dusting for prints and there's a full palm print on the living-room table, with a lot of dents around it. Looks to me like someone has been busy with a hammer."

"That would account for the broken fingers?"

"It could," Eiríkur said. "I'll have to check against our victim's prints, but it looks like everything has been swept right off the table and onto the floor. It's a real bloody mess in here. Has our boy said anything?"

Gunna looked around and wondered how long it would take to change Maris's dressings.

"Not a single truthful word. He claims he was moving a wardrobe and it fell on his hand."

"Bullshit. There isn't even a wardrobe in here." She could hear a door creak open. "There's one in the bedroom, but you can see it hasn't been moved for years. For fuck's sake . . ."

Gunna distinctly heard a crash through the phone.

"Eiríkur, are you all right?"

"Yeah, I'm fine," he answered after a pause. "I opened the wardrobe door and a load of stuff came crashing out onto the floor. All electrical stuff, drills, that kind of thing. There must be a dozen of these things. Why would anyone need a wardrobe full of power tools?"

"Stolen goods?"

"Looks like it to me. Listen, I'll have a proper look through all this stuff and get back to you."

"Fine. You do that while I have another chat with our friend. You'd better see if you can rustle up a squad car from the Hafnarfjördur station to help you if there's a lot of stuff there."

"Wow, a DeWalt cordless, I always wanted one of those."

"Eiríkur, keep your mind on the job, will you?"

"Hell, there's a few laptops here as well, all sorts, and a couple of those computer games consoles. It's like a treasure trove."

"Write it all down, there's a good boy, and call me back when you're done."

There was no water anywhere, but a stream that chattered and bubbled past the ruined farmhouse was good enough. With no cup to drink from, Jóhann had no choice but to kneel on a flat rock and lower his face to the water that startled him with its chill.

The building itself was a wreck, abandoned more years ago than he could imagine, its gaunt concrete walls pitted by sun and frost and with deep cracks running from the ground like the branches of a tree to fade out higher up. The roof seemed intact and Jóhann looked with disquiet at the grey clouds that had replaced the bright dawn sunshine, threatening rain. The stillness of the dawn that had woken him had also been replaced by a cool wind that cut like a knife.

At the back of the building what he guessed had once been pasture had been filled with a framework of rough wooden poles, nailed and lashed in place, with hundreds of cross bars running from side to side. Each of these was hung with fish drying in the wind. He stood helplessly underneath, staring at the headless fish hung tail up on the bars and it was a long time before the thought struck him that this was food.

He scrambled as best he could up a triangular trestle at the corner of the structure. Halfway up he realized that he was faint with hunger and wondered just how long he had been there. He had long since given up wearing a wristwatch, relying instead on the phone that had become his constant source of data from messages to traffic updates to the simple concept of tracking the time. But now the phone was lifeless in his pocket. Had he been there a day or two days? He had no idea; he was only able to judge that he would collapse soon if he wasn't able to eat. The thought spurred him to climb a little further and he reached out to snatch at one of the closer fish drying on a beam. A pair of them came away in his hands, one in his grasp and the other falling to the ground below as the twine holding them together parted. He was surprised at how light the fish in his hand was.

On the ground he tore at it with his fingers, ripping it apart and retching. The strips of white meat were hard, far tougher than the dried fish in chunks that he occasionally bought in plastic bags to offer at conferences to foreign colleagues as a typical Icelandic delicacy for them to chew their way through.

He chewed manfully and the fish gradually became a pile of desiccated skin and bone on the ground. Still hungry but no longer starving, Jóhann trudged back to the house, carrying the other fish that had fallen to the ground in his hands like a prize and wrapping his jacket around him like a shroud.

Orri was relieved to have the place to himself for a change. He yawned and lifted his feet onto the table as he clicked the TV into life and scrolled through the channels. He had checked the camera he had fitted in the unused postbox opposite his own, bluetoothing the files in its memory to his phone and he checked the short video files one by one. The camera was motion-activated and he could see from the clips that it started to record its sequences as the outside door swung open or when someone came down the stairs.

Mostly they showed people walking rapidly straight past, while some stopped to check their own mailboxes. One showed the rather superior elderly lady from the ground floor standing in the lobby where she daintily picked her nose with a crooked little finger as she waited for a taxi. The clip that showed the capricious teenage daughter of the couple on the top floor checking her lipstick and adjusting her ample chest to display maximum cleavage before going out was the one he watched several times with a grin on his face, but there was nothing to show anyone putting anything through the slot in his mailbox, apart from the postman with the handful of envelopes he'd already collected.

They were all bills, none of them big ones but they were still outgoings, and his night-time activities that would normally have brought in extra cash had been curtailed, in spite of the windfall of cash the Voice had put his way and which he felt could not be relied on to continue for long. He might have to dig into his savings, he thought with misgivings, standing up to make his way to the kitchen and see if there were the makings of a meal in the fridge.

He found himself wondering where Lísa was, almost admitting to himself that he preferred it when she was there even though she talked too much. She liked to cook and that was what gave her food a spark of energy that the stuff he made lacked. Orri liked to eat and it was only after Lísa had elbowed her way into his life that new things had appeared in his diet, a variety of new flavours he had been suspicious of at first but soon found himself missing when he had to cook for himself.

He was bent over the contents of the fridge when the door rattled and slammed.

"Hungry, are you?"

"Starving," he admitted, hauling himself upright to give her a kiss. "Are you cooking anything?"

"Men." Lísa snorted. "They're only interested in two things, and food is the other one."

"Beer, you mean?"

"Yeah. Right."

"Well, we can discuss the other one after dinner, if you like?"

Lísa shook her head and rummaged in her bag. "This is for you," she said, handing him an envelope.

"What is it?"

"How should I know? Your name's on it."

He read "Orri Björnsson, c/o Elísabet S. Höskuldsdóttir" typed on the envelope.

"Where did this come from?"

"It was under the wiper on my car. Don't ask me who's sending you letters through me. Seems stupid, considering they could have just posted it to you."

She banged a pot onto the stove and poured water into it. Orri saw that she was annoyed and pretending not to be curious, although she looked sideways to see what was in the envelope as he ripped it open.

"What's so special about that?" She asked, mystified, looking at the grainy print of Orri's back, his hands in the unused mailbox. Orri stuttered in incomprehension. They knew he had tried to catch them out but had beaten him to it. There was nothing else in the envelope, no note, nothing that might indicate where it had come from.

In the lobby, with the print in his hand, Orri looked around frantically, trying to figure out where the picture had been taken from and finally noticed a glint behind one of the mailbox grilles on the opposite side of the entrance hall, where a tiny electronic eye was watching him. He hammered at the steel front of the mailbox and pushed his fingers as far into the slot as they would go, but with no chance of reaching the contents inside. He raced up the flights of stairs and clattered back down with his lock picks, telling himself to be calm and take it easy.

The fine pick refused to slide into the lock as it should have done, and squinting into the barrel, Orri saw the lock had been filled, he guessed with fast-setting glue. His shoulders sagged in defeat. The lock would have to be drilled out and he could hardly get the surly old man who looked after the block's maintenance to force open a mailbox that wasn't his.

He went up the stairs slowly and while Lísa looked on with concern, he filled a litre bottle with water and took it downstairs with him. Looking outside to see if anyone might see him, he poured the water into the mailbox slot, hoping it would short-circuit something in the tiny camera and stop it spying on him.

"What the hell are you doing?" The querulous voice behind him was filled with fury. "Are you mad?"

240

"Someone's put glue in the lock," he explained plaintively to the elderly woman who had appeared from her flat, recognizing her as the one who had stood by the door exploring the inside of her beaky nose with a little finger.

"What? Then get the maintenance man to come and look at it."

"I'm trying to wash the glue out," Orri said frantically as the last drops of water dribbled from the bottle into the mailbox. A puddle of water had already formed at his feet as it leaked down the front of the steel door.

"I'm going to report you," the old woman hissed. "You're a vandal, that's what you are."

She slammed the door behind her and it suddenly occurred to Orri that the whole exchange had probably been recorded, along with his frantic attempts to get at the spying eye behind the grille. He trudged back upstairs to where Lísa was waiting in the doorway, arms folded.

"Orri Björnsson, will you tell me just what the fuck is going on?"

The car was deliberately inconspicuous. It had been drilled into Alex that gangsters could treat themselves to gold trinkets and eye-catching sets of wheels, but a man with something to hide was better off being inconspicuous, and Alex had a sinking feeling inside that he had attracted more attention than was healthy.

He brooded, leaning on the wheel with the engine running, looking up at the dark windows of the flat.

There was no doubt the heavies who had come calling the day before weren't the brightest pair, and the message was intended for him. But what was the message, and who the hell were they?

He closed the car door and walked silently around the building in the twilight. With a stiff wind blowing salt off the sea, there was nobody about. He almost tripped over the twisted frame of an abandoned bicycle, cursed and pushed open the door. The block of flats was an old one, with external walkways along the front leading to the individual flats. He hated these as they had filled up with snow last winter, and it was too easy to see who was going to which flat.

With yet another sinking feeling, he saw that his flat was sealed. The lock had been changed and a police seal fitted to the door. That idiot Maris must have blabbed, instead of sticking to the story Alex had told him to tell before he put him in a taxi. Not that Maris had been in much of a condition to make sense the night before, Alex reflected, his face grey with shock and his teeth chattering.

He tried his key, even though he knew it wouldn't fit. The lock was too new. He already knew that a credit card would not slip past the door's deep frame, and he smiled grimly at the idea of getting Orri to come and open it for him. But now it was important to know what the police had seen, or even if they had seen anything at all, so he stepped back as far as the balustrade would let him go and kicked, aiming, as he had been taught to do, as close to the lock as he could. The door creaked and buckled.

Alex stepped back again. This time he took his time, aimed more carefully and let fly with a kick that saw the door crack open. Pushing at it with one shoulder, he saw that the lock was intact, but he had managed to splinter the tired frame. Not that it mattered, he decided.

He left the lights off and went through the place rapidly. He was sure he had left nothing that would identify him when he'd gone out the night before, but Maris had probably spilled his guts, as expected. The place had been cleared out. There was nothing in his bedroom wardrobe and all the stuff he had been getting from Orri and which he knew he should have passed on was gone. It wasn't a huge problem, just a minor irritation, but he knew that Bruno would not be pleased.

He pulled the door closed behind him and tiptoed down the stairs. Outside he again walked round the building to approach his own car from an unexpected angle. With the engine running and the heater on at full blast, he opened his phone and dialled a number from memory.

"It's Alex," he said when the voicemail kicked in. "Call me. We might have a problem."

Maris looked less happy as Gunna knocked and entered without waiting to be asked. The smile had gone from his face and he looked drawn with pain as she sat down and made herself comfortable.

"So, Maris, how are things since we spoke this morning? Feeling better?"

"It hurts a lot. But it'll be all right in a few weeks."

"You really think so?"

"Yes. Going home soon. The consul was here, they're going to get me a flight home."

"You want to go home, do you?"

Maris nodded. Gunna decided this was a young man who had taken his misfortune badly. She had to steel herself to deliver bad news.

"That might not be possible."

"What? But the consul said . . ." he floundered.

"This is the way it is, Maris," Gunna explained in a patient voice, looking into the young man's anxious brown eyes which reminded her of the sheep being herded into the slaughterhouse at Vestureyri when she was a girl, convinced that behind the sad eyes was the knowledge that they would not be coming out again. "The health system in Iceland is hugely overburdened and you've managed to get yourself a very nasty injury that's going to take up a huge amount of resources to put right, not to mention all the treatment you're going to need afterwards to get your hand back to being of some kind of use one day. I don't know what the doctor has told you, but your hand has been smashed and it's going to be months or years before it's any use to you," she said and paused to let her words sink in as tears began to well up in his eyes.

"You're going to need a huge amount of therapy," she continued. "And it's going to take months. So you can understand that the health service would really prefer you to go home and get treated there. You see what I mean?"

"Yes, I know all that. I pay for my flight home. My family know I'm coming."

Gunna jerked a thumb at the door. "They want you off their hands. You can understand why, can't you?"

Maris nodded and Gunna pointed a finger at her own chest. "On the other hand, I have a problem with that."

"How?" he asked with a blank look. "Why is that?"

"Because I know that a crime has been committed; not a trivial one, but a brutal attack. You get my meaning? I have a pair of thugs running around my city who are probably going to do this again to someone else before too long, and I'd like to catch them before that happens. So I'd like you to tell me who attacked you and why."

This time he looked bewildered and Gunna wondered if he was going to cry.

"I can't tell you."

"In that case, you'll be staying in Iceland a long time. I can withhold your passport, don't forget. I'm not letting my key witness leave the country," she said as the first tear made its way through the brown stubble on Maris's cheek. "And on top of that we have the little matter of why your flat was crammed with stolen goods — that also requires a little explanation."

CHAPTER
TEN

Orri stayed curled in a ball under the duvet as Lísa left for work at five for an early shift. He wanted to go downstairs but didn't dare, certain that he was being watched. His phone buzzed and he left it where it was. When he finally uncurled himself from his bed, he pointedly didn't even look at the phone on the floor with "new message" on its screen, and kicked it under the bed on his way to the bathroom, where he stayed for a long time under the scalding shower.

A mug of coffee and a bowl of cereal later and he started to feel more awake. He had spent the night playing out all kinds of bad dreams in his head, wondering what the Voice would do if he simply ignored instructions. The Voice knew so much about him and he knew absolutely nothing about the Voice, except that its owner was ruthless — and clever. Or was he? He turned over in his mind what might happen if he were to ignore instructions and he was painfully reminded that the Voice knew where his sister lived, and clearly knew where to find Lísa.

He liked her well enough and would never have wished her harm, even though she could sulk on an

246

infuriatingly colossal scale on occasions, but discovering his fondness for her took him by surprise. He decided as he downed his second mug of coffee that he didn't dare ignore the Voice. The pang he felt when he thought of Lísa coming to harm was an alien feeling he hardly recognized and it felt thoroughly disconcerting.

He brushed his unwelcome feelings aside as he lay on the floor and stretched an arm under the bed to find his phone, blowing the dust and fluff from it before peering at the screen and the message.

Good morning, Orri. The cafe in the shopping centre in Hafnarfjordur. Be there at 10.30. Sit facing the counter and don't look round. Reply with a blank message to confirm.

He looked again and this time he saw that it had been sent without the number being withheld. He hit the reply button and immediately heard the electronic voice intone that the user's phone was switched off and he should try again later. Orri dropped the phone on the bed and sat with his head in his hands. Time to call the police, maybe? Would they believe him? Could he tell them without letting them know that he had been quietly breaking into people's houses for the past few years and making a tidy living out of it?

There was a fatigue deep inside him that he didn't recognize and which unnerved him. He sat up, shook his head violently and stood up to go to the kitchen and splash his face with cold water, telling himself that it was time to get a grip and go to work. He'd go to the meeting and damned well face up to the Voice, whatever the bastard's real name might be.

Alex kicked the duvet off his feet. It was hot and for a moment he wondered where he was in the darkness until he heard Emilija's steady breathing next to him. He dozed off again and it felt like no more than a few seconds later that the alarm buzzed.

"What the fuck . . .?" he snarled as he hauled his head from the pillow.

A shaft of light from the street lamp outside found its way through a crack in the blinds and he felt Emilija stir and sit up. She yawned, stretched her arms above her head, her thick brown hair loose for once from its plait and hanging around her shoulders like a curtain.

"No," she said, slapping away a hand intent on pulling her onto him. "I have to go to work and so do you."

A moment later she was in her jeans and pulling on a shirt as she left the room.

"Sigga! Time to get up, sweetheart!"

Alex lay back and reflected sadly that single mothers really were the business: a night of action and still up for work at the crack of dawn. He was already looking forward to the mournful expression that he would expect to see on Maris's face as he recounted Emilija's enthusiasm in the sack when he remembered with a sinking feeling that he wouldn't be seeing Maris for a while, and wondered how he was. Then he wondered what Maris had said, and searched frantically for his phone when he also remembered that there had been no call after he had left his message the night before.

He heard the rattling of crockery from the kitchen and Emilija chivvying the children into wakefulness. Anton was awake and chattering while Sigga was quiet and watchful as she spooned up her cereal. Eggs boiled in a saucepan and Emilija sliced bread for Sigga's sandwiches.

He arrived in the kitchen fresh from the shower, poured himself coffee and took a seat at the table next to Sigga.

"School today?" he asked, trying to sound friendly.

Sigga shook her head and said nothing, while Anton chattered to himself. Emilija put eggs and slices of bread and cheese on the table. Alex helped himself.

"It's Sunday. Sigga goes to basketball practice and Anton's going to my friend's while I'm at work," Emilija said.

"When are you finished work?"

"I'm not sure. It depends how much there is to do, and I might have an evening shift as well."

"I'll drop by later, then."

"No, Alex. I'd prefer it if you didn't."

His face set in a petulant frown. "Why not?"

Emilija sighed. "Alex, you're a sweet boy, but I'm not what you want. We've had our fun, so let's call it a day, shall we?"

"What do you mean?"

"An older single mum with a saggy bottom and two kids? Come on, Alex. Find yourself something younger."

"Maybe you're what suits me," he said. "How would you know?"

"I can see it in your eyes. Eat your egg before it goes cold."

Emilija plaited her hair behind her neck with nimble fingers and threw it over her shoulder while Alex and the children ate in silence.

Alex drained his coffee mug and crushed his eggshell onto a plate. "I'll see you tonight," he said defiantly, heading for the door with his car keys dangling from one finger.

"No, Alex. Don't."

He curled an arm around Emilija's back and pulled her towards him, his other hand snaking behind her to cup a buttock as he ground himself against her. "Don't tell me what to do."

Emilija squirmed out of his grasp. "Alex, how many times do I have to tell you? It was fun but I really don't want you coming round here."

"That's not what you said last night when you wanted me to screw you again."

"Shhh. The children . . ."

"So what's the problem?"

"You really want to know?"

Emilija took his elbow and steered him into the hallway and out of the children's earshot. Standing by the front door, she looked earnestly into his eyes.

"Because in five minutes there'll be some sweet young thing along who has time to paint her toenails and who'll catch your eye, and Alex'll be gone. I can do without the heartbreak that goes with all that. That's reason number one. You want the other one?"

Stunned and truculent, Alex leaned against the wall, his arms folded. "Go on. Tell me."

"Because you're up to no good. I don't know what you're doing, but it's not honest and I can't afford to get involved in anything illegal. Ingi and I get on well enough most of the time, in spite of everything, but his mother loathes me and she'd do anything to wrench the kids away from me. Sleeping with a gangster is just going to give the dried-up old bitch the ammunition she needs. So thanks, Alex, but no thanks."

Eiríkur patted the baby's back and listened to it gurgle happily while Svala spooned yoghurt into the toddler, hardly keeping up with his appetite.

"Are you working today?"

"This afternoon."

"I thought you didn't have a shift today?"

There was a note of accusation in Svala's voice and Eiríkur felt a pang of guilt, knowing that she expected him to visit her parents with her, a Sunday afternoon ritual that was rarely broken.

"Shall we get them ready and go and see your mum and dad this morning?"

Svala turned the idea over in her head. Both she and Eiríkur were creatures of habit.

"I don't know. I'm not sure they'll be up early today."

"Well, I have a shift at two. Shall we go to Ikea for lunch and I'll drop you off?"

Svala sighed. She had preferred Eiríkur as the student she had met half a dozen years ago, a man who lost himself in textbooks. She was still wondering why he had abandoned his studies to join the police, and the idea of her husband as a detective was something she was struggling to come to terms with.

"If you like," she said. "Will you pick us up after your shift?"

"That won't be until ten," Eiríkur said.

"Why so late?"

"That's a normal shift, two to ten."

"If you must." She sighed and spooned more yoghurt into the little girl, who had begun to voice her disapproval at the interruption in supply.

Eiríkur's phone buzzed and he stretched to extract it from his pocket without disturbing the baby on his shoulder.

"I mean, I can go with you to the old folks and maybe you can get a taxi home later?"

"Maybe," Svala said. "Or maybe Dad can drive us back."

"Or you could leave me at the station and take the car," Eiríkur suggested. "I'll get a lift home with someone."

"Æi. You know I don't like driving with the children in the car."

"Up to you," Eiríkur said, and his eyes lit up as he read the message.

Hæ Eiríkur. The car you're looking for was parked in the Selar district last night. Gimme a call.

He saw it was from one of the traffic officers and immediately dialled the number while Svala tutted her disapproval.

252

* * *

The night had been bitterly cold. Jóhann huddled in the thick overcoat he had found himself in the day before as dawn again woke him and he wondered if it was seven or nine o'clock. He shivered and his stomach howled its displeasure at the scant meal of nothing but dried fish the day before.

He tried to lie still for a few minutes but thirst drove him up and out of the broken farmhouse to the stream where he lapped water like a dog. It stilled the pangs in his stomach for a while and back inside he tore at the second fish he had pulled from the drying racks.

With his need for food temporarily assuaged, Jóhann began to think, surprised at how the previous day's concentration on food and water had driven practically every other thought from his mind. He walked slowly around the building that had once been a handsome farmhouse. It must have been abandoned years before, but how many? Thirty? Fifty? There was nothing to give him any clue.

A rutted track disappeared downhill and vanished past the curve of a low hill that sat beneath the shoulder of a higher mountain with snow on its upper slopes. He sniffed the wind and felt that there was a faint fresh smell of seaweed to it, so maybe the sea lay that way? But were there people there? A village maybe? Or even a house with a telephone?

He racked his brains wondering what to do and which way to go, or maybe he should just to wait until someone came. There were faint tyre marks on the ground beneath the racks of drying fish, but he had no way of telling if they were recent or if they had been there since last year, any more than he could tell if the fish hung to dry had been there for a month or a year. He could tell roughly which way was east by the sunrise, but knowing the direction without having any idea of where he might be was of little use.

"Early for a Sunday, Gunnhildur?"

"It is, but there's stuff to be done," she told Ívar Laxdal without turning round. At long last she had taught herself not to let the unexpected sound of his voice take her by surprise.

"And overtime to be had?"

"It doesn't come amiss."

"Progress?"

"This way," she said, leading the way to the detectives' little coffee room and filling him a mug without asking. "Yesterday I spent most of my time dealing with a Latvian with a smashed hand. First he said it was an accident, but after I leaned on him, he finally admitted that two thugs had muscled their way into the flat he lives in and smashed up his hand with a hammer."

"Any particular reason? This wasn't some kind of anti-foreigner thing, was it?"

"No. He couldn't tell me who had done it, and eventually I realized that he simply didn't know who they were, or why. A little more leaning and it seems they were looking for his flatmate, who he finally admitted had put him in a taxi and told him to say he'd had an accident."

254

"Ah. With friends like that . . ."

"Exactly. Who needs enemies? So now I'm in search of Alex Snetzler, who also appears to be the owner of the impressive stash of stolen electrical goods that Eiríkur has been going through for serial numbers to see if we can match it up anywhere. From what Maris said, Alex is selling this stuff on, and he gets it from a local character."

"No name or description?"

"No. Maris said he comes to the door and Alex always answers. The guy never comes inside to hand stuff over and sometimes he just leaves it outside."

"You have an alert out for this Alex?" Ívar Laxdal asked, picking up a sugar lump and lodging it behind his teeth to filter a mouthful of coffee through.

"I do. But first we need to go and pick up the headcases who smashed our Latvian boy's hand."

"I thought you said he didn't know who they were?"

"I showed him a lot of mugshots of likely candidates. So this is going to be fun."

"You'll get some uniform backup, won't you?" Ívar Laxdal asked with a hint of concern on his heavy face.

Gunna drained her coffee cup and cradled it in her hands, feeling the warmth ebb from the porcelain.

"I will, once I've asked a few questions."

Orri nursed a mug of coffee that he had no appetite for in the shopping centre, surrounded by women with pushchairs, squabbling toddlers and a few aimless teenagers with expensive phones in their hands.

His coffee was cold and he looked at his watch. As it ticked over to ten thirty, the phone in his pocket buzzed and he looked at it quickly.

Now go to the fuel station opposite the port entrance and wait there in your car. You have five minutes, he read. He quickly downed the cold remains of his coffee and hurried out to the car park.

The road was a quiet one, leading to industrial units and the harbour gates. Halfway along was a self-service filling station that he could see was deserted as he pulled in. Orri sat and waited, the engine running as he tapped the steering wheel with his thumbs and scanned the deserted road.

His phone buzzed again.

Go 200 metres further along. On the open ground. Park facing the road.

He swore under his breath, telling himself that a filling station equipped with CCTV was never going to be the right place for them to be seen. He drove slowly, looking around him carefully, and drove onto the waste ground, the crushed black lava crunching beneath the van's wheels as he did so, taking deep breaths and trying to stop his hands from shaking.

A small blue car was already there. Orri took care not to look as he parked parallel to it and sat looking ahead at the superstructures of the line of ships at the quay in the distance, beyond the high fences of the port area.

The van's passenger door opened and shut quickly. Orri looked incredulously at the man in a heavy

256

overcoat and an old-fashioned hat as he sat next to him.

"Good afternoon, Orri. We are pleased that you made it," the man said in stiff English. His mouth opened and he tried to speak, but found he could say nothing. "You have done quite well, Orri. Good work, I think."

"Who the fuck are you?" Orri demanded when he finally found his voice. "Why have you been making me do all this stuff?"

"I thought it would be obvious. Because you love your sister and your girlfriend." The man raised an eyebrow as bushy as his clipped moustache.

"Who are you?"

"Ah, that's a question one should never ask. It's embarrassing to have to decline to answer. But as you don't normally move in our circles, I'll make allowances for you. Just don't ask again and don't bother trying to find out for yourself. It's not healthy."

Orri sat speechless and furious. He toyed with the idea of putting the van into gear and driving away with the man a prisoner next to him, but this old thing had no central locking and he would be able to jump out easily somewhere. "So why are we here now?"

The man smiled. "Because we are wondering what to do with you. Can we trust you to do what you are asked to do?"

Orri's eyes bulged as he suppressed his fury. "What the hell do you mean? What do you think I am?" He struggled to stay calm, infuriated by the man's placid smile.

"We would pay you, of course," the man said, as if dropping a careless remark. "Probably quite handsomely by this country's standards."

He had been ready to yell at the man but found his anger suddenly gone. "How much?" he asked quickly.

The man smiled and Orri regretted having asked so fast, knowing he had lost a point.

"Enough for you to be comfortable, I would think. But I'm not here to discuss anything specific."

"And if I say no?"

This time the man smiled broadly and chuckled. "You think you have a choice? I think you have an idea of what we are capable of and how far we will go. Do you really want to turn down such an interesting offer?"

"If I don't have a choice . . ." Orri growled, his frustration returning.

"Listen. We may need you for an assignment occasionally. Sometimes several times in a single week, then you may not hear from us for a long time. It's simple enough work and you have already demonstrated that you can do it without a problem. You will be paid for this work, and no, you don't have a choice."

"So what are you going to do if I don't play ball?"

The man looked into Orri's eyes. "I don't have to tell you what would happen to you. My associates wanted to dispose of you the night we found you sneaking through our apartment, and I assure you that you would have disappeared without trace."

Orri gulped. "Then I guess I'd best say yes."

258

"A healthy choice. Continue to go to work as usual. It's important that you remain unobtrusive. Don't stand out. Don't try to follow or trace us as you did before. That shows initiative, but once is enough. You'll be well paid so don't screw up. You have a phone number. Don't call it. If you have a problem or need to be in touch, send an SMS and somebody will contact you. You will get instructions. Money will appear a few days after each operation. Cash, probably. What's your preferred currency? Euros? Dollars?"

"Er . . . I don't know. Krónur."

The man snarled disparagingly. "Icelandic money. Please. Have a little imagination, Orri, and let's make it Euros. Your krónur are worth nothing," he said and pulled the door handle to step out.

"Hey . . . before you disappear."

"What?" The man asked, his head still inside the door and the cold wind snatching at his coat.

"This is a stupid question, right, but why are you paying me to do this stuff?"

"That's the first sensible question you've asked," the man said with a sinister smile pulling one corner of his mouth sideways and down. "Let's say you're a skilled operator and your skills are valued. We don't particularly want you to be caught and I expect you not to compromise what you're doing for me by supplementing your income with a little thieving. When you're doing a job for me, you're working only for me. Let's say it's to keep temptation at bay."

He made to pull the door shut as Orri stopped him with another question. "What do I call you?"

"Why?" He asked, and Orri saw him nonplussed for the first time.

"You know everything about me. I know nothing about you, not even a name."

"So?"

"Hey. One more thing."

"What now?" There was a trace of irritation in the scratched voice.

"I need to know, what if I get caught?"

"Caught? Who by?"

"Anyone. The police, maybe."

The man shrugged. "It's up to you."

"And if I tell them everything?"

He saw a smile tug at the corner of the man's mouth. "Orri, you can tell them whatever you like, because once it's checked out, they won't believe a thing, believe me," he said and shut the van's door. "Oh, and before I forget, here."

He handed him a plain envelope and winked, leaving Orri sweating in spite of the chill air as he watched the little blue car drive away and decided that trying to follow it might be a seriously bad idea.

They had parted coolly. Svala had been silent all morning while they looked around Ikea and there had been none of her usual chatter while Eiríkur had pushed the buggy and she had carried the baby in a sling over her chest. It had been a relief to leave her and the children with Svala's parents, who had immediately sensed the tension between them.

260

He wondered as he drove into the car park if they were even now being regaled with a litany of his shortcomings, but dismissed the thought as uncharitable. In spite of her routine of visiting them every weekend, Svala and her parents were not particularly close, and he guessed that few confidences were exchanged. Maybe that was what had brought them together, he mused as he inspected the cars parked outside the block of flats. His own parents were elderly, old enough to have been his grandparents, he'd often thought as a youngster. Both he and Svala had awkward relationships with their parents. His parents found it inconceivable that their son should be a police officer while her teacher parents instinctively distrusted authority. Eiríkur often found them difficult to understand, a couple who were happy to demand their rights but ready to denigrate the authority he felt was there to protect those rights.

There was no grey Ka to be seen anywhere in the windswept car park. Eiríkur wanted to grind his teeth at being too late, and wondered where it could have gone on a Sunday. If Elísabet Höskuldsdóttir really was a chef, then she could be at work, he decided, and told himself that he could check back later, just as his phone rang and Gunna's number appeared on the screen.

"*Hæ.* I'm on the way."

"Meet me at the station, would you? There's someone we need to pick up and it's a job that needs two of us."

"No problem. I'll be right with you," Eiríkur said, putting the car into gear and heading for the main road as a white van bumped down into the car park and stopped outside the block's door. In the mirror he caught a brief glimpse of dark green fleece jumping out of the van and into the building, and stamped on the brakes. He quickly reversed, wondering whether to follow the figure in the fleece or head for the hospital as he had been told to do.

He decided it would be as well to do as he had been told, and quickly jotted down the van's number before plugging his communicator in and driving away.

"Control, zero-four-fifty-one."

"Zero-four-fifty-one, control. What can I do for you, Eiríkur?"

"Check a number for me, can you?" he said, taking his eyes off the road for a moment as he read out the number jotted on the back of his left hand.

"White Trafic, registered to Green Bay Dispatch. All legal. Anything else?"

"Is there an address?"

"It's in Bæjarhella, out at the end of Hafnarfjördur."

"Thanks," Eiríkur said, a fist clenched and pounding the wheel in triumph.

It was Valmira's first day back at work and Emilija sounded the van's horn outside her house, concerned that her friend would not be ready to come back to work so soon, but her fears disappeared as Valmira opened the door and smiled warmly as she settled into the passenger seat.

262

"You don't want to drive like you normally do?"

"No, you drive. It makes a nice change to be a passenger." She looked closely at Emilija. "Are you all right? You look tired."

"I'll be fine. A bad night, that's all," she said, pulling away into the stream of traffic. "And you?"

"I'm fine now," Valmira said, her face hardening. "A difficult couple of days, but that's over now. Are the children keeping you up?"

"I had a visitor last night."

"A welcome visitor, or the other kind?"

"Alex."

"Alex? The guy who ate everything and then disappeared?"

"That's the one."

Valmira's mouth set in a hard line. "He's a bastard, Emilija. You know that. Did you . . .?"

Emilija sighed and nodded.

"Get rid of him, Emilija. You know he's going to let you down."

"I know," Emilija said, eyes on the road, fumbling for the wiper switch to clear spots of cold rain from the windscreen. "Alex is a shit. But he's such a charming shit when he wants to be."

"Did you do this place yesterday?"

"I did it with Natalia. It only took an hour."

"So why are we doing it again today?"

Emilija grinned. "Because Viggó made a mistake. He wrote three hours every day on the work sheet. So we do three hours every day."

"But the place was cleaned yesterday. There should be nothing to do."

"Exactly. There's a nice bakery across the road where we have a coffee and some breakfast, and get paid three hours overtime for it."

An eye appeared at the window and again as the door opened a crack.

"G'day. Is Oggi home?"

The woman with the washed-out face kept the door open only as far as the security chain would allow. She looked Gunna up and down and then her eyes quickly scanned the windows of the terrace of houses across the street, checking for her neighbours peering out from behind their curtains.

"He's not here. He hasn't been here for weeks."

"So you don't know where your little lad is, do you? Not hiding upstairs?"

"Go away. He's not here and if he was I wouldn't tell the law."

The howl of a motorcycle being revved mercilessly ripped through the air. Gunna glared at the woman and hurried around the side of the house, throwing herself flat against a wall as a trail bike screeched past, its rider yelling from behind a black full face helmet that contrasted incongruously with the battered bike.

Gunna ran after the bike as its back wheel spun in a muddy puddle in what had once been a garden, losing traction and almost stalling as Eiríkur and Gunna hurried towards it. The rider revved the engine furiously.

"You bitch! You fucking bitch! Don't let me down now!" The rider yelled, muffled under his helmet as the engine refused to give him full power, revving and dropping away. With Eiríkur only a couple of steps from grabbing the rider and pushing the bike off balance, its engine burst back into life and the bike gave a full-throated roar as it spun its way out of the mud and gripped the road surface.

Gunna stopped, panting with exertion, and clicked for her communicator. "Control, ninety-five-fifty."

"Wankers! Fuck you!" Gunna heard the motorcycle's rider scream at them, turning and cruising past them out of reach.

"Ninety-five-fifty, control."

"A red trail bike. Rider wearing a full-face black helmet, grey sweatshirt, black jeans, can't see the number. Heading towards Réttarholtsvegur. Any chance of some support?"

The bike revved again through its cracked exhaust as it picked up speed and the rider twisted round in his seat to give the hopelessly pursuing Eiríkur a single finger held upright as a token of his opinion.

"Ninety-five-fifty, control," the calm voice responded in her ear. "On the way. Is he heading north or south?"

Eiríkur stopped to catch his breath after sprinting in the bike's wake.

"Losers!" the rider shouted, but his yell became a howl of frustration as the bike's front wheel hit a broken skateboard that had been left lying by the kerb. The bike slewed to one side as the rider's single hand on the handlebars was not enough to keep them steady. Eiríkur jogged triumphantly towards the tangled heap that had been bike and rider a second before. The rider rolled from the mess, his helmet bouncing across the road. This time he howled in pain, clutching at his ankle with both hands, and Gunna saw his mother approaching as well, her front door gaping wide open as she splashed through the puddles towards him.

"Oggi!"

"Control, ninety-five-fifty," Gunna said into her communicator. "Cancel the intercept, will you? But we could do with a patrol and an ambulance. Our idiot's just fallen off his moped."

Ingi Antonsson sat in the back office of the 10–11 shop he managed and his hands shook. Gunna stood by the door with her arms folded, as if to ensure that this innocuous man didn't try to make a run for it between the aisles of soft drinks and sweets.

"You've been keeping tabs on your ex-wife for a long time, have you?"

"Since we split up. Three years."

"Any particular reason?"

"It's the children. I thought she'd leave the country and take them back to Latvia, and then they'd never see me again."

Gunna watched Ingi tremble.

"You've never been in trouble with the law before, have you?" she asked and Ingi shook his head.

"It was a guy who comes in here who said he'd scare Alex off for me. I knew Emilija had been seeing this gangster for a while and I hated my children being near that bastard. It was driving me crazy. I was losing weight, couldn't sleep."

"This guy's name?"

"I don't know his real name, but he's called Oggi."

"A little chap with a sharp nose?" Gunna asked and Ingi nodded. "Óli Grétar, otherwise known as Oggi. We know him well. He offered to frighten Alex off for you? How much did you pay him?"

"A hundred thousand."

Gunna sighed. "You idiot," she snarled. "I'd like to throw the book at you. Your pair of thugs found the right place but got to the wrong guy. So there's a man in hospital with a hand that your friends smashed with a lump hammer who has never even seen your ex-wife. So you've screwed up his health for life and Alex gets away scot-free. Well done. That's a fine job."

The blood drained from Ingi's face and he gulped air, reminding Gunna of a fish on dry land.

"What? I had no idea . . ."

"What did you expect?"

"I thought they'd just push him around a little, maybe a black eye. I never thought . . . Shit, what have I done?"

Tears cascaded down Ingi's hollow cheeks.

"Come on. Back to the station and we can get this dealt with there," Gunna said, reaching for her phone as it rang in her pocket. "Gunnhildur."

"Laxdal. Where are you? We have a problem."

The white van was still parked outside, rain pattering on its roof as Eiríkur shrugged himself deeper into his coat.

"I've been here before somehow," he complained.

"How so?" Geiri asked, hunched forward over the wheel to look through the drops of rain on the windscreen at the block of flats.

"Knocking on doors to find out which apartment some deadbeat lives in," he said glumly and passed a print of the CCTV image of the man in the green fleece to Geiri in the front seat. "That's what he looks like. We don't have a name, but we know where his van's registered and presumably that's where he lives."

"Pick him up at his work?" Tinna suggested.

"As the van's here and it's a Sunday afternoon, I think we can be sure he's not at work," Geiri said, trying not to sound acid. "Come on. Let's make a start, shall we? There are eight flats in the block, so we start at the ground floor and work upwards."

Eiríkur checked the lobby first, noting down the names on the mailboxes and hoping to see Elísabet Sólborg Höskuldsdóttir's name there, though he wasn't surprised when it didn't appear anywhere, before walking around the building outside to check for the fire escape that a building of this age didn't have.

268

Eiríkur was already in conversation with a sharp-faced elderly woman on the block's first floor as Geiri and Tinna came up the couple of steps leading to the landing.

"Keeps himself to himself, that's all I know," the sharp-faced woman said. "I like to mind my own business and not interfere with other people, but he's an odd one, that Orri."

"That's his name? Orri?"

"Orri Björnsson. That's his name, all right. Up there on the third floor on the right."

"Do you know if he's at home?" Eiríkur asked.

"I haven't seen him go out."

"And I'm sure you've been keeping an eye out. Come on, let's see if your friend's at home."

There was no answer as Geiri rapped on the door.

"Police!" Eiríkur yelled. "Open the door, please. I know you're there."

"Nobody home," Geiri muttered in disappointment and turned to go, but Eiríkur stayed put, hammering on the door.

"What now?" Geiri asked.

"Either he opens the door, or we stay here until he or his girlfriend shows up," he said, banging the door yet again. "Orri Björnsson! Open the door, please. Police!"

He stared intently at the door and was rewarded with the briefest flash of movement behind the spyhole.

"I know you're there, Orri. Open the door," he called. The lock rattled and the door squeaked as it opened.

"Orri Björnsson?" Eiríkur asked needlessly and the man nodded as he looked back, his face composed.

"Yeah, that's me. Sorry, I was asleep and didn't hear you knocking. What can I do for you?"

Bára opened the door to the suite at the Harbourside Hotel.

"Where's her ladyship?"

Bára looked at her watch. "She's been in the bathroom for just over forty minutes now."

"And no sign of Jóhann?"

"Nothing so far. No replies to calls."

"And what does Sunna María make of it? Is she worried?"

"It's hard to tell. I've only seen a little of Jóhann, but they make an extremely odd pair. He's fifteen years older than she is and they've both had a string of affairs over the years."

"She told you that?"

"After her fourth Baileys on the rocks yesterday afternoon," Bára said with a grimace. "In detail. She told me how she was the other woman who wrecked his first marriage and since then she's been determined not to let anyone wreck hers. So they have a tacit agreement and they both play discreetly."

"But they stay together for the sake of the money?" Gunna asked. "How sweet. So Jóhann was last seen on Friday and only now she decides she wants to make a song and dance of it? What the hell's going on?"

Bára cocked an ear. "She's out of the bathroom, so she can tell you herself."

270

"I'm wondering how concerned she is about Jóhann. It doesn't seem right to me. She should be frantic by now. I would be."

"She's a cold fish, I think. Either that or she can bottle it all up or compartmentalize things very effectively. Their accountant was here yesterday and she was as bright as a button. You wouldn't have imagined for a second that her husband had just walked out and that she should have been worried witless."

"Good morning, good morning," Sunna María said, breezing into the room with a smile that looked as if she had carefully put it on. "Any news?" she asked, giving Gunna a steely gaze and pouring herself coffee.

"I was going to ask you that."

"Nothing."

"Are you concerned? Why are you in such a rush to report your husband missing now?"

"What kind of a question is that? Of course I'm concerned."

"You didn't seem concerned on Friday. Has this kind of thing happened before?"

"That's an intrusive question."

"Your husband walked out of here unexpectedly two days ago and you haven't seen or heard from him, which doesn't sound like normal behaviour to me. So you can see why I'm trying to make sense of this, can you? Has this happened before?"

Sunna María stood with her back to the window, saucer in one flat hand, coffee cup held delicately in the other. She was dressed for business, an ivory blouse buttoned to the neck and a fine silver chain artfully arranged over it.

"Jóhann and I had a row on Friday after you were here, if you really must know," she said, and Gunna could sense her gritting her teeth at the admission. "Normally that ends with one or other of us storming out, and this time it was him. It's not the first time and I don't suppose it'll be the last."

"Are you telling me you're not worried about him?"

"He's never been away more than twenty-four hours like this. And by the way, I'm checking out of here today and going home."

"You're reporting Jóhann as a missing person?"

"Yes. He took his mobile phone, his passport and credit cards, but he should be back by now. I'm hoping he's fine; he's probably holed up somewhere comfortable for a few days while his temper settles. He might even be on the next floor," Sunna María tittered and the cup in her hand rattled musically against the saucer.

Gunna stood up. "In that case, I'd appreciate it if you could let me know what your movements are. As far as I'm concerned, there's still an element of danger as the killers of your business partner haven't been identified."

Sunna María flashed pearl-white teeth. "Come on. This is Iceland. People don't kill each other in Iceland."

The photograph of the little pile of gold lay on the table between them.

"It was my mother's," Orri said simply, hardly looking at it. "I needed the money, so I sold it."

"This was stolen from a house in Kópavogur a couple of weeks ago. The owner has identified it as hers and we have pictures of her wearing it, which prove it had been in her possession. So how did you get hold of it?"

"Like I said, it was my mother's and she had it from her mother. They're both dead now. It came to me from my mum's estate and I just left it in a drawer for years. Then I needed the money so I sold it."

Eiríkur sat back and surveyed Orri Björnsson. There was no bluster to the man, just a quiet, dogged refusal.

"You're going to have to come up with a much better story than that," she said. "The evidence is against you. The clasp's owner has identified beyond any reasonable doubt that it's hers and she has pictures to prove it."

"Then the shop has fucked up somehow. I sold this stuff, but I didn't steal it."

"The woman in the shop has identified your photo as the seller and we have CCTV images of you going to the shop that bought this stuff."

"Really? You mean you have some pictures of me walking along a street?"

"Close enough, Orri. It ties in with the shop manager's statement. So why the false name? Who's Halldór Birgisson?"

Tinna looked up from the kitchen cupboards. She had emptied every cupboard and drawer while Geiri watched impassively. There were packets of porridge and the usual items you would expect, as well as exotic things — galangal, chillies and fresh ginger — things that Eiríkur reflected played a limited part in Svala's cuisine.

"Not a lot," Tinna said in answer to Eiríkur's unspoken question.

Eiríkur nodded. "Living room next."

This time they switched roles. Geiri and Tinna together went carefully through every drawer in the old-fashioned dresser while Eiríkur sat with Orri and watched for his reactions while he asked questions.

"So I don't get a lawyer, then, like they do in the movies?"

"I told you the moment you sat down that you have the right to a lawyer at any stage of the proceedings."

Orri shrugged. "Whatever. I haven't been arrested, have I?"

"Not yet. Why did you give a false name to Aunt Bertha when you sold the clasp?"

"I suppose I thought they might declare it to the taxman and I already give the government enough of my cash."

"Good answer, Orri. But not good enough. You still have to convince me and you haven't done a great job yet."

"It was Mum's. She's dead now and it came to me."

"What are these for?" Eiríkur asked as Geiri placed a set of lock picks on the table.

Eiríkur thought he saw the briefest flash of concern in Orri's eyes as he saw the picks, although he hid it well and shrugged.

"I've had those for years. Somebody gave them to me and they've been in that drawer ever since."

274

"Who's this?" Eiríkur said, pointing at a picture of a woman with facial features so similar to Orri's that they had to be relatives. Apart from a Bruce Springsteen poster that Eiríkur had seen tacked to the back of the bathroom door, the woman with her two children in their Sunday best was the only picture in the place that showed any people.

"My sister and her kids," Orri said.

"You have a sister? I'm wondering why something like a gold clasp for a set of national dress would go to you rather than to your sister?"

"I don't know. The old woman didn't give us anything much."

"When did your mother pass away?" Eiríkur asked as Geiri went down on hands and knees to check under the sofa

"She didn't pass away. She rolled a car on Hringbraut and broke her neck when I was seventeen," Orri said savagely. "She never had a lot of time for us and I don't miss her, and neither does my sister as far as I know."

"You work at Green Bay Transport, right?"

"Green Bay Dispatch."

"What do you do there?"

"Drive the van, drive the truck, drive the forklift, stack boxes on pallets, listen to the old guys whine about how great the old days were. That kind of thing."

"Done," Geiri announced, standing up. "Let's take a quick look at the basement, shall we, before we go to the station?"

He shivered and gnawed at the fish. Once he had eaten most of it, he knew that he would have to use the strength it gave him to get more from the rack. This time climbing the rough triangular frame at the end was easier and he came down with four fish, which he put on the table in the old kitchen.

It was the glittering of the intermittent sunshine on the stream as he bent to drink that gave him the idea. He gathered handfuls of dry grass and in the most sheltered spot he could find he made a small pile on top of the dried skin of the cod he had just eaten. Desperately trying to recall what he had learned as a scout fifty years ago, he held his glasses between the sun and the dry grass, experimenting to focus a spot of light and finally watching a wisp of smoke rise from it.

The grass smoked and died. Jóhann cast about for more grass, added it to the pile and tried again, cursing as the sun vanished behind a cloud. He waited impatiently for it to return, collecting handfuls of heather and some crumbling sticks of rotten timber from under the racks of fish.

As the sun appeared again, he set to, kneeling over the kindling and concentrating on keeping the bright spot focused in one place until it smoked and smouldered. Remembering long-forgotten skills, he lay full length with his face inches from the ember and blew the gentlest of breaths on it until tiny flames appeared, which he fed with more clumps of grass. Finally tongues of flame ate hungrily at the handfuls of dry heather he added to the little fire.

The slivers of wood were quickly devoured and Jóhann realized that the fire would burn itself out if there were no more fuel. In spite of being light-headed from hunger, he hurried back to the racks and gathered as many splinters and offcuts of wood as he could, using his shirt held out in front of him as a basket.

The flames demanded constant attention. More grass and more heather were needed constantly until the fire gained strength enough for bigger pieces of wood to be added and these sent up acrid smoke. Inside the old house he hunted for anything that would burn and a smashed window frame in one room became more fuel as he huddled as close to the glowing warmth for as long as he could, eventually retreating inside as darkness fell and wrapping himself in the overcoat once again.

Gunna found the number of the taxi she had written down and it was the work of a few phone calls to track down Snorri Helgason. She found him at the bus station with a mug of coffee and a doughnut that he had sliced carefully into cubes.

He shrugged as Gunna showed him Jóhann Hjálmarsson's picture.

"Maybe. It's been busy these last few days. You sure it was me?" He asked with a supreme lack of interest, popping a morsel of decimated doughnut into his mouth.

"Friday morning, outside the Harbourside Hotel. A few minutes after eleven."

"Could be, darling. What's he done?"

"I'm not your darling and if you don't start remembering, we might have to take this down to the station."

"Whoa, no offence, darling." Snorri Helgason's eyes widened and he rapidly backed off. "I'm due back on the rank in ten minutes when the bus from the north gets in."

"Then start remembering quickly."

"Picked him up outside the hotel, like you said."

"A call or were you waiting?"

"I was just in the queue. I stopped and he got right in."

"Did he say anything? Where did he want to go?"

"That's all he said. 'Ármúli, thanks.' Then he sat there with his nose in his phone and didn't look up until I asked where on Ármúli he wanted to be dropped off."

"And?" Gunna said, not bothering to mask her impatience.

"He didn't want Ármúli at all," he said with satisfaction, chewing another chunk of doughnut. "He wanted to go round the corner and I dropped him off outside that big block on the end instead, the one next to the hotel there."

"Did you see him go inside?"

Snorri Helgason shook his head. "He paid in cash and walked off, still looking at his phone. He went that way, but I didn't see him go inside."

Gunna's heart sank. The block was at least nine storeys high and she guessed that it housed dozens of offices, any one of which could be where Jóhann Hjálmarsson had been heading.

"And he didn't say anything?"

"Only 'keep the change'. That's all." He smiled, showing off a gap between his teeth. "So what's he done?"

"Listen to the lunchtime news and you'll find out," Gunna said, handing him a card. "If you remember anything else, call me."

The first security guard was an overweight young man with dead eyes. His reservations were overcome by Gunna's warrant card, throwing his hands in the air in despair and calling his supervisor when asked for security tapes. Ten minutes later a flustered but slightly less corpulent young man appeared, shaking off a jacket that was a size too big for him. He checked Gunna's identification before closing the door to pointedly shut out his junior colleague.

"What can I do for you?" He smiled ingratiatingly.

Gunna produced the picture of Jóhann Hjálmarsson. "I have reason to believe this gentlemen walked in here a few minutes after eleven o'clock on Friday morning last week. So, to start with I want to get that confirmed as I see you have a CCTV camera covering the entrance, and then I'd like to know where he went and what he did."

"Oh, right." The young man's fingers flickered over a computer keyboard and he called up footage of the lobby. People walked back and forth with speeded-up steps, oddly foreshortened by the camera looking down on them. It took a few minutes to identify Jóhann Hjálmarsson walking in with a jaunty step and a smile on his face. Gunna was surprised that a man with a price on his head should look so cheerful as he walked through a set of revolving doors and out of the frame.

"Now what? Where's the next camera?"

"By the lifts," the young man answered and the image switched to a bank of doors as people entered and left. He speeded up the replay and caught Jóhann Hjálmarsson entering a lift on his own. "There you are. He went upstairs at . . ." He peered at the screen. "Eleven fifty-one."

"And you have cameras on the other floors as well?"

"No, we don't. Individual companies can do that for themselves. We just watch who goes in and out. What happens up there is their business."

"So there's no way of telling which floor he went to?"

"No, I'm afraid not."

"Hell."

"Well, not as such," he said, and he went back to the computer. He recalled the footage of Jóhann Hjálmarsson getting into the lift and ran it slowly. The doors closed and he pointed at the indicator.

"Your friend got in the lift on his own, so you can see the light above the door? That's the number of the floor."

"I can't see the number, it's not clear enough."

"Look. It's on one for ground there. So if you watch the indicator, it flashes every time there's a new number."

They both watched intently as he slowed the replay down and counted.

"I make that eight," he said finally. "It hasn't moved for a while, which means the lift stays where the last person got out, until it's called to go either up or down."

"And what's on the eight floor?"

Orri sat back in the interview room chair, his hands in the pockets of his fleece.

"Nice sweater," Eiríkur said, looking at the logo on the right side of the chest. "Where did you get it?"

"It's my girlfriend's. It's too big for her, so I wear it."

"It's distinctive, isn't it?"

"I suppose so," Orri said, the distrust in his voice coming to the surface as he wondered where this was leading.

"I have it on very good authority that someone wearing a fleece exactly like this one, including that distinctive logo, was seen on six occasions walking along Kópavogsbakki in the last couple of weeks."

"Kópavogsbakki? Where's that?"

It was Eiríkur's turn to sit back. "Nice try, Orri. You're a driver. Don't try telling me you don't know every street and alley in the city, including Kópavogsbakki."

"So what? There must be hundreds of fleeces like this one around."

"Not so. The Kjölur Equestrian Club in Selfoss had a hundred made about five years ago and they still have about half of them. So that means there are another fifty in circulation, and more than half of those women,

281

I'd guess. That means that at a rough guess there are twenty-odd men with fleeces like this, most of them living near Selfoss and with no reason to be anywhere near Kópavogsbakki."

Orri shrugged and said nothing. Eiríkur leaned forward and looked into his eyes. A flash of uncertainty appeared and was immediately hidden as Orri regained his impassive expression.

"I need to borrow your fleece for a few minutes."

"Why?"

"We need to compare it with what our witness claims to have seen."

"And if I say no?"

"Up to you. You haven't been arrested, so you have every right to," Eiríkur said. "But it would confirm for me that you're lying through your teeth."

With a sigh of resignation, Orri pulled off his fleece, emptying his pockets of keys and oddments as he did so, and hung it from one finger to hold it out.

"There you go."

"Thanks. I'll be right back."

"No luck," he said. "I've watched the whole footage for the rest of the day and the guy you're looking for hasn't come out of the building. At least not before five o'clock."

"There's only one exit?"

"There's a service entrance."

"And a fire escape?"

"The service exit is the fire escape," he said. "It's an old building."

"Right, but first you were about to tell me who's on the eighth floor of this building."

Gunna left the lift and stepped into a wide corridor with glass doors to the right and left. On one side the door had "Ath!" etched into the glass in a splash of lettering that looked as if it had been done with a broad brush. On the other side the opaque glass of the door was etched with an image of a schooner under full sail, which she guessed must have cost a fortune. There was a group of companies sharing office space and the names were immediately ones she recognized with a feeling that she should have spread her net wider and earlier.

The doors were firmly locked on Blue Steel Investment, Sólfell Investment, Blue Steel Management, Bright Spring Shipping and Sólfell Property. She rattled the door and rapped on the glass, but although there was a distant light on somewhere deep inside, nobody came to answer the door. A distant telephone that nobody answered rang for a long time inside and finally gave up. After half a minute's silence the ringing resumed, and Gunna decided not to wait for anyone to answer it.

Back downstairs the security guard had reached the end of the day's recordings.

"The door's locked at six and people use the service entrance to get out," he explained.

"And if someone needs to get in?"

"Then they call whoever they want to see, and they'll have to go down and open the service door for them."

"And there's no CCTV at the back."

"I'm afraid not. People aren't supposed to use the service entrance for day-to-day stuff, and hardly anyone does anyway, so I suppose we don't worry about it."

"Maybe you should. After all, it's the people who don't want to be seen that are the ones you might want to check up on, not the law-abiding types at the front."

Orri got out of the police car and slammed the door without a word. He scanned the car park and saw with relief that Lisa's car was nowhere to be seen. He had no desire to spend any time evading her questions and made for the stairs just as the door of the bottom floor flat creaked open.

"The police were here today," the sharp-faced woman who lived there told him with satisfaction. "I suppose it was you they were looking for?"

"I expect you know damn well it was, you nosy old bitch," he snapped at her without breaking his stride and took the flights of stairs three steps at a time. "And I bet you showed them the way," he called back down.

He locked the door behind him, kicked off his boots and soaked in the shower, washing away the smell of the police station and that sarcastic bastard who'd asked all the questions. Sitting on the bed and drying himself carefully, he told himself to think straight. The police had found him through that stupid clasp he should never have sold like that, he decided; he should never have allowed himself that moment of sentimentality.

He wondered if he should contact the Voice and tell them what had happened. Maybe the Voice would leave him alone if he thought he was a risk?

He shivered at his recollection of the steel in the Voice's measured tones he had heard in the cellar of that house on Kópavogsbakki. There was no mercy there, no room for doubt. If they thought he was a risk, just how ruthless would they be? He decided that he should just tell them he had been questioned. He wouldn't mention that the police had placed him on Kópavogsbakki.

Call me, he wrote in a text message to the number the Voice had given him. We might have a problem.

The back of the building bore no resemblance to the glass and steel of the front. An unloading bay for catering trucks ended with a steel roller door that was firmly shut and a set of double doors next to it. A couple of cars were parked close up against a wall, but otherwise there was a windswept space that was empty on the office block's side. On the far side of the yard was the back of a row of shops, some of them little more than a blank wall with a door set in it, others sporting grimy windows, but every one of them with a huge bin on wheels outside.

Gunna walked along the row, looking hopefully for CCTV cameras, but none was to be seen anywhere. Each door also had its own quiet smoking spot out of the glare of the customers at the front, with a scattering of cigarette butts on the ground or an ashtray neatly placed by the step.

The sight gave her a pang in the centre of her chest that was instantly dispelled by the smell as she walked along the row of doors. At the end she stood in thought as one door finally opened and a man in a grubby white apron stepped outside, lighting up and taking a deep drag on his cigarette. He did a sudden double take on seeing Gunna stalking towards him in the glare of the security light and she could tell that an innate sense told him of the presence of the police.

"G'day," he offered, cautiously rather than with any outward sign of nerves.

"*Hæ.* You work here, do you?" Gunna asked.

"No, officer, I just come here for the fun of it."

"Sarcasm will get you nowhere, I'm afraid. Tell me, what's on the other side?"

"This place, you mean? It's a sandwich bar. Lots of offices round here and hungry office types after their decaffeinated sandwiches and free-range coffee."

"But quiet on a Sunday evening, surely?"

"Not as busy," the man admitted, jerking a thumb at the office block opposite. "But we do a good few takeaways and you'd be surprised how much business there is at weekends with all those suits and flunkies doing overtime."

"Were you here on Friday? Around midday?"

"I was. Why? Who's asking?" he said with a sour note in his gravel voice. "Not that I can't guess."

"You've probably guessed right. City police, CID. And you are?"

"I'm Finnbogi Finnbogason. I don't suppose you're here to do a health and safety inspection?"

286

"Far from it. But I'm hoping you might be able to help me."

Finnbogi Finnbogason looked back at her with narrowed eyes as he drew deeply on his filterless Camel. "Go on."

"How many shops are there in this row?"

"Half a dozen. Why?"

"Smokers in every one?"

His face creased in suspicion. "Near enough, I reckon."

Gunna jerked her head towards the block of offices that towered over them. "I'm wondering if you see much of what goes on next door, comings and goings from that place."

"It happens. A good few people use the back door as a shortcut, and there's a guy from the insurance company on the fourth floor who leaves arm-in-arm with his secretary while his wife's sitting in her car out the front waiting to catch them," he said with a laugh as dry as rustling paper. "She'll figure it out one day, and that'll be worth watching."

Gunna took out the picture of Jóhann Hjálmarsson from her pocket. "I'm looking for this man; he probably came out of that door sometime on Friday."

Finnbogi's eyes narrowed even further. "And what's he done, may I ask?"

"You may ask if you like, but I reckon you know I shouldn't tell you. Let's just say that we're concerned about his safety. It's no secret. He'll be on the evening news tonight."

This time his eyes widened. He dropped the butt of his cigarette and quickly ground it out under his toe. "Dead?"

"I hope not. I'm looking for when he came out of there and who was with him."

"I didn't see anything."

"No, but you could ask around among the staff and the people who work in the other shops."

His lip curled. "You're asking me to do your police work for you?"

"Not at all. I'm asking you to be a public-spirited citizen who doesn't want an unexpected visit from environmental health. I'll drop by tomorrow and see what you've found out." She handed him a card. "Or call me if you find something."

He shook his head and grinned, as if accepting defeat with good grace. "Strange women giving me their phone numbers doesn't happen every day, sweetheart," he said, tucking her card into a pocket and patting it. "I'll give you a call if I hear anything. Hell, I might give you a call even if I don't hear anything," he added with a lewd wink.

"Eiríkur let him go?"

"He did," Gunna said. "We could have arrested and charged him for the theft of the clasp that came from Aunt Bertha."

Ívar Laxdal looked dubious. "And why didn't you?"

"What's the hurry?" she asked, looking up as Eiríkur came in and hung his coat on the back of his chair. "We can pick Orri Björnsson up whenever we want, but all we have to charge him with is an offence that will get him a suspended sentence, and that's assuming it even gets to court."

"You have all the evidence."

"We do, but a smart lawyer could argue that the old lady is too senile to know what day it is or that there's a reasonable likelihood that Aunt Bertha could have mixed things up," Gunna said. "Plus, he's worried now. He knows we're interested in him and I'd like to keep him worried."

"It's up to you, Gunnhildur. I'd have charged the bastard and made it formal, myself."

"That's not a problem. We can pick Orri up and charge him whenever we feel like it. Eiríkur, I hope you don't feel you've had a wasted day?"

"What? I've watched that evil bastard Oggi fall off a motorbike and break his ankle. That's a great day as far as I'm concerned."

Gísli looked more uncomfortable than Gunna thought she had ever seen him before, his broad shoulders hunched as he sat on a stool in the corner. She felt a sudden pang at the sight of him, the uncertain, lonely teenager suddenly brought back to life as if he had never been away, but instead of the skinny boy there was a brawny man with a goatee in the corner.

Soffía and Drífa sat together on the sofa, chatting animatedly.

"Wow! How many stitches?" she heard Drífa ask Soffía as she pushed open the door to see plates and cups all over the table, Laufey spooning yoghurt into

Kjartan Gíslason and Steini lying on the rug tickling the soles of a laughing Ari Gíslason's bare feet. The only one who didn't seem to be having a great time was Gísli in the corner.

She stood silently in the doorway for a moment and took in the scene of her two grandsons together in the same room for the first time. Gísli was the first to look up and notice her. He stood up and went across to wrap his arms around her.

"*Hæ*, Mum. I tried to call you yesterday," he said as his embrace slackened and Gunna regained the breath he had squeezed out of her.

"I know, sweetheart. I'm really sorry, but everything's gone arse-shaped at work these last few days and I didn't have a chance to call you back."

She perched on one of the stools by the little breakfast bar and poured herself a cup of coffee. Gísli sat next to her and did the same as they watched Laufey and Steini play with the children, while the two girls seemed to be sunk in conversation.

"Are you all right, Gísli?" Gunna asked, the hangdog look on his face stabbing her through the heart as she appreciated the turmoil he must be going through as a result of the same sight that brought her so much pleasure.

"Yeah, I'm OK, I suppose," he said with a wry smile that showed just the opposite. "Been working a bit too hard recently."

"You're still on the freezer, are you? They kept your berth open, didn't they?"

"Sailing next weekend."

"A shame you couldn't finish college."

"I know. But there are mouths to feed now and I can go back next winter and finish."

"Make sure you do," Gunna said, patting his hand. There were hundreds of questions she wanted to ask, but this was neither the time nor the place for it. Gunna desperately wanted to know which of the two girls he planned on staying with, assuming that either of them still wanted him. She imagined that the sharp and independent Soffía would have some serious reservations on that score.

"Thanks for looking after Drífa and Kjartan, Mum. I know she's been as lonely as hell away from her own family."

"I gather she still hasn't spoken to her mother yet," Gunna said in a murmur as their heads came close together over the coffee cups.

"No. I had a call from her, though."

"From Ranna?"

"Yep. She was very drunk and absolutely steaming with rage. Called me all the names under the sun."

Gunna took a deep breath. "That's no big surprise. Ranna's never been what you might call even-tempered."

"I really screwed up, didn't I?"

"You could say that."

"You're not angry?"

"Gísli, of course I'm upset. But there's nothing I can do about it now except make the best of it. I can't turn the clock back and I can't make things any different. Look, you have two handsome boys. The

291

circumstances might have been easier, but just be satisfied that they're both healthy and being looked after properly."

Gísli sighed. "I suppose you're right, Mum."

"It's up to you to make sure that you stay part of their lives and don't just fade into the background."

"Like my dad did, you mean?"

It was as if an electric current had jolted through her.

"Yes," Gunna said with gritted teeth. "I'm afraid your father wasn't much of a role model, was he?" She paused. "Why? Have you seen him?"

"Not for a while," Gísli admitted. "I know you didn't want me to, but I did go and find him a couple of years ago."

"And?" she asked with trepidation.

Gísli shrugged. "To be honest, I wish I hadn't taken the trouble. He wasn't particularly interested. I went to visit him a couple of times and felt I was more of an embarrassment than anything else. His wife wasn't impressed."

"She didn't appreciate a long-forgotten child from her husband's past showing up all of a sudden? I can't say I'm surprised. And I'm even less surprised that he wasn't interested in seeing you. He didn't want to know all the years you were growing up. Oh, and if you do see him, you can maybe tell him that he still owes me about fifteen years' worth of maintenance."

"Really, Mum?" Gísli's brows thickened in dislike as his eyebrows merged into one dark line across his forehead. "If I'd have known that, I wouldn't have bothered at all."

292

"It's probably best you did," Gunna said, patting his hand again. "Just don't follow his example, all right?"

He awoke with a clearer head. The headaches of the previous days had gone and Jóhann decided that the withdrawal symptoms from his life-long caffeine habit had dissipated remarkably quickly. There was no buzz in his ears. The low sun was peeping over the distant hills and today's stronger wind from the west brought a tang of the sea.

This time lighting a fire was a quicker job and he was determined to do it before the sun rose into the clouds and out of sight. He hurried to collect grass and the lumps of off-cut wood that the men who had built the huge drying racks had dropped.

Jóhann cursed the lack of any tools. He needed something more substantial than his fingernails to split the wood and fell back on pounding them with some of the round grey rocks that were everywhere until pieces came away. The dry grass smoked into life and he lay flat to blow the fire into flames, which he nurtured with handfuls of heather until it was burning robustly enough to be given pieces of wood.

He threw everything on the fire, deciding against keeping any wood for later. Today was the day to leave, he decided, gnawing at one of the dried cod he had snatched from the racks the day before. The only worry was would it rain? It was something he had never had to think about before. Rain could be an inconvenience between the car and the door, or something that could mean bringing the party indoors. It had never occurred

293

to him before that a good shower of rain could kill him rather than being just an occasional annoyance on the golf course.

Leaving the ruined farm would mean abandoning shelter, such as it was. Wearing only the office clothes he had been in when he left the Harbourside Hotel and the filthy overcoat he had woken up in, he was painfully aware that these would give him little protection against the weather. A decent downpour could result in hypothermia and a quick death out here in the wilderness.

Maybe that was the intention? He had tried to avoid thinking about what had happened to him, preferring to concentrate on survival, but now, with the fire burning merrily in the lee of the wrecked house and a half-eaten fish in his hands, those thoughts came flooding back to him.

He had gone to the lawyer's offices as he had agreed to. He had taken a taxi that turned up as if it had been called for him, but that was not unusual outside a busy hotel. He would probably have just walked, he reflected, if the taxi hadn't turned up, and wondered if that might have made a difference in some way.

Someone he knew had been there, he was sure of that. Had anyone else been present? It was hard to be sure. He wasn't even sure who, but somehow the man's ridiculous moustache had remained fixed in his mind. Jóhann suddenly felt tired and sat back against the rough wall of the farmhouse as thoughts of Sunna María flooded into his mind. Would she be missing him? Would she be distraught? More likely, would she

294

simply be angry, he wondered, clawing at his memory for fragments that might tell him what had happened. And what about Nina? She would worry at his unaccustomed silence and that knowledge gave him a pang of deep regret.

Through all this, the question that burned was why? Why had they dumped him up here in the wilds to die? If the intention had been to do away with him, why had they not done it quickly? Why transport a man to the back of beyond to starve?

Gunna arrived to find an impromptu conference in progress. Sævaldur's face was redder with frustration than she had ever seen it, and Eiríkur quailed in the face of his fury while Ívar Laxdal mediated.

"I don't call it poaching from under your nose, Sævaldur," he said quietly, fingers entwined into a bridge below his square face. "I'd be more inclined to call it an excellent piece of police work that gets you closer to the villain you've spent weeks looking for."

"Months I've been chasing this housebreaker, and this lad whose balls have only just dropped turns up on a Monday morning and gives me his name and phone number?" He gurgled and coughed, sitting down and pounding his chest with a fist to get his breath back. "It's a bloody cheek," he said finally.

Ívar Laxdal took off the glasses he wore for reading and pointed with them, emphasizing his point. He looked up to see Gunna.

"Gunnhildur, we have a minor disagreement."

"Problem, boys?" she asked, taking off her coat as Sævaldur spluttered.

"Your boy has only gone and found the bastard I've been after for months," he said. "And then let him go."

Gunna sat down and opened her notes on the table in front of her.

"We could have charged him yesterday, in which case he would have been released anyway within a few hours. We have all the evidence, witness statements and the rest of it. We know where he works and where he lives. So what's your problem? A golden opportunity for you to gather evidence and build a convincing case, I'd have thought. Or did you just want to gloat over him for an hour or two before you'd have to let him out anyway?"

"Don't talk shit, Gunna. I'd have made the little fucker sweat and confess everything he'd ever done from primary school onwards."

"And then watched him walk out of here," Gunna said, trying not to sound sarcastic. "Now. Alex Snetzler. I've just had a visit to the hospital on the way here and apparently the guy who lives in the flat is called Alex. He's from Latvia, the same as Maris." She looked up. "Eiríkur, have you filled Sævaldur in on our broken-fingered Latvian?"

"I haven't had a chance," he said in a hurt tone.

"In that case, Sæsi, for your information, a Latvian called Maris had all the fingers of one hand smashed by Big Oggi and his brother the other night. The interesting thing is that we found a pile of stolen goods in the flat, mostly electrical. The flat is rented by Alex.

Maris was only staying there temporarily while he was looking for a place of his own, or so he says, and it seems certain that we're looking at mistaken identity here."

"Alex?" Sævaldur demanded with a growl. "There's a lowlife called Alex who works for a freight company down at the other end of Hafnarfjördur who's definitely been fencing stolen gear. That's someone else I've been trying to get my hands on for a while."

"A link between a thief and a fence?" Eiríkur mused. "What could be more convenient? Guess where our Orri works?"

Green Bay Dispatch was quiet on the outside, while once inside the big sliding doors Gunna could feel the tension. An elderly man with a scarf around his neck yelled from the seat of the forklift at two men stacking boxes onto a pallet and a thickset girl in a high-viz vest over a bulky fleece marched past Gunna into the building and offered a curt greeting on her way.

"G'day," she said and made for the forklift.

"Hey," Gunna called after her. "You work here?" she asked as the woman turned.

"Just for today. Why?"

"I'm looking for the manager. Any idea where he is?"

"That's who I'm looking for as well. You're agency?"

"Not quite," she said as the elderly man jumped down from the forklift and hurried over to them.

"I'm Dóri. Looking for me, are you?"

"It seems we're both looking for you," Gunna said.

Dóri dug in his pocket and handed the muscular girl a set of keys. "Ragga, isn't it? You've been here before, so you can take the flatbed. It's loaded and fuelled, and the key is in the cab. We'll sort out the paperwork afterwards," he said in a rush.

He turned his gaze on Gunna and wiped a bead of perspiration from his forehead. "And what's your name, sweetheart?"

"I'm Gunnhildur."

"All right. We're a van down today so I'll have to give you the lunchbox instead."

"Lunchbox?"

He jerked a thumb at a small, square van outside. "We'll have to use that one. Just be careful not to overload it. We can do without any attention from the police."

"In that case, I'd better let you know that I'm not here as a relief driver. I'm from the police."

Dóri looked her up and down, noticing the uniform trousers and deflating as his shoulders sagged.

"Hell. Just what I need. What can I do for you, in that case?" he asked with exaggerated courtesy. "Two of my guys haven't showed up this morning and it's bloody bedlam, in case you haven't noticed."

"Hence the agency driver, I presume? Well, this may take a while, but it's because of your missing guys that I'm here."

"Mind your backs!" a voice yelled and Dóri stepped smartly to one side. A forklift whizzed past, missing Gunna by inches.

298

Her eyes narrowed. "And I suggest that you tell that clown to slow down; I'll have his licence off him if he comes that close again," Gunna snapped. "Now, where can we go that's quiet?"

She followed Dóri past the closed office door and into the canteen, where paperwork was spread over one table and cups and plates were strewn over the other.

"What does this company do?"

Dóri sat at the table that served as a desk and glared at her with suspicion. "We move stuff."

"Tell me more, will you?"

Dóri sighed and pushed aside a stack of computer printouts. "We have two lines of work. One, we transport fish. That goes by air and it's simple. We turn up at a factory, the boxes are loaded and we take them to the airport in a refrigerated truck where they go onto a plane and go to somewhere in Europe, normally Belgium or Germany."

"And the other line of business?"

"That's general cargo. If somebody wants something moved, then we move it. It could be a spare part for some machine that has to go to Kópasker, or it can be the entire contents of someone's house that has to be moved abroad. There's been a lot of that these last few years with the middle classes deserting the sinking ship," he added.

"You do everything?"

"We can. If necessary we can turn up and pack up a whole house into boxes, put it all in a container and have it shipped to wherever. But most people just get a container parked outside their house and load it themselves."

"It's your staff I'm interested in, especially Alex and Orri. I believe they both work here. They haven't turned up today?"

"Orri has yet another of his frequent appointments with the dentist this morning, As for Alex, well . . ."

"Let's start with Orri, shall we? How long has he worked here?"

"Longer than I have. Five, six years. Something like that."

"You get on with him? What sort of a character is he?"

"He's all right. We get on fine because normally he's reliable. There's an occasional lapse, but not often," Dóri said and sat back. "He keeps to himself and doesn't say a lot."

"You mean he's unfriendly?"

"No. I mean maybe he values his privacy. He keeps to himself and isn't chattering all day long like some I could mention."

"How about his private life?"

"It's just that," Dóri said shortly. "Private. It's none of my business and I don't ask. I know he has a girlfriend although I've never met her. I know he had a difficult relationship with his family, but I don't know any details. That's just what I've put together over the last few years from odd remarks, and to be honest, I'm not comfortable sharing this stuff with the police."

"Does he strike you as being short of money? Has he ever said anything about that?"

"No. Not that I recall. Look, what's all this about? I'm answering all your questions and maybe I deserve a little information in return?"

Gunna sat back as Dóri folded his arms, elbows on the desk as he rested his weight on them.

"I can't tell you much. It's not that this is classified stuff, but I'm hunting for information. All I can say is that both their names have come up in connection with investigations."

"Separate investigations?"

"No comment." Gunna smiled without getting one in return. "Now tell me about Alex. Where's he from?"

"Latvia."

"He has an identity number?"

Dóri extracted a sheet of paper from the pile on the table, turned it over and pushed it in front of Gunna. "They're all legal here. Nothing on the black."

"Pleased to hear it," she said, jotting down Alex's number and noting that the flat where the attack had taken place was his legal residence. "He's a good worker?"

Dóri grimaced. "He's all right. He's not punctual. He's a cocky little bastard, to tell the truth."

"And he keeps his job in spite of that?"

"Arrogance is not a sacking offence."

"But not showing up for work on time can be if you do it often enough."

"Maybe, but that's not my decision."

"Maris Leinasars. Does that name mean anything to you?"

Dóri shook his head. "That's not a familiar name," he said after a moment's thought.

"And where's Alex today? At the dentist as well?"

"Who knows? He's not here and that's all I can tell you."

"You're the manager here?"

"I'm the foreman. If I was a manager, I'd have an office and wouldn't have paperwork all over the canteen would I? If you can't tell me what these two jokers have been up to, you could at least let me know if they're likely to be at work tomorrow, or are you determined to lock the pair of them up?"

For a quiet, exclusive street, Kópavogsbakki hummed with unaccustomed noise and activity. Men in blue overalls and carpenter's tool belts swarmed over one house while a concrete truck was parked at the side of the other site further along, its drum revolving while its driver stood next to it, eyes hidden behind sunglasses and his jaw rolling a piece of gum in time with the concrete drum's slow revolutions.

Gunna squeezed the car past the vans parked by the road and stopped further along where things were quieter.

Bára answered Sunna María's door.

"Morning," Gunna greeted her. "How's her ladyship?"

Bára wrinkled her nose. "She's all right. Confused and worried."

"Well, take me to her, then."

Sunna María had a phone at her ear and another in her hand, and her eyes bulged for a second as she saw Gunna appear in the doorway of her long, sparse living room.

"Yes, of course. I'll settle that at the end of the month as long as we're ready for the next stage," she said, jaw firm and her words clipped. She stabbed at the phone to end the call and put the other one to her ear. "Listen. I said Monday, not Wednesday, and not Monday next week," she said in the same brusque tone. "No. As soon as possible. That's right," she said and ended the call before looking at Gunna.

"What can I do for you?" she demanded.

"Any news of your husband?"

"Nothing. I haven't a clue where he's gone. He's walked out. That's what I think."

"Leaving his laptop on the table? Did he take his passport? Credit cards?"

Sunna María looked blank for a second. "I don't know where his passport is, so I assume he took it. Of course he had his wallet and cards in his pocket, and I'm sure he can find himself a new laptop easily enough."

There was a road of sorts. It was deeply pitted and ran mostly downhill, which Jóhann hoped meant he was heading for the coast, facing the distant faint tang of salt water as he walked through a tranquil landscape. The track looped several times. At one point he decided to take a short cut, scrabbling down a loose scree of red earth and stones over a slope that was frighteningly steep once he'd started down it, but as soon as the loose earth had begun to crumble under his feet, there was no way back. Jóhann tottered and fought to stay upright, bouncing the last few yards downhill on his back, terrified that his precious glasses would be lost as more loose stones rattled down the slope and came to rest around him.

He sat dazed in the little landslip that had deposited him on the road sixty yards from where he had started, having saved himself half an hour of walking, he guessed, but at the cost of having ripped the sole from his right shoe, which now flapped as he walked, attached at the heel but with loose stones and gravel now constantly under his foot.

He stopped and sat on a boulder. He laid aside the overcoat he'd wrapped around himself like a cloak and took off his jacket. He picked at the seams of his shirt, a flimsy item that was fine for city wear, but had no practical use out here. He gave up trying to unpick a seam with his broken fingernails. He took off the shirt and ripped both sleeves clear off, one after the other, surprised at his own strength and the noise it made in this quiet landscape.

With the now sleeveless shirt, jacket and overcoat back in place, he used the sleeve to tie up his shoe, hoping it would last as he set off yet again, picking at one of the dried fish he had filled his pockets with before leaving the ruined farm.

The track widened gradually and even became enough of a road to sport a makeshift bridge over a bubbling stream where he stopped and drank. A little further along he encountered a dilemma in the form of a crossroads where he knew the wrong choice could prove fatal. The sun was high in the sky behind grey cloud and he guessed that at least half of the day had gone. He would need to find some kind of shelter for the night if no help could be found before dark, and to start a fire he would need sunlight as well as fuel, and hunting for fuel would be a time-consuming task up here where nothing but moss and heather grew.

He studied the road, trying to work out which direction looked to have been the most used, and therefore more likely to carry some traffic and the possibility of a lift to civilization. Downhill was tempting as that had carried him this far, but this time the uphill direction was the one that seemed more likely to take him seawards, judging by the vague smell of the sea.

It would have to be uphill, he decided, promising himself that at least this would give him a vantage point to spy out the land, and if there was nothing up there, he could at least turn round and hobble back downhill instead.

A pair of coal-black ravens flapped slowly past and Jóhann felt that they were looking for him, waiting for him to give up as he trudged towards the brow of the hill.

Stepping out of the lift on the eighth floor, Gunna immediately saw the familiar nameplates etched into glass in sharp letters in a door that was locked up tight in front of the still darkened office. She knocked and tried the door, and then wrote down the names of half a dozen companies listed below Sólfell Investment's name on the window.

On the other side of the lift a more inviting door stood open. There was no indication what business Ath! was in, but smooth musack played from a loudspeaker overhead and there were brochures on an unattended reception desk. A stylish computer gleamed on a table to one side, and with no keyboard to be seen, there were just two words visible on the screen.

Gunna touched it with her fingertip, as the words had commanded, and the computer's screen dissolved into a cascade of pixels that resolved themselves into the Ath! name. She was nonplussed by the images of smiling professionals with perfect skin, hair and teeth that paraded across the screen, extolling the virtues of Ath! and was still none the wiser by the time the presentation had ended and the screen had returned to its former shade of blue with the words "Touch Me" emblazoned across it.

"I'm sorry to keep you waiting. Can I help you?"

A smiling young man in a polo shirt had appeared behind the desk, the shirt embroidered with the same Touch Me logo in discreet stitching on one arm.

"What is this place, then?" Gunna asked. "What does Ath! actually do?"

"We're a communications solutions provider."

"Public relations, you mean?"

"Well, yeah. If you want to be old-fashioned about it," he said with a hurt look on his face. "PR, advertising, that sort of stuff."

"I'm looking for the people who run the company next door. Are they about anywhere, do you know?"

The smile faded. "You're a bailiff?"

"Far from it. Police."

"Oh. I've no idea. I think the guy who runs it is out of the country at the moment and I haven't seen his secretary for a long time."

"How many people work there, do you know?"

"There's a few of them who come and go, I think. I don't pay a lot of attention. There's the guy with the moustache, the little one with the grey hair and there's a blonde woman who's there occasionally."

"You know their names?"

"The grey guy is called Elvar, I think. Haven't seen him for a while. I don't know about her."

"Anyone else who shows up there regularly?"

The young man made a show of thinking hard. "There's a cleaner. She's here once or twice a week. Then there are a few other people who come and go. Like I said, I don't pay them much attention."

"When did you see anyone there last?"

"End of last week, something like that."

"Friday?"

"Could be."

"And was that Elvar or the blonde?"

He shook his head and pouted. "I'm not sure, the moustache guy, I think. There were voices, so there must have been more than one person. That's all I could say. I don't sit here all day watching out for next door."

"I didn't expect you would. But why did you ask if I was a bailiff?"

"Because you wouldn't have been the first one."

The couple of restaurants and takeaways were lit up for the start of the lunchtime trade and as she parked behind the office block on Ármúli again, the smell of something spicy wafting from the open door behind one of the shops suddenly told her that breakfast had been a long time ago.

Finnbogi Finnbogason sent her a smile as she walked in.

"You're not here to order a taco, are you?"

"Depends what you've found out for me."

"I'm a little busy at the moment. See you round the back in a few minutes?"

"Can do. I don't have long."

"I'll be as quick as I can," Finnbogi said, hands busy behind the counter. He handed her a closed carton with a plastic fork tucked into a loop in the paper handle. "Here. Something for the wait."

"What's that?"

"Beef with noodles and pad thai sauce."

"How much is that?"

Finnbogi shook his head. "Don't worry about it."

"I shouldn't."

"It'll go in the bin otherwise."

The aroma from the carton that sat hot in her hands was overwhelming. "All right, but sell me a bottle of water to go with it, will you?" She said, digging for change in her coat pocket.

"So how were the noodles?" Finnbogi asked when he found her ten minutes later. He sat next to her in the car, the same grubby apron folded in on itself and stowed between his knees. He spied the empty carton in the footwell.

"Excellent," Gunna said. "I don't normally do quite that hot and spicy, but that was great," she said, swigging from the bottle of water and feeling the heat still on her lips. "I hope you've had a few minutes to chat with the other smokers along here?"

"Yeah."

"And?"

"Not a lot. We've seen the same people as always come and go. But there's a guy who works at the chicken and chips shop along the street. He said he saw a van on Friday afternoon that he hasn't seen before and it was being loaded with a lot of stuff, as if some company was moving out."

"What time?"

"Mid-afternoon, he said."

"I don't suppose he got the registration?"

"No idea. I'm not a copper. You'll have to ask him yourself. He should be at work now."

For the first time, Jóhann wondered if it was hopeless. He sat on a rock at the side of track that stretched away into the distance behind him and debated with himself whether or not to turn back to the crossroads. He longed to do it, and somewhere inside a nagging feeling told him he had gone wrong.

The day was drawing on and there was no sign of any shelter anywhere in this bleak landscape. He looked up from the fish and saw with surprise that a pair of black eyes were staring curiously back at him before their owner looked quickly to one side and ran.

Other than an eagle that had circled high in the sky earlier in the day and the malevolent ravens that he felt were dogging his steps, the sheep was the first living thing he had seen. He wanted to despair but made himself stay rational, forcing himself back to his feet to continue.

Now he was looking for shelter. There were spots of rain falling, pattering on the overcoat wrapped around his shoulders. The landscape stayed blank. The road itself was better, almost wide enough for two vehicles, but not quite, and he listened for the rumble of tyres to tell him that someone was on the move.

The road that had dipped began to climb upwards again, and with it the temperature fell until he reached the top of a small pass and saw a sight that gave him extra strength. The land dropped away slowly and in the distance he was sure he could see the sea, while the wind blowing off it convinced him.

Now he was walking faster, his broken shoe flapping loose once again as the track showed signs of recent traffic and the new marks of heavy tyres cut deep into the soft sides of the road. As the road rounded a rocky escarpment, a sight greeted him so welcome that he gasped with relief. A steel hut had been erected on a patch of ground cleared from the rock, its door firmly padlocked, and next to it was a digger and a bulldozer.

310

Everything looked as if it had been untouched for days or even weeks, but it was at least a sign of activity and that there had to be a road, a real road, not that far away. Now it was starting to get dim and there was a threat of real cold rain as the drops began to fall with a heavy smack.

The digger and the bulldozer were both locked. Heavy padlocks swung from hasps on the cabs. He turned his attention to the steel shed, which had a similar lock hanging from a steel loop that held a metal plate flush with the door. He rattled the lock hopelessly and cast around for a tool of some kind, any tool that could help him break in. But the road menders had cleared up well and there was nothing to be found. It was as if they had swept, hoovered and polished everything before leaving, he thought bitterly.

It had to be a rock. Over by the road he found several that looked suitable, heavy enough to do some damage but light enough to be handled. Repeated blows on the lock began to twist it and the first rock he had brought eventually fell apart in his hand. The second fared better and the padlock began to look decidedly unhealthy by the time the rain started hammering down. Jóhann shivered, pulled the overcoat over his head like a hood and attacked the lock with a frenzy he did not know he had in him, battering it until he had to give up through exhaustion, dropping the rock at his feet.

As he was ready to give up and crawl under the bulldozer for shelter, the door swung open and he saw that the padlock had survived the onslaught but the hasp itself had been battered clear from the door. Inside the rain beat furiously on the roof as Jóhann curled up in a corner of the dim interior and gnawed on the last rock-hard piece of fish.

The man was tiny and Gunna felt that she towered over him with the glass door between them. His jet-black hair was shorn in a ragged crew cut under the white hat and his black eyes were impassive.

"We closed," he said shortly, hand on the door.

"I'm not looking for lunch. Are you True?"

She saw his eyes flicker left and right. "You police, right?"

"I'm from the police, yes," Gunna said.

He opened the door and Gunna had the feeling he wanted to hurry her inside and out of sight.

"Finnbogi along the street said that you saw something unusual on Friday. Is that right?"

"We go out back," he said, picking at a pocket inside his white tunic and extracting a cigarette. Outside the back door he patted the pockets of his checked trousers until he found a lighter and clicked it repeatedly. Eventually he exhaled a long stream of blue smoke into the damp air. He pointed at the loading bay.

"There," he said. "This isn't going to be trouble for me?"

"No trouble," Gunna assured him.

"Big car. Van. A man fill it with stuff."

"When was this?"

"Friday. They were here some time. Two, three hours. Boxes, bags. All kinds of stuff."

"Can you describe the man?"

"Tall. But everyone is tall in Iceland," he said with the first hint of a smile.

"Young? Old?"

"Middle-old. Forty-fifty. Grey, with big nose."

Gunna took out the photo of Jóhann Hjálmarsson and True peered at it. "Is that him?" she asked, knowing already that the description would not fit.

"No. That's the drunk man."

"Drunk?"

"Yeah, There was a drunk guy hanging around. He sat on the wall and talk to the guy with the van."

"Did you see where he went?"

"No. I come out, smoke, see him. Next time I come out here, he was gone. Didn't see him again."

"But this is definitely him?"

"Yeah. That's him. He was really drunk that day. He could hardly stand up," True said with disgust. "In the middle of the day, and he didn't look like a loser."

"I don't suppose you remember the van's registration?"

"No, sorry."

"Anything special about it? What make?"

"It was a hired van."

"How do you know?"

True looked at her as if the question was a particularly stupid one. "On the side, Borg Vehicle Leasing. Big letters."

It was far from warm in the steel hut, but Jóhann reminded himself that it was much warmer and more comfortable that it would have been outside with the rain beating down at intervals. The wind moaned as darkness fell, rattling the roof and occasionally showers lashed the hut with a deafening onslaught, magnified by the bare steel roof. It wasn't night yet, but the thick black rain clouds had blotted out any sunlight and it felt much later than it probably was. He huddled deeper into the stinking coat that he felt had probably saved his life, and now that he was at least under cover and somewhere within striking distance of civilization, his mind wandered to how he had found himself in this situation.

He fought to reach elusive scraps of memory that were probably only a few days old but which felt as if they were in the distant past. Jóhann wondered why he had gone out, leaving Sunna María with the blonde security girl with the tight bottom and an air of competent menace about her at the hotel. He was sure of that, and sure that they were thought to be in some kind of danger. He recalled that Vilhelm had been murdered and he shivered, although he had never liked the man much. He had been a friend of Sunna María's, just like Elvar; boys from some small fishing village who had made a pile of money selling scrap tonnage before they'd made the pile bigger by making the tonnage work instead of scrapping it.

He felt that Vilhelm had always been a dangerous friend to have, someone with only one real aim: to make money by any means, watchfully sizing up the world around him through those frameless glasses and attaching a mental price tag to everything he saw. Elvar

314

was much the same, he decided, more easy-going on the surface, but with the same ruthless drive for cash underneath.

He thought fondly of Sunna María and hoped that she was missing him, or at the least, was worried about him. She had been deeply upset by the violent death of her friend and he could tell that she was far from her normal self, preoccupied and her thoughts clearly not on him in the few days between his return to Iceland and his disappearance.

They needed a holiday. It was time to reconnect, he told himself. There had been lapses on both sides and he assumed Sunna María imagined that he had no idea about her occasional fling with a young man and on one occasion with a brash young woman. He wondered if Sunna María was aware that his own lapses had all been long ago. He felt that she distrusted Nina, the German widow he had been doing business with for some years importing dental equipment, and he was sure that Sunna María felt there was something more there than a business relationship.

Jóhann admitted to himself that a few years earlier he would have jumped on Nina joyfully and added a notch to the respectable number on his bedpost, but he was an older man now and he valued Nina's friendship as well as her business, and business and pleasure rarely mix, he told himself, his mind straying back to somewhere warm.

Greece, maybe, he decided. Once he got back to Reykjavík he would book a couple of weeks on some island in the sun where they could sleep and read, drink rough wine, eat simple food and cement their faltering relationship before it was too late. There were more important things in life than business, money and expensive toys, he told himself as he nodded off to sleep under yet another assault on the hut's tin roof.

The man looked older than Orri remembered from their only previous meeting. The bushy moustache looked greyer and the artificial light of the shopping centre accentuated the lines on his face.

He stirred sugar into his coffee and smiled at Orri in a way that made him look sinister rather than friendly.

"Tell me the story, Orri."

"All of it?"

"I'm a good listener."

"The police have been asking me questions. They reckon I sold some stolen jewellery to an antique shop."

"And did you?" the man asked, sipping his coffee with his little finger cocked at an absurd angle.

"Well, yeah. I did."

"I recall advising you to keep out of trouble."

"This was before. Weeks ago."

"I see."

He sat for a long time holding his coffee cup in front of him, looking past Orri's shoulder at the window behind him. Orri wondered what he was thinking and what needed so long to consider.

"You know this place better than I do," he said suddenly. "What do you think? Do you think they may have linked you to anything else? Note that I'm not asking what else you might have on your conscience."

"I don't think so. I've always been very careful and I don't take chances unless I have to."

"But you did that time? Why didn't you dispose of the jewellery through your usual routes?"

Orri opened his mouth and closed it again. He thought quickly and wondered if the man would understand that the gold clasp reminded him of the grandmother who had been there for him when his own mother had no time for her children. The thought of something so old and precious being melted down had gone against the grain in a way he couldn't explain and which had also taken him by surprise. He twisted uncomfortably in his chair and looked behind him, pretending to see if they were overheard.

"Nobody's eavesdropping on us, Orri."

"I'm getting paranoid," he said with a short laugh, having seen nothing except a man reading a tablet computer on the far side of the otherwise empty café.

"Where do you usually dispose of your merchandise?"

"Through someone reliable."

"Someone at your workplace?"

Orri stared, wondering where else this strange man would cheerfully wrongfoot him. "Could be."

"You are aware that Alex works for the owners of Green Bay Dispatch and he does a little freelance work on his own account?"

"What? How do you know?"

"Let's say that we are aware of Alex and what he does."

"So you're from Latvia as well?"

A smile flickered under the moustache. "Very clever, Orri. You're a smart operator," he said and his face returned to its previous stony expression. "As I said to you before, don't ask questions when you're better off not knowing the answer."

"Fair enough."

"But now that you're here, I have another job for you." With one gloved finger he pushed a box and an envelope stiff with notes across the table. "Take care. Don't take chances. Withdraw if you feel it's safer, but send a message to me if you do. Understand?"

"Understood," Orri said, in spite of his misgivings eagerly pocketing the cash in a swift movement that didn't escape notice.

Ívar Laxdal stopped her outside his office, his brawny arms folded over his chest. "I don't believe in coincidence. Everything happens for a reason."

"True enough. But people's paths can cross by chance," Gunna said. "But I can't help being worried about all this."

Ívar Laxdal looked long, hard and unnervingly into Gunna's eyes, snapping his fingers in thought and looking away a fraction of a second before she was ready to give in and blink.

"In what way? What worries you more than usual?"

"You know as well as I do that the local criminals sell homegrown dope and home-made booze. The Baltic types deal in speed. They both do burglaries and all kinds of stolen-goods scams."

"Yes. And?"

"I'm hoping there isn't some kind of turf war brewing. One crowd or the other looking to steal the other's business. That's what's worrying me."

"Because it would get nasty?"

"Exactly. I like a quiet life, and if it happens, we'll be right in the middle."

"Is there anything you need? Do you want to recall Helgi? I feel that you should."

"Helgi will be back next week anyway. I could do with a few things that I'm not allowed, but traces on a bunch of phones would be useful. Apart from that, I'd just appreciate it if you could keep Sævaldur out of my hair."

"I can do that. Give me the names and numbers and I'll get the warrants as soon as I can."

Gunna scribbled in her folder and handed him a slip of paper. "I'd love to be able to put a tracker on Orri's car, but I guess that's against the rules?"

Ívar Laxdal allowed himself a wintry smile. "I'll do what I can, but don't expect too much, Gunnhildur. Don't expect too much."

"I'm hoping that this isn't the start of a feud between the local underworld and the Baltic villains. That really could be a nightmare."

Ívar Laxdal nodded sagely. "A shame we can't just sit back and leave them to it, isn't it?"

CHAPTER
ELEVEN

Orri's car was nowhere to be seen, but Eiríkur was pleased to see that Lísa's car was parked outside the brooding block of flats.

"You're from the police?" she asked in surprise. "Why? What do you want with me?"

"You live here now?" Eiríkur asked, ignoring her question. "I have your address as Stafholt nineteen?"

"Yeah, well. I still live there, but I'm here a lot of the time."

"You recognize this?" Eiríkur asked, showing her a picture of the green fleece and its distinctive yellow logo.

"Yeah. I used to have one like that."

"Where did it come from?"

"A riding club I used to belong to before I moved to Reykjavík. Kjölur. It's near Selfoss."

"And where's the jacket now?"

"My boyfriend wears it mostly," she said with a twitch of her lips. "I, er . . . I lost a lot of weight after I moved to Reykjavík and it was just too big for me. You know?"

"So now Orri Björnsson wears it instead?" Eiríkur asked.

"If you already know, then why are you asking me?"

"How long has he been wearing this fleece, would you say? A couple of weeks? Months?"

Lísa stared at him in confusion. "Do you mind telling me what this is all about?"

Eiríkur looked at her closely. He could make out the tiny scar on her lip where she had once worn a ring through it.

"It's been identified in connection with a crime. So how long has Orri had this fleece to wear?"

"I don't know. A few months. When the weather started getting cold after the summer."

"September?"

"Something like that."

"How long have you known him?"

"A couple of years. A little longer, maybe. Why are you asking me all this stuff? Is Orri in trouble?"

"What are his movements like? Does he have regular habits? Do you know where he is all the time?"

Lísa's lip curled in anger, while inside there was the nagging reminder that no, she frequently had no idea what Orri was doing or where he was, and then there were the mysterious texts and phone calls that Orri carefully kept to himself.

"We lead our own lives. I don't own him," she snapped.

"So he keeps regular hours, does he? Tucked up in bed by midnight every night?"

"If he's working the next day, yes. He starts at seven, so he has to be gone by six thirty."

"He drinks? Smokes? Takes drugs?"

"A glass of wine or a beer sometimes. He doesn't smoke and he certainly doesn't do any drugs."

"You're very sure."

"I've been practically living with him for long enough," Lísa said coolly. "There's an old boyfriend of mine who had trouble in that respect, so I think I'd recognize the symptoms."

Eiríkur closed his notebook. "I'd like to take a look round the basement."

Lísa shrugged. "The key's on the hook by the door. Help yourself."

"You'd better come with me."

Jóhann woke with the dawn light creeping through the half-open door. He felt chilled to the marrow and faint with hunger, regretting not having made the effort to carry more of the dried fish with him from the abandoned farmhouse. It took him a while to drag himself to his feet and his legs felt weak.

Outside the hut the fresh breeze made him shiver. He wondered what the time was, and then wondered what day it might be. The last day he remembered before waking up on a bed of straw had been Friday, but he had no idea how long he had been out cold there. One day, or two? No more than two, he decided, and then tried to work out how many days he had been at the farm before walking away from it.

He knew he could hardly be far from the sea, as a producer somewhere had taken the trouble to fill those racks with fish for drying, so somewhere not that far away had to be a harbour with fishing boats, but how far? Not far for a truck or a car could be an impossible distance for a starving man with leaking shoes. He had no idea how far he had walked the day before, but it felt like a million miles. His legs ached, both from the unaccustomed exercise as well as from malnourishment, and he forced himself to face the fact that if he did not find help today, then his chances of survival were probably as good as zero.

Jóhann wondered briefly what he looked like and ran a finger over the stubble on his face. He tried to remember the last time he had started a day without shaving and smiled as he realized that Sunna María would hardly recognize her husband after only a few days without access to all the usual luxuries they took for granted.

He rummaged in his pocket and pulled out his phone. He switched it on and watched with excitement as it started up. The screen appeared for a couple of seconds, the phone buzzed, flashed a warning signal and switched itself off, but in that moment he had seen that the time was just after seven and that he was within signal range. He couldn't be that far from civilization, surely? But which way?

The day was greyer even than the day before with spitting drops of rain from spent clouds that had emptied themselves overnight, leaving the road outside the hut running with red water thick with dust. He turned round slowly, trying to gauge through his cracked glasses where the sun might be behind the grey, and decided that uphill would again be the most likely direction as he set off, his shoes immediately filling with water.

Lísa pulled on a shapeless sweater with baggy sleeves longer than her arms and went down the stairs, her wooden clogs clicking on the concrete. The ground floor flat's door opened a whisker and an eye peered out as they passed.

"Nosy old bitch," Lísa muttered to Eiríkur, just loud enough for her voice to carry.

In the basement she opened the storeroom and stood in the doorway with her arms folded while Eiríkur went through the drawers of the dresser, examining the old trinkets, worn-out tools, an obsolete computer and even a pile of ancient schoolbooks.

Lísa shuffled her feet after a while. Eiríkur opened all of the cardboard boxes in a stack and found nothing but old clothes and shoes.

"It's his mother's stuff," Lísa said. "I've never understood why he doesn't throw it all away."

"She's dead, right?"

"Yeah. A long time ago. He was quite young."

"He doesn't talk about his upbringing?"

"What are you, a psychologist?"

He stepped out of the storeroom and let Lísa lock it and pocket the key. "No, but I'm trying to get a picture of a person who is much more complex than he might appear on the surface. That's all."

She went up the stairs, arms still folded and Eiríkur followed behind.

324

"Is there anything else?" Lísa asked as they stood in the lobby by the mailboxes, making it plain that she had no desire to answer any more questions.

"No, that's everything for now."

"So Orri's in the clear now, is he?"

The ground floor flat's door had been left ajar and Eiríkur jerked his head towards it. "I'll be in touch if there are any questions," he said and pulled open the heavy outside door just as someone else pushed it from the other side. An elderly man with a stick and a carrier bag came in, rain dripping from the brim of his hat, which he tipped to them both as he passed.

"G'day."

"Morning."

The man stopped on the third step and turned stiffly. "Lísa, my dear, would you ask Orri to come and have a word with me when he's in from work?"

"Yeah. No problem. He should be back around four today."

"That's wonderful," the old man said, already on the next step up. "It's just that we need to settle up for the store that he rents from me downstairs."

"Excuse me, what did you say?" Eiríkur asked as Lísa's jaw dropped.

Eiríkur and a uniformed officer stood under a single dim bulb by the storeroom with the elderly gentleman who was still wearing his hat. Lísa stood by the stairs, her arms folded tightly around her and a bewildered frown on her face.

"You're telling me you knew nothing about this?" Eiríkur demanded.

"Of course not. That's Orri's storeroom there," she said, pointing with an arm that did not extend beyond the end of her sleeve at the storeroom they had already examined twice.

"And this one?"

"Hell, I don't know. That's between Orri and . . .?"

"Steinar," the old man said politely. "Steinar Atlason at your service," he added with exaggerated old-fashioned courtesy, looking at Lísa with a twinkle in his eye. "And you are?"

"You know who I am," she retorted.

"What's the story, Eiríkur?" Gunna asked, appearing in the doorway and not delighted at being called to Orri's basement storeroom again.

"It seems that Orri has more than one storeroom down here. This gentleman says that now he's a little unsteady on his legs, he doesn't use his storeroom any more and he actually rents it to Orri, which Orri conveniently forgot to tell us about."

"Your young man is quite right," Steinar chipped in. "I can't get about like I used to, so my son cleared my storeroom out and this young lady's husband asked if he could use it. For a consideration, of course," he added. "Now you're not going to tell the minister of finance about this arrangement are you? To my mind he wastes enough taxpayers' money as it is and I've no intention of giving that young fool any more."

326

"Don't worry. Your secret is safe with us," Gunna assured him. "But I'd appreciate it if you'd open the door."

"I can't. Orri put his own lock on there."

"Lísa, do you have the key?"

"There isn't one."

"No key?" Eiríkur said.

"If you look carefully, you'll see that's a combination lock," she said with a sour expression. "And no, I don't have a clue what the combination is. You'll have to figure that out for yourselves," she said over her shoulder as she made for the stairs, her arms still wrapped around her.

"This is definitely your storeroom?" Gunna asked old man.

"It is."

"You have any objection if we look inside?"

"Well . . ." Steinar Atlason looked uncertain. "It's young Orri's belongings that are in there, so it would be wrong to open it without his permission as well."

Gunna scratched her head and wanted to bark at Eiríkur.

"It's up to you," she said. "If this gentleman agrees, then you can get an angle grinder and have that lock off right now." She saw the uniformed officer brighten at the chance of doing some damage. "Or you can seal the store now, fetch Orri and get him to open it in your presence, which might be a better way of going about things," Gunna said, turning to leave them to it.

"But now I'm going up there for a word with Lísa, and to make it clear to her that calling Orri right now to tell him the law's on his doorstep isn't a helpful move. Let me know what you find in there."

"I let Bára go," Sunna María said. "I don't feel I'm in any danger."

"It didn't occur to you to let us know that you'd dispensed with your protection?"

"No," she replied crisply. "I don't feel there's any hazard to me. I don't need protection in my own house, thank you. But what I'd really like to know is what you're doing to find my husband."

"Without knowing where to look, it's not easy to mount a search," Gunna said. "And I recall that a few days ago you weren't worried about your husband and didn't seem keen on the idea of the police looking for him. Do you maybe know something now that you didn't yesterday?"

Sunna María stared back at Gunna blankly. "I don't know what you're talking about," she said finally. "The last few days have been . . ." she paused as if looking for the right word. "Stressful in the extreme. If I gave the wrong impression, then I certainly didn't mean to."

Her phone rang and she stalked to the desk below the window of the long living room to snatch it up.

"Yes," Gunna heard her snap. "Just get on with it. All right, another four per cent is acceptable, but that's my last word. You know how far behind schedule all this is already?"

Gunna looked out of the window and watched as a mixer truck pulled up. The driver got out and lit a cigarette. A cloud of cement dust seemed to envelop

328

him as he stood and waited. A man in blue overalls appeared and they both looked through a handful of documents, gesturing and pointing animatedly.

"I'm sorry," Sunna María said without any apology in her voice. "Things are getting busy and there's a lot to be doing."

"The construction work?"

"Yes. The house that's weatherproof is for someone else but I'm acting as the owner's agent. The other one's ours. Work stopped last year when it started to get cold, but it's warmer now so they can get to work on the foundations."

"Another one to let?"

"Or sell. It depends on the market once the roof's on and the windows are in."

Beyond the construction site along the street, white horses danced on the sound between Kópavogur and Gardabær.

"I'm wondering why work is starting just now, with your husband missing."

Sunna María drew herself up and opened her mouth to speak, but stopped herself and thought. "It has taken a while," she said eventually. "I've been negotiating with the contractor for weeks. The original construction company went bankrupt at the end of last year, so I had to find a new one, and they finally started on Friday."

"And the finance?"

"I have enough to keep business afloat, thank you."

"Who's this guy?" Gunna demanded, unfolding a sheet of paper she had taken from her pocket while Sunna María was on the phone and pointing to an indistinct passport photo of a hawk-faced man with swept-back hair looking at the camera with amusement from behind a bristling old-fashioned moustache.

"I . . ."

Gunna watched Sunna María's confusion, determined not to miss anything she might let slip in her surprise.

"I've really no idea." The moment's hesitation told Gunna more than Sunna María had wanted to let slip. "Why? Who is he?"

"That's what I'm wondering. I'd be interested to know how he rented a van for two days last week and paid with a credit card belonging to Sólfell Property. Jóhann Hjálmarsson's credit card. After all, it's not as if they look alike or as if the names on the card and this man's driving licence even match, but as the hire company didn't look closely, off he went with a van."

"I honestly have no idea," Sunna María protested weakly. "If I could tell you, I would."

Gunna folded the paper back into her pocket.

"Intriguing," she said, looking out of the window at the occasional drop of rain hurled against the glass by the wind. "I feel like a walk, so I might have a look at your construction site."

He trudged almost in a daze. The hunger cramps had abated, kept at bay with mouthfuls of water from the streams that clattered through the rocks. Jóhann stared at the grass by the track, wondering if grass could be eaten or if it would just make the ache in his belly worse. He remembered hearing somewhere that Iceland was a nightmare country for vegetarians, with a cuisine that consisted largely of lamb and fish. Nothing other than potatoes would grow in Iceland's short summer, but at least there was enough grass and heather to support all those sheep.

He spied a couple of scruffy ewes watching him with suspicious eyes from far up the slope and he wondered if he could catch one, dismissing the thought immediately. He had no idea how to kill a sheep even if he were to catch one, let alone how to turn a dead sheep into something edible. It was the wrong time of the year for any kind of berries and he guessed it would be too early for the eggs of ground-nesting birds.

The ravens had returned and he was certain it was the same mean-eyed pair that had followed him the day before, always somewhere in the distance as the track had gone up hill and down. Jóhann knew that his strength would not last. Sooner or later he would have no choice but to sit by the side of the track and wait for someone to come to him instead of using up precious energy trying to find help before it was too late. He was uncomfortably aware of a clock ticking in the distant back of his mind.

He thought of Sunna María, imagining her concern, daydreaming of her voice and the throaty laugh he loved to hear as her clothes slipped to the floor. He still liked the idea of a week or three in the Mediterranean sunshine once he had got to safety, but it was now the idea of safety, a square meal and a night's sleep that was preoccupying him more than the thought of a holiday.

Deep in thought, he hardly noticed the cattle grid until he stumbled and fell, one foot twisting in the process as he cried out in pain and swore to himself.

He sat by the side of the road with his back to a fence post as he massaged his ankle and it was some time before he realized the significance. A fence post meant a wire fence snaking off into the grey distance, and that had to be a sure indication that he had to be somewhere close to human habitation. In spite of the nagging pain in his ankle, which he told himself he could not afford to worry about, Jóhann felt buoyed up by the thought that a fence meant a farm somewhere nearby. Now he felt it was just a matter of time before he found himself sitting in a farmhouse kitchen with breakfast in front of him.

The track went steadily downhill in a gentle gradient, allowing him to see the landscape far ahead when breaks in the weather allowed. Jóhann had never before had to deal with weather. Weather was something that people outside worried about and he was coming to the conclusion that the elements were far more important than he could ever have imagined in his comfortable city cocoon that allowed him to shut out the climate at the touch of a button.

As the track rounded the curve of a hill and there was still no friendly pastel-shaded farmhouse roof anywhere in sight, his euphoria began to ebb as his ankle throbbed. He dared not stop or rest for fear that he would not be able to start off again. The ravens seemed to be there all the time at the edge of his field of vision and he felt they were coming closer, stopping to perch on rocks as he hobbled along the pitted track. He was sure they were waiting for him to falter and he pulled the ragged overcoat tighter around his shoulders, promising himself that if the worst came to the worst he would wrap it around his head to protect his eyes from the razor beaks that would go for the softest target.

"You can't come in here without a helmet, sweetheart," a man in a yellow vest, his own helmet perched on top of a woollen hat, told her.

"I think you'll find that I can," Gunna said, showing him her identity card.

"Oh. In that case I suppose I'd better watch what I say. The lads are all legal," he added as Gunna marched past him.

"How far have you got?"

"Still doing the footings. The ironwork's all in place and we'll start pumping the rest of the concrete in a minute. Then the princess will have her foundations," he said with a gap-toothed smile that gaped from ear to ear.

The site stretched away across a patch of ground scraped from the slope. The basement of the house had been dug and shored up with rough plankwork and a lattice of supports ready for the walls to be poured.

"When was this dug?" Gunna asked.

"Last year some time. Gvendur Bjarna started the job, but then he packed it in. Had a heart problem and had to shut up shop, plus I hear there was a liquidity problem somewhere. So in we came."

"By princess, I assume you mean Sunna María?"

"That's the lady. The fashion icon in person. She's been keeping us on our toes."

"Why haven't you been here earlier?"

"We would have been here a month ago, but it's taken the princess a while to stump up the cash." He tapped his nose. "Not that I know anything about that. You'd have to talk to the big man about all that stuff."

He followed as Gunna strode through the mud around the edge of the new building, looking into the trenches with a layer of fresh concrete in the bottom, from which brown iron frames and blue plastic pipes sprouted.

"When was that done?"

"Yesterday. That's just to anchor the metal before we fill in."

Gunna turned to face him. "When's that supposed to start?"

"Right now. The mixer truck's here."

"In that case, I'm about to ruin your whole day. Do you want to tell your princess or shall I?"

Everything was wet and as darkness fell, floodlights illuminated everything with a harsh, unearthly brightness. Gunna huddled deep into her parka and felt rain drip from the rim of her helmet onto her shoulders. Sunna María watched from the sidelines on her side of the police cordon, her furious discomfort palpable even from a distance.

"Gunnhildur."

Ívar Laxdal's appearance always caused people to sit up straight and take notice. She had observed the

334

phenomenon many times and the sight of Eiríkur and the others unconsciously straightening their clothes and their backs as Ívar Laxdal entered the room always made her smile. He unfolded a printout and handed it to her.

"From Riga, with love."

Boris Vadluga's slim, crop-headed face stared out at her in the light of her torch. There were intelligent cornflower-blue eyes, the skin crinkled around them as if he had smothered a smile to provide a straight face for the camera.

"A good-looking man," Gunna said appreciatively.

"That's as may be. A very smart businessman with fingers in a great many pies. He's into logistics mainly, trucks, shipping, containers."

"Does he have a record?"

"As clean as a whistle," Ívar Laxdal said. "On the surface, at least. He has investments in Iceland and Denmark and spends a lot of his time in Copenhagen these days. He's big in fur as well."

"Fur?"

"That's it. Mink. He has a mink farm in Denmark and has been involved with one here as well. On the other hand, I gather he's the elusive partner in Sólfell Property and his connection with Iceland is largely due to his relationship with guess who?"

"Vilhelm Thorleifsson and Elvar Pálsson?"

"And the dentist and his lovely wife."

"I see. Anything on Alex Snetzler or Maris Leinasars, or even the mysterious Juris?"

"I've already emailed it all to you," he said. "The famous Alex has plenty of form, minor violence, drugs, burglary, handling stolen goods and all the rest of it, a really pleasant character. Maris, nothing at all. He's a failed medical student, no criminal record, but his association with Alex and the fact that he's been on Boris Vadluga's payroll means he has been given some attention. As for Juris, not a word. He doesn't appear to have returned to Latvia."

"Hell," Gunna swore. "And there's no record of anyone of that name leaving the country. "So if he didn't leave . . .""

"Another body somewhere?"

"I hope not. We have enough as it is, thanks. And the other man, the one with the nose?"

"Waiting for confirmation of who he might be, which means we're hoping that someone in the Riga police sees the photo and recognizes him. So, what now? You'll be interested to know that some of the stuff from the flat has been traced to burglaries over the last few months, and forensics identified small traces of amphetamines there as well," Ívar Laxdal said, glowering. "We need a tent," he decided. "It's too damned wet for this."

Four officers in heavy overalls stood around a fifth, a burly man who handled the jackhammer as if it were no heavier than a wooden spoon in his huge hands. Lumps of broken day-old concrete had been piled on a sheet high above the trench as the newly laid foundations were broken up piecemeal. The metal frames had already been sliced off with an angle grinder and heaped by the road.

"Break off," Ívar Laxdal called. "Give them half an hour and we can get a cover rigged up while they eat their pizzas," he ordered. "I still want to know if you seriously expect to find anything here, Gunnhildur?"

"You know, I'm not certain," she said. "But the pressure's working over there," she added, jerking her head towards Sunna María, swathed in an ankle-length coat by the perimeter.

"It's a damned expensive way of applying pressure, if you ask me. Have you any idea how much all this is costing?"

"We can't not look," Gunna replied, turning to follow him back to the road, where neighbours had lined up in spite of the rain to watch the fun. "Her husband vanishes and a few days later there's a trench next door being filled with concrete."

"Hey!" One of the officers in the trench called.

"What?" Gunna yelled back over the roar of the generator.

"There's something here."

Water had collected in black pools at the bottom of the trench between jagged edges of concrete.

Gunna squatted down at the top of the trench and peered into the darkness "Where?"

One of the officers adjusted a floodlight and illuminated a training shoe emerging from the broken concrete.

"A shoe?" Ívar Laxdal frowned.

"Yeah. And there's a foot in it," the officer at the bottom of the trench called back.

This was a very simple job, Orri decided. He had taken extra precautions, parking off the road and walking across the rocks in the dark. The place seemed to be deserted, with a ghostly feeling that he was being watched, which he immediately told himself was just superstitious claptrap.

His mother had believed in aliens and vampires, and that was all rubbish, he reminded himself. But his grandmother had held a belief in the people who lived in the rocks to the end of her long life. Orri reminded himself that the old lady, who'd been one of the few people who'd had time for him as a youngster, had never lied to him or made anything up, so maybe there could be something in it after all?

He walked around the low building. There were no obvious security cameras and no alarms, not that anyone was likely to hear an alarm with the nearest house a kilometre or more away. His picks made short work of the elderly locks on both outer and office doors, which were so worn he could almost have opened them with his own house keys.

Somewhere in the distance water dripped intermittently. The place was cool, but not cold, and the radiator had a little warmth in it, so he guessed that someone had been there that day. He made quick work of the job in hand, pulling plastic bags over his shoes to stand on the desk and replace the smoke alarm in the corner with the new one from the knapsack worn over his chest, guessing that these contained some kind of recording devices but not bothering to check, and using a chair to reach the second alarm in the lobby outside.

He had finished when the roar of an engine outside shook him and he froze. The engine died and he heard the rattle of a key in the lock. Orri looked around quickly. The door on the far side of the office was the only available escape route and he closed it gently behind him as the outer door opened, banging against the wall as a blast of cold air came in with it.

In the long room that Orri found himself in, he hurried along the rows of racks in the near darkness without wondering what they might be, searching for a door that would take him back outside before stepping smartly sideways into a smaller room. Behind him he heard someone whistle in time with heavy footsteps. Orri stood with his back to the wall, his ski hat rolled over his face and ready to take to his heels if he were seen, but the footsteps passed by and the whistled tune became faint in the distance.

Orri peered with caution around the door and saw that the long room was empty. Whoever it was had taken themselves out of sight, and he wasted no time in going back the way he had come, through the office and out into the yard. The quad bike parked by the door still had the keys in the ignition and for a second he considered taking it before dismissing the idea as a stupid one. If he were to disappear into the darkness, then nobody would be any the wiser, he reasoned as he rounded the end of the building and set off back across the rocks towards his car with the familiar triumph at a job well done returning.

"You were right, Gunnhildur," Ívar Laxdal admitted.

The operation at Kópavogsbakki had suddenly acquired a new urgency. Every available officer had been drafted in to help. A tent had been erected over the site and more lights added. Two officers guarded the perimeter to keep the growing crowd of curious bystanders at bay and the road had been blocked off to stop any traffic, apart from the one neighbour who had started ferrying mugs of coffee to the police team.

"Who do you think it is?"

"I'd be surprised if it wasn't our mysterious dentist, Jóhann Hjálmarsson, Sunna María Voss's husband. He's been missing since Friday," Gunna explained grimly. "I managed to trace him to a last sighting by an office block on Ármúli around four o'clock on Friday and a hired van that was returned on Sunday morning. Apart from that, nothing."

"What's your best guess?"

"That someone gave him a Mickey Finn, trussed him up and dropped in in the trench there just in time for the concrete to start flowing yesterday. It's just as well it's fresh concrete, otherwise it would have been like breaking through iron in a few days."

"And the wife? A suspect?"

"Who knows? Maybe not in person, but certainly someone close to her, I'd say. Too early to tell if it's with or without her knowledge."

"You're going to question her this evening?"

340

"Not sure. I'm inclined to let the pressure continue to build for the moment."

Ívar Laxdal's famous frown returned. "I'd have a word. It's her property and she ought to be kept informed, suspect or not."

"You go, then. You're the senior man."

Ívar Laxdal preened for a moment. "You're right. Why not? I'll just assure her that everything's under control and she'll be kept informed."

"Perfect. Now I'm going over to that nice lady over the road who's been dishing out coffee for a quick chat."

"What for? Is she involved? Or maybe she's seen something?"

"More than likely, but that can wait until we start knocking on doors. Right now there's a more pressing issue. I could pee behind a bush like the rest of you, but I prefer not to cause a scandal."

The truck had given him an extra day of life. He had seen the wreck squatting a little way downhill from the road and wondered what it might be. With dusk not far away and no other option, Jóhann stumbled across the tussocks to where the shape stood out against the darkening landscape.

It had been a lorry once, one of the kind that had been common in Iceland in years gone by but which had now long disappeared. The wheels had been taken off and there was only one door, but it provided shelter from the wind. Mercifully, the windscreen was still in place and unbroken.

He curled up where the driver's seat had once been before everything had been stripped out. He guessed that the old Bedford had long since broken down up here and had been rolled off the road before someone had stripped it of the spare parts that were any use.

It wasn't warm in there and Jóhann wondered bitterly how long it was since he had last felt comfortable. At least the rusting remains of the lorry's cab kept the wind and rain at bay. As he pulled the overcoat tight up to his neck and wrapped his arms about him, Jóhann watched the sun set through the grimy windscreen, thankful that it had given him another day, although he was sure that now he was on borrowed time and that the day to come would be his last chance.

It was late and most of the bystanders had drifted off when the call came. Gunna and Ívar Laxdal stood side by side with Sævaldur hovering behind them. A forensics team was ready to start work, dressed in their white suits, although the team leader had already expressed his doubts that there would be much that could be done after the work of breaking up several tons of concrete had taken place.

Gunna clambered down a ladder into the trench where it was suddenly quiet. The jackhammer had stopped and the sound of the chattering compressor in the street was muffled. The body had been freed from the concrete, wrapped in a carpet and black plastic bags, and transferred as gently as could be managed to a stretcher to be lifted clear.

342

She made her way carefully over the sharp ridges of concrete and the officer who had wielded the jackhammer parted the carpet at the head end and exposed a shock of sodden dark hair.

Gunna looked in surprise at an unfamiliar face.

"It isn't Jóhann," she called up to Ívar Laxdal.

"What? Who the hell is it then?"

"Alex," Sævaldur said with distaste, the brim of his hat pulled down over his face. "His name's Alex."

"So that's why he hasn't been at work," Gunna said, shivering.

CHAPTER
TWELVE

"Good morning, Maris," Gunna said in a cheerful voice that contrasted sharply with the expression on her face which instantly made Maris quail.

"Hello," he said slowly and Gunna swung a chair across the floor, planted it backwards next to the bed and herself firmly on it, arms folded on the chair's back.

"The good news is, we've found your friend Alex. The bad news is, Alex is dead," she said and watched the blood drain from his face. "He was murdered, probably two days ago, and now you're going to tell me every single thing you know about Alex Snetzler. Who were his friends? Who did he hang around with? But we can start with who was providing you two with stolen goods and who was your buyer?"

"I don't know," Maris said, still half asleep and running a hand through his tousled hair. "That was Alex's business. I didn't have anything to do with it."

"You expect me to believe that?"

"It's the truth. I've been here for a few months. Alex has been here for a couple of years. The flat was already full of stuff when I got here, and stuff would go and more junk would arrive. I didn't pay it much attention."

"You knew Alex before you came to Iceland?"

"No I didn't."

"So how come you were living with him?"

"It came with the job. I came here to work for Mr Vadluga and I guess it's his place."

"Where are you working?"

"It's a place called Vison, just outside the city."

"Vison? Doing what?"

"It's a mink farm that's just starting up."

"Tell me about Mr Vadluga."

"Boris Vadluga. He's a businessman in Latvia, all kinds of businesses. He owns the company where Alex was working as well."

"Green Bay? The transport company?" Gunna asked, reaching for her phone and standing up.

"That's the place."

"I'll be back in a moment," she said, her phone to her ear and closing the door behind her. "Don't go away."

"Eiríkur?"

"Yep."

Gunna could hear him trying not to yawn. "Listen. I need you to check out a company called Vison. Maris Leinasars works there. The missing dentist and his wife are involved with it, plus the same Boris Vadluga who owns Green Bay Dispatch."

She could hear Eiríkur come to life. "Where Alex Snetzler worked?"

"Precisely, and Orri Björnsson. I'm at the hospital with Maris. You check on Vison, I'll go to Green Bay."

"Will do," Eiríkur said smartly. "Oh, and a bit of extra information for you. Guess who's the owner of the flat where those two jokers were living?"

Maris looked at her with wide brown eyes as Gunna shut the door behind her again.

"When did you last see Alex?"

"The night this happened," he said bitterly, lifting up his splinted and bandaged hand.

"How was he? Did he seem worried before this happened?"

"No, not at all. He was going out for a beer somewhere. He seemed happy enough."

"Who was he meeting?"

"I don't know. His girlfriend, maybe."

"Alex had a girlfriend?"

Maris looked uncertain. "Well, maybe not a girlfriend exactly. He was seeing a girl. Emilija, her name is. She's from Latvia as well. He liked her, but he told me he didn't like her kids. They got in the way, he said."

"There are traces of amphetamines in the apartment you and Alex were living in, found in the living room and some of the clothes showed distinct traces. Where did that come from?"

Maris looked too innocent for Gunna's liking. "I don't know. Alex, maybe?"

"Look, you've gone from being a victim to a suspect, so let's do without the bullshit, shall we? These were in the bag of clothes in the living room. Your clothes. Alex had the bedroom. This tells me that someone had been handling respectable amounts of the stuff, not for personal consumption."

Maris started to shake. "I don't know," he whispered, cradling his smashed hand.

"We also found some traces of precisely the same stuff in a house in Kópavogur."

"Not me. It's nothing to do with me."

"Look, Maris. Have you been inside a prison? Icelandic prisons are great, very comfortable. Central heating and three meals a day. But if you don't start to co-operate then I'll make sure that one day you get sent home to sit out all of your sentence in a Latvian prison. How does that appeal to you? You're not a criminal, are you? No friends there to make life easier? I'm telling you, you won't enjoy it."

There was a roof in the distance. Jóhann was certain of it. He had become more familiar with Iceland's landscape than he had ever expected to be and he knew that there are no straight lines in nature. Everything natural is made up of elegant and subtle curves that turn and sway with the wind and rain.

But far ahead there was a straight line that jarred with the view he had become used to over the last few days. It was too far away to be distinct yet, but he was sure that it had to be a roof of some kind and hoped that it was a farmhouse with a plump farmer's wife inside a centrally heated, well-stocked kitchen with a hissing percolator in one corner and the promise of a hot shower and an even hotter breakfast.

The thought helped him overcome the pain in his ankle as his pace increased. The track twisted over the base of a hill that spread out in front of him and the uphill gradient was hard work. He stopped to catch his breath a couple of times, leaning on a stick he had pulled from the fence by the cattle grid. Jóhann told himself repeatedly not to be too hopeful and that the dream of the plump lady farmer who bore startlingly little resemblance to Sunna María was a vision he could not afford to allow himself.

He was right. It took more than an hour before the straight line of the roof hove close enough into view for him to make it out. His pace slackened as he finally made out the low-slung farmhouse's blank windows, like empty eye sockets in a dead face. The place had been abandoned years ago, just like the ruin he had already left behind him. This time there was at least a sign by the road; its paint was long gone but the raised metal letters announced that the place it pointed to had been known as Brekka.

He felt crushed by disappointment. Jóhann wanted to howl at the injustice of it. He had walked for two days, slept in a steel hut and wrecked truck, yet the sanctuary he had hoped for had been swept away. The plump farmer's wife and her kitchen had been snuffed out in a second as soon as he saw the farmhouse's blind windows.

He walked slowly, his energy eaten up by disappointment and his feet sore as he almost tiptoed along the road. Now each pebble underfoot hurt and he felt the gaze of the ravens that had retired into the distance earlier in the day suddenly closer than ever.

There was nothing to indicate where Vison was and Eiríkur found himself backtracking more than once along dirt roads that made the Polo rattle and rumble alarmingly. When he finally found the place, he was already irritated at having wasted time.

He parked in a yard between two long buildings where the lack of any other cars told him there was little likelihood of anyone being about who might be able to answer a question or two. He knocked and tried the handle of the first door he came to and found it locked tight. Another door marked Vison Ltd, Office & Reception was also locked and there were no lights to be seen. He shivered as he rounded the end of the building, stepping into the cold wind that stole down the hillside, and rattled the handle of yet another locked door.

Something about the place unsettled him. Eiríkur had always tried to fend off superstition, but found himself a victim of it when presented with dark and unfamiliar places. He had the inescapable feeling that he was being watched and walked back the way he had come, keeping his eye on the car. He walked quickly around the second long building, apparently identical to the other. Again there was nobody to be seen, and a perfect full moon still visible in the thin daylight between the torn clouds racing over the sky added to his discomfort.

He clicked his fob and the lights of the Polo flashed comfortingly as the silence was broken and a quad bike roared into the yard.

"Can I help you?" A heavy man in a blue padded overall asked as he got off the bike, removing his helmet and hanging it on the handlebars.

Eiríkur opened his wallet quickly, not giving the man enough time to read the contents, just as he had seen Gunna do. "Eiríkur Thór Jónsson, city police."

"Aha. And what does the law want with this place?"

"Just being curious. The name came up in connection with an investigation and I thought it best to take a look."

The heavy man looked at him through narrowed eyes. "Which name? This place has only been Vison for a few months. Before that it was just called Akur."

"I can't give too many details, but it's a name connected with this location. What's your connection with this place? You work here?"

The man grinned and unzipped the overall that had been closed tight to his neck. "Ásgrímur Stefánsson. I'm the manager. At the moment, anyway."

"Which means what?"

"Ach. It's complicated. You want a look around, do you?"

"That's the idea."

He unlocked the office, clicked on the lights and pushed open a second door, beckoning Eiríkur to follow. He found himself in a cold, dark space, his breath visible in the chill. There was a moment's

350

disquiet and then the lights shimmered into life and he saw the room stretching away into the distance.

"This is it," Ásgrímur said, hands in his pockets as he nodded towards the rows of steel cages that filled the place.

"This is for mink, right? No animals?"

"Yep. Mink. The animals won't arrive for a while yet. We're still setting up."

"So this is a new place? It doesn't look new."

Ásgrímur barked with mirthless laughter. "You want the full story?"

"Go ahead."

"This was a mink farm years ago, back in the eighties. My family built the place and when the market fell to pieces we shut up shop. Closed down."

"It went bust?"

"That's what we should have done, but no. It would have been easy to just file for bankruptcy and let the bank pick up the pieces, wouldn't it?"

"I suppose so. But you own this place?"

Ásgrímur's heels clicked on the concrete floor as he strode along an aisle between the cages with Eiríkur next to him. "My sisters and I own the land and the buildings, but now I'm just an employee of the company that's setting up here. That's Vison. You're from the police, you said?"

"That's right."

"Just as long as you're not one of those bunny-hugging vegetarians."

"Why's that?"

351

"Back in the eighties those were the people who screwed up my livelihood by destroying the fur market. So I went to work in Denmark for a long time. There are fur farms still running there and I wanted to stay in the business."

They reached the final row of cages and a door at the far end.

"What's in there?" Eiríkur asked.

"Cold storage for feed when we finally get up and running in the summer. Storage for bedding and there's a small lab for quality control in there as well. That's all waiting to be fitted out."

He tried the handle and the door swung open, but the lights refused to obey as he clicked the switch by the door.

"The circuit breaker's popped, I expect," Ásgrímur grunted. "There's a lot needs to be done yet before we start up."

"When's that happening?"

"June, if everything goes according to plan."

They walked back between the cages, their clouds of breath preceding them in the chilled air.

"So how come you came back from Denmark? The market improved, did it?"

"Simple. The gentleman I worked for in Denmark wanted to expand, and he knew I'd farmed mink in Iceland. Times have changed. The fur market has picked up now. Costs in Iceland have fallen and the exchange rate since the crash means we can be competitive on exports again. So he wanted me to set up here."

"And fortunately you still owned this place so you're a partner in this?"

Ásgrímur grinned, displaying gaps between his teeth that made Eiríkur wince. "I'm getting on for sixty, and I can't be doing with all the paperwork and all that shit. Once the place is up and running I'll manage it for a few years, and when the lads are trained to do everything, I'll step back and retire. That's the grand plan, anyway. Right now I do what I do well and get paid for it, plus they lease the site off me. That's enough for me."

"So Mr Vadluga is putting a decent amount of money into this venture?"

Ásgrímur's eyes narrowed again. "You've been doing your homework, I see."

"It's not difficult. The company's in his name."

"If it's something to do with fraud, then I can tell you Boris is straight. Everything's up front. Cash on the nail, accounts, the lot. That's the way the farm in Denmark was run and that's the way this one runs as well. Or will run," he added.

Out in the yard it felt warmer than inside the echoing building. Eiríkur shivered and nodded towards the second row of buildings.

"What's over there?"

"Nothing much at the moment. You want to look?"

"I do."

Ásgrímur found a key among dozens on a ring and opened the door. Again lights flickered on. A sports car with its bonnet gaping open and a hole where its engine had once been sat sadly in a corner. A row of filing cabinets lined the far wall. Lengths of timber had been stacked here and there.

"This lot all has to go." Ásgrímur sighed. "My brother-in-law's antique Porsche has been in there for the best part of twenty years and if he doesn't get it sorted out soon I'll put it on eBay. That's the paperwork going back to the old company here. That can all go as well."

Eiríkur took it all in. "In that case I'll be on my way and leave you to it. By the way, how often does Mr Vadluga come here?"

"Almost never. About two years ago was the last time, when he wanted to take a look at this place."

"So he hasn't been to Iceland for a while?"

"No, he doesn't travel a lot these days. Not like he used to do."

"You know a young man called Maris Leinasars?"

"Yep, he's been working here for a few months, helping get set up. A decent enough lad. Works hard."

"Where is he now?"

"No idea. I had a call saying he wasn't well and he'd be off for a few days."

"I think you'll find it might be more than a few days," Eiríkur said.

This time Orri did have a lawyer, Gunna saw as she put her head around the door, a plump young woman she had often seen in the interview rooms, and nodded to her.

"Mind if I sit in?"

Eiríkur ushered her in and announced her presence for the benefit of the recording. Eiríkur and Orri sat opposite each other; Eiríkur with Sævaldur at his side, red-faced and seething with badly suppressed anger, while the plump lawyer sat at the end of the table.

"Want me to recap? he asked.

"If you would."

"We've established beyond any doubt that Orri has been using Steinar Atlason's storeroom in the basement of Ferjubakki twenty. We have Steinar's testimony to that effect and we have fingerprints from the storeroom that are being analysed at the moment. There's a heap of iPads, games consoles, laptops, drills and whatnot that Tinna and Geiri are checking for serial numbers so we can trace the owners and find out where all this stuff came from."

Gunna jerked her head at Orri as if he were a piece of the furniture. "And what's our friend's story on where all this stuff came from?"

"He claims he was storing it for a former work colleague who has left the country."

Gunna grinned. "That's almost as good as 'the cheque's in the post' or 'of course I'll still respect you in the morning', isn't it?"

The lawyer looked cross but let the comment pass while Orri grimaced in anger.

"His name's Juris. He used to work at Green Bay until a few months ago."

"All right, and where is Juris now?" Eiríkur asked. "Gone back to Lithuania or wherever?"

"He left in a hurry and asked me to look after all his stuff for him," Orri said.

"What's his full name?"

"I don't know. Juris. That's all I know."

"Very convenient, and a little unbelievable, surely? You store a load of stolen goods on behalf of someone whose name you don't even know? You expect me to believe that?" Eiríkur said in a soft voice that Gunna knew would be more likely to trip up lies than Sævaldur's habitual bluster and noise.

"That's the truth. It's up to you to prove otherwise," Orri said and the lawyer looked at her hands.

"So when did Juris disappear?"

"Two, three months ago. I can't remember."

"In that case it'll be interesting when we trace some of the owners of all that stuff and find out that it was stolen less than two months ago, won't it?"

"But you don't have that kind of information, do you?" the lawyer challenged. "Can we stick to what's established fact, please?"

"Why not?" Gunna said with a wink to Eiríkur and looked at Orri's hands with the sleeves of his dark green fleece tugged down over his wrists. She nodded at his hands, clasped together in his lap. "I can't help noticing the scabs on your wrists, Orri. Anything you'd like to tell me about?"

There was a look of fear that passed over his face. "No," he said quickly. Too quickly, Gunna decided.

"They've been there for a while I'd guess and I'm fairly sure that those were some nasty cuts on your

356

wrists. In fact, I'd go so far as to bet folding money there's a matching set on your ankles as well."

Orri went pale and leaned over to mutter something to the lawyer.

"My client and I need to confer. Ten minutes break?"

"Let's make it half an hour, shall we?" Gunna suggested. "I could do with conferring as well."

Storm clouds were heavy overhead and Jóhann knew the ravens were behind him in the twilight, waiting for him to falter and fall. By sunrise he knew they would have picked his eyes out and he shed bitter tears at the thought of dying out here alone. Hunger was a constant ache in his belly and he could hardly feel his feet any more. The sole of his damaged shoe had come completely adrift and the sock beneath it had worn right through, leaving him squelching through the puddles with only the other sleeve of his once smart shirt wrapped around his foot for protection.

A spot of light in the distance gave him a moment's hope until it flickered out of sight and he wondered if it had simply been an illusion brought on by his own despair. There was a humming noise that he could hear occasionally and he dismissed it as yet another figment of his imagination, along with the flashing green and red lights he had begun to see in the sky.

Blinking spots of white light returned intermittently, teasing him as he squinted through his rain-spattered glasses.

Eventually he told himself that enough was enough. Full darkness would be upon him soon and he had run out of places to shelter. He no longer had the strength to walk and the only remaining option was to sit in the road and hope that some time in the summer someone would be able to identify whatever might be left of him.

Gunna had watched the previous evening's TV news on her computer and saw the request for sightings of Jóhann Hjálmarsson, fifty-four years old, grey hair and glasses, last seen on Friday in the downtown area of Reykjavík. Sunna María and Jóhann's sons had been warned that the appeal would be broadcast, and while the two sons, both of whom had entered middle age early as far as Gunna could see, were deeply anxious, Sunna María was agitated and distracted, angry at her husband rather than concerned about his whereabouts.

She closed her laptop and went back to the interview room where Orri had been given a meal. She expected him to be held overnight and transferred to prison at Litla Hraun the following day.

Back in the interview room Eiríkur went through the formalities. Orri still looked pale as his lawyer sat next to him making notes.

"My client has a statement to make," the lawyer announced, fiddling nervously with a necklace that straggled round her neck.

"Let's hear it."

"He accepts that the goods found in his basement may have been stolen, but is not prepared to accept responsibility for them as they were given to him by Juris, surname unknown, to look after for a few weeks. That was at least four months ago and he has not since heard from Juris and attempts to contact him have been unsuccessful. With reference to the scabs on his wrists, he would like to state that these occurred during a session of bondage with his girlfriend Elísabet Sólborg Höskuldsdóttir," the lawyer read from her notes, her voice quavering and her cheeks glowing pink. "He states that this was entirely consensual and is not prepared to discuss this sensitive personal matter," she finished, her voice an octave higher than it had been at the start of her speech.

Gunna smiled broadly. "Very interesting, for what it's worth. Of course, I'll speak to Elísabet Höskuldsdóttir and ask her to corroborate your client's testimony. I take it you're not going to be in touch with her the moment you're out of here to warn her what kind of questions she's likely to be asked?"

"That would be highly unprofessional," the lawyer said.

"She won't tell you," Orri said with a shrug. "Lísa's a bit uptight about that kind of thing."

"Not too uptight to tie you up? I'm intrigued," Gunna said. "I must say, you don't strike me as the kinky type. Was this your idea or hers?"

"Hers."

"Like I said, I'll ask her." Gunna tapped the table. "Now, Orri. We have sightings of you on Kópavogsbakki on half a dozen occasions and to my mind that means you must have been around that area a good few times, assuming that not every visit was noticed. What were you doing walking around a residential street that's miles from where you live?"

359

"Not me. It must have been someone who looks like me."

"The interesting part is that someone was assaulted in one of the houses on that street a week ago. There's some compelling evidence to suggest that person was you. Fibres found at the scene match perfectly those of your fleece. There are bloodstains on the floor and I would imagine that the DNA sequencing will show it's yours. Any comments, Orri?"

"It wasn't me. I was at home on Tuesday night."

"You'll notice I didn't say the assault took place on Tuesday night. We were called to the scene on Wednesday, but it could have been any of several days or nights before that."

"You said a week ago, so I assumed Tuesday."

"So why Kópavogsbakki? I have a list of sightings with times and dates over the last couple of weeks, although not one in the week since the mysterious assault took place there. I suppose you'll be able to tell me exactly where you were on all these occasions, as you weren't walking around Kópavogsbakki?"

Orri shrugged again and looked blank. "I don't know. Like I said, nothing to do with me."

"You know Alex Snetzler."

"Yeah, He works with me."

"Where is he?"

"Search me."

"You're not aware that Alex is dead?"

Orri's pale face rapidly went paler. "No, I didn't know that."

360

"You're a dangerous person to know, Orri. Juris worked at Green Bay Dispatch and was fencing stolen property, and he's disappeared. Alex works at Green Bay Dispatch and his flat was stuffed with stolen property, and now he's dead."

"Excuse me, officer," the lawyer broke in. "Are you insinuating that my client might have something to do with the disappearances of these men?"

"I'm keeping an open mind," Gunna retorted. "It strikes me as too much of a coincidence that two fences appear to have come to sticky ends."

"I don't know. I reckon Juris went back to Latvia. I don't know about Alex. We work together but we don't get on all that well."

"Any particular reason?"

"He's a loudmouth. I don't like people like that. He does his work. I do mine. Otherwise we don't get in each other's way."

"And you don't know how he came to have a wardrobe stuffed full of stolen laptops and iPads. That's just wonderful. Orri, it just beggars belief. You're all over the place. There's stolen gear in your basement that you completely forgot to tell us about, plus you sold that gold clasp to Aunt Bertha —"

"It was my mother's," Orri said.

"No, it absolutely wasn't. It belonged to a lady whose house was broken into sometime in the last couple of weeks by someone who took a couple of envelopes of foreign currency and a smart wristwatch that looks remarkably similar to one of the half dozen or so watches we found in your basement with all the other bits and pieces. Tomorrow my colleague will be asking its owner to identify it and if that goes the way I expect it to, then that places you right there."

Orri sat silent and the lawyer pursed her lips in frustration.

"Enough," Gunna decided and stood up. "Eiríkur, will you finish up, please, and then escort this gentleman upstairs to the executive suite?"

Orri opened his mouth and glanced at the lawyer sitting next to him. "I, er . . ." he mumbled.

Gunna sat down again and glared at him. "What?"

"I want to speak to you in private. Just you and me."

"Orri," the lawyer began. "This isn't clever."

"Without prejudice," Orri said. "That's the legal term, isn't it? I have stuff to tell you, but no recordings, no witnesses. Just you and me."

"You know I can't do that."

"I'm advising you against this," the lawyer said sharply.

Orri shrugged, looking Gunna in the eyes. "Up to you. I'll go off to Litla Hraun and keep quiet if you don't want to hear it."

Gunna hurtled out of the city with the wipers fending off the spring drizzle that had left the roads slippery with water. Passing through Gardabær she overtook more cars than she should have done and told herself to slow down, rattling a fingertip rhythm on the wheel as she waited by the lights outside Hafnarfjördur.

She curbed her impatience on the slope and put her foot down to surge past a truck the moment the road was wide enough, again reminding herself that there was no need for this kind of speed, but frustrated with herself that her mood demanded it.

She crunched the car to a halt in the gravel outside Green Bay Dispatch and hurried inside, spying out Dóri immediately a second before he saw her and grimaced at the sight of her.

"Dóri, a word," Gunna demanded and swept him along in her wake to the canteen. "Out of here please, gentlemen," she ordered unzipping her coat and opening her wallet to show them her warrant card.

"When did you last see Alex?" Gunna fired at Dóri as he limped into the canteen and she shut the door behind him.

He looked at her suspiciously, pushing his wire-framed glasses up to perch them on his thinning crown.

"Alex was here on Friday. He hasn't shown up since."

"He hasn't asked for any holiday or anything like that?"

"No, nothing. Why? Where is he?"

"And Orri? When did he leave yesterday?"

"He went home as usual yesterday and hasn't been back. What's going on?"

"Just so you know, Orri is in a cell right now and Alex is on a slab at the National Hospital. He was murdered some time at the weekend, I guess, and his body was dumped in a trench that was about to become the foundations of a new house."

Dóri went pale and sat down, shaking his head in short, sharp movements, as if unable to comprehend.

"Is there anyone here that Alex used to go around with?" Gunna demanded. "Any special friends? How long had he worked here? And while I'm asking awkward questions, who is Juris?"

"To start with," Dóri said, "I'll answer your questions in order if I may. Alex and Orri are the youngest staff here and they both kept fairly much to themselves. Alex has always been a sociable sort of character, but no. No particular friends as far as I'm aware. He started here a little under two years ago. Juris is a young man who used to work here and who left suddenly. One day he was here and the next he wasn't. He left a forwarding address for his outstanding wages to be paid by cheque, which as far as I know was done. What else would you like to know?"

"Alex spoke reasonable Icelandic, right? So he must have been here in Iceland for a few years. Do you know where he was working before?"

"Building work. That's all I know. But his work permit was in order."

"Orri and Alex, how do they get on?"

"Well enough, I think. I gather there has been some tension on occasions, but nothing they weren't able to sort out between themselves. We're all adults here, you know. It comes from having an older workforce." Dóri looked dazed. "This is serious stuff, isn't it? What happened to Alex?"

Gunna extracted a print from her pocket. "Recognize this face?"

"Sorry." Dóri shook his head. "Should I?"

"Not necessarily. It was a long shot," Gunna said and poured herself a coffee from the flask on the table without being invited. "What did you make of him? Be honest."

"Alex? A sweet enough boy, but he was a crook."

"Why do you say that?"

"I'm an observer of people, officer. I haven't always been a clerk in a transport company, you know. I was a teacher for many years. You grow a sixth sense after dealing with adolescents for all those years and I was rarely wrong about which ones would come off the rails somewhere. I could sense it with Alex. He was charming enough, but abrasive at the same time. My suspicion is that he was shipping things that weren't part of the company's regular business."

"Stolen goods? Drugs?"

"I don't know. I need this job so I take care not to ask."

"What brought Alex to work here?"

"He just appeared and I was told he was the new driver."

"Who told you that?"

"Óli Hansen. He owns this company. Or rather, he's one of the owners now," he said as Gunna raised an enquiring eyebrow and he continued. "None of us have been told this, you understand, but we see things change and it's easy enough to find this stuff out if you know where to look. The majority shareholder now is a gentleman called —"

"Boris Vadluga," Gunna said, finishing his sentence for him.

He felt unaccountably warm, for the first time in days. He carefully opened one eye and found himself somewhere dark, but swaddled in something heavy. His stomach was complaining and he realized that the smell of food had woken him.

Jóhann put out a hand and felt for the side of whatever it was he was lying on. He found to his alarm that his clothes had disappeared and the rough blanket he had under him was making him itch. His head swam as he put out a foot to the floor, but he pulled himself upright, his eyesight getting used to the gloom.

He found that he could stand, although his feet were sore. A table in the middle of the room had the remains of a meal on it and his hands shook as he poured milk into a cup and drank it, savouring the sweetness of it. He immediately felt stronger and let himself drop onto a chair. The rest of the table swam in to view and he wondered what had become of his glasses as he squinted at the loaf of bread in a plastic bag, a pot of yoghurt and some slices of cheese under a plastic wrapper.

The taste of the cheese was so sublime it almost brought tears to Jóhann's eyes. He tried to remember how long he had been without food other than the dried fish he'd pulled from the drying racks where he'd woken up, how many days ago now?

Sunna María had lost none of her usual bluster as she sat, straight-backed, in the interview room. "I suppose you want me to answer all kinds of questions, do you?

If that's not Jóhann you found under the concrete, then I have no idea who it is."

"Were you expecting it to be Jóhann?"

Her cheeks reddened in anger. "Of course not. Who is it, anyway?"

"Who was it, you mean," Gunna said, opening her notes and taking out a file. She gave Sunna María a print of Alex's face, enlarged from the driving licence in his pocket, gazing into the camera with a louche smile. "Anyone you recognize?"

This time the reaction looked genuine enough, but the momentary hesitation and the flash of uncertainty in her eyes told Gunna that Sunna María was stalling. She handed it back with a shake of the head. "No idea, sorry."

"Alexander Snetzler," Gunna said and thought she detected a tremor in Sunna María's face as she continued. "He's a Latvian citizen. Any ideas?"

"None whatever."

"Vilhelm Thorleifsson and Elvar Pálsson were doing a lot of business in Latvia, weren't they, with a company that you and your husband were partners in? I understand that Sólfell Investment crashed leaving a lot of people out of pocket. They are both dead, your husband has vanished, there's a dead criminal in the foundations of a house you're building and you're telling me you have no idea what's going on? Don't give me bullshit, Sunna María. I can smell it a mile off."

Sunna María froze and Gunna wondered how many years it might have been since anyone had spoken to her so abruptly.

"I'm sure I don't know what you're talking about. Jóhann handled our business affairs."

"Except that he didn't. You were at university with Vilhelm Thorleifsson and Elvar Pálsson. You all did business studies, but they both dropped out and you finished with a very good degree. So don't pretend to me that all this business stuff is too complicated for you. Who is it that has a grudge against you? Who killed your friend and has probably done the same with your husband in a slightly more subtle way? And why do a not very good job of hiding the body of a small-time Latvian criminal in the basement of your house? I'm wondering if whoever did that actually wanted to get rid of the body or if they wanted to implicate you?"

Sunna María's mouth hung open. "I didn't think of it like that," she said with an effort and after a painfully long pause.

"Where is Boris Vadluga?"

"Latvia, I guess. He travels a lot."

"And do his travels coincide with Jóhann's, maybe?"

"I have no idea."

"You and he are pretty good friends, I understand?"

"He's a business acquaintance. That's all."

"You seem happy to do him favours, such as supplying an apartment for his staff to live in."

"Well, yes. Look, it wasn't easy for foreigners to buy property in Iceland back then and he was looking for somewhere for his staff. So we bought the place and rent it to Boris."

"Who's this?" Gunna laid the blurred screengrab of the hook-nosed man on the table.

"I haven't a clue," Sunna María said immediately, eyes darting to one side.

"Bullshit. I think you know exactly who this is, and I suspect that this person also knows exactly where your husband or his remains are to be found."

Sunna María burst into tears. "You don't understand," she sniffed eventually.

"I'm starting to think I do. Where did the money for all this construction come from?" Gunna demanded. "Your husband pulling teeth doesn't pay for this kind of venture. So come clean, where did it all come from? Who did you rip off?"

"I don't know what you mean."

"In that case, who are the two men who rented the house at Kópavogsbakki fifty, the ones you told the estate agent were friends of yours so he didn't need to go through any formalities?"

"That was Jóhann."

"No. Óttar Sveinsson the estate agent told me himself: 'Sunna María told me she knew them and we could skip the formalities.' That was you. Someone was brutally assaulted in that house just before those people left. Who were they?"

"Boris asked if we could accommodate some friends of his. I don't know any names."

"They paid? Bank transfer? Cash? To you?"

Sunna María nodded and Gunna tapped the picture of the hook-nosed man on the desk. "This man?"

"I don't know."

"So why did they repaint the whole basement from floor to ceiling?"

"What?"

"You heard. The whole of the basement was repainted from top to bottom. Walls, floor, ceiling. Óttar Sveinsson says he had nothing to do with it. So why would two tenants do a thing like that?"

True to his word, Eiríkur had tracked Emilija down and she was sitting fearfully with him in the section's hired Polo as Gunna drove in.

"Why am I here?" Emilija asked as Gunna approached. "I have done nothing wrong."

Gunna took her arm and propelled her through the door into the building, with Eiríkur behind them stumbling over the steps in his efforts to keep up. Instead of using a formal interview room, Gunna sat Emilija down in a quiet corner. The now much-folded picture came out and she turned first to Eiríkur.

"I sent this to our liaison officer in Riga yesterday but haven't heard back yet. Check if there's been a reply, will you? We really need to know who this man is," she said and Eiríkur departed at a trot.

"Now, Emilija. When did you last see Alex?"

"Not for a long time."

"Alex is dead."

Emilija's eyes bulged. She stared at Gunna, who watched her shake her head violently and her small fists clenched into tight balls.

"No! Alex? How?"

"He was murdered. His body was found late last night."

"Who did this?"

"I don't believe your ex-husband is involved, although he certainly had a grudge against Alex. When did you see Alex last?" Gunna repeated.

The reply came grudgingly. "Sunday morning. He stayed the night."

"You didn't see him or hear from him after that?"

"No. I told him not to come back," she said in a blank voice. "But I expected he would. Alex doesn't give up."

Gunna considered what Emilija had said. Alex had been alive on Sunday morning. His body had been uncovered on Tuesday night and must have been placed in the trench before the concrete had been poured the day before. He had probably been murdered within a few hours of leaving Emilija's bed, she decided.

"Did Alex say anything? Did he mention where he was going?"

"I thought he was going to work as usual."

"Was there anything unusual that morning? Tell me what happened and what he said."

Emilija flared in resentment. "It's not every day a man stays with me, if that's what you're thinking."

"It's not," Gunna snapped. "It's Alex I want to know about. Why did you tell him not to come back?"

Emilija's anger subsided. She sighed. "I suppose I can tell you. He was doing something illegal. I don't know what. Alex always had money, more than enough money. More money than someone in that kind of shit work should have."

"How do you know?"

"He used to buy presents for the children, really expensive toys, until I said stop. He used to buy me things. Never anything useful, but perfume, that sort of stuff." She reddened. "Underwear," she whispered. "Expensive. Designer. But it wasn't comfortable so I never wore it."

"I understand," Gunna said. "What else?"

"He didn't work long hours. Half days mostly. So where did all that cash come from?"

"You never asked him?"

"Why?" Emilija snorted in derision. "Why ask a question when you know the answer will be a lie? Sometimes it's best not to know. So I didn't ask where his money came from."

"Drugs?"

"I suppose so." Emilija shook her head. "But what do I know? I've been wrong so many times that you shouldn't take my word for much," she added bitterly. "I would never have dreamed for a moment that Ingi would stoop as low as he did, unless it was his bitch of a mother pushing him."

"Alex was driving the day you last saw him?"

"Of course. He had his keys in his hand as he left. He had a red Accord. I don't know the number, quite an old one."

"What time did he leave you on Sunday morning?"

"Around nine thirty. That's when I left for work as well. I know he should have been at work earlier, but being on time never worried Alex much."

Jóhann had no idea what had become of his own clothes, but he pulled on the outsized shirt and trousers

372

that had been left folded by the couch he had slept on. With food in his belly, not too much as he knew that overeating would be as bad in his condition as starvation, he hobbled around the chalet on painful feet. It was tiny, one room lined with bunks and bookshelves, and with a small bathroom at one side and a verandah at the front.

He had no desire to go past the door, and simply watched the rain course down the window against the unbroken blackness beyond, revelling in being warm and no longer hungry. He had found his glasses, phone and wallet on the windowsill, but there was no charger to be found that would fit, so his phone remained obstinately dead, refusing to give him more than a second of life before the red warning flagged up on the screen and it died yet again.

In the chalet's only comfortable chair, he sat hunched with his arms around his legs, reflecting that a week before he would have been frantic at not having checked his email for more than a few hours, but now he was thankful to have simply escaped the ravens; the thought of them made him shudder.

"You're awake, then?"

The door banged open and an elderly man and a younger woman came in, kicking off their boots by the door.

"Don't stand up, man," the woman said, as Jóhann struggled to get to his feet. "Helga Dís," she said, giving him a hand to shake and then opening the fridge to throw packets onto the table.

"Jóhann Hjálmarsson."

"Bjarni," the man said, proffering a calloused hand. "You look better now than you did last night, I must say."

"I don't remember. Where was I? Was I still conscious?"

"You were in the middle of the road, spark out as far as I could see, like a bundle of rags with that old coat wrapped around your head. What the hell happened to you, then? How did you find your way up here?"

"I'm really not sure. What day is it?"

"Wednesday today."

"Five days," Jóhann said, suddenly animated. "It's been five days since I was abducted."

"What's that you say? Kidnapped?"

"I think so, I don't remember very well. Where am I?"

"Geirsmörk."

"I'm sorry. Where's that?"

"Borgarnes is that way," Bjarni said, a hand waving towards the door.

"I passed a place called Brekka yesterday, I think. Or maybe the day before."

"You were a long way up."

"I don't know where I was. I've been walking for days. I'm not sure how many."

"I know," Helga Dís sang out. "We gave you a bit of a scrub yesterday and put you to bed. I'll bet your feet are sore, aren't they? How far have you walked?"

"I really don't know."

"It must have been a distance if you passed Brekka?"

374

"I was at a place with a hill behind it shaped like a loaf of bread, with a lot of fish in drying racks next to it."

Bjarni cracked his knuckles. "Sounds like you must have been at Vatnsendi. It's not that far from here across country, but the road goes the long way round to get there. How the hell did you get all the way up there? Hardly anybody goes there from one year's end to the next."

"And all that dried fish?"

"It's been there a few years now. I think they must have forgotten it's there. Anyway, if that's what you were eating, then you really are very fortunate to be alive."

Jóhann sat in silence for a moment, digesting what he had heard as cups and plates clinked on the table.

"You don't have a phone here, do you?"

"We're out of range. Even the radio reception isn't that good up here."

"Oh. Is there any chance of being able to get to town?"

"Not now," Bjarni said. "It's dark and you'll be in no condition to go anywhere until the morning."

"Explain, Gunnhildur." Ívar Laxdal scowled and shook his head. "But sit down, you're making me nervous pacing up and down like that."

"It's a drugs operation."

"What is? And how have you figured this out?"

"I haven't figured it all out," Gunna said, sitting uncomfortably. "Just the outline of it all, Maris cracked when I asked him a few uncomfortable questions and mentioned having him sent to a Latvian prison."

"Go on."

"It's a speed factory. Maris was here to make dope. His family got into some serious debt a few years ago and the only way they could pay it off was by him agreeing to work for the same people who were doing the loan sharking. Vison is financed by this character in Latvia, Boris Vadluga, and it's a pretty clever operation. The speed is made in Iceland, which is what Maris was doing. Alex works at the transport company . . ."

"Green Bay Dispatch," Eiríkur put in.

"Exactly, Green Bay, which was about to go bankrupt a year ago, when Boris Vadluga stepped in and bought two thirds of the company. Alex collects the fish that's being air freighted to Europe, and he replaces the cold-gel packs in the boxes of fillets with sealed bags the same colour."

"But packed with amphetamines?" Ívar Laxdal suggested.

"Exactly. Iceland's the perfect place to smuggle something out of. You'd expect drugs shipments from southern Europe or the Middle East. But Iceland? So the fish boxes hardly get looked at and Maris said they've been careful to ship their gear only with every third or fourth consignment — so far as they haven't been producing big amounts."

"But they're planning to?" Eiríkur said excitedly. "Vison? The fur farm?"

"That seems clear enough. The place even has a lab of its own for quality control. They were producing this stuff in the basement at Kópavogsbakki fifty, but it was too small and too close to people who would notice the smell sooner or later. So that was packed up, the place was painted from top to bottom, and they moved out, leaving it pristine."

"Except that the cleaners found that someone had broken in and stumbled across more than he'd bargained for, you mean?"

"That's it."

"So who killed Vilhelm Thorleifsson? Where's the missing dentist? Who murdered Alex? Fair enough, you've found a dope factory. Let's hand that over to narcotics to deal with and concentrate on the two dead people and three missing ones, shall we?"

"It all ties in together. If the drug squad bust them now then everything's wide open and my guess is that we'll never find the killers. In any case, there's nothing to bust. The dope lab at Kópavogsbakki is gone. We might find a few traces if we strip the paint off the floor, but I wouldn't bank on it, and the new lab they're setting up under cover of the mink farm isn't a speed factory yet."

Ívar Laxdal rubbed his chin. The rhythmic rasp of the back of his hand against his chin was like sandpaper on a wooden floor. Gunna thought he looked deeply tired for the first time since they had started to work together almost three years ago.

"All right, Gunnhildur. How do you want to do this?"

"I don't know," she fretted. "The last definite sighting we have of Alex was leaving his girlfriend's house fairly early on Sunday morning. After that we have nothing to go on, and my best guess is that he was dumped in those foundations on Sunday night, as the construction team was there to start work early on Monday morning."

"Could he have been put in there on Monday?" Ívar Laxdal asked.

"No. They put a layer of concrete at the bottom of the trench on Monday."

"Without noticing the body at the bottom?"

"It was dark at that time of the morning and I don't suppose they make a habit of checking for corpses before they throw concrete down there. I suppose it wouldn't have been that hard to hide the body with a layer of earth or gravel. No, Alex was murdered on Sunday, and he must have been disposed of by someone who knew the trench was going to be filled in the next morning."

"Sunna María?"

"You see her with a cosh and a black mask? She wouldn't do anything that might risk laddering her tights. I don't get the feeling she's exactly giving us bullshit, but she's evading a lot of questions and there's a whole load of stuff that she's not telling us. I want to know why Alex? He was fencing stolen goods, almost as a hobby it seems, and he was a cog in the delivery part of the speed business. So why kill him?"

Gunna was out of her chair, smacking one fist into the palm of the other hand. Ívar Laxdal watched her pace to and fro while Eiríkur stood by the door.

"Alex had made a mistake, maybe?" Ívar Laxdal suggested.

"More than likely, but what? And how do Sunna María and Jóhann slot into the puzzle? Why has Jóhann vanished? Is he dead as well? Who's next on the list? What about this other joker who seems to have vanished off the face of the earth and who the combined police forces of northern Europe can't find?"

"Elvar?"

"That's him. Has someone already bumped him off, or is he the next body we're going to stumble across?"

"You think there's more to come?"

"Don't you?" Gunna shot back. "What's going on here? Is this a turf war between Boris Vadluga's Latvian operation and some local criminals? That doesn't strike me as likely as we'd have heard the rumblings for a while by now. Or are we watching some old scores being settled?" She stopped and her hands dropped to her sides. "On top of that we have Sævaldur's burglar in another interview room, and I know perfectly well he's involved in all this, but he's keeping his trap firmly shut. Any ideas? Because I'm running out."

"Arrest everyone connected to this and bring them in?" Eiríkur suggested.

"We hold them for twenty-four hours and then let them go again? No, we may as well just tell them to hide every scrap of evidence and shred their bank statements right away. Ívar, you tell me. It's your investigation," Gunna said. "Do you want to keep them under surveillance until the dope factory is up and running and then let narcotics grab the whole lot of them red-handed, assuming we haven't scared them off already? That means a pat on the back all round. Or do you want to push these people hard right now and hope it leads to the killers before they kill someone else?"

Steini yawned and laid aside his book.

"Any good?" Gunna asked, looking up from the television.

"Last year's Arnaldur. Not bad at all."

"I thought you'd already read that one?"

"That was the one before. This one's better. You've had a tough day?"

"Not the easiest day's work I've ever had, but I'll manage," Gunna said, lifting her feet onto the edge of the table and stretching. "How about you? A boiler suit in the washing basket tells me you've been doing something dirty."

"The perils of living with a detective. There's not much gets past you, is there, Sherlock? We got the engine on the *Ísborg* running this afternoon, so Svenni's a happy man now."

"How long has it taken? Three months?"

"That's what comes of having an antique engine. He had to get the spares from a scrap yard in Denmark."

He hauled himself to his feet and padded to the kitchen, returning with two bowls.

"As you've been busy, I thought I'd do you a little treat."

"You wouldn't be after something, would you, young man?"

380

Steini laughed. "Young. I like that. No, pure altruism on my part."

"Just the goodness of your heart? What a man," Gunna said, taking the bowl and a spoonful of the fruit salad with a generous lump of ice cream on it. "Not good for the waistline, though."

"We can't have you wasting away, can we?"

"There's no danger of that," Gunna grunted, dropping her feet to the floor and sitting up straight. "Steini, you picked up Gísli the other day. What did he have to say?"

"He's on your mind, isn't he?"

"Rather more than the case I'm working on," Gunna admitted. "I'm his mother. I can't not be worried about him."

"You think I hadn't noticed?"

"Touché, Sherlock."

Steini nibbled at a wafer. "He's worried, as you can imagine. He did ask about you and I told him the truth."

"Which is?"

"Like you said, you're his mum. You can be as pissed off as hell with him, but you're still his mum."

"I see."

"It's about time you two made peace, don't you think? I know you're as hard-headed as each other, but it's affecting everyone else. Laufey's walking on eggshells because she doesn't want to say the wrong thing and upset you, Gísli's lost his way because you're hardly speaking to him and Drífa's nervous around you as well."

"And you?"

"You're not as much fun as you used to be, but I'm older and a little more patient than the youngsters, so I can recognize that we'll have the Gunna we know and love back soon enough."

"Ever the optimist. Keep up the treats and she'll be back before you know it, especially if we catch this devious bastard before too long."

"Difficult case?"

"Horrible. Some very unpleasant people, as well as mister über-chauvinist chief inspector Sævaldur Bogason, who is in the running to be the least pleasant of the lot. I'll call Gísli in the morning and see if we can meet in town for a change, away from the various girlfriends and offspring."

CHAPTER
THIRTEEN

Orri rubbed his eyes as Gunna flipped the peephole cover to wink at him. The warder opened the door.

"You don't need to lock us in," Gunna said as the door swung to behind her. "Orri's not going to do anything stupid."

Orri sat up with the duvet wrapped around him and blinked.

"Been in here before have you?" Gunna asked. "Breakfast will be along in a minute."

"I'm going to Litla Hraun today, am I?"

"I expect so. You've not been there before?"

Orri snorted through his nose and rubbed his eyes.

"I have, actually. Visited both my parents there at one time or another. Not at the same time," he added. "But I've never been a prisoner, if that's what you mean."

"You'll be all right. Keep your nose clean and I don't suppose you'll be there long." Gunna sat down on the bunk next to him. "Now, before the lawyers turn up and before my colleagues get here, strictly between you and me," she said. "You have something to tell me."

"Yeah," Orri said slowly. "I've been thinking about it all night."

"And you still want to talk? It's up to you."

"Will it help my case?"

"I can't say, and it depends what you want to tell me. But I don't imagine it would do any harm."

"Right," Orri said and yawned. "Is there any coffee?"

"On the way. You're the notorious Reykjavík housebreaker, aren't you?"

"Could be."

"Come on. If you're going to play hard to get, then I'm wasting my time."

"Yeah," Orri grunted. "That's me. Been doing it about two years now."

"You've not done a bad job of it. No prints, no traces. You've been very careful, haven't you? But you realize your career's at an end now?"

Orri looked blank.

"My colleague Sævaldur has been running around the city like a headless chicken for the last year trying to track you down. So you can bet your last penny that whenever there's a burglary in the next ten years, he'll be knocking on your door. You broke in at Kópavogsbakki fifty. What happened? Where did the blood come from?"

"I was taken by surprise," Orri said slowly. "There was someone there with a gun. I was tied up and questioned. Honestly, I thought they were going to kill me."

"Was this one person?"

"I think it was two. I can't be sure. One of them did the talking, in English. Then I could hear them muttering to each other, so I guess there were two of them."

384

"Did you see either of them?"

"No." Orri hesitated. "I just heard the voice, that's all."

"Nothing that could identify these people?"

"Just a voice in English, with an accent. He didn't sound like he was English or American."

"Russian? Scandinavian? An Icelander, maybe?"

"Could be. I couldn't tell."

"And what was this questioning all about."

"They wanted me to work for them," he muttered.

"Work for them? In what way?"

"Breaking into places and planting bugging devices."

"Good grief? And they paid you for this?"

"No, of course not," Orri lied. "But they told me they knew where I live, where Lísa lives and where my sister and her kids live, so I didn't dare say no. Now I've told you, and if they find out we're all going to need protection."

"Where did you plant bugs?"

"There was an office in Kópavogur, near Hamraborg. I can't remember what it's called, but I could find it. There was a house in the Thingholt district and there was that bikers' place in Gardabær."

"They wanted a bug in the Undertakers' clubhouse? You're kidding."

Orri shrugged. "It's there. It's hidden in the electrical conduit in their boardroom."

"That's all?"

"No. There was a place up past Mosfellsbær, a farm of some kind. I don't know what it is, but it's out in the country."

"Vison?"

"I don't know. I put a bug in the office ceiling there. There were a whole lot of metal cages in the long room there."

The door swung open and a warder walked in carrying a tray.

"Breakfast," he announced, handing it to Orri, who placed it on his knees, still keeping the duvet wrapped around him like a cloak.

"And definitely no idea who these guys are?" Gunna asked as Orri sipped his coffee.

He shook his head. "Well," he said after a moment.

"Well, what?"

"I think I saw one of them, but I'm not sure, a day or two before."

"Where? At the same house?"

"No, further up the street. The one where the dentist lives."

"How do you know it's the dentist's house?" Gunna asked.

"I do my homework carefully," Orri replied. "They live at Kópavogsbakki forty-two and own a couple more houses in the same street. I saw a man go in there who definitely wasn't the dentist, and I was there again later and the same guy was screwing the dentist's wife up against the wall."

Gunna fumbled in her coat pocket and came up with the photograph of the hook-nosed man.

"Him?"

"That's the guy," Orri said with the first hint of a smile on his morose face. "But listen, you didn't hear any of this from me, and if you ask about it again, I'll deny every word." He tapped the photograph with one finger. "Unless that guy's locked up as well."

Jóhann hung on for dear life, his arms wrapped around Helga Dís, pressing himself close to her as they shuddered and vibrated.

"All right, are you?" she yelled.

He could only nod his head in reply. His arms were still weak. Sitting on the back of the quad bike, he held on tight as the wheels transmitted every pothole and lump in the road straight through his spine to the back of his head. He sighed with relief as the bike finally hit the main road and he could see cars and signs of civilization around him.

Helga Dís seemed to drive more slowly on the better roads, but he decided that had to be an illusion. He recognized the hills, and with relief realized that Borgarnes was closer than he'd imagined. As they by-passed the cluster of shops and filling stations, the rain began to come down hard, drops bouncing off the visor of the helmet he had borrowed from Bjarni as they rolled into the town.

"I'd better come in with you," Helga Dís said, looking behind her when they stopped outside the police station.

Jóhann dismounted stiffly and she helped him off with the helmet. Helga Dís carried both helmets in one hand and took his arm with the other, supporting him through the door. Jóhann was surprised and frustrated at how weak he was after his experience. He wanted to sit down but leaned instead against the reception desk.

"Good morning, Unnur," Helga Dís greeted the officer manning the station. "I've brought someone to see you."

Unnur took off her glasses and looked at them. "Good morning, Helga. You're about early." She looked Jóhann up and down. "And who might you be?" she asked.

"My name is Jóhann Hjálmarsson and I believe you might be looking for me," he said with an effort.

"Tell me about your relationship with Boris Vadluga."

"That was Vilhelm and Elvar," Sunna María said stiffly. "We were sleeping partners, Jóhann and I."

"But still partners. You were directors of Sólfell Investment. Mr Vadluga could hardly have been happy when his money went up in smoke."

"I don't know. I didn't get involved."

"You're a director, so you're involved. Not reading the small print doesn't absolve you of any responsibility."

"Is this going to take long?"

"It'll take as long as it takes, and my colleague from financial crime would like to speak to you as well. Of course, you're free to leave at any time," Gunna said, folding her arms, and Sunna María instantly scraped her chair back across the floor. "But then we might have to look at other options, and if you decline to co-operate it won't reflect well when we find ourselves in court."

388

"When? You mean if."

"When," Gunna assured her. "Two people dead? If it doesn't come to court, then something's seriously wrong, I'd say." She laid the photocopy of the hook-nosed man's driving licence on the table between them. "It's a faked licence, naturally. I'd be interested to know this man's real name."

"I have no idea. I told you that before and I'm getting tired of telling you this."

"You're absolutely sure you've never seen this man?"

"Yes, yes," Sunna María repeated. "I don't know him."

"Now that's odd," Gunna said softly. "This is the man I suspect may have abducted and possibly murdered your husband, and I have a witness who has seen him in your company. On one of those occasions under circumstances that would indicate you're quite intimately acquainted with him."

Sunna María opened her mouth and closed it again.

"In that case, there has to be some mistake," she said finally. "It happens, I'm sure."

"He and another man were living at Kópavogsbakki fifty until recently."

"We have nothing to do with the letting. Óttar Sveinsson handles everything."

"Óttar told me you knew this man. How do you explain that? And how come the basement of Kópavogsbakki fifty had been painted? Surely that's the letting agent's job, but Óttar said he had no idea that the place had been painted."

389

Sunna María's face twisted into something that was a long way from a smile but was clearly supposed to be one.

"You'll have to ask the tenant that, won't you?"

The squad car emerged into the daylight and Unnur Matthíasdóttir brought it to a halt in the lay-by outside the Hvalfjördur Tunnel's southern exit. Reykjavík could be seen dimly in the distance across the bay beneath scudding spring clouds. She got out of the car and went round to open the door for Jóhann, helping him out as Eiríkur hurried across from his own car.

"Jóhann? Eiríkur Thór Jónsson from CID," he said. "You have no idea how pleased I am to see you in one piece."

"Thank you," Jóhann said with tears in his eyes, bewildered by the attention he was getting. "I'd just like a lift home, if you don't mind."

Eiríkur helped him into the Polo and shut the door. He saw Jóhann huddle into his borrowed coat and reach forward to turn up the heater.

"What's the story?"

"To be honest, I don't know. The lady who brought him in has her sheep and horses miles up in the highlands at a place called Geirsmörk," Unnur said. "She and her father had been up there for a few days and they stumbled across this guy in the road the night before last; they took him back to the chalet they have up there and warmed him up. She said he was too weak to be moved yesterday. It seems he was at a place called

390

Vatnsendi, which has been abandoned for at least fifty years. How he got up there, who knows?"

"How is he?"

"He's very weak. I wanted to take him to hospital, but he wouldn't hear of it and wanted to go straight home. We had already had an alert about this man, so I called and here you are."

"Thanks. We'd more or less written him off."

"Did he walk out, or what?"

"It seems he was abducted. Hopefully he can tell us how he managed to get to somewhere that far up country. Have you asked him any questions?"

"Only to make sure he was feeling all right and wasn't going to have a seizure on the way. So now he's all yours," Unnur said with a bright smile.

"Thank you," Eiríkur said. "I'd best get him to Reykjavík and we'll see if we can work out what happened to him."

"Are you telling me my wife may have had something to do with this?"

Jóhann's eyes were wide. Anger and surprise made his voice lift in pitch. Gunna could see that both of his hands trembled. A drip had been put into one arm below where the borrowed shirt that was several sizes too big for him had been rolled up high above a skinny forearm.

"We don't know, but for the moment I really don't want anyone to know that you're alive and well."

"I see," he said, subsiding thoughtfully. "What's today? Thursday? Is it almost a week?"

"What happened last Friday morning? Tell me every detail you can remember."

His brows knitted. "It's hazy," he admitted. "I've been trying for days to remember everything."

"It's important," Gunna reminded him.

"You don't need to tell me that," he shot back in irritation. "I had a message asking for a meeting at the old Sólfell offices at twelve."

"How? Email or text?"

"Email, I think. I'd have to check my computer. But it was no problem, so I got a taxi up there."

"That fits. I traced you that far. Who were you going to meet?"

"So I went up to the office on the eighth floor. I can't remember. It might have been Óttar or one of the property managers."

"Óttar Sveinsson?"

"Yes. His company leases our property and Sólfell also rented its offices through him. But I can't be sure. It might have been one of his staff. So when I got there the place was open and there was someone there I didn't recognize, but he said his name was Boris."

"Boris Vadluga? The man you were in partnership with?"

"That's him. Well, I was surprised."

"You had never met Boris Vadluga?"

"No, we'd spoken on the phone a few times, but Sunna María saw to all that business with Vilhelm and Elvar. All I did was sign the accounts once a year."

Gunna took a photo from her folder of notes. "This man?"

392

"Who's this?"

"This is Boris Vadluga."

"Definitely not him. This fellow was older, I thought."

"This man?"

The driving licence photograph was indistinct, but Jóhann almost jumped from his chair when he saw it. "That's the man! I'd recognize him anywhere," he squeaked and calmed down quickly, his breathing laboured. "If that's not Boris, who is it?"

"That's just what we'd like to know as well. So what happened?"

"We chatted, had a coffee. He was clearing stuff out of the office since the company had folded."

"Didn't you find that strange?" Gunna asked. "Wasn't it odd that he should be doing something like that himself. Wasn't it odd that he should be in Iceland at all?"

"I did find it very unusual, but he said something about being here on other business. Then I started to feel very strange, unsteady on my feet. It was as if I knew there was something very wrong but couldn't do anything about it."

"You were doped," Gunna said. "As soon as you'd drunk that coffee, your friend didn't need to worry any longer about being convincing. A witness saw a man answering your description leaving the building with this man on Friday afternoon. He thought you were drunk. So you wake up in the wilderness and then what?"

"I think I'm lucky to be here. I don't believe I was intended to survive."

"Maybe he got the dose wrong," Eiríkur suggested.

"We'll probably never find out what it was he gave you. Most of these drugs are out of your system after a day or two and this was a week ago. Rohypnol, ketamine, there's plenty to choose from."

Jóhann shuddered as he thought back to the moment he woke up in the distant ruined farmhouse.

Gísli fidgeted as the waitress took away the empty plates, casting glances around him.

"Why this place?" Gunna asked. "Not your usual stamping grounds, surely? I thought you would have preferred the place by the dock."

"Actually, I would have. But here there's less chance of seeing anyone I know."

"Don't want any of the guys to see you out with an old lady?"

"Come on, Mum. It's not like that. If we'd gone to Kænan then there'd be someone around I'd sailed with or worked with, or someone who knows Steini. We'd just be talking boats and engines."

"Instead of what?"

Gísli sighed and looked up as the waitress brought them fresh cutlery. He stayed silent until she had gone, shredding a piece of bread between his long fingers. A craftsman's fingers, Gunna thought, like his grandfather's.

"I'm not a complete slob, you know, Mum. I do like to go to smart places occasionally. I came here with Soffía once or twice," he said wistfully.

"How is she?" Gunna asked.

"Soffía's fine. For a skinny little thing she's as tough as old boots."

"It's something that hadn't escaped my notice," Gunna said as the waitress returned with steaming dishes. Pasta with chicken for Gísli, grilled fish for her. "Looks good," she said as the girl vanished silently into the background.

They were silent for a few minutes as each made inroads on lunch. The restaurant was quiet, with only a few lunchtime customers holding quiet conversations over their meals beneath subtle lights and sprays of dried flowers on the walls between dark abstract oil paintings. The quiet suited her. Conversation at the table had never been encouraged when Gunna had been growing up in a large family where food had to be eaten before it disappeared into two hungry big brothers, and the same custom had been unconsciously carried on in her own household.

"The pasta's a bit overdone," Gísli said eventually and Gunna stared at him.

"Overdone? You can overcook pasta?"

"Sure, mum. Haven't you seen Steini timing it every time he does pasta?"

"I suppose so. I hadn't noticed that."

"It should be *al dente*, so it still has a little texture to it, not boiled to death like . . ."

"Like I do?"

"I wasn't going to say that. I meant like a ship's cook does it."

"In that case you can be forgiven."

Gísli cleared his plate first and fidgeted again while Gunna finished her plaice.

"Not bad," she said, downing her knife and fork. "Gísli, what's bugging you? I know there has to be plenty, but what in particular? Soffía? Drífa? Any decisions? I know I'm only your old mum, so I'm the last one to get any information, but it would be nice to know what's going on."

"I know Soffía would be your choice, wouldn't she?"

"I like the girl a lot. There's bone in that nose."

"And Drífa?"

Gunna took a deep breath. "She's lovely, but she's a child."

"She's growing up fast. I think she needs me more than Soffía does."

"You don't have to tell me. I see more of her than you do." The words slipped out and Gísli flushed. "I'm sorry, Gísli. I didn't mean it like that. You have to make your own choices and decisions."

"Like you did, you mean?"

Gunna frowned her eyebrows into a dark bar. "In what way?"

"Like when you and my dad . . ."

She sat back and looked him in the eye. "Your father was a mistake on my part."

"So I was a mistake?"

"I didn't say that."

The waitress sensed the tension as she collected their plates. "Would you like to see a dessert menu?" she asked shyly.

Gísli shook his head. "Just a coffee for me."

"I would, thanks," Gunna decided. "As I'm being treated."

"Sorry, Mum. I didn't mean to snap at you," Gísli mumbled. He reached across the table and placed a hand on hers.

Gunna wanted to snatch her hand away but resisted the temptation.

"Listen. Your father was five minutes of madness. I should have known better, but I wasn't much older than your little sister is now. I was sixteen when you were born."

"You must have been . . .?" Gísli said and stopped, colouring.

"You can work it out easily enough," Gunna said sharply. "A month or so short of my sixteenth birthday if you must know."

"You weren't . . . together at all?"

"Are you joking? Your father was in the process of divorcing his first wife and the last thing he wanted was to be shackled to a wayward teenager. Why? You've seen him, haven't you? What's your impression?" Gunna scanned the dessert menu the waitress handed her. "The fruit salad, please. And a coffee."

"Latte, expresso?"

"Just ordinary coffee will do nicely."

"He's a charming man," Gísli said. "In his own strange way."

"I wouldn't say charming," Gunna said after a moment's thought. "He's a fascinating man, and when he was younger he was a remarkable character. But there's a dark side to everyone and your father's dark side is very close to the surface. So what did you make of him?"

"Disappointed," Gísli mumbled.

"Why's that?"

"Because he wasn't interested, like I told you before."

"He must know when your birthday is but he never sent a present or a card, never tried to maintain any contact. But to his credit, I suppose, he never tried to claim you were nothing to do with him. You thought he'd have been waiting all these years for you to come and find him? Think again. He could have had access when you were a child but he didn't want to know then. So why would he now? I'm afraid Thorvaldur Hauksson is a rather self-centred character."

"Have you seen him?" Gísli asked.

Gunna let the fruit salad the waitress delivered sit untouched on the table in front of her as she wondered whether to tell Gísli the truth or not.

"He left Vestureyri before you were a year old," she said finally. "It wasn't exactly a healthy place for him to stay. He had an affair with a woman whose husband didn't take kindly to it when he heard. So he left town and moved to Reykjavík, taking only what he could pack in the back of that old American gas guzzler he had at the time."

"That's the last you saw of him?"

"After I moved south to go to the police college I heard of him around town, but we didn't run into each other, which was probably just as well. You were being looked after by your uncle Hafsteinn's Anna Sigga at the time. They had three children of their own, so she said one more didn't make much difference. It was very generous of Anna Sigga, I realize now."

Gunna toyed with the fruit salad, but her appetite had deserted her, while Gísli sipped his coffee.

"I saw him once," she said slowly. "You must have been about six or seven, I think. I was at the Hafnarfjördur station at the time. Two of the guys had been to a fight at a club and rounded up everyone who'd been involved, herded them into the back of a meat wagon and brought them down to the station to be charged."

"And my dad was one of them?"

"He was the only one they had to handcuff," Gunna said sorrowfully. "It was a shock to see him sitting there having his details taken, sloppy drunk and with his hands behind his back. Someone had smacked him and given him a fat lip. He didn't recognize me, I don't think. At any rate, I didn't say anything and just left the boys to it. I suppose he must have been turned out first thing the next morning because they were all gone when I came in for the next day's shift." She forked up a slice of guava. "That was the last time I saw your father."

"You didn't say anything?"

"Not a word. I thought I'd leave the poor bastard a bit of dignity without having some young copper crowing over him," Gunna said and reached for her coffee. "So, how is he? He must be past fifty by now."

"Fifty-six," Gísli said. "He's tired, I think. High blood pressure and he smokes like a chimney."

"Like a coal-fired sidewinder, as Steini would say," Gunna said and was relieved to see Gísli smile.

"Something like that."

"You want some of this?" she asked, pushing the fruit salad over to him and watched him spoon up what was left.

Outside the restaurant Gísli hugged her. "Thanks, Mum."

"For what?

"You know," he mumbled. "Nothing. You're going back to work?"

"Oh, yes. I have to go and make some decisions before Ívar Laxdal makes them for me."

"Well, you've a track record of making tough decisions, I suppose. I'll see you tomorrow."

Gísli walked down the street and Gunna affectionately watched his broad back as he made his way downhill, car keys hanging from one finger, until he was no longer in sight. When he had gone, she shook herself, recalling their conversation and setting off towards the Hverfisgata station where Orri Björnsson was waiting in a cell for the hour-long ride in a police van to the prison at Litla Hraun.

"No! Absolutely not."

Sævaldur's face had gone an entirely new shade of red that Gunna had never seen before. Lunch with Gísli had driven Orri completely out of her mind for an hour and she felt raw after the long talk with her son, but deeply relieved that they had gone some way to making peace with each other again.

"All right, give me one good reason, will you?"

"Because I've been chasing after this bastard for the last year and I want him to stew in a cell for ever. I don't want him to see the light of day ever again."

Three years of working with Ívar Laxdal had given Gunna an insight into his character, and she recognized the glint in his eye betraying that he relished the sight of Sævaldur Bogason in full furious flow.

"That's still no reason," she continued. "He's been arrested and he's been charged. He's no danger to anyone but himself and he's hardly likely to go on a last burglary spree now, is he?"

Are you off your fucking head, woman?"

"Ívar?"

"My feeling is that Gunnhildur is right," Ívar Laxdal said. "It hurts to let this character out, but he's been charged and in any case his lawyer can argue convincingly enough for bail. He'd get it, no doubt, as far as I'm concerned. He's not a violent criminal and I can't see him hurting anyone."

"Have it your own way," Sævaldur said, his frustration evident. "But I hope they throw away the key. Not that they're likely to give him more than a pat on the back and ask him nicely not to do it again for a while," he added bitterly. The door banged behind him.

"He's not a happy camper, is he?"

"No, Gunnhildur, he's not, and I understand his feelings entirely. But if you have to, I suggest you get this done quickly."

A few minutes later Gunna stood at the back of the least comfortable interview room as Eiríkur gave Orri back the contents of his pockets.

"Sign here, will you?" he said, spinning the form around and placing a pen on it.

Orri looked bewildered. "What does this mean?"

"It means you're being released," Eiríkur told him. "Pending recall for further questioning and a court appearance."

"But . . . I thought . . ."

"Thought what? Thought you were going to be shipped off to Litla Hraun? Count yourself lucky is all I can say."

"But I don't want to be released," Orri blurted out.

"What? You don't want to be let out? Listen, we get drunks turning up asking for a cell to crash in often enough, but you must have a good reason to want to be inside, surely?" Eiríkur said with interest. "What's the problem?"

Orri deflated in confusion. "Nothing," he said finally. "It's all right." He switched on his phone and listened to the chime of it starting up before he stowed it in his pocket. He scrawled a signature on the form to confirm his belongings had been returned.

"I'm going that way myself," Gunna said. "I'll even give you a lift home."

"What the hell's going on?" Orri demanded. "Why is this happening?"

"Why are you so suspicious?" Gunna retorted. "I'm going to Hafnarfjördur anyway. I can drop you off on the way. But if you'd rather go over the road and wait for a bus, that's up to you. I'll be downstairs in ten minutes," she said and left the room, leaving Eiríkur to deliver Orri to the car park.

Gunna discreetly glanced in the rear-view mirror to make sure that Eiríkur was in sight while Orri sat slumped in the seat next to her.

"I shouldn't have told you anything," he said as the Golf swished through puddles on the way out of town.

"You didn't have to. Listen, Orri. What's the problem? Go back to work."

"That's what I don't understand."

Gunna slowed as they approached a set of lights. "What don't you understand?"

"I don't understand why you're being so nice," he sneered. "That fat bastard wanted to lock me up for ever."

"Sævaldur? Yeah, he's a bit extreme. But we're not all like that."

"So why the nice cop, nasty cop thing?"

The traffic crawled to a standstill on Miklabraut as a large four-by-four with tinted windows caused a furore of horns as it stopped across two lanes at the intersection.

"If I wasn't busy, I'd pull that idiot over and give him a ticket," Gunna mused. "Because that's the way we are. Some of us are rougher round the edges than others. As far as I'm concerned, you haven't been charged with any violent offences, your passport's been impounded and it's not as if you're going to skip the country. So I don't see the point in keeping you fed and watered at taxpayer's expense. Do you have any idea how crowded Litla Hraun is these days and how much it costs to keep someone on remand?"

"Well, I suppose."

"Keep your nose clean. You'll probably get a year when it finally comes to court and you'll be out in six months. After that I hope never to have to cross your path again in a professional capacity."

Orri sat up and looked happier as Gunna accelerated and then didn't speak again until she had taken the turning along Nýbýlavegur towards the far end of Kópavogur.

"And if you do?" he asked suddenly.

"If I do what?"

"If we have to meet in your professional capacity?"

"Then I'll throw the book at you and hang every unsolved break-in I can find for the last twenty years on you. Does that answer your question?"

Orri finally allowed himself a wan smile. "Yeah. It does."

"Go to work tomorrow. Make it up with with Lísa. Keep your fingers clean," Gunna said, turning off down the rutted road leading to the block where Orri lived and checking as she did so that Eiríkur had driven past. She pulled up next to Lísa's Ka. "Now piss off and make the most of your few weeks of freedom before the courts get round to your case."

CHAPTER
FOURTEEN

Gunna lay in the dark and wondered if she'd done the right thing. Sævaldur was furious, not least because of his complete failure to uncover any leads on the murder of Vilhelm Thorleifsson, his frustration compounded by Eiríkur finding the culprit behind the wave of burglaries around the city that had become his own personal mission over the last eighteen months. Gunna's decision to release Orri when Sævaldur would have relished grilling him for hours in an uncomfortable interview room at Litla Hraun had practically given him palpitations. Much as she disliked working with Sævaldur Bogason, she could understand his feelings.

She knew she should be asleep, but the makeshift bed was unfamiliar and the flat was a small one. Gunna stretched out, feeling something hard digging into her back through the sofa bed's thin upholstery. Thoughts of Sunna María, Orri and Jóhann kept nagging her, especially Jóhann's chagrin at being asked to stay in hospital instead of going home, and his bewilderment when Gunna had told him how important it might be not to let anyone know he had survived his ordeal in the wilderness.

Eventually she had relented and Jóhann's sons, one a younger version of their lanky, curly haired father and the other a bearded barrel of a man, had both been told that their father was alive, but sworn to silence.

Gunna padded across to the kitchen and keyed a message into her phone: Anything yet?

She toyed with the idea of making herself a cup of coffee, but immediately decided against it, knowing that a hint of caffeine would definitely rule out sleep.

In the other room, ten-month-old Ari Gíslason moaned in his sleep and Gunna could hear Soffía clucking and cooing to him as she rocked him back to sleep. Her phone buzzed discreetly on the kitchen table.

Nothing so far, she read. Had she made a huge mistake? She was sure this time Ívar Laxdal's head would be on the block along with her own and she wondered why he had allowed her to take such a chance. She punched in another message.

Seen anything?

This time the reply came back almost instantly.

Silent as the grave, she read and smiled grimly to herself, wondering how Eiríkur was feeling outside on a cold night like this.

I'll come and relieve you in a couple of hours, she wrote back and looked up as Soffía appeared with Ari on her shoulder.

"He won't go back to sleep?"

"He's hungry," Soffía said, yawning, and sat down, cradling the little boy and lifting her shirt to attach him to a nipple. "Can't you sleep?"

"No. I had a couple of hours, but woke up and couldn't get back to sleep again."

"Something big going on?" Soffía asked. "I know I shouldn't ask . . ."

"I'm really not sure. I may be barking completely up the wrong tree, but I expect we'll find out in the morning. All right, is he?"

"He's fine," Soffía said fondly. "He normally needs a feed around this time."

"So when did you last get a full night's sleep?"

"About this time last year."

"I remember all that like it was yesterday."

"I spoke to Drífa yesterday. I'm going to drive out to Hvalvík and see her again at the weekend. We need to let these two little reprobates get to know each other," she said. "I think he's asleep already," she added, shifting the baby gently. "And it was lovely to see Laufey and Steini again. It's a long time since I saw them. I've missed Hvalvík," she said wistfully. "I like being back in Reykjavík again, but I miss the quietness in Hvalvík."

"Laufey spends a lot of time with Drífa these days."

"Good. She must be lonely. I don't envy her being in that position."

"We tend to be difficult in my family, I'm afraid, and my Gísli is no exception," Gunna said and started as her communicator buzzed.

"You there, Gunna?" She heard Eiríkur's voice in the earpiece she hastily stuffed into one ear.

"I'm here. What's going on?"

"Not sure. There's someone moving around."

"Can you see who it is?"

"No. Just a shadow in the dark. What do you want me to do?"

"Do what you think's best. Observe but don't take any chances. I'm on my way." Gunna stood up. "Time to go, I'm afraid."

"A short night for you."

"Yep. Someone's going to be grumpy in the morning." She grinned. "So feel sorry for any villains who have to deal with me tomorrow. Thanks for letting me stay."

"You're welcome. I won't make the sofa up, in case you need somewhere to crash in the morning."

Eiríkur was swaddled in a coat that came up to his chin and a hat that came down to his eyebrows.

"Where's Tinna?" Gunna asked as soon as she saw him.

"She went to check the street."

"All right, what did you see?"

"Someone came along the street, walking towards the car. Dark clothes, tallish. Disappeared between the houses."

Gunna peered into the gloom between the patches of light cast by the few street lamps erected in the half-finished length of Kópavogsbakki. "Between which houses?"

"There and there," Eiríkur said, pointing to one of the two houses being built for Sunna María and the completed villa next to it. "Tinna went that way and I went to check Sunna María's place."

408

"All quiet?"

"Nothing to be seen. Any luck?" he asked as Tinna, the uniformed officer he had been paired with for the night's surveillance, appeared from the darkness.

"Nothing," she said with a shake of her head. Nothing to be seen and nothing to be heard."

"No movement or lights at Sunna María's house?"

"The lights went off not long after midnight."

"No visitors before that?" Gunna said.

"No, looks like she's been there all evening."

"Unlike her to be home alone, I'd have thought. Oh well, keep an eye out and see what happens, but watch that back door," she warned as her phone buzzed.

Something's going on. Give me a call, she read on the screen, and immediately dialled, walking along the street away from Tinna and Eiríkur as she did so.

The phone rang once before it was answered.

"Communications. Siggi speaking."

"*Hæ*. Gunna. What's going on? Any calls to any of those numbers?"

The communications officer on the other end of the line muttered to himself and she could hear him shuffling sheets of paper. "Your friend in Kópavogur had a text message, in English. It reads: Meet tomorrow? Does that make sense to you?"

"Not a lot. Is that all there is?"

"The reply reads: Can't meet. Been arrested."

"Any more?"

"There's a message back again that says: We'll be quick. Same place."

"And?"

"That's it."

"And the number it came from?"

"An unregistered pay-as-you-go mobile."

Gunna walked faster, turned and walked back towards Eiríkur and Tinna as she talked. "Can you trace the locations?"

"Your friend's mobile has been on the same mast since four this afternoon. The other one's somewhere downtown and hasn't been moving about either."

"And our friend hasn't replied?"

"Hold on." Gunna could hear the clicking of a keyboard and Siggi's heavy breathing into the phone jammed under his chin. "Just now. He sent one back that said: Time? There's been no reply to that one yet."

"All right. Thanks, Siggi. Let me know as soon as something happens with either of them, will you?"

"I will. I'll brief my relief when he arrives as well. This has priority, right?"

"Absolutely. Our friend's friend is someone we definitely don't want walking the streets. So top priority, please," Gunna said and ended the call. "Eiríkur!"

"Yes, chief?" he said, looking expectant.

"It seems Orri's meeting someone in the morning, and I have a feeling it's the guy who abducted Jóhann."

"You know when?"

"That's the fun part of it all," Gunna said. "We don't know when and we don't know where."

"Gunna."

She heard the voice calling her from a distance. A soft, welcoming voice that begged her to open her eyes.

410

"Gunna."

This time it was more insistent, firmer, and she resisted the temptation to find out who wanted her so badly. She rolled her shoulders and huddled deeper into the borrowed anorak when the hum of an engine starting up reminded her that she wasn't asleep in her own bed and a heavy hand shook her shoulder.

"Gunna, our friend's on the move."

She was awake in an instant on the back seat of one of the car pool's unmarked Golfs. Big Geiri, who had been watching the door of the block of flats where she had delivered Orri the previous afternoon, was taking the car along the track towards the main road with the lights off. Looking through the windscreen she could see Orri's rust-coloured Toyota in the distance in the glow of the street lights. Drizzle fizzed in the dim spheres of light around them and the wipers swept the windscreen clean.

"Keep behind him, but not too close," Gunna instructed needlessly. "What time is it?"

"Six ten."

"Hell, he must be going to work."

"Where's that?"

"Off Reykjanesbraut, just outside Hafnarfjördur."

"That fits, he's going right."

"Don't lose him, Geiri, this one's important," Gunna said and Geiri put his foot down as soon as he had a chance, keeping his eyes on the lights of Orri's car while Gunna clicked her communicator.

"Zero-four-fifty-one, ninety-five-fifty. Eiríkur, you there?"

Ninety-five-fifty, zero-four-fifty-one. Got you."

"Heading for Reykjanesbraut. Our friend's moving."

"Orri?" Eiríkur asked sleepily.

"My guess is he's going to work. Any movement at Sunna María's place?"

"This early? Nothing."

"All right. Give her an hour and then bang on her door. Make sure she's still in one piece."

"Will do."

Gunna leaned over the seat to peer through the windscreen. "You can still see him?"

"Right there," Geiri growled. "And over the speed limit in this weather."

"Definitely looks like he's going to work. I'll duck behind the seat if you want to get closer. We can't let him see me."

The Golf spun through the sheets of water forming on the roads and Orri's car came gradually closer until Geiri caught up with it at an intersection outside Hafnarfjördur. As the lights changed he ran a light that had just gone red to keep up and then allowed another car to filter across between them, still keeping Orri in sight.

With Hafnarfjördur behind them, Orri's car sideslipped onto a feeder road and Geiri took his foot off the pedal to create some space between them.

"He's coming off."

"I thought he would. Keep an eye on him as far back as you can."

Geiri slowed and waited until Orri was already down the sloping curve before he followed, letting himself lose sight of Orri's car for a few seconds, and at the same time letting Orri lose sight of anyone who might be following. Now it was obvious where he was going and Geiri pulled up in the parking lot of a neighbouring building between a couple of vans, far enough from the Green Bay Dispatch unit to be inconspicuous.

"What now?"

"I need another half hour with my eyes closed," Gunna said, handing him the pair of small binoculars from the back seat. "Our boy will probably come out and drive off in one of those vans. When he does, wake me up."

Gunna's communicator came to life at the same time as the Golf did and she felt the car move as "Ninety-five-fifty, zero-four-fifty-one" crackled in her ear.

"Zero-four-fifty-one, ninety-five-fifty," Gunna answered as she looked around. "What's happening, Geiri?"

"Our friend's moving off. The white Trafic up there." He pointed with a thick finger to the van in the distance.

"OK, good, don't lose him," she said blearily and clicked her communicator again. "Eiríkur, what news?"

"Nobody home, chief. No answer when we banged on the door and the home phone isn't answering either. Nothing to be seen through the windows."

"Hell. Where's the damned woman got to?"

"I'm starting to wonder if it was her we saw last night."

"Why do you think that?"

"It was someone who knew their way around, I reckon, and slipped away in the dark. We were looking for someone going to her house, not someone coming from it."

"Use your discretion. Get inside if you can without doing too much damage and check if she's there or not. If there's any comeback, we can truthfully say that we were concerned for her well-being. All right?"

"Sure, chief. After sitting here all night, Tinna really likes the idea of breaking Sunna María's windows."

Gunna wanted to laugh, but stopped herself. Her head was starting to pound. "Up to you, dear boy. But you'll have to answer for any damage. Let me know when you've had a look."

The van was making sedate progress back along Reykjanesbraut towards the city through the swelling rush hour traffic that Gunna reflected she would also be in the middle of on a normal day. Geiri hummed to himself, easily keeping the high-sided Trafic in sight as the streams of cars stopped and started, pushing his way across into the other lanes when he needed to and once flooring the accelerator when the van took an unexpected turn, pressing Gunna into the seat in the back.

She reflected that it was as well Orri drove fairly responsibly, and wondered why she was still in the back like a passenger in a taxi. As the van approached the intersection with Vesturlandsvegur and Geiri watched Orri join the lane of traffic heading for the city's northern region and the countryside beyond, Gunna's communicator clicked.

"Gunna, you there?" she heard Eiríkur call, for once forgetting proper communications protocol.

"Yep, I'm here. What's the score?"

"The house is empty. Nobody here."

"Sure she's not been dumped in the freezer?"

"Already checked. She must have gone out the back door, around the house and walked away. There's a footpath between the two houses and she must have gone up there."

"Hell and damnation."

"Want to put out an alert for her?"

"Not yet. Her car's there?"

"There are two cars in the garage, and guess what? One of them's a dark grey Audi A5, the same as someone saw in Borgarfjördur the night Vilhelm Thorleifsson was shot. It's registered to Jón Vilberg Voss."

"Who has been in Paris for the last three months. Very convenient."

Gunna felt the car slow down and looked up. The white van with Orri at the wheel had pulled into the exit lane and climbed a slope to the lights at the top, where it waited, eventually hauling itself past the lights and across the intersection bridge to another set of lights.

"What's happening, Geiri?"

"Not sure. Looks like he's heading into Grafarvogur. Unless he's figured out he's being followed and is doubling back on himself. We'll see when the lights change."

"All right," Gunna said and went back to her communicator. "Eiríkur?"

"Here."

"If there's nothing happening, then get over to communications. Check the traffic on Orri's phone, the mysterious one he's been in touch with, and see if Sunna María's phone can be tracked as well. I've already requested warrants for a bunch of mobile numbers, so check with the Laxdal if they aren't there yet."

"Will do. And you?"

"We're tailing Orri in his work van. We're up near Höfdabakki at the moment and it looks like he's just driven into that new shopping centre there."

He had to admit to himself, it didn't feel bad to be back in the van and back at work. Dóri had been surprised to see him, but refrained from dropping the sarcastic comments the others let fall. The place had changed in the last couple of weeks, but with all the fuss of the police and being arrested a couple of times, he had hardly noticed it.

The old boys had a subdued feel about them now, nervous that their jobs were about to fall through, and while nobody missed Alex and his abrasive manner, the fact that he had died in such circumstances had left a clear mark on the staff.

Dóri had given him a couple of easy collections that would keep him busy for a few hours. He was still undecided about meeting the Voice. He felt he was in enough trouble already and he was nervous that he might not come out of a meeting unscathed, but meeting somewhere public should be safe enough. Of course, it wasn't his fault that the police had caught up with him like that. Well, he admitted to himself, it had been his fault, but he could hardly be blamed for it.

As the van made its stately way up Vesturlandsvegur to the first pickup of the day, Orri wondered how long it would be before the police came calling again and how soon he would be hauled before a court. The thought had kept him awake last night, along with all the other question marks he felt had dropped into view in the last few days.

He had called Lísa's phone twice and she hadn't picked up. Would she come back? Could he persuade her to come back? He certainly missed her presence far more than he could have imagined, even though her pernickety ways sometimes irritated the hell out of him. And what about the Voice? The thought kept coming back to him and he wondered what was going to happen there.

He was already starting to regret having sent the man a message the night before to let him know he was temporarily free. It would have been so much simpler if the police had just shipped him off to Litla Hraun and helped him drop out of circulation for a few weeks; hopefully the whole thing could have blown over while he took it easy behind bars.

The ticket for the first pickup was at the top of the pile of four, the address in the newish shopping centre at Bíldshöfdi. No problem. Orri sat back and turned up the radio, trying to shut out all the unanswered questions he dearly wanted answers to.

There was a prickly feeling in her eyelids and she was certain that her eyes were red-rimmed after not enough hours of sleep. She knew that Geiri must also be close to exhaustion, having watched Orri's flat all night, but he sat in the driver's seat and looked over his shoulder at her.

"What now?"

"What time is it?"

"Just before nine."

Gunna got out of the car. The shock of the cold air made her gasp and she quickly got into the front seat next to Geiri.

"You're not tired?"

Geiri shook his head. "Yeah. But good for a few hours yet."

Gunna wondered if she had ever seen him out of uniform before and decided she probably hadn't. It seemed odd, sitting next to this bear of a man with as much stubble on his face as on his cropped head. Without his uniform, he looked like the kind of thug she would normally be wary of.

"Our boy knows me, so I need to keep out of sight. How about you go inside and see if you can scrounge two cups of coffee from the bank?"

"There's a bank in there?"

"Yep, opened a few months ago. There's a coffee pot by the door for customers. I'll buzz you if our boy shows up."

Geiri walked towards the shopping centre's entrance and the doors hissed open for him. Gunna's heart was in her mouth as Orri came out of the same open doors, pushing a trolley in front of him stacked with a dozen boxes on a wooden pallet.

"Shit," she cursed as Geiri went straight past Orri without looking at him, and made for the glass-sided bank in the bottom corner of the block-like shopping centre, where Gunna saw him chatting and flirting with a woman filling the coffee machine. Gunna ducked down as far out of sight as she dared and watched Orri load the van, stacking the boxes one at a time in the back before going back inside with the trolley and its empty pallet.

A few minutes later Geiri emerged from the building, a plastic coffee cup in each hand, with Orri behind him.

"Here you are. No sugar," he said as he got back in the driver's seat.

"You took your time. Didn't they want to give you any coffee unless you opened an account?"

"Talked her into it." Geiri grinned. His coat was half open, making the police emblem on his T-shirt visible. "And the cashier gave me her phone number."

"She's probably looking up your financial records this minute to see if you're trustworthy," Gunna said as Geiri allowed Orri's van a head start.

Orri took the van back the way he had come. Gunna sipped her coffee and felt herself relax slightly as Geiri dropped back as far as he could without losing sight of the van in the distance. She glanced at her watch and saw that it was approaching ten o'clock. The rush-hour traffic had thinned and the roads were quieter now, but with faster-moving cars throwing up screens of water from the road behind them.

Geiri accelerated to close the gap again as the Reykjanesbraut intersection approached. He stared ahead intently at the white van as it dropped into the slip road.

"Going back the way he came," he grunted, holding his hand out for the cup of coffee that Gunna held for him.

"A long way to go for a few boxes."

"Someone's paying, I suppose."

"Let's see if he's going back to the yard," Gunna said and spoke into her communicator. "Zero-four-fifty-one, ninety-five-fifty."

"Ninety-five-fifty, zero-four-fifty-one," Eiríkur responded smartly.

"Still awake, then?"

"Yeah. But Tinna's taking a nap. I'm at comms. Nothing to report. No communications with the mystery phone and it seems to have been switched off at around six in the morning downtown. Orri's phone has been tracked up to Höfdabakki and back towards town. Looks like he's on Reykjanesbraut now."

"I know. We're right behind him. And Sunna María's phone?"

"We don't have a warrant yet to track it, the Laxdal's working on it but it might take a while. But I can tell you it's in Kópavogur."

"She may have left it behind, I suppose, but it wouldn't be like her."

It was another shopping centre. This time Orri parked in Hafnarfjördur and sauntered into the shopping centre, leaving the van in the public car park.

"What now?"

"One of us is going to have to keep an eye on him, and it can't be me," Gunna said.

Geiri nodded and pulled on a wool hat that came down to his eyebrows. "Let's just hope I don't look too much like a copper out of uniform, eh?"

"Out of uniform, you look nothing like a copper," Gunna assured him. "Be discreet and let me know what he's up to."

She fretted in the car, wondering if Orri had noticed the tail back and forth through Reykjavík, and concerned that Geiri would look suspicious in there. Gunna fidgeted with her phone and checked her text messages, trying to think through what Orri might be doing and why.

Her phone ringing startled her and she answered immediately. "Gunnhildur."

"Orri's in the café. With a woman. Tall, blonde," she heard Geiri mutter.

"A woman? It's not Sunna María, is it?"

"I don't know. I can only see the back of her head and I daren't go any closer."

"Where are you now?"

"In the kiosk opposite, looking through the magazines."

"OK, keep an eye on them, but not for too long."

421

Orri had expected to see the hook-nosed man. He looked around the café, his phone in his hand, searching for him, but his heart skipped a beat when he saw a blonde woman smile at him. The last time he had seen her was when she had been on the other side of the hall doorway with her legs wrapped around the man he knew as the Voice.

"It's Orri, isn't it?" she said in a slightly husky voice that was undeniably the same as the one he'd heard that night through the door. "Bruno asked me to meet you. I hope you don't mind? I'm having a latte. What can I get you? The same?"

"Er . . . just a coffee. Where's . . . ?"

"Bruno? He'll be here shortly. He asked me to meet you as he's been held up for ten minutes. Would you like something to eat as well?"

Orri sat down, confused. Why was the dentist's attractive wife here to meet him? "Bruno?" he asked himself as he sat at a table and looked out of the rain-splashed window at the car park where the van was parked, telling himself that he could manage twenty minutes or so before his next collection and then back to the depot. Not seeing the Voice was a surprise and it had shaken him to understand that the dentist's wife and the Baltic thug were clearly working together rather than straightforward lovers while the dentist was out of the country.

He looked round and saw her at the counter, pouring milk into a mug and dropping a wrapper into the bin next to it. She smiled broadly as she appeared with a

422

tray, placing a mug in front of him and arranging a tall milky concoction for herself and a plate with strips of rich Danish pastry between them.

"I must say it's nice to meet you properly," Sunna María said, sinking perfect white teeth into a slice of pastry.

"We haven't met before, have we?"

"In a strange kind of way, we have," she said and Orri wondered if she knew he had been in her house more than once. The smile became glassy as Orri took a mouthful of coffee and she watched approvingly. "Want some?" she invited, pushing the plate of pastries towards him. "I'm terrible. I never have breakfast and then I'm always starving by mid-morning."

He nibbled a pastry without much appetite. "So if we have met, where was that?"

"You want a refill?" Sunna María asked, nodding at his mug.

"All right, then."

She stood up to return with a second mug of coffee and put in front of him.

"You didn't answer my question. Where have I seen you before?"

"You've been to my house, Orri," she said sweetly. "And to the house I own along the street. I have a few motion sensor cameras here and there, and it wasn't that hard to figure you out."

"Oh," Orri sat crestfallen, wondering what to say as she reached out and patted his hand. He tried to draw his hand back but his fingers felt numb.

"Then you appeared one night and we met in the cellar. I thought Bruno was a little harsh on you, but that's his business."

"That was you?" Orri wanted to stand up and overturn the table, but found himself welded to his chair, watching Sunna María bite into another slice of pastry.

"It was, I'm afraid. Are you feeling all right, Orri?" she said, standing up and dusting crumbs from her fingers with the same enchanting smile. "I'll help you back to the van. You don't want to embarrass yourself in here, do you?"

Big Geiri hurried out of the shopping centre and sat heavily in the driver's seat.

"There's something odd going on in there. Our boy's had a funny turn or something, and she's helping him out," he said, switching on the engine and watching over the steering wheel as Orri came out of the shopping centre, unsteady on his feet and with Sunna María, an arm firmly around his waist, propping him up and steering him towards the van.

"What the hell's going on?" Gunna muttered to herself. "He looks drunk."

"He had two cups of coffee and that's all."

"Zero-four-fifty-one, ninety-five-fifty," Gunna called into her communicator. "Speak to me, Eiríkur."

"Ninety-five-fifty, zero-four-fifty-one. Nothing new here."

"There is here. Listen, I want some backup ready in the background and I reckon we're going to need an ambulance as well. You can follow me on the tracker, so I want them ready when I need them. Got that?"

"There's a traffic unit round the corner on the main road and a squad car at the Hafnarfjördur station. I'll get those ready to go for you. What's happening?"

"I have Sunna María and Orri apparently heading towards Green Bay's van and it looks very strange. I really want to grab the pair of them, but I don't want to move until our mystery man shows up," Gunna replied. "If he shows up, that is." Gunna impatiently wiped the windscreen with her sleeve. "Can you see what's happening, Geiri?"

"No, looks like they're round the other side," he replied, letting the Golf creep forward. "There's something going on round there. Hang on, he's moving."

"Sunna María isn't. Surely Orri's not driving the van if can hardly stand up?" Gunna said, pointing to the blonde figure in a belted raincoat getting into a black Mercedes four-by-four. "So which one do we keep track of now?" She clicked her communicator. "Eiríkur, still there?"

"Listening, chief."

"We have two people to follow, Sunna María in a Mercedes four-by-four," she said, reading out the car's registration.

"Got that?"

"Got it."

"And Orri in the white Trafic. You have the number, don't you?"

"Got that as well."

The Golf moved off as the van swung out of the car park. Gunna put a hand on Geiri's elbow. "Wait a second. Let the Merc go as well," she said. Geiri stopped and the four-by-four sped too fast through some puddles and followed the van. "Now go," she said, as the Golf was already rolling forward.

"That's not our boy driving the van," Geiri said. "There's someone else there and it's not him."

"You're sure?"

"I think so. It's someone who sits higher than the guy we were tailing before, and whoever's driving isn't wearing a high-viz vest like our boy was."

"Right, keep in sight," Gunna said as they followed the van and the four-by-four along the waterfront and then up the hill. Instead of taking the turnoff to the main road, the van carried on towards the trading estate where Green Bay Dispatch had its depot.

"Back to the yard, it seems?"

"I don't like it. Why's Sunna María going that way as well?" Gunna growled, reaching for her mouthpiece. "Eiríkur? What's the situation on backup?"

"The squad car's a few minutes behind you."

Geiri again slowed down as the van took an unexpected turn at the roundabout at the edge of the trading estate. "They're going along the Krýsuvík road."

"What the hell?"

"That means we can't easily tail them without being seen."

"Hang back as far as you can, then," Gunna said, and speaking into her mouthpiece. "Eiríkur? Is there another squad car available? Or anything?"

"It doesn't look like it."

"Can you re-route the traffic guys? It looks like we're tailing them along the Krýsuvík road, and I'm trying to second-guess where the hell they might be going. Can you get the traffic guys to go down the Kaldársels road from Hafnarfjördur?" she said, thinking fast and trying to remember the lie of the land on these little-used country roads.

"That way we should be able to head them off if things start to get sticky."

"Yep. Will do."

"It's not the same driver," Geiri said, shaking his head.

"Sure? How so?"

"This guy's not as cautious as our boy. He's throwing that van around as if nobody's going to have to drive it ever again."

The ink-black rocks with patches of lichen hanging on to them for dear life sped past as Geiri drove faster to keep the two vehicles in sight. Tangles of dormant trees, leaves long fallen and their buds waiting for some spring warmth before breaking into new life, were scattered by the roadsides at intervals, with the occasional forlorn evergreen conifer here and there. Now they were in open country where any kind of traffic was a rarity and the road was rough after a winter of heavy weather. It spat stones and water back at them while the Golf's wheels struggled to get a grip on the wet road surface. In summer, this was a popular enough place with walkers and cyclists, but on a cold spring day with winter still very much in evidence, the area was deserted.

Unfamiliar with the district, Gunna tried to think where they might be going at such speed.

"They're throwing up that much water that they won't be able to see anyone following," Geiri said. "Now they're slowing, and turning again. That's the road towards Hvaleyrarvatn."

"Eiríkur. You can see us on the tracker?"

"Got you."

"They're turning along the Hvaleyri road. Warn the traffic guys, will you?"

"We have company," Geiri said. "Look in the mirror."

Gunna leaned forward to see that a four-by-four in police colours could be seen in the distance, its headlights dipping and bouncing as it negotiated the pitted road, while Geiri again slowed as the brake lights on Sunna María's Mercedes glowed bright beneath the layer of grime they'd already picked up along the way.

"If we can see them," Gunna said, pointing back at the police four-by-four and forward to Sunna María's car. "Then they can see us."

"If they're looking, and I don't imagine they are," Geiri said. "Another turn. If you want to head them off, now might be the time."

"Where are they heading now?"

"That's the road that passes south of the lake. There are only a couple of turnoffs to summer chalets and the like."

"You're sure?"

"Sure enough."

"Eiríkur, they're taking the road south of the Hvaleyri lake. Get the traffic guys onto it from the other end, will you? This has gone far enough, I want them stopped."

"Will do, chief," Eiríkur said and Gunna could hear him relaying instructions on the open channel. "Warn them to be careful. This guy may be nasty."

"Armed?"

"I don't think so, but take care."

The gravel road began to disintegrate as a burst of rain came down hard. Geiri switched the wipers on and they scraped pathways in the corrosive mix of water and black volcanic dust that coated the windscreen as he leaned forward to peer through the murk. The road could hardly be seen in the sudden downpour that pebbledashed the road ahead and battered the roof of the car.

"Where the hell . . .?" Geiri cursed, and Gunna wound down her window, pushing her face half out to see what was happening.

"Geiri! Back up!" she yelled.

"What?"

Gunna almost bounced up and down in the seat in frustration. "Over there, they pulled off the road." She pointed towards a narrow track half hidden by a clump of fir trees, meandering away from the main road and down a dip.

The Golf shuddered to a standstill, reversed at top speed, and the four-by-four behind stopped in a flurry of stones and flying water. Geiri put his foot down, spinning the wheels through the lakes forming in the road as he rounded a bend, meeting Sunna María's jeep coming the other way. Gunna caught a glimpse of Sunna María's face behind the wheel, white and tense, her mouth open in astonishment. Geiri spun the wheel and hauled at the handbrake, dragging the long-suffering Golf into a screeching turn that left it flat across the road as the four-by-four came to a halt.

As Gunna jumped out of the car, the acrid smell of burning was unmistakeable, and she looked around quickly to see a pall of greasy smoke from behind a low hill. She could hear the agonized rattle of the four-by-four's gears failing to engage as she ran to Sunna María's car, where she pulled open the driver's door, caught a handful of coat and hair and hauled her bodily from the car, dumping her in a puddle. Only then did she look up to see the man with the hook nose and moustache glaring back at her. She sensed rather than saw the blow coming as she reached for the keys. The flat of his hand caught her on the side of the head instead of in the face, making her stagger back and trip over Sunna María lying where she had been dropped.

The man leaped into the driving seat, slammed the door and gunned the Mercedes along the track, the engine whining in complaint as it raced and the wheels spinning in wet gravel before it jumped and was gone in time to meet the police four-by-four coming the other way.

For a moment, Gunna thought the squad car was going to veer and politely let the Mercedes past, but it stopped across the road, lights flickering in the wet gloom, and the two officers in it jumped out, one with his baton already in his hand. A siren could be heard in the distance as the hooknosed man slowly got out of the Mercedes, his hands in front of him but still with a smile on his face, as he realized that the odds were against him.

"Geiri!" Gunna called, still dazed from the blow, panting with exertion as she ran towards the pall of black smoke. The Golf coughed and spluttered as it sped past her and around the bend to where the white van was in flames, pulling up with a crunch of tyres. Geiri hauled open the Golf's boot and pulled out a fire extinguisher.

"The back of the van! Geiri, open the back," Gunna yelled, searching her coat pockets for the gloves she knew should be there and pulling them on as she ran through the puddles. Smoke was pouring from the white van's cab. Geiri lifted the extinguisher as if it were a toy, smashed the driver's side window with the base of it and let fly with the contents into the van. Gunna wrenched at the rear doors, pulled one open and coughed as a gout of black smoke erupted from inside. After a few seconds it cleared a little and she jumped inside with her eyes watering and one hand over her mouth.

There was little she could see, but among the boxes that Orri had stacked in the van that morning, a foot could be seen in the gloom. Knowing she had no more than a couple of seconds at most, Gunna grabbed the foot, pulled with all her strength and found herself falling backwards out of the van into Geiri's bear-like embrace with an unconscious Orri in her grasp.

"Get him clear, will you?" she gasped, coughed and doubled over, retching onto the black lava gravel as Geiri swung Orri over his shoulder and laid him on the ground next to the Golf. He came back for Gunna, helping her to her feet and half-carrying her to the car as the flames burned even more fiercely in the van, illuminating the little group in an unearthly light as the gouts of black smoke blotted out weak sunlight that fought manfully to break through the clouds after the downpour.

Gunna still felt dirty and the smell of burning clung to her in spite of a shower and clean clothes. Ívar Laxdal looked at her with respect as she dropped herself gingerly into the visitor's chair in his office.

"How's Orri?" she asked.

"Sorry, Gunnhildur."

"Shit. You mean I was too late?"

"I wouldn't put it like that."

Gunna scowled and smacked a fist into the palm of her other hand. "I knew I should have acted sooner. I should have grabbed the lot of them before they got out of town, before they had a chance to set that van on fire."

"Gunnhildur, you couldn't have known."

"I should have known that they weren't taking Orri somewhere for a sauna and a massage."

She sighed, suddenly exhausted, and slumped in the chair, while Ívar Laxdal looked brighter and more cheerful than she had seen him for weeks. Gunna realized that the pressure on him had been relieved once Sunna María and the man with the hook nose were in custody. Ívar Laxdal could expect his superiors to be quietly satisfied that a difficult matter had been dealt with, and it occurred to her that she still had no idea of the man's name.

"So who is he?" she asked abruptly.

"Ívar Laxdal looked uncomfortable. "Our mystery man? He says his name's Bruno Kovalchuk, and what's interesting is that he claims diplomatic immunity."

"What? He's embassy staff?"

"It's a bizarre claim, considering his country has no diplomatic presence in Iceland. He claims to be from Belarus, which doesn't have an embassy here. But we have no choice but to jump through the hoops, so I've happily passed the whole headache over to the Ministry of Foreign Affairs, which can deal with the Belarusian Embassy in London or Helsinki, or work through our consul in Minsk; not that I'm expecting anything to happen fast, and in the meantime he's already been charged with assaulting a police officer."

"Me, once again."

"As you say, you. That's enough to keep him locked away until this mess is sorted out."

Gunna pursed her lips. "You're not going to let him disappear, like . . ."

"Absolutely not, and as soon as wherever he comes from gets the idea that he was running a drugs operation, I don't expect they'll want to remember who he is. I'm half expecting them to just say his passport's a forgery so they can forget about him."

"It was a speed ring, then? That's what it was all about?"

Ívar Laxdal sat back, his face relaxed for the first time since Vilhelm Thorleifsson had been gunned down in his summer house.

"That's what it seems. According to the dentist's delightful wife, Bruno was getting rid of members of the group who had doubts about expanding the business or who might have wanted a share of the profits."

"You mean they were getting rid of their business partners one at a time? Has she said anything about Elvar Pálsson?"

"I don't know. You'll have to ask Eiríkur. He's been in there with her since they were brought in. You want to sit in, or have you had enough?"

Gunna yawned. "I've had about four hours sleep in two days, so while I'm tempted to lean on Sunna María or Bruno, I'd probably be best off going home and seeing if any of my family actually recognize me. But, Alex? That was this Bruno guy, was it?"

"So Sunna María says. She believes Bruno and Alex between them murdered Vilhelm Thorleifsson, and she thinks Bruno murdered Alex because he was unreliable. It sounds plausible to me. The question is how much she actually knows and how much she's guessing."

"We know Bruno abducted Jóhann. What about the Latvian business partner, Boris Vadluga?"

Ívar Laxdal smiled humourlessly.

434

"As clean as a whistle, ostensibly. Unless Bruno decides to say something and implicate him, then we have only his financial involvement with these people as a business partner and the main investor in the Vison fur farm. So it appears that Bruno Kovalchuk, Sunna María and others were using Boris Vadluga's businesses as a front for their drug operation. I'll have to leave it to the financial crime division and the police in Latvia to decide whether or not he was part of all this."

Gunna stretched. The day's tension and the tumble from the black four-by-four had left her stiff and aching, although she was delighted that Sunna María had broken her fall. "So what's your plan of action?"

"We have to establish that Bruno Kovalchuk, whoever he is, really did murder Vilhelm Thorleifsson and Alex Snetzler, what happened to Juris, and if Elvar Pálsson is still alive or if he has been disposed of as well. We have evidence that he abducted Jóhann, so there's no question of bail."

"And how much of all this was Sunna María party to?"

"Precisely. What are your thoughts on that?"

Gunna pondered. "My guess is that she knew nothing about Alex. When we dug up the body in the foundations of her house, it was obvious that she was frightened and surprised. So was I," Gunna admitted. "I expected to find her husband under there. But I reckon she knew damned well that Jóhann had been abducted, although that's something else we have to get to the bottom of. Dumping a city dweller like him in a place like Vatnsendi is tantamount to murder in my book. The man's extraordinarily fortunate that he survived, and that's another whole line of questioning I'm going to have to deal with."

"Where is Jóhann? Gone home?"

"I gather he's left hospital and is staying with his son. I don't suppose he's in a hurry to go home to Kópavogsbakki."

"He's aware that his wife may have tried to murder him? I wonder why they didn't just dump him in the foundations like they did with Alex?"

Gunna shrugged. "Who knows? Maybe they wanted to maintain an illusion that Jóhann had walked off and vanished into the countryside in a fit of mid-life crisis? Your guess is as good as mine, but between them, I'm convinced we have the two of them responsible in one way or another for all those killings and probably a few more that we don't know about yet."

"I'm looking forward to seeing your full report."

"Probably as much as I'm not looking forward to writing it. But are . . ." Gunna raised her eyes briefly towards the ceiling. "Happy with you now?"

"They're happy with us, shall we say, Gunnhildur? They're happy with us."

Jóhann looked frail and Gunna thought he had a chastened air about him as he sat surrounded by plants in the conservatory of his son's house, wrapped in a thick sweater in spite of the place being uncomfortably hot. He cradled a glass of juice in his hands and looked at Gunna blankly.

436

"My son tells me that you were searching for me all last week. Is that right?"

"You haven't spoken to your wife, have you?" Gunna asked, ignoring his question.

"No, of course not. You were very insistent that I shouldn't and I still don't understand why."

"In that case, I'll tell you," Gunna said, sitting down without being invited as the dentist's son and his wife fussed in the background. "Your wife is right now in an interview room at Hverfisgata where she's tying herself in all kinds of knots. Any idea who Bruno Kovalchuk is?"

"Never heard the name. Should I have?"

"Bruno Kovalchuk, assuming that's his real name, is the man who presumably drugged you at the Sólfell offices and dumped you miles up country, where I imagine you were expected to die of hunger or exposure. You'll also be interested to know that we arrested him and your wife earlier today, and we weren't quick enough to save the life of the young man they had apparently drugged and abducted. Both of them are going to be in custody for a long time while we try and get to the bottom of all this. So if you can tell me anything that would make it easier to unravel this mess, I'd appreciate it."

Jóhann's son and daughter-in-law discreetly left the conservatory, the door closing silently behind them.

"I'll tell you whatever you want to know," he said, staring into the distance behind Gunna's head.

"Did you have any idea of what was going on at Vison?"

"It's a fur farm. Vilhelm put us in touch with Boris Vadluga as he wanted to invest in fur in Iceland. Boris runs a car-rental empire, which is where his money comes from, but he has other businesses, including logistics and fur. He has owned a large share in a mink farm in Denmark for many years."

"Did you have any inkling of what was going on in the background?"

"What do you mean?" Jóhann looked first confused, and then irritated. "I'm not interested in playing games."

"All right. That suits me. It appears that Bruno Kovalchuk may have been working for Boris Vadluga, although I'm not sure in what capacity. They were running a small amphetamine factory in the basement of the house they rented from you. As business was doing well, they wanted to expand. So the Vison fur farm was the camouflage for a speed factory, with a transport link through another company owned by Vadluga to shift the goods to Europe. You're with me so far?"

This time Jóhann nodded wide-eyed. His mouth opened, and then quickly shut as he floundered for something to say.

"It's plain to me that your wife and Bruno Kovalchuk were the ones behind the scheme. So what I'm fishing for is how much you and Boris Vadluga knew about all this? Were you and Vadluga also partners in this, or were you unwitting dupes? And why was Vilhelm got rid of?"

Jóhann sat open-mouthed for a long moment. "I . . . I'm at a loss. I had no idea," he gasped at last. "I should have known that anything that came through that soulless little bastard Vilhelm couldn't be honest."

"They're pretty ruthless people," Gunna said. "Vilhelm was shot, and my guess was that he wanted a slice of the pie, although we'll probably never know exactly what went on there. They also disposed of two other people."

Jóhann seemed to be having trouble breathing. Gunna poured water from a jug into a glass and handed it to him. He took it gratefully, holding the glass in both hands as he gulped the water down.

"And they wanted to get rid of me as well?" he whispered.

"So it seems. It appears you were surplus to requirements. How come?"

Jóhann looked into the glass in his hands before putting it on the table. His fingers trembled.

"You were aware of your wife and Bruno's relationship?"

"I knew there had been one or two," he said eventually. "I didn't know about this one in particular."

"But had you any idea of the direction their business was going in?"

"None whatever," Jóhann said, finally with a little fire in his voice. "And if I had, then no, I certainly wouldn't have gone along with it for a moment." He sighed and his shoulders slumped. "I hope you have grounds to back all this up, officer, and that you're not just spinning me a lot of hearsay."

"That'll all come out in court, although it might take a while and your wife's lover is steadfastly saying nothing."

"And Sunna María? What has she said? Has she admitted all this?"

"In a roundabout route," Gunna said. "She's blaming Bruno for everything, although it'll be interesting for both of them when they find out that you're still in one piece."

She killed the engine and sat in the car, looking at the front door for a minute, listening to the engine tick and wondering where the Passat in the street opposite had come from. Gunna closed her eyes and felt the tension of the last two days drain away. She thought about Sunna María, flustered and distraught, while Jóhann's world had collapsed around him over a few long days of hardship and Bruno Kovalchuk sat silent with his arms folded in the interview room chair, refusing to say anything other than to confirm his name.

Finally Gunna stepped out of the car and her key scraped in the lock of her house. She listened for a moment with the door open a crack and was relieved that there was no sound of voices or small children, although the lack of any cooking smells was a disappointment.

"Hæ, Mum," Gísli said awkwardly from the end of the sofa where Steini normally sat. The book Steini was reading was still open, face-down on the arm of the sofa.

"Gísli, I didn't expect to see you here," Gunna said. "It isn't that I'm not pleased to see you," she added. "It's just a surprise, that's all. Been to see Drífa and Kjartan, have you?"

"Well, no."

He shuffled awkwardly. "Laufey's over there with Drífa at the moment, and I wanted to catch you without anyone else about."

Gunna's eyes narrowed. "Problem?"

"No." He coughed. "Not exactly." He gestured to the chair at the far end of the room and Gunna saw a young woman with blonde hair in plaited and beaded cornrows sending her a bright smile.

"Hi, you're Gísli's mum? I've heard so much about you."

Gunna shook the girl's hand in bemusement.

"Mum, this is Naomi. She's from New Zealand." He coughed again. "I'm thinking of moving there to live with her."